"*A Spy in the Ruins* implicates its reader in the rich multiplicity of a solitary, all-encompassing soul as it lives out an entire lifetime in one shuddering moment. In vivid, almost succulent, yet powerfully controlled prose that frequently rises to exquisite poetry, Christopher Bernard holds a mirror to the artist of his generation and immerses him in the endlessness of childhood, the loneliness of adolescence, the anguish of love, the joys and torments of a mind awakening in the political ferment of the sixties and seventies. A Bildungsroman hallucinogenic in its intensity, *Spy* is an extraordinary literary experiment."

— Anna Sears

$\mathcal{A}$ SPY
in the RUINS

$\mathscr{A}$ SPY
in the RUINS

CHRISTOPHER BERNARD

$\mathscr{A}$ Caveat Lector Book

REGENT PRESS
OAKLAND, CALIFORNIA

ISBN: 1-58790-111-0

Library of Congress Control Number: 2004099086

First Edition

0 1 2 3 4 5 6 7 8 9 10

Design by Roz Abraham: Regent Press
Photograph of author by Alexandra Karam

A Caveat Lector Book

Regent Press
6020 – A Adeline Street
Oakland, CA 94608
www.regentpress.net

A SPY

in the RUINS

Strive to ascend into yourself, gathering everything broken and scattered from that unity that once abounded in its power. Bind together into one the ideas born within you, clarify those grown confused, draw the obscure into the light.

— Porphyry, *Ad Marcell.*

Any life, no matter how long and complex it may be, is made up of *a single moment* — the moment in which you find out, once and for all, who you are.

— Jorge Luis Borges

*It hit like a hammering on a door lifting the room on its edge and
rattling it with an imaginary break a moment at the tip before
dropping it into a long ferocious shaking like a bone in the mouth of
a dog books slithering from a case the phone scattering over the rug
CDs slipping from the shelves as the kitchen rang with breakage the
room's frame creaked and squealed around you torquing in the ground
roll wave following wave cracking the plaster across from you as you
crouched in the doorway the doorframe bends the door slowly swings
away something booms far below the building had been raised on a
single square of concrete you imagine the long diagonal fork of black
lightning split its face yet you feel almost calm riding a wave as you
used to do as a child throwing yourself into the curl of the surf crashing
toward the foam of waves already spent in a chug of spume and froth
and it keeps rolling the apartment building across the street sways gently
like a giant cradle as you see the squares of transparency fall like large
glassy snowflakes from the building's face and you realize it is windows
falling and you hear the squish and rattle of the rain of shattering glass
along the street and the rolling seems to go on endlessly until as abruptly
as it hit it stopped.*

*And silence and darkness fill the room the evening air outside suffused
with pale luminescence white as the moon edged yellow-pink with
sunset and the street you look down (from the window you hastened to*

as soon as the shock ceased and you could keep your balance) the street
is shadowy with houses sagging into the darkness of the defile as far as
you can see dimly east and west small grayish smudges that only with
an effort you realize are people dazed walking their eyes stare up into
the air perhaps the shock fell from the sky and more might come from
there the smudge of smoke and fog that usually lies torpid over the city
half hides the towers downtown rising blank and lightless in the twilight
and only then do you hear moving across the city from all around you
wave on wave of the wailing of sirens and distantly across a multitude
of blurring and deepening roofs a blacker smudge turns toward the
dusk like a fist of darkness slowly unclenching toward the sky the yellow
red spark in its grip the only answer to the evening star which at that
moment opens its red eye over the shaken city as the fires begin …

And wake and stare into the darkness around you. And wait for
the shaking to begin again the spasm and stab again the seed of
the nightmare again to burn in the darkness of a sleep that will
not come. But it too does not come. You wait for the burning of
the city the fire that eats you the loss of love of happiness of hope
the wreckage of a life at the edge of your life that you now inhabit
that now inhabits you like the larva of a wasp eating you from
within at the same time laying you waste under bombardment
and disappearing in a haze of sirens and cries you pass the rubble
through your fingers like sand and disappear in a smoke of blazing
hair try to fold your body back to sleep like a knife hoping the
nightmare won't resume hoping it will hoping against hope for the
abandonment to day hoping against hope against the abandonment
to day. But it does not come. As on every night and breaking into
fragments many of your days. Even when it does not come. As
now. Hoping to find in the dreams between sleep the thread that
snapped in the scissors' teeth the palace that fell and fired in the
loss of joy the city that burned to the grave of its memory the
kingdom that collapsed between the battle that lost the war and the
whispering of blind historians who insult its memory by trying to

revive it. And you wait. In the wreckage of a life contained like a seed in the wreckage of love. Since that is what it is meant to have been all about. Wasn't it. Was it not. Where is it. The nightmare again. Flung. Out. Far. Across a wide and opening field as of seeds or stones or birds dispersed by wind or the force of migration or a series of swift kicks. The sound of shouts driving seagulls up a beach. With a storm coming. The shadows on a summer porch. A pattern of sycamore leaves. The trash burning in a tower of stones. That. Yes. Yellow rocks. He smears his tongue with the ash. I smear my tongue with the ash. The sky opening like a palm cut with crescents where the fingernails bit into the skin. Sand in your cuff a conch in your hand. A broken pattern taking its. Revenge. An execution rose. Encrypted in panels

of sand crumbling as you read them

                                        sifting

sifting through your fingers the words

            sifting through your

                        through your eyes

the web of dust in the toolshed at the bottom of the

                        property where the solitary one

sat long ago in a back corner against the rotting

            joists

            staring into the shadows of the rafters

                        the smell of rot piercing sweet

like the gull decaying on the levee rampant

                                    flaring into the earth

            smelling of the earth your mother

whom you have never known

1

Dazzling.

Light from every compass point.

In the outback at the edge of the frontage road the sky opens like a long-clenched fist. Offering a suddenness of generous blue and constantly changing clouds. Or reaching out to sternly grab someone's hand. Or pointing to an error in a serene-looking notebook. Or about to slap someone's frightened cheek. Or ...

Are we ready for the next lesson have we learned anything from the last. The eyes blink rapidly they can't take it all in. Frozen watching. Waiting. Vast perspectives on all sides. There is no end to the horizon.

Who is in control here? You or you or you? Someone overtaken someone taking over. Surprised as the egg of the lark spiraling up to nimbo-cumulus imagined from inside the shell....

You are unseen but guessed at.

Shh, he's finally sleeping now, leave him, let him sleep, go, go …

You think so do you let him forget. But he can't forget. Ah where is senility when you finally need it....

Behind the rivulets of laughter ice and the smell of sex the list of humiliations I went over each night before I slept.

No. Hosannas....

A narcissus in a small clear bowl. Yes that.

On every side the boundaries were collapsing. At the time. The border guards stood like torches of pitch. You were drawn without your knowing it. Into the conspiracy.

The net flying beyond its reach. Adenine guanine cytosine thymine. Cartilage cleaver bone. Shell. Cage. Jail. Wings.

Into the tide ...

O the astonishing novelty of dawn.

The screen goes blank with beauty it was so great a joy we vanished.

A spare swath of light crosses the hallway table. That!

Why we could never quite remember the lesson and so must keep repeating it.

The head has no voice only whispers furtive signatories to the treaty you made with the past. Hand-flocked mail sent to a blocked address and the cartouche that will not disappear from the monitor screen.

The solitary one moves across the bottom of the aquarium collecting trace bubbles rising from the oxygenator.... A glint of bluefish through the tidewater.... The air rising from two open hands....

What you remember what he remembers is the pain in detail it cannot have been all suffering you reasoned why can't I remember the happiness.

Let the door pull you through. As you approach the threshold you grow immense and slow never to be seen to attain it.

If esse est percipi you will not ever be.

As you dive into the shadowy heart of the rose. A cross fleur-de-lys on a banner. A tide of grasses moving over a plain. The boy not seen that day....

I think he's really sleeping now. His eyelids are quivering. Yes, of course, if you like. Stay.

Take the turnoff to Lock among the ghost towns in the hills beyond the city.

See the shadow of a condor. From April to November waterless earth. The sun nailed at noon. Creek beds smooth as.

The counterpane you can see it from above knobby with hill ranges like the knees of teenagers sleeping in the hot afternoon. A Cessna whirrs oblique to the horizon. Whistles sound in the burdock glen. The birds are strangers to me you announced. The keys clattered to the floor.

The peculiar range of sound in the country the chuff of tractors I could almost hear you from there. The exhilarating scent of compost. There were many horses but they were all silent. An open palm shining with moisture. The woods arched over me like hands. Pale as. Dark as. Thought of winter at the center of summer brightness. A daydream of snow. Flash of water skis an arm waving. The roar of the motorboat beyond the jetty. At the heart of the winter dream in the silence of summer the memory of other summers cocooned in snow. The taste of seawater. Everywhere….

The soft hour of the sandpiper in the distance the pier that collapsed section by section over the decades but never entirely fallen.

The ship's log lying open in the antechamber.

Coordinates in parallax psychopomps terns.

Whitecaps.

A thin layer of sand on the linoleum a bend in the tide reflecting the clouds. Foam crowns the shell of a horseshoe crab lying on the beach like the helmet of the fabled dead German soldier. With tail.

Retorts. Why retorts?

The fumes cleared the chemistry wing in long-lost adolescence why that now.

The shouts of the walking psychotics as they scream in the night. That you should pity but can't except in retrospect.

A tangle of undercurrents the Portuguese man-o'-war the sharks. Airborne. Off the port of tempests. Cape Hatteras and the flight to the islands of Malatesta and the coast of. Campana the call of the horns. The review closed with a corps of dancers strutting to strident reprises of Semper Fi. Consume your reserves in the night. That you have been given many of. Gifts.

Our altars burned with offerings. The hammers formed a circle their handles point toward the center. A suspicious stare at the passport the airline ticket your shoes your look of innocence that no longer convinces it could be anyone. Here. Now. The fog closing in. A flare of coins a string of buoys. A plangent moan as of a snoring giant the sheet shifting over the harbor of his bed.

Oh what was his name? Nomen Dubium. Or nomina nuda!

The solitary one removes his hand.

A velocipede is overturned in the driveway.

Representations of social power in the land of the living were inflected through docile bodies panopticon of the net Argus made supreme polymorphous perverse expressed through the search for the multiple orgasm. Again. To erase the assertive I and the it. Parry riposte. Hit. Do not spare the heart. Whip. Tied to the finials of a bed. The humiliations the too-powerful pay for. The sexuality of the atom was to implode. We had a wanton tenderness phemes of repulsion and a drive toward nescience. We were counting bone samples in the art department. For catastrophe theory how the mosquito's wings in the Maldives upset the tech stock rates on Nasdaq. A tear in the unified field. As collapsible as charm. Toward a cast party in the Balkans. Or the collapse of Bam. Or where the road for Cabeza de Vaca spanned. The bain-marie spilled on the countergirl's thigh. El Camino Real to its end in the Ohlone graves. Tension between accomplishment and. Intention. The result never in doubt. So that everything can now happen at once. What was meant by the end of distance. There was no more there. Unto the tenth generation. Immediate demolition why wait.

Ah whoever is waiting?

The solitary one closes his book. Then casts it lazily into the flames on the café hearth. "I have written" you said "in invisible ink." As if you could have known. You were caught in a glass brick signaling in the latest dead language.

How tall the young were they had the serenity of those who cannot imagine the future. The rent due for months she keeps her back to the millennium. There is acquaintance rape in his eyes. If I ignore him he may not go away but he will not be there. Between her lips a red medicinal Campari edged with rind.

At the time there was retrodisco at Julie's Supper Club we were dancing just out of reach of each other's arms.

Not robust he had the features of a mouse of prey. A woman was dancing with her own hands. There were three undrunk martinis. The glitter ball fell between us then surprising both of us bounced away. Even the growing tangle of gazes across the packed dance floor could not be sliced by a single hard thought. It was a virtual orgy. Ramifications of the appearance of mass traffic in the suburbs of Petra. Gridlock of mutually exclusive. Blossoming. What brought you here. Baiting us with frustration. An aphrodisiac cocktail of denial. Placental camisoles flip-flops thongs. Cars of silence and overhead the quiet rattle of a patrol helicopter circling. The spotlight caught you at an especially embarrassing moment. You were never good at the tactics of seduction. She was overly proud of her sexual career never having learned how easy it is for a woman. The man must work the woman need only fall. Back into the grotesqueness of remorse. A lemon-colored blotter. The hermit crabs returning at night to their stolen shells.

Midnight silence in the wards. The soft tread of the nurses. They think I am dead and are trying to ignore me.

The eulogy was brief enough. Someone spoke and what he said was what no one would have expected. To pass on. To remove. To erase your words before they were spoken. Like a sculptor of air. With all the self-destructive honesty of eros. These emblems of worship provided the earliest signs of their civilization. The gathering in the atrium expressed its grief through the attenuation of expression its calm even cheerfulness. There were no tears. All the more overwhelming was the devastation within. Subordinate accuracy to politeness but respect nothing. Of strange presumption there was among other examples that could be mentioned the chapel awkwardly placed on the university campus. I wore my hopes like a life preserver that didn't fit but would have to do. What does happen when two become one. The elaborate emptiness of the ritual the ritual hypocrisy of the priest the priest who had never after all even met her.

You did not look dead even the last time I saw you. Refuse circulation stuff it in your mouth place one then the other over your eyes. The pilot at the ferry landing in the shadow of the prison. Not quite. The prison is due north. Always regnant in sun from there. He collected bribes from the timid among them.

A grotesque pause.

Like an inconvenience. Into the trash of a life. Such clarity was a form of deception after all. There was an alibi but you disposed of it when you. Which means less now than what it might have meant at the time. The flatworm cut in two was resurrected twice.

What was that? I thought he just laughed. Shh. His eyes are quiver-ing.

Partly hypocritical praise yields to jokes at the banquet followed by singing though no dancing. Reflecting morning sunlight the eight points of the Maltese cross as it spins snakes spirals. The ashtray in my hand is the shape of a lotus in glass. Her name falls through the air. Weakie thrashing on the dinghy seat. Save as. Give it a name. Then close it. Nail it down. Now.

Floating hovering a total openness where everything is available all closure relative all certainty tentative suspense of intention held breath of possibility the resolution into meaning delayed or not so much delayed as shied glanced at acknowledged caressed. In embryo moving toward birth.

You are my possible lover. But not now.

Not yet made whole but soon to be made whole. Some day some hour. Metaphors of immanent transcendence and other oxymorons. Flickering. Fritillary. A strange attractor graphs a butterfly.

Available in the dark whole brightness. Empire of holy tragic of happy. Memorialized by the one not to release the many. In your hand. In the white ink well of. Glory. Back alley of grunge the smell of decayed bananas not forgotten. In your face. A rage of tenderness.

What better way to express desire's paradox than the oxymoron. Thirst was the desert's happiness. Cloud chamber of the night. Shrunk to naked singularity the genesis event. From an original tranquility serenely exploding. Etc. The self turned inside out like a sock. The solitary one plays in a sandbox of galaxies. Building bridges to emptiness which then plodes. Like a piñata in a park. Crowded with happiness oh smothered with joy. A sundae. Hot fudge. Lots of fun. Tag you're it. Your time your way your side your fault your turn. Great America. Terrific Milky Way especially with nougat. Making love to the air. In order to exist at all she had to have sex with the universe. At the center of her cunt burned God. In ecstasy. Forever. How could you not love. Her. She did not believe it she could not let herself believe it.

The solitary one pushed down the walls of the sandcastle. To expose a pair of clam shells pressed together like hands in prayer. The stink of stagnant water in the tidepool. At the zenith the Perseids scratching the night. The night a tunnel beneath the road. The hunger of being in pursuit. Smell of panic. The eyes turning to you as you sleep.

What is love.

The solitary one caressed his thighs remembering. His head was eaten by the moon. Salt heart. Unknown the void between mountain and mountain. The cable dazzled us away. We were airborne for half the night. She leaked blood and tasted of sweat and tears. I licked the shadow beneath your mouth I sucked the sweetness of your nipple I feasted on the starvation of your loins. Until you took me. And shattered me against your heart's stone.

You were a blank screen of contradictions. You were a scavenger of happiness. You sifted your life through your mouth like sand. And cannot die because he never lived.

The heart is the size of a loosely clenched fist. Gray tells you so. The lambent blue of a western mountain flower. What color are my eyes today. White.

He cried. Wake him up. I can't. He cried.

Glass spy.
Ruins of the kingdom.
Far far away far flung.

The village at the bottom of the road was where the rooster could no longer be heard. Velvet as the creek bed the embrowning layers of leaves. A tremor of waterskate. A shape of spire surrounded by maple. Long long the distant siren. Crack of shotgun in the dazzled glen. You tasted the hot cross bun before the butter. Enchanting. But what was the cause of the anxiety that passed between our eyes? One speaks there only when one is lost.

Look. The farmer raised his cap in greeting. It is a friendly place the talk is mainly about the low prices for farm products and rising real estate taxes. The soft stench of the cowstables of milk and manure and their comfortable stares. Moo cow. Lovably ponderous tender and dumb. The rotted barn door opening to the blanched fields. Gone. Sky. Road. Rolling thunder of traffic. The hand riding the slipstream. An ensign snapping at the mast. Green blur of roadside whipping past. Swift plunges into the forest darts of sunlight on flashes of meadow shafts of brightness a fugue dream of the kingdom thought of the ornateness of leaves the netting of branches the dropped jewel boxes of wild flowers the weaving of the songs of the birds. Enframed in blur slipping by. Velocity. The automobile as an aid to daydreaming. Between any two cities there is a reverie. The hum of cement. Fly cast in amber. A special flair for knowing where to be at what time. Pigeons perched on his shoulders for the slightest reason. He dipped the zinc pail into the vat of milk. All you needed to do was make a list and you had an order. The peacock shrieks beneath the willow. The little girl drops her fork to the restaurant floor. A blow of ocean breeze makes the awning snap. The half-open door creaks in. If you listen you can make out what they are shouting on the beach. The laughter. The officious whistling of the lifeguards. A soothing roar of surf. Lapped with little pools of quiet. Your feet in the water your eyes on the clouds your mind in the city your heart in the forest. Your soul on the back of your tongue.

There we were all crammed into a multivalent now here always. Then that is to say at that time. How wrong we were! Curled around the jugular nonetheless. Polysemic. Suffocating.

Nothing was not available. Electronic hysteria glossolalia of the chatroom elusive but multiple tasks. There were subordinate questions such as who tied the solitary one to the bedposts. The exquisite happiness of public humiliation fed absolute pride. The random constellations of public chaos organized according to fire codes and usage zones. Woman was the principle of disorganization man the imposer suspect in the urban ghettos of repealed order.

She again. Who dared you to set her boundaries. Who lashed according to absolute moments. Living in a present without past without future. Demanding submission to pity. Inciting the stallion to the thrust of light. A hand on muscle. Strain without object. The strenuous drive toward the normal. The ordinary an irresistible dare.

She again. We dreamed of each other for days. Again. We stalked each other like prey our fear equal to our despair. Again. You stood before me like a pillar of darkness in the wilderness. Wherever I reached for you you disappeared in a play of fire and pain. You burned me. There was nowhere to go. The shed collapsed in the back of my mouth…. The titular leader advanced to the front of the march. And there spoke to the line of winter police. Our job is not to move. Our ice is your boundary.

In your hand the possible adventure. That must come out. Like an afterwards of stark beauty. A bed of vastness. Caught in a constabulary of sheets. Wild nights of memory and a litter of squibs. Larks of irresponsibility. Rocket flowers in the community gardens. Nothing but name to back it but that was enough. At the time.

The solitary one returned to his solitude with a hurried bouquet of thankfulness. To briefly coin his joy.

A spiral of heavenliness rose from his lamp.

She danced in the pocket of the meadow thinking she was alone. Purslane. A long sigh between beats of night. Being taken with. Being overtaken by. A portfolio of elevations for an ideal city. Gargoyles prone with chin in palm on malachite consoles. Glass caryatids holding the tablets. A line of prophets speaking words of stone.

We could hear everything. Those of us alive at the time that is. Nothing was more amazing than the way things came and came. The wonder of the night was that it recurred there was always a sky above him the clouds marshaled thought into ranks of possibility the stars uncurtained the hallways of the night there were infinite perspectives of assurance. The glorious freedom of the dream.

They felt themselves expand to the ends of the universe the musicians of quantity told them had no end. Though only in thought it was enough. For you to have it. To turn your back on the shattering. The moon a flocking of swallows the sun an arrow of tenderness. Where could they meet but on the sand. But you told me to. And I did it. Here. See.

Tracing the path of the unknown one the silent one in another part of the city. For we moved to a city. Then.

Back and forth the cat's cradle of blue threads of light.

Ubiquitous tangents of the real.

Valance. Vectors. Corrupted sectors. Prime time. Brief psychotic breaks.

Healing followed the same pattern.

He still felt the occasional stab of a barely endurable anguish in the phantom heart.

I know it is not there and yet I feel it.

Useless notes from the director applied to a hopeless production.

And yet the paradox held. The swinging bell in the great cathedral near the pension where we stayed in that ancient city. Built over centuries weird pockets of light on the entablature where the grotesque peeked at the world between the averted loins of the beautiful.

You turned toward me in sadness away from me in joy. That was a hard time.

Knots of the impenetrable hung like lianas in our room. Unbearable the brief openings of light. Seeing was. Between starlight and the seapaths of the moon. She stepped on darkness timidly gathering her hands each clutching a different fear to her small and withered breasts.

Cross.

Aching to and unable to. Behind him the ghosts of his unborn children. We received with clenched hands the offerings. We were showered with blessings. We held our hands over our heads to protect them from the sun. We pleaded for exemption.

By that time love had become unendurable.

The low iron railing around the small temple.

More crows.

At the time the orans presided the slim figure on the catacomb wall rose before him as he turned the corner her arms raised in prayer. The surprise of it. The wonder of a prayer that is not stooped to the knees head bent hands clasped the body clenched in the body language of pleading or contrition.

Not a supplicant a celebrant. Of what mystery you could not see in those eyes.

The beardless Christ the lamb against the white wall of the alcove. Fascinans. The tenderness of her. Presents. What was that unknowingness other than the search for. Scintilla. Where the body met the gleaning of its desire. Caligine. Hard love. Broken softened worked to usefulness. But whose use. Contemplatio. Coincidentia. If there were god what then. What if not. Where put her longing. In hopeless quest for justice in the empty courts of the world. Squeezing the stone for blood. She lived in unquenched thirst in unslaked hunger. The ten thousand beings were not enough without the one thing needed. What is that. What is that. There was no way. Oppositorum. She murmured god not knowing what she said. She murmured all not knowing what she said. She murmured you not knowing what she said. Her arms made a cross of her body. A gesture of powerless wings.

At the center of her devotion burned a banked but incurable fury.

In the memoirs of the assistant nothing has been revealed. We will seek in vain for a persuasive justification. The main events are scanted the relief is of trivia against a background of confusion.

You never said you would tell me.

Given the arbitrariness of the cornerstone to the baptistry of conversion there was little telling what the eventual construction would amount to before collapsing. Piezo. Volta. Cell. Into the casuistry of ordinances and the dark faded mold where. Figural discourse reverted to a slightly quaint abstraction. Picking at instances of law and statistical aberration. The turtle's shield. Hiding from the interaction of the egg.

And when one was erased. Cities of infusion the cries of the crazy in the alley which reverted to euphemisms in the café. The night inversions. The male into the female connection to secure.

Resolved we thought we were enough.

Vast cope of twilight. Foundations rocking on the air were not beyond settling into the sea's. The sea's children heard almost laughing. Through the night shaft. Noises you mistook at first for desperation. Yes laughter.

My neighbor's face appeared suddenly on the back of my hand.
You cannot move further in. We found a coil rusting from a kind of
oxidized nostalgia. Of crystallized blood. It prevented us for years from
recognizing the future in the oak tree by the currents of the road....
Twenty years would pass before he woke. In the barranca. Inhabited
by only the shy natives of the past. Under the burning star.

In every rhetoric of explanation there was a trope of dismissal.
No mathematical system being both consistent and complete.
Incongruent topologies variant geometries of possibility taxonomies
of doubt leaving everything possible again. For example the taste
of your name in my mouth. Of salt and bay leaves. Unfinished
rosewood. A lock of chestnut hair shot with lianas of gray. Of white.
An irrational at the heart of counting.

Infinitely caressed endlessly aroused.

Moving toward the lightning of is followed by endless thunder.

A term that designifies god.

A broken curtain of rain covered the jungle mountain.

Having taken the absolute we were left with wheels of partial the
luminous individual flecked with drops of light.

The absolute contingent in the fragrance of the momentary.

The wilting tea rose in the bud vase.

Infinitely slow what had gone in a moment.

Whirring like a desert of butterflies rising off the coastal
islands.

Origami twisting in the fog.

A court of matriarchs passing judgment in the church cellar.

In the southwestern quadrant a smudge of comet like a smear of
chalk wiped by the night's finger.

The pristine attempt at a calculation not based on the imposition
of an identity.

Thralled. Parataxis. Metaphor.

I take you for what you cannot be.

Dusty grammar. Dusty grammarian.

Like pink dead worms on black asphalt after the autumn rains the words appearing beneath your hand. Then forgotten. Should anyone hear there being no difference since all is hidden in a code without cipher. The street washed clean next day. The crown of roads.

What story to tell. Is there a motion toward. Is there possibility. We live ones never knew when we set out we simply went. Between channel walls of expectation down flues of obligation anxiety and desire. Fear that we could not know. Could not be. Or have less than what we needed. Considerably less. Our being after all small sealed repositories of recurrent need. For nourishment protection the respectful greetings of friends. The family of toleration. And the blank terror of other people's gestures. To let us fall without our knowing into the nihilism of friendly manners. How we could be erased. At will. Our total dependence at the time to which we must at all times lie. Convincingly. With enthusiasm.

And take what power we might.

The last definition of freedom you repeated to me over a midweek lunch at Zingari. Is the freedom to fire. And immediately flames surrounded the small flat in a nondescript part of the city. Dancing ecstatically. Like a mummer in a drunken August cakewalk lighting the drug that had transcended our eyes. Laughing loud they carried you enthusiastically to another part of the city where they dumped your unconscious but still breathing carcass between a trailer of unintelligible ideals and a forklift.

He woke to the ululation of denials where what he admitted only proved what he never would. That was the story he had to tell. Tearing up the cards of his solitaire game one at a time until none are left. Of us. Of you.

Let tenderness advance as the answer to uncertainty if all this escapes your understanding. For it certainly escapes mine. As it escaped his. Battlements not so much needed as granted without asking. Gunwales against which the fishermen slept. There were banquets every evening and a gift for quiet laughter. Students met in the garden and rehearsed the ideas of millennial exploration. Most wrong turns were not denounced as much as welcomed with a gracious baffled smile. For every labyrinth had a santos at its heart. The couples on the tombs were holding hands. But you were left alone with your happiness. Guilt was considered a rumor yet even it was given a room where it might lay its head for the night. Shame blushed at its posterity of joy. Little boys met in secret covens of adventure where revenge against the dragon was plotted where ciphered screeds were rolled in expectant corners. Back lots were empires haunted houses challenges to our paladins neighboring woods enormous and unexplored frontiers. We played Indians in the yellow weeds.

There were signs in the sky above Lock.

Our lives were unfolding symbols lined with promise and warning. Vast green and enormous blue were the theater for our shadow plays. A drama was an incitement to glory. The small beauty of the snapdragon was the signature of an all-powerful tenderness. Shadows stalked the earth beneath the vast keels of the clouds. There was no hardness that did not have in mind our happiness.

God was in the wind. No sooner doubt it than doubt your doubt of it.

Pirates laughed in the beech trees. The cavalry irrupted from stands of bush. Adventure was the taste of the morning as comfort was that of twilight. Happiness was no promise for tomorrow happiness was perpetual now.

Our castle held us like a hand its corridors were roads to the edges of the sea. Its walls were hung with tapestries designed in abstract brocades of rich hues threaded with mineral. Wolfhounds slept near the fire twitching at dreams of prey. The high roof suspended kingdoms and opened at the vanishing of the sun to show us the vast entanglement of the stars.

Snow was the frame for our wonder.

Silence. Silence. Yet more silence. He is listening no longer.

At the bottom of the stairs lay a head like a peeled heart. We set the traps with human bait.

In the stalls hung the split carcasses of hogs. Stink of flies above the catchment. No stimulant more vitalizing. It edged the mind with a strange unwholesome clarity. There was nothing to see but the revulsion of the audience. Of doubtful sincerity. For they were fascinated by the roadside sandwich of bodies pressed between the slammed cars.

A skein of cues and forgotten lines. An attack of stagefright in a hermit's den.

The legerdemain of power the hostile examination of language.

The birth of innocence.

Roadkill.

Jersualem cross targets.

The iniquity of the page followed you like a lovesick dog.

Text for midrash.

Squatting in the sweat lodge baying at the points of the compass. Some might consider it a euphemism for hysteria. And other attention deficits. A naked muttering accosting a prim silence. And we lifted like the ash of a burning moth. You cupped your hand around the thought of my pain. Then carefully pressed the scalpel in.

In the first of the twenty-three layers that constituted the ancient city before the conquest by Scipio Africanus lay the undressed stones of a temple in its original foundation. Teneo te. Terra mea. In the turbulence of no peace. A branding. Lamb on the altar pulled splay. Army lined along the ridge. Tossed banners flickering in a crosswind.

Nothing more a threat than the moment of incarnation. The tangle of roots edged into us from variant wildernesses of phoneme and radical the rangers stood watch in the towers of spiders. Facies zone.

Women were the generators of insoluble problems.

Their goal was the demolition of what they called the crystal dome. It was strenuous and there was no standard of success. The obsession and frustration of the overachiever. Delayed resolution of the chord. The dream of your death unknown to me. Behind my back suddenly erased. I had not dreamt of you in years. Not since our awful love began. Was it love it was love. The nave turned around itself in the choir. I had come to the end point of land in the sound there was nowhere to turn but back. And in that moment you disappeared.

The soundless words chipped into the low stone wall. An admonition you no longer remember. Yes. Towers.

The soft book grew beneath your hands. One by one the leaves unfolded across the binding in the palm. Patient eyes wondering if there was a story there and if so when it would begin. Catching at the melody as if at a thread. Echoes. You dozed off for a moment. The liminal threshold where most dreams are remembered. Rapid eye movement. Saccade. If there is an attack into sleep. Barren plains. The percentage of remuneration times the interest on your debt. What if your love letter to the world is unreadable sweet foolish romantic. Connections fall on every side rise unscaleable walls. Of glass and snowpack.

Resist the seduction at your peril. Licking your lips. You love. What was there about. To possibly. Tantalus. Wading though mercury a mirror of sea. It gilds the flanks of Venus. There is nothing to want he said primly because there is nothing to have. There. Hole surrounded by flesh. She heard. And fled. Doors slamming down the hall. You know too much. It was a long tale compressed into a few words. A catherine wheel. A stocking. A metal box. Because you didn't. Not once. Ever.

His emotional level was that of an underdeveloped graduate student. No one he had loved had yet died. It was bound to go on forever. Our power was infinite. We were going to show them how it was done. One of the gifts of age is that you learn to forgive the young their unforgivingness. We became at last kind to ourselves. In their eyes danced the splendor of the absolute. Success was mandatory. Grandeur vaulted on every side. The universe opened like an enormous theater and beckoned you to the tables of honor. Hosts of women gazed at us from cushions along the palace corridor. A hand gently and thoughtfully attended your advance into wandering. Although our secrets were held in a polished vanity chest locked with gold and inlaid with mother-of-pearl we consulted them only on the soft occasions when our judges were safe to ignore us. Bliss was it. The enameled park. A molted feather lay on the stoop. I put forth my hand fearfully and tenderly.

The heavy snows were after all the first promise of spring.

The solitary one briefly rejoiced in his hard-won aloneness and listened with affection through the decaying wall to the ghosts.

Nothing whatever could stop us. Every conversation dissolved into music. The thrush on the locust tree in the darkening courtyard sang for you alone. Walking the streets was a triumphal procession. Joy was not as much an anticipation as an embarrassment. I was almost ashamed of my happiness.

We were giants and wrapped the crowds in our arms. She ached to give. He was the banner of his own victory. You moved from temple to temple seeking a god adequate to your worship. The only source of a deepening sadness was the thought that you would never be adequate to your love. There were so many clouds.

And the sun and an assault of laughter. Aimless shafts vaulted into the white dandelion air. The hunters knocked at the sky's mother-of-pearl. The springhouse. The feel of cold water on her ankles. In the left hand was an oyster shell in the right hand fields of summer corn. Intensities of endurance and the demand for an instant heroism. Marked the intolerance of the young ones.

So that we learned to thank.

What before left us fitting fragments into a pattern that might suggest a symbol out of the luminous trash of the past a night road to the future.

The solitary one smiled in the darkness of the shed. Among the branches the spiders were weaving a signature across the sky.

Fears crossed the field in clouds of fireflies. Lambent anxieties fox fire. Immense spires. A flock spiralling across the autumn bells. Agate and rose that. That there were helices where asymptotes had been denied. Begging ever closer. Truth functions and the elegance of symbolic logic revealed to have been forms of political torture. The ascent of equality led to the even distribution of pain across any given population. *If everyone is unhappy.* What is daunting is the prospect of joy. Instinct for leveling and the vertigo of the spectacle. Tropism of the valley peeling away layers on layers of mountain. Intoxicating view. The point was to be reasonable beyond the tolerance of pain. Avoidance theory propounded the law of the deflection of bodies proportional to the square of their desire. The fear of sex was the fear of dissolution. We paused in astonishment. The century was just beginning to end a new one to begin. To millennial strains. How could one hold so many symmetries in one hand.

You made a sign to keep me from staying. But it was a language I had not mastered. There was no response. Yesterday's signs of romance seemed embarrassing today. They had made us. It was time to lay siege to the city but all we had were catapults of oak and gut and battering rams from an old millennium.

Daydreams spinning into sunlight.

It was a hackneyed phrase but so true so true.

The wilderness of their bodies. He wondered if he should be ashamed. All my life I sought the woman who all my life would flee. Perhaps after several years of celibacy it was time to end. Is masturbation a form of celibacy what after all is the survival value of the opposable thumb. You turned from me appalled. No one like you should have desire you said. I will save you I will screw you I will dump you. The sequence rigidly followed. My heart committed suicide several times. It was easier than murder. Like life itself. To erase the memory of love with great slowness.

The gods of adequacy were laughing you could hear it at the head of the stairs.

The theory of chaos after all was not a theory of chaos.

Words clustered according to structures of grammar over which the speaker had no ultimate control. Association was free only to a point. Which was as frustrating as it was reassuring. Or will be. The roses on the trellis near the birdbath in the forgotten corner of the garden. Night light. I played a game of stones on a sort of frame of random parallels. We bared our bleeding wrists to the moon and the long sleep of the bees.

Evensong.

Arrows of geese. The plangent honk and responding laughter the hug of the enormous ground.

Windmills.

The smell of drying oils.

It gave you your first sensation of a life ruined by art hunt for phantoms craft of illusions obsessive assertions of rejected self the seduction the strange liminal joy.

A life devoted to the masochism of romance.

For thou art. Glory. And I worship thee. Power. Bless me. Again. Splendor. Show thyself. In glory. Make me. Yours. Destroy me. Again. He said. And she heard. You noted this in your yellow notebook of suspect themes for future research.

He felt as though he were walking down the streets of a vanishing life with a bomb ticking between his thighs. A terrorist of love. You have been condemned to kill all in your vicinity in a series of virtual suicides. Though years had passed. And harm was not after all his intent. It was more like redemption. Not health the goal kept firmly in mind but transcendence.

Precession of paradoxes in testimonials of exhausted desire. Sated with self-love they turned back to the world with enchanted eyes.

How could one not have suspected them of predatory habits given their way of life their income their neighborhood their diet. The calcified victim found after exploratory surgery in the alimentary canal. Of course we were vegetarian that year. It was all we could do to suspend our purity for a summer. There is nothing as ludicrous as self-confidence. Our lives were pratfalls of faith. We kept stubbing against the thresholds of our perfection and raged in tears all night over our book of failures.

We never forgave the mirror its serenity.

For the source of our relentless feelings of guilt was our inability to rise to our own standards for longer than it took to reveal them. Then we collapsed. Yet the sun hung above us so blinding and so clear. Our hatred of life you must understand was the purest expression of our love. We had no hope and yet we were prickly with moods and tenderness. It was an askesis of being. Existence then was a murderous joy. Truth was no longer possible and yet was our only hope.

Our hands bled from handling the stars. The larval stage of being was the rat on the threshold of maturity. Effloresence. Denial. Erasure. What was our life it was the politics of the everyday the abandonment of expectation the reality principle defeating the pleasure principle in single combat.

Ocean.

And love if not a hand held out to the impossible as to an abandoned child. Folded clothes locked in a winter closet. The smell of mildew and mothballs. And the child left to die on the night hillside. Faced it once then turned away. The twisting neck of the owl. Its cry like that of a woman's shriek as she comes as she gives birth as she dies as she attacks. As the blood freezes into being.

The night is so silent. Did I fall asleep? He's moved. Yes, I'm sure he's moved.

Compline.

The ice cross of the moon blanches the winter fields of what was once your home.

Distant barking.

The edge of light at the bottom of the architect's lamp moves unsteadily as he draws it near. A careful deleting.

A blade sweeps the strings of a harp.

The invincibility of the human is terrifying. That is why she ignored it. Raised in a center of darkness the breasts of gift. Needing to give. Pulsating with the most generous of frustrations.

There was nowhere to stand where she drowned. Flailing between knots of driftwood. The sand loosening between her fingers. She sailed like an angel into the sea. And he was left to his despair watching.

That's too easy despair is easy death is easy what is hard hard is reaching out holding on drawing in is life is hope is love she proclaimed all heroism the violets falling from her eyes.

She wept in her anger. I will not give up I will not she broke down I will not not not. He stroked her hair from far away from across the sea he reached out and wiped the tears with his finger. He held her in the world of his arms. They did not settle for less than everything. They scarred each other's hearts with diamonds. The dream of each was the storm in which the other wrecked and drowned.

There were those who refused all sorrow their faces were fixed in a purity of mad joy. You met them in the hallways of the university they were often surrounded by admirers. The mind was its own place they shouted in the square there is no loss that is not gain the erasure of earth is the birthing of a star behind each love there is another.

Ill wind.

You looked at them bewildered with hope you longed to believe. Chaos is unspeakable joy they said sorrow is a chatterbox. Her tears had no place in the dictatorship of fulfillment happiness is the only imperative happiness is success success is the moment's victor follow it. Wipe memory from your lips with the kiss's fervor lick the body that desires you enter pleasure engulf joy go crazy with absolute clarity.

She writhed on the dance floor like a snake of banners blotting out the past the future the latticework of obligation and care crumbled in the moment's fire such power raised such love from the flames.

Among the flash-fire cities the shimmer of landscapes the flicker and vanishing of empire and continent and ocean and world turned and dissolved the face of every person she had loved o pyre of essence o woodland of flames.

Sudden palaces.

She could not stand she could not walk she could not lie so she danced on the floor of embers secretly hoping for a quick end to all. Which cannot be given like every too-passionate desire.

The smell of burning skin.

They smeared their bodies with water and ash. Where there had been a body there was a vanishing. In the garden a wood dove flickered between the trees.

Plush consoles and amber ornaments the caught fly of an extinct species clearly articulated in the polished sepia-brown oblong.

Porcelain objects aligned with studied negligence on shallow glass shelves.

Shafts of light supporting the ends of long afternoon hallways.

Motes hung above the carpets.

They were shrewd and manipulative at that time. It was the result of a cunning ancestor's unscrupulous and patient accumulation of a jealous futurity.

Stocks and bonds.

It was a chained freedom but it was freedom.

I had always assumed wealth. What a shock.

The flattering placement of mirrors on landings at the ends of brief corridors above the mantel of the rarely used fireplace.

Her ears were indeed translucent. Paper nautilus of light.

The pinking shears on the formica table top. Zigzags of cloth. A hum and throttle of sewing machine. Domiciliary habits and cares the round paper lid of the glass milk bottle. Thumb and finger. A closing refrigerator door the breath of cold. That made one feel briefly warmer.

Snow outside.

Such happiness.

And when the rains came we dawdled in doorways and played endless games on the scattered rugs gin and monopoly and magic tricks and marbles and jacks for the girls and quarrelled because reconciliations were so nice and ran away though there was nowhere to run our universe was infinite and bound.

Tranquility over the waters of the Cher. Chenonceau my castle of murmurs. What a theater it is you said. What I asked. And embarrassed and happy she said our life. Oh yes that yes our life I said should we be grateful she said or ashamed.

The long climb out of the valley of nettles and ice streams toward the village on the summer plateau.

Pockets of schist and huge knuckles of moraine like the remains of.

The oblique angle of anticipation.

Although they were uncertain how their adventures would turn out and disaster was always a prospect.

The pleasure of not quite knowing what might happen next.
Politics.
The possibility of imminent collapse.
A shadow propped against a corner of the empty living room.
Why after a certain age one ceases to feel.
Unknown to them they had blossomed.
The beach was littered with fallen roses.

And the stones rose between the cedars in a gray pile of incoherent elevations and scrambled floorplans. You made your way through as though it were desire's maze. Every corner offered an enthralling spectacle in prospect an illusory dead end. For pessimism was never entirely justified. Nor optimism though there was always hope on that island despite every setback and there were many. The roads you drove down were defined by the ditches you fell into. The tangle of mist resolved for a moment into a map a circuit board of currents carefully engineered to offer you a way out or at least the thought. Here was a door there a window we were given much scope. On the porch the rockers in the cellar a winter's load of coal. A curtain in the draft. A statistical average of contentment between extremes of nightmare and ecstasy. Unsheathed nerves and the tenderness beneath the callous.

It was advised to render not too much even to the heart if you would know contentment.

A view of mountains seen before only in photographs and movies.

It was a vastness one could not even dream. Nor remember except as a stifled exclamation.

Cold and unbroken.

White heights.

The fishermen returned home at nightfall bearing presents from the sea. A shoal of blues had caught in an undercurrent past the windward islands and drove down the coast past the sparkling lines. The men with their waiting hooks. In patience the bait was a window the capture a charm. And possession a means of honorable seduction.

They flailed in the buckets but could not escape. Not then. The panting of the gray gills the flanks the spasms of hope the cold eyes in retreat.

Arc of terror.

To leap from your hands into the sea. To escape anyhow anywhere and keep escaping. As though the world were a bucket the sea a crowd of hands clasping them as they flee the medium of their escape their prison. In those eyes unmistakable panic.

We were the fishermen and the sea and the baited hook and the caught fish and the longing to escape and the hunger and the nourishment that fed us. A ubiquity of incomprehensible yet the charge was to discover. Slated in commands of chalk.

So she fed herself on her fear.

He sliced the fruit and raised each piece to her lips.

What he found in the book that he had removed without help from the high shelf in the school library was a maze and tangle of highly wrought phrases that described a cast of experiences by turns agonizing and ecstatic without clear cause enigmatic to the ignorant reader.

He was made to feel like a child listening to the incomprehensible conversation of adults the shorthand of an uncanny omniscience.

These were the beneficiaries of power.

His only certainty was that he would be put in the wrong and made to pay for it.

The penalties came randomly and severely.

You had to make up your mind though mind was what you did not yet have.

He stood on the threshold unable either to enter the room or turn on his heel and leave.

The darkness at each moment promised to break and did not.

Phase transition into being.

The war against reality.

It was like a dream and you wanted to awake and were not allowed to.

Words wedded in luminous arcs chains of laughter lightning and music promised a gift even as they dimmed to haunting possibility brightened in the air between two eager faces rose from the pages of an afternoon garden then out of nowhere broke like a pod eaten by parasites clashed in the twilight scattered like fireworks fell into pockets of ash and brightness memories of regard grails of understanding burned the ear with anger and fear shimmering in splinters of incomprehension.

All was in suspense it was thrilling at first and for long after not knowing or caring to know not seeing ahead more than the next curve in the road the spine of the next hill against a cloud forming on the horizon a charge of lights down a night road a crowd of shadows massing around your head your hand held out for an alm of the mystery.

But then one wanted it to resolve into something firm and clear a plinth of stone a crystal even a door of lead to batter against in exhausted frustration for it was mortally wearying to chase it over those icy meadows there was nowhere to rest there was nothing to believe there was nothing to know but no it stayed quick and fluid and slipped from his grasp like a joke he was not meant to understand the book the solitary one read was his life at that time it abandoned him to questions he could not answer yet needed to urgently it tantalized him with every conceivable answer and

therefore

no answer at all the binding dissolved in his hands the print appeared on his palms he read the runes of his veins until he was half blind.

You wanted to run away but there was nowhere to run.

This was escape and there was nowhere to escape from that.

Any attempt to stop the wheel merely made it turn faster.

The world spun like a nail inside his head. It drove down through in out the axis of a top a pain just barely endurable.

Nothing was allowed to make sense.

The hammer descended without ever reaching the vase.

Neither creation nor destruction but a state between the two suspended.

The unmerited punishment of love.

Silence. Or is it the hum of an iron lung? But do iron lungs hum?

Or have you too fallen asleep.

Then you will never know how she contracted bliss that summer. There was nothing that was not real. She wore sun dresses and woven sandals and her hair in a long braid or loose bun and large floppy hats that hid her eyes from the sky. She carried her heart between her lips. A silver anklet sparkled at the back of her mind but she feared that wearing one might make her meaning too clear. She had the painful tenderness of those who are both timid and sincere. She told herself bitter truths in the desolation of her solitude as though picking at a wound that would not heal. She was moral to a fault. She was in love with God. She was ashamed of the blood between her thighs. She wore no lipstick on the day it started it was as though she were doing penance for something she had forgotten she ached to remember. Her mother had not told her how it hard it was to be a woman and why were men so unaware. She opened her eyes with all her might she fed on light as a vampire does on blood and yet we saw nothing at the time. Her body was a wall between herself and the world. And yet there were times when the wall collapsed and light streamed in from every side bathing her darkness and penetrating her with wave on wave of joy.

Where did it come from where did it go.

There was amazement in the day. Anything could happen anything did happen. Her body shifted with the tides her body perished in the arms of the moon from those same arms her body was reborn her body was her tyrant her body was her lover her body was her betrayer a locus of tempests the principle of chaos the fault line passed through her she was the problem that no one could solve she carried a twister in her womb. Beneath her silence there was laughter shaking with tears. She felt like an aircraft doing somersaults in the air always on the point of lunging into a dive the crowd would be astonished amazed horrified with an eerie feeling of privilege that they had witnessed the tragedy they would never forget that day.

Salto mortale.

She sat quietly in a corner and felt herself spinning out of control.

It was when she was happy that we worried most when she was desperate we shrugged at what we called her moods.

She walked in unsteady balance over the abyss of her body trying not to look down.

What will you do he asked himself on the other side of the partition.

The light had fallen from the day.

Between his desire and his desire there was fear it was like a page written in words of shame.

There came a time when he was afraid to let himself believe.

Golden was the arrow catching up with him as he vaulted toward the clouds. Gentle were the fingers of the bars. So he wrapped himself up between his walls.

It was love that then ripped him from himself and returned to him shame and joy he walked each day across the splinters of his heart the scabs became scars the scars became callous eventually free of the bandages and the splint he hobbled outside again to the open air.

Birdsong emptiness.

She does not love you he said to the morning and grew calm.

He returned the precious object to the shelf and steadied his nerves with a drink that was tasteless and clear.

He had lost often enough to play without hope he had given up hope he was tranquil. Not joy not despair he thought anything but joy and despair.

He discovered the reassurance of control.

What after all was contentment not obtaining what one desires but not having desired or gained. Satiety and peace though this contradicted what he had just thought.

He began smoking again.

He picked his heart to pieces and then shook the pieces over the ground they lay there dazzling in the sunlight splinters of glass and flames as he stood blanked out in the sun. There was nothing to do but give up I am not a saint I am not a hero he repeated to himself over and over.

In the mirror he saw her bitter look.

Equipoise between two hindrances paralysis before the fork in the road which way leads faster to damnation one cannot tell from here the depth of the fall. So he thought at the time. He had grown.

Nothing appeared as grand as what had never been but might be. The air was transparent as possibility it smelled without the pungent stimulating stench extremely pleasurable (piercing sweet) in small doses of reality.

It was now clear. There was no smog at all between himself and his eyes. His movements his words were painfully awkward his thoughts his feelings were dazzling swift all powerful they swept the night in enormous dreams oh what will life hold in store. He was in love with life he could hardly bear the joy of taking in a breath the deep penetration of the light. He felt the hand of God beneath his feet each thought was touched with grace he felt the terrible privilege of living. He heard the hosannas of the angels welcoming him into time he shook in thankfulness. He felt so happy he was almost ashamed. They whispered among themselves and tittered softly the young women. The solitary one felt no solitude rather a rustling of wings and whispers that followed him everywhere. Desire burned in his hand. The torch procession grew out of the darkness he watched it moving toward him the songs grew louder there was drunken laughter it was a wedding procession they were bearing the newlyweds to their tent somewhere at the edge of the darkness. He stood off to the side wondering when it would be his turn to join in. The waiting grew longer it stretched into years it threatened to become his life he was paralyzed watching. Act act cried the voice inside him to which he could only reply how? All action was self-canceling. Turn to her embrace her take the beloved face between your hands and kiss. Her. Oh that. Oh yes. Take the fiery iron in your hands it will scorch the skin from your hands like paper but it will also illumine. The deep shaft of being the dark well of her body. The night that lies behind her eyes. Take it enclose it as a glass does water contain it in a firm grasp and do not let it go. She will flee you but it will be mock flight. She will thrum at the bars you draw around her and fall back into your arms. But you must act says the voice or earn the punishment that is self-contempt and burn in its unforgivingness.

So he heard at that time as he stood on the threshold looking out at the day.

Shavings on the floor of the woodshed. The sweet poisonous smell of gasoline. And cautious the spider descends from its tangle of logarithms and surds into the resplendent darkness cautious and daring. Like a folly of mountaineers up the Nameless Tower sheer face a thousand meters up. Up into the crystal enormousness. A vault of leap into the sky. Spectacular. Toward the cauldron. That darkness nameless with radiance. Her undeniable pain. Which he could only gaze at paralyzed with pity and longing across the battlefield of the room. As she picked her way through the dead. Singing.

The solitary one marked each spot favored by his solitude with a flower of bent iron. These marked the shrines of his happiness even when he had known love especially when he had known love. For he gathered his love to him in his solitude and relished it there far from others far from the other far even from the beloved.

She danced and whispered in his mind's theater its hidden balconies where transcendence transpired shadowy boxes generous stage. His eyes flickered with memories of her he used her for his own joy. He suspected this was not quite fair but he wished to be happy not good he had noted the abject cheeriness of good people the relaxed serenity of the profoundly selfish.

His central passion was to love he cared less to be loved in return being loved was a prison and a torture being loved was to have your skin removed a layer at a time by the loving eyes being loved was to be locked inside the cage called you and not let out except in anger.

To love was to grow a cloud of wings to be loved was to be buried alive.

There was something wrong there he knew but what was it in his mind that baffled him from that happiness.

He sat quietly in his room and listened to the breathing. Tantalizing to feel so vaguely guilty and serene. As if this removal were a deliberate abandonment but was not. Not deliberate it was not. Not deliberate abandonment with its accent of betrayal. Not that. No. But liberation.

But from what the solitary one asked the vacancy. And an answer came but from where.

From only human love.

A dust storm rose on the horizon the birds wheeled in ragged flocks.

There was nowhere to go that was not there.

The sun sucked up the darkness leaving behind blindness and nakedness. To be absolutely seen yet blind they could imagine no greater. Pain.

They moved alone across a field.

The farther they fled the tighter they were bound.

The grass pursued them burning. The walls of their eyes were blackened with bands of ash. It was a withing of weed and steel.

When will come the day when it will freeze into a shining of ice and cold detached and ponderable. As massy and solid in the hand as this stone. Remote as the history of an ancient century whose suffering inspires nostalgia for a time one never knew unreal and far and strangely pleasing in its depiction of struggle and victory followed by annihilation.

Into a cold and magnanimous page.

As they walked through the night of their love like torches.

The fishermen plucked their lines and there was a trammeling of fish. In the ozone above them the islands of depression had just begun to bend inwardly. Embossings of emptiness slippery with the sun.

Over the hill on the other slopes the village straggled to the edge of the forest. Fields enameled the borders of the farms. The sound of tractors tooted through the spring. The summers were silent with growth. The tractors chuffed with melancholy satisfaction sated sheaf-heavy in the fall. Kids were crying out as they played in the evening the occasional fight graced with theatrics of reconciliation. The neighbors pretended to despise each other but didn't poison the borrowed sugar. It was a happy time spiced with impatience for the future.

Cans of air stood on small grocery shelves in the fluorescent aisles of supermarkets.

We were without grief or guilt though obscurely frightened in that time of unrepentant optimism.

The television laughed like a household god the dishwasher hummed the toys smiled from the shelves the car lay supine in the garage. There were martinis waiting in the evening. Cartoons tickled Saturday mornings. Feasts regaled the gourmet nights and music defined the shifting of moods. Homework bored the kids with grudging reassurance. Teachers nasalled bullies leered girls goaded boys pretended to ignore them and struck their bats.

The hundred-year-old oak spread toward us its big gray boughs.

Sirens taught us to bow our heads under the ugly student desks.

Great clouds began invading our dreams.

The sky was tendentious with visions of rockets pointing at us like accusing fingers.

But we were innocent how could we deserve such a punishment. We were pursuing happiness it was a God-given right it was mandatory.

So we learned to deny everything.

The hedgehog disguised as a fox it was his best trick.

To seduce serenity.

Caretaker of breeding generator of the sunrise.

The girl on the beach with the ocelot.

The surfers in the tunnels of the waves.

The acrobats of sticks and platters.

The bright hip shakers of hoola hoops.

The conquerors of bicycles.

The cards spread on the table.

The disdainful minx in the sand.

Childhood? The lost paradise? What was that?

There was so much more to come. I stared hungrily at a tin can called tomorrow placed up on a high shelf. There was no opener sharp enough. There was no ladder tall enough. There was no tomorrow far enough away for me not to dream about it. Oh how happy I would be how happy. So happy I sped beyond dying and what would heaven be what was the greatest happiness I could imagine. It was this to live over again and over every instant of my little life from birth to dying every moment in an eternal chain forever forever forever.

What joy. What unspeakable joy. Life. Life.

Between those two states of twilight a flare of darkness woven with flashing at what moment did the brightness of the night the comfortable darkness of day start? Not from this porch was the line across the sky visible it paled out on either side connecting moon and sun like scales balanced against a pale blue screen. The roof and pillars formed a frame expanding the vastness the open never quite gave rather contracted.

Perceptual puzzle.

As grammar by framing time expands it. As time unordered contracts and withers away aimlessly. Luminous the larval stage of being if it had ever been anything else. You turned on your heel in the doorway and found yourself spinning forever. Only thinking back was there the crystal. Only looking back was the shadow thrown against the clouds majestic monumental that was I. Wow. As the mist vaporizes into evening. Something unknown defined you. What was to come. His ignorance drew a wiry line around him exact as a blade. I am because I do not know. How retrieve the redemptive ignorance he thought how forget the future. Overthrow the tyrant. Liberate the nation. Break through the palace gates. Kill the guards. Seize the temple. Conquer happiness. Draw back a step at a time blissfully into unknowingness. Toward where he stands now at this moment staring down.

(You pored through the snapshots the old documents seeking a thread that might bind them together. It's the morning of the next day. What made the day before a whole or seem so all the days before up to this one the decades. A lance across a windowsill. What I possess at the moment a confusion of papers and days. That doesn't quite fit. That don't quite fit. Bills invoices postcards letters uninformative from family and friends vaguely threatening or speciously friendly but deeply sincere from businesses requesting cashflow from you. Journals. Drafts of letters never sent. Glossy paper stained with white shadows. The one sure thing the oblivion before birth. Stuffed with movies and reading. And less certain the one to come. Oblivion that is. Dickered with guessing. Your life a deceptive confusion between. Suggesting order but never. Not sure even of that. Your prize possession your uncertainty. And nebulous fantasies obscure memories consigned to paper. Or computer screen. What a lark the literary life. Who is "he"? Who is "she"? Who is "you" or "I"? A vastness echoing with the sighing of cars birdsong half-heard speech the sound of barking dogs. Even that. Back into it you must. Lie between dreams. Guess at recall. Go.)

They're all sleeping. Even the guard, look at him. No, it's all right. Just stay here. Sometimes he says something in his sleep, but I can't tell what it is. Listen if you want. I'll bring you a ...

Home. It marked the pattern best. Their household. A fixture between the villages. The slide at the back a swing set an archery target one spring put up against bales of hay. He sat on the grassy bank and gazed across the fields. A dreamer. Nothing made him happier than staring at the clouds. Or the delicious shallow-sea illusion of summer cornfields moving under the wind. Early summer. Late spring. Beginning of the fall. He was convinced he had been made to be happy. A difficult prejudice to shake. And yet it seemed so obvious so clear. For he was happy then.

The lights in the house across the night field.

Always distance however close always the horizon edged with trees and the far point of light sparkling on a hill's darkness that made you dream of that distant happiness those lives you could only guess at. And preferred guessing knowledge always a. Only the dream. Nothing more. Enough.

Thus dreams were protected there. Honored. A happy childhood. It comes to you now with surprise given. The place where he went to hide. From them all. Could. Can. Shall. The dogwood blossoming in the picture window.

Until he disappeared. Out of joy.

Deeper in. Further.

For there was money oh one was not supposed to mention that it was not sex one hid one's salary or the salary of one's parents one's father at the time. And the money behind that. One always assumed sufficient funds there was no question folly the mulch of happiness. Behind the battlements of one's parents' faces stood the brightly shining edges of the mint always unfathomable unmentioned and presumed the good life security false or real. The garden bed. Flowers falling to the hand fruit bending to the mouth. The laziness of expectation will ruin your future. But he does not know then. He dreams. Not knowing the decline from an extravagant wealth to the genteel pretensions decorating the poverty of his domicile to come.

Wealth.

Decor.

Sun.

Exterior.

Day.

The frame of childhood where the little boy with the crewcut stands looking hopefully into your eyes. Up. Smiling as if for a photograph. Straining just a little. Slightly uncomfortable self-conscious. With unquestioning and boundless trust. Of course I believe the face says frowning a little. I've seen it.

What.

In the clouds that cross in the stars picking light from in the turmoil of in the hills the cornfields in the woods the face and hands of. No. Don't give it a name. A gesture only. What. That. This. The all of it although I know only this only that. Pinched between moon and sun. Pageant moving in unending circle. Always returning to its place yet shifting. Always returning yet always. New. Beyond us containing us. Small and foolish and proud. Reflecting it. Even death no object of fear. Even oblivion no reason for. For the single one lives only through the all of it only the all of it. Counts. Cradles the dead one like a child folds around it its arms taking it in. Tenderly. Perhaps. So he thought when he found the body of bird or rabbit or mouse as he walked the fields through the woods near the back of the house after school. For even in the dead one there was life it became nourishment gave back as it had been given. Given. Death was a justice not a punishment. You missed the point it is not here for you you (the small boy thought) are a little gold thread in a vast fabric draping the shoulders of you have your place you are not all you are the center you are not the center either way it makes no difference if you do not know this the universe ignores it either way.

And yet thought the boy how many. Suffer. And make suffer.

And he remembered photographs and films he had seen of dead naked bodies found in large walled and fenced camps after a recent war. And the pity and horror that had then touched his forehead.

And the woods said nothing.

But why don't you teach me? thought the boy.

You will learn or not you cannot be taught you children with the poison of adults you will destroy whatever you can out of boredom pride envy crazy-eyed optimism look at the clever ones what trouble they get into someday they will grow up and become dangerous there is a storm of godlike laughter.

And woke hearing his own voice echo in the room.

The solitary one walked the fields intent on the sounds.

The sounds of broken straw in the wind of single birds whistle and chuff of wings of old leaves clapping on the gray boughs or singing across the ground.

Whistle of wind through an old bone.

The fallen trunk rotting in the yellow grass.

The vivifying odor of decay.

All the life of the land mulching inward into the land.

The bustle around an anthill.

The vagrant buzz of a late bee.

The tingle of a cobweb against his cheek as he walks between two apple trees.

Unending net of connective across the mud and air.

Deepening weave of loom in loom. Fabric. Carpet. Spell. The wonder of it. Hidden and woven and teeming. Unregarding him anything human. However spurious even transcendence. Illusion whatever price.

Drunk and happy he walked from end to end of his solitude to where the fields broke up into gray and welcoming woods.

Where he shot his look up suddenly to confront the sky's absolute eye.

And the cold fell.
Deepening weft of light and dirt.
Fabric become stone field.
Carpet become.
Spell.
Crystallizing wonder.
Hidden woven teeming frozen.
Still not regarding anything you.
However spurious.
Periphrasis in snow.
Empire of the inhuman.
Winter twilight.
Plunging mercury.
Venus raging in the east.

2

Couldn't hold on the substance escaped you a scum on your hands after popping soap bubbles airy light multicolored dancing nothing left after but echoes of ridicule and rebuke the light quivered with shame all that poetry doubtlessly pretty wisdom questionably profound what's it worth when you find yourself moneyless on the threshold of your life beaten humiliated abandoned by family lover friends but did you have any family lover friends to do the abandoning your employer sought means to replace you with something cheaper your landlord looked for legal means to evict you for someone richer you were a walking wound a mass of blisters boils in continuous abscess an emotional hemophiliac your presence on the street mortified you saw yourself in rags and filth stinking up the air a blot on the street leaving a trail of slime wherever you went carrying pestilence the eyes of suspicion examined his movements picked him up with vague curiosity put him down with quick distaste filed him in the drawer of incorrigibles smirked with satisfaction over his ineluctable failure here was little promise of anything worthwhile barely maintenance of a roof over his head food in his belly let's glory in his shame pride ourselves on his downfall against his darkness our light shines all the more brightly against such ugliness what radiance is ours our beauty shows all the more astonishingly he is the foil that brightens us the dazzling sun that makes the moon glow in the night dazzling sun they're mocking you pitiless angry envious behind its elegant colonial and Beaux Arts facades a city that never left the depression a reporter once said it wasn't called the city of brotherly love for nothing how does your wisdom answer that at the moment the pain slips into you like a razor beneath your fingernails where has it gone disappearing in a scream of rage.

The abrupt change from shelter to abandonment in the nightmare filth and blur kicked from the portals of the sky sudden horror out of the green paradise smelling of jasmine and cut grass out of the weedy shade the glistening dew out of childhood heaven into the psychotic shriek stench of garbage the homeless man on the sidewalk screaming at a strip of sky between office towers. Broken in two their life a snap of green wood and asphyxiating fire. Sudden pinching and shrinking darkening and lowering as if draining a country lake into a sewer sudden collapse from the house on the hill to the tight apartment in the city the water stank of chorine lukewarm like an unwanted kiss you barely saw the sun marking time above skyscrapers. Giant tombs of human hope. Loss of promise in the labyrinth. Concrete concrete. Metal glass. Streets straight and narrow as graves. A prison three million strong stretching as long as the horizon. The nights ringing with sirens and sleepless moans of traffic a patient in pain with cries. A pustule a fist a vast cesspool stinking with the. An ineradicable scar of the humiliation of. Dark and abrupt as the head of an ax as it fell between your possibilities your impossibilities your impotence on each face reflected the image of what might be and what must and shall. Absolute brutality of the real.

Human. Reduced precipitate distilled to. The least. The subtending bond that. Skin. Gristle. Need.

Laughter stuttering in the kitchen.

Voided what promise had made perennial confusion lambent change a handful of loose coins on the dresser keys severed locks.

Tirra-lirra-la.

The sounds of girls playing hopscotch drifting up from the alley.

A view of ginkgos.

Paste of gray in the sky.

Fetid odor of whiskey mash floating from the river an alkaline phlegm of rain.

Hopelessness you fled into the silence of music forest of books white paper.

The solitary one quiet one child collapsed inside his skin he would have to learn how to lock his eyes.

There was no she there only hardness meeting sparks splay in the air flint against glass sharp meeting sharp in a paralysis of furies. Strenuous and athletic hopelessness spitting delusions of. Encounter of cacophonies self-imposed gymnasts of. Exultant in their capacity for cynicism and survival. Laughter of unjoy. Exalted demonic desperate. Crossing every promise with a vindictive defeat sucking each other into a contest of. Obloquy. Monologs carried on inexhaustibly panted gasped unending hoarse in relentless refusal to stop gripping the mind in a vise squeezing into submission the silence of the pavements black pointlessness of an infinite grid of streets. Nothing returning to them everything moving in that chaos nothing changing as the prisoners threw themselves periodically against the walls of their cell but there was no way out for there was no way in no gates windows ingress egress the wall closed over their heads like a dome someone had taken pains to lock closed the sky. Panic. Horror. Rage. Despair. Resignation. Resentment. Until no longer able to take it they once again began to wring the necks of their neighbors. In the latest glaring of hope.

Who. Why the octopus of maggots.

My folly for was I not human why deny revile or try to escape the human was shoved down your throat.

Grab what is offered.

In random possession.

Filth depravity viciousness there was nothing the child could see especially beautiful about. The homeless woman shrieking curses in the afternoon. A dampness of rot hung from the ceilings. A cat hissed in one corner a dog growled in another. Each departed for a room no longer his own. They met in mutual loathing marked by periodic fits of delusion. Of liberation. The light from the lamp on the table was slowly erased. The towers beyond the window hung rows of yellow lights oblongs of a suspect luminosity that deflected imagining. Imagine the squalor behind the pane. Imagine the curl of stained sheets the smell of urine and vomit. The eyes of stupor. Or worse the prim gentility spiteful defensiveness of a dead-end career shredded family collapsed life attended to in a narrow grave furnished from thirty years ago.

Evade.

Escape.

Run.

Into self-imposed silence.

Bits of the past behind that past arranged on a blue tablecloth embroidered in white. Fragments large and small slivers and shards the shape of Mexico or France others like little men in oversized suits others the profiles of half-forgotten women. A bird in flight or balanced on a wire singing furiously. A spider suspended in a bathroom doorway. (No cockroach nocturnal innovation among vermin yet ancient as the horseshoe crab skittering behind the sugar jar. Yet. Here.) No. The shape of the light in a shaft of dust. There. A hand sweeps a towel hanging on a clothesline out of range of your sight. The sour taste of unripe grapes an almost black blue despite the fuzz of fungus on the skins. Theft. The pleasure of. Mr. Carter's grapes you must not steal them. Must you.

There was that small corner in the backyard where you always felt hidden though you weren't. As though there visibility had been secrecy. A kind of safety. Or a little throne of stones. Ochre. Where on boring afternoons you could be more tolerably bored. Smearing your hands on your pants. Negligently exposing the stain of your crime.

At times the pieces are swept from the table with cavalier violence and you must build fragments from the air as if nothing had ever been.

A pattern of white flowers on slate blue.

Or rather a list of miscarryings. The melancholy woman with the long leash of dogs. Gone. The spokesman of anarchy on the indifferent corner. Now. A young girl in a tartan jumper and white socks sears the air with mockery. A grocer stares at the vacancy of your request. In a pharmacy a fat black girl full of anger and laughter. A slinking middle-aged queer with furtive and defiant eyes. The defensive Italian bellows silently at traffic. The Irish teenager eyes the sidewalks with predatory anguish. Anxieties of pigeons locked in a recursive loop they flock pointlessly in the lengthening autumn their genes summoning them to a migration they can neither pursue nor escape.

The light goes on. It could fill volumes of brick asphalt and antique glass could bulge from the libraries of tar warped window jambs creosote roofs gray raining sky. A book ducked in a puddle bloating obscenely its pages open like a whore from her inner elbow a needle slips into the gutter near her hand. Tiny cake of blood. Oil on the surface of the water. Tangled hair and cigarette butts in the sewer drain. A newspaper shouts that a politician has lied to it. A bus exhausted to a standstill vomits an irritable clot of neighbors. Viscera of unease. Tighten. Smirks at the back of good morning. A battlefield littered with undegrading mines. To say nothing of the tedium of waiting for the next eradicating discharge.

Ring the bell. Memory over winter fields. The crack of a shotgun came to you from a fissure in your sleep followed by the echo. In dream memory loomed. The castigations of the luminous. Buried in the forbidden territory of the real it blazes.

The solitary one withdrew into silence there was nowhere now to hide. Building a honeycomb of stillness around him he kept the others at bay behind a wall of stiff smiling. They treated him like a child he would behave like a child. Yet he was a child. I ask no forgiveness I give no quarter. Proud and ashamed of your conceit in your mind yours was a heroism of solitude. I hugged it to me like an honor or a scar. The rings of silence opened around him pulling in the winter birds to nest in the branches. A falling star burned through a leaf and ignited a forest into acres of fire. And I stood within it singing at the top of my lungs. The wet streets smeared with scattered trash.

For the air was jammed with signal. The heliotrope in the ghetto lot sagged in tangles of glare and amazement. Plethora. Bricks stuck to mortar and aimless encounters. A fist closing around a tube of wax. Sculls skittering down the river like huge waterskates. A centipede in the bath tub. Migrating colonies of roaches. Scrambling rats. The walls sweated vermin and sardonic ripostes. A family in that place was a form of organized insecurity.

No doubt.

In immanence a patient god lies in the paper under your feet. Speaking without sound in the slang of the city's misery. Without pause.

Well the sortie was made. The platter shield up the basin-helm cocked over the brow. A cat's cradle of stares linked across the subway stations. The casual swipe of the train. Entire generations never made it upstairs.

A fit of paranoia on a regular basis was only natural.

Given that the family itself was on the verge of collapse. In the swarm of darknesses vying with futility. The gymnastics of desperation as though one were not even allowed to die so told the cry rising from the street. We are not allowed so you are not allowed.

Commands from all sides countermanding commands from all sides. Of hope for example in general and in some cases particular. Which was as in other such cases of dubious account.

Lament become customary. The muzak of the neighborhoods.

You will eventually not even notice it or notice it only when it isn't there the eerie silence of the countryside those rare times you are able to visit it dependent as you are on others' transportation. Outside the raucous rural night that is. Where is the music of despair I hear nothing the silence is like a love song in a death camp have you ever heard a love song in a death camp haven't they been told why are they not grieving why the macabre merriment of the birds secretive spectacle of the woods harrowing fertility of the cornfields chastened megalomania of the hill-ranges whispering death has made its peace with life and they lie together now under the crippled carrousel. How can this be embracing the trash of them. Come kiss me now so I will forget. Wrap me up. Cradle me. In the arms of. Of a morning I have forgotten.

And panic gives you the slap no you must not let yourself be taken in every belief however small touched like a pin and boom in consequence the sweet rose path down the fragrant garden to the woodpile where you were beaten into submission stripped to bare buttocks and strapped stripped to shame weeping with laughter.

From love not from love no love never love. A certain boy had a peculiar talent for stimulating unaffection even as a child he could see it in the startled look on their faces. Cagey askant. Wincing suspicious. Disconcerted. Discomfited. Disgusted. Any more? At what he asked himself. The face that met his gaze in the mirror repelled him wasn't that enough. The haughty brows the prim shapeless mouth tilted fleshy nose blond mop. Ice blue the little pupils opaque and vague crooked eyes. Greasy paste of hair. Black heads white heads inflaming the surbase of the nostrils lower cheeks and chin. An odor of disdain emanating from him followed him he could sense it obscurely. Self-hatred absorption obsession contempt. Naked and writhing within a camouflage of sarcasm and pride. Crying out yet loathing every offered hand. Stupid and willful and preening and desperate. Gardening his despairs (thought it was despair he did not yet know the meaning of despair) like a promise.

Every she who came to visit his days had no time for the immolating ego to say nothing of the groin.

The no-self that looked so much like an all-self.

The all-self a no-self ah wisdom had he known.

As he tried to suck the world into his pit.

The beatings. Not entirely random yet not always foreseeable. The back of the brush against the naked buttocks. The slap against the face. The gagging of the mouth with soap. The bending of the waist across the knee. The only remembered meeting of skin to skin surely not the only but the only remembered ones. The slap against the side of the head. Spankings. So called as to be a regular event. Weekly. Sometimes daily during particularly demonic seasons. And deserved. They were not unearned or unjust. They cut the limit to his and his siblings' spasms of anarchy. They formed a wall against which one could lean. The sureness of punishment almost a consolation. The ways of rage fortified thus against the evil that raised them. Would raise them. Might. Could. If only will.

From the labyrinth of woods to the rat's maze of the. Reduced to five at that time they had come. The beautiful hysterical mother who was not his mother yet who if not her was that mysterious absence who inspired shy pity for him for the stark irreplaceable loss the sardonic insecure sister half sister the brother half brother of the perpetual smile. Yourself withdrawn nebulously defensive. And the father of ice and style punctuated with slaps. An equatorial tension reigned flanked with Mr. Frostees. Berthed in rows of rotting wharves. An alarming but vivifying stench. The house was buttressed with light shafts the apartment barred with shadow and brick. The lawn stretched clear on all sides the streets were jammed with vacancy. The only noises there were distant shouts and dog barks the asthma of a tractor weaving about a field the only silences here were between the siren's howling and traffic's backlash angry shouts.

Silence at the head of the table broken by irascible lectures. Elegance and a cold tolerance veiling vast despising. Sumptuous food. Riotous candor on one side of the dining room table meeting timid duplicitous silence on the other. The mother-yet-not-mother's nerves the father's nightly yelling at her for once again forgetting the salt. The hectoring self-pity across the table. Sitting next to the skinny grin. Your childish smirk little arch comments. An occasional relapse into giggling. The occasional irruption of unheralded fury. But usually the volcano remained silent just smoking. An atmosphere of anxious social superiority assumed by the father still to be proven for the mother who was yet not mother. We were part of the decor of reassurance. The need to dominate one's neighbors as the only way to tolerate having any. The same to dominate the world the only way to support the inanity of family life a subadult world that kept the parents nailed to the infantilism of the kids. The false sense of power pretense of authority the childlike grandiosity of parenthood. To say nothing of the marriage cage though at that time such cages were beginning to split with increasing ease. You did not know this at the time do not know this now only guess as you pick at straws of understanding to figure what got you scribbling associations onto a tablet in an otherwise empty room between bouts of staring into space like. A bump on a log. As they used so often to characterize you from their perches at each end of the table. Often justly such was your talent for laziness daydreaming later on passiveness futility self-demoralization if that is a word it shall be a word. Over your peas.

An elegance cold and angry. Translated without a hitch from country to city. Fibrillating with nerves the feminine half.

A repletion of scorn arrogance and disdain made for a sustaining spiritual nourishment.

Almost hidden behind the mother's nervous loving unhappiness fringed with frustration and spite. That you sensed nothing of oblivious to all but your confusions. As the quarrels increased in frequency and violence in the tight apartment.

I did not let myself be aware.

It was easy to hide behind the eyes.

And the sibling antics made for a scintillating sideshow. Oh how the laughter masked the rancor oh how the mask slipped oh how the face unhinged with rage stabbed the air with its teeth.

No more. An acane favor given for uncertain at best highly suspicious reasons. The justifications carefully nailed down airtight waterproof. No jury would convict on such slender grounds. All we need do is put you on the stand they won't believe you you did it you could have done it you are fully capable of having done it indeed of doing it then indeed of doing it indeed of doing it now not him your honor must be kidding he's a total wimp. Although you did and we know you did. Juridical persiflage. A modest pride in the capacity for crime. Against your past against yourself. And all the cutouts hanging on the rope that extends from your window down to a pulley in the garden. Multiple avatars of Her.

Anger became him more than kind.

To say nothing of his literary style.

The solitary one gropes for his solitude like a blind man. He cannot feel it cannot find it. What. Around him there is only bitterness and air. Nothing but eyes.

She had made the transition without ease hanging by her fingers on to the escarpment. Transition into an endlessly delayed maturity. Childhood was pushed from her with the budding of the mounds on her torso the distending of the papillae ragging of the pudendum trickling then flooding of the blood. Which from all men must be hidden they faint so easily. The thread down the inside of her knee that humiliated her one afternoon in the school hallway. Set her mother crying when she told her in the evening. It left red spots behind her on the tiles. It led up to her a bleeding leaky mess with a blatant trail behind me. I am disgusting. Hide me. The powders the perfumes the hairdoes the hankies the combs the jewelry the squeegees dresses laces clogs the pumps the stockings the garters the jumpers panties petticoats the blouses the barrettes the bustiers the flowers in the hair cute little hats the darling pendants disguises for the blood camouflage false face theater to fool them from the repellence of this flaccid ugliness smelly and bleeding that surrounds the fallopian nausea. The filthy moon of my body. Brain-dead who says he loves me knows nothing when he finds out he will run. Away. Off. Gone. After another disguise.

Women are filth men are idiots.

Help me. I can't bear it anymore. Help me please God help me.

The edge of the escarpment bit her fingers where she hung over the bright abyss.

Greetings from the fire. There we handled with care for it was breaking at the folds this blueprint for an invasion of the past. Her fingers flickered in and out of the flames. At the other end of the city where the incinerator belched. A smoke wattled in and out of the air a weave of bark in whose chinks shone crosses of sunlight.

We were helpless so we prayed. Heroism not being an option however demanded. We had no choice but to take the boot in the face. No one else felt our mortification. That was consoling. To be human at that time was to live in a state of shame. For we destroyed everything we loved. We touched. And were instant ashes. Good King Midas of fire. Grinding the sea into a great pillar of salt. As we gazed rapt happy frozen behind. No power there had ever been to match our weakness. We drew all with us down.

Oh to melt into each other's skins. What rapture. To vanish into the hour of our gazing. What delight. They were no more and yet they were.

The mind learned to match the world that did not match the heart. A slow learner or rather a recalcitrant student. No. But two plus two and so forth. Make three. You must grow up sometime. Never. You are going to have a hard life. Over my dead body. Ah!

Demonic attachments have their place. Frankly. Honestly. Eye to eye. Without flinching. Callous was called for it will come with time. With disappointment. When.

The desire to penetrate a woman and keep penetrating her without end in view. Forever or a close facsimile. So this is where it belongs this hitherto deeply frustrated thing. But what a payment plan! The worst crime to give yourself your pleasure on her of course. The pleasure you gave and took. Crafty she never did admit the joy of. You the accused in her holding cell. The mug in the box.

So she crushed you slowly between her loins for the privilege. Little knowing the links. Or chain. Her own dissolution taken on trust. Into fulfillment. Or ecstasy.

You the love I have come to destroy. Forever more or less.

The place where they camped on the edge of the kaldera. Curling tongs of loathing officious of no explanations. Glancing witheringly down. He was a beaten dog about the legs. Kept his eye on the cold faces. Studied his tricks. Gamboled at whistle. Made his A's. Received his imperial approval however detached. Was only slapped by the father once in these later years. For not purchasing the gift for which he had no money.

Skeletal weeds strummed the windows. Nervous dogs of the neighborhood bayed at the passing cars.

I saw my first cockroach the egg sack sticking out behind the vestigial wings. It was a memorable day. Though disgust was followed by dismay. Rotten fruit outlined the edges of the palace. Knives piled up like a house of cards ready to crash down over my little solemn head. I saw the future a flat darkness stinking of rotting banana.

They giggled together nervously in the white kitchen.

The meals remained sumptuous long after the wind had ceased to rattle the windows. They were aware somewhere of a flaw diffracting the perspective but could only infer what no one was allowed to see.

The fingers pointing in the distance from the caravans of traffic. As if the only mirrors waved into the grotesque and the only allowance was for repellence. Their eyes smears on glass slides checked by unmatriculating lab assistants through uncalibrated microscopes. All the vivid microbial life hidden in their tears. Lachrymae rerum. Revealed by a simple stain.

Mud fell from the sky smearing its fingerprints on the windows. The city waited patiently outside like a cat burglar. The corruption had already begun. Yet you were growing soaring awkward passionate though immobile. Everything you touched brought amazing pain or joy. Ecstasy and misery were your closest companions. I didn't know where I was.

I found my solitude unimpaired in the throngs. The city was the home of my anxiety. Everything advanced into an ambiguous hope. The world was scaled to my measure and my measure was infinite.

I gazed longingly at the clouds framed between the towers. They bellied like sails against an azure sea. The sun railed at the city.

Trapezia retreating in perspective.

No loss that was not loss of all.

And at the base of it such mad hope such uncompromising happiness.

We were never wiser than in the folly of our youth never more faithful than in its cynicism and mockery. What generosity burned in our eyes. We spread our nonexistent wings and plummeted blank and giddy. The air whistled past us obscure with hallelujah. We never learned till we were almost wiped out and what we learned then was worthless. Prudence. Circumspection. Duplicity. They were not yet our second nature. Our foolishness was our glamor our self-absorption was our gift. Our infinite self-centeredness the panels of our armor. We were breathtaking. We destroyed each other like children. We wore the mask of corruption of adults. We took as far as we dared and then collapsed. It took ten years to explode our fireworks each day sending up a regiment of stars shaking the house and banishing night yes for ten long years. As though the supply were everlasting and the applause must roll forever. We dug our hole cheerfully and jumped in shrieking with laughter. The world shook in our embrace and wouldn't let us go. Unbelief was not available to us except as an extravagant charade. Because we were the gods.

At that time.

At whatever time was available to us.

As he walked at the edge of the crowd longing to become one of us.

He sought a place to pray in but there was nowhere there. The churches mocked the divine the surrounding city cursed it. He walked until he was exhausted in his search for a mark of the holy. There was only the humanly obscene. Nowhere reflected back the delicacy of a face.

The breath of a god murmured in the trees and passed over his head beyond him. The sky was out of reach of his hands. He stretched his mind until he thought it would snap. He sought the place where there was no one. Beyond the air. He remembered bitterly the silence of the woods the darkness of evening by the sea. In these eyes there was no paradise.

He shouted voicelessly through the streets. They responded with equal eloquence. Innamorata divina. He wept without tears or so he thought. But there was nowhere.

And still he sought. Like the child he still was. In the silence of music. The whiteness of books. The darkness of the stroke of a pen on paper. There. Sharpened to a form just beyond his sight. There brightened and fluttered a vanishing hosanna.

Oh to be thankful for the writhing labyrinth of life how could he be he who had been at one time so joyfully grateful for the gift life's gift in this. In this.

He shook the locked casket of his past listening to the bones rattle. Inside must be the key to the secret of his loss of. He shook. Only as a last resort would he take a hammer to it. And out of it emerged a cloud of moths dusting his face with their wings.

To crawl one goes on bended knees. Lowers the forehead to the ground. Raises the voice in. Lamenting the loss of. What.

One must live one's punishment in the burnt-out garden. At the edge of the garden are the walls at regular intervals the towers where the guards keep watch along the top of the walls is a sparkling of splintered glass and a snow of peach-colored petals. The further they advanced toward the walls the farther the walls moved. And the heavier was the scent of lilacs roses and honeysuckle it made the air drunk slowly drove them crazy. They had thought they were inside the prison. When they finally escaped the trap tripped with the sound of a shot.

A crystal garden of cement and glass. It rose all around him uncanny stalagmites. Clawing its way toward an unreachable sky. Into which the oak does not grow. One expected it for oneself however infinite and unending growth. The feeling of youth was the feeling of surge. Every wall was a test. Smoothly laughing. There shall never be no more worlds. To conquer. Even in the brick encampment of the city. In such weakness was such power. Such sense of power. Such mad and drunken glory. There was a heaven to be found in that particular insanity. So be it. For nothing else had one broken the shell. In this seed dwelled this sun. The air was dense with light. You were a bottomless lake at the heart of the mirror. And the sun as it rose cried love. And the sun as it set cried love. And the haze of stars drew the moon through the night like the sparrows the chariot of love. He could not believe it was not so. Frail brave little boat he blindly rowed. All happy. Singing softly to himself so that no one might suspect. No one know. No one envy. And no one knew no one envied no one suspected no one saw the sudden fall toward the sun beneath him.

Winter grew and the birds escaped from her hair to the abandoned forests. All hollow in the place's heart. Pinging gently like a bell made of eggshell. She walked the woods chanting from her book. Listening to the silence's answer. All echo. And the souls of unborn birds sang in her mind for she was their maiden and protector. Butterflies clustered on her lips. And leaves dangled like hands. In offering in benediction in plea. Of her honey drank the mist. Small animals curled against the ache of her breasts and they sucked and drank. And stared into the summer of her eyes.

Neither here nor not here. Neither there nor not there.
You woke from your dream gasping for air.

They sat in order around the table. It was in the age before the microwave. To nourish the family properly required at least one meal per day taken in togetherness. A ritual of napkins and silver. The head and foot traded solemnities for barbs. The peanut gallery tittered on the flanks. Upstaged at every opportunity. Flattered the fertility of the adults. Injunctions prohibitions ejaculations and jibes wrinkled the candles. The kids were never slow to attack. The reward was thunderstorms of laughter. Anger tested in grins and teeth set on the edge of grievance. Into the Yorkshire pudding vanish in delicious savory. Every evening was a festival. It was the high point of each day's happiness if happiness it was. The kitchen smelled of basil rosemary thyme olive oil bay leaf garlic. Minced onions sautéing in butter. The wolves were kept beyond the firelight for an hour. The thread between the father and the mother was cautiously thrummed the note moving from rumble to trill depending on the day's mood and pitch. It was examined surreptitiously for fraying. A sudden tension would send the tone out of earshot. The quiet that followed made the small bones in our ears tingle.

Freeze.

Entelechy or rebound to the teleology of darkness. Speckled agape like marbles. Overarching the heavens. Unless their peculiar psychology was secure and there were indeed final things. A moment that in a fit or seizure stopped time and split it like a coconut. Big rip. To draw out eternity like milk.

God to our solitary child had become a rumor what had been a transparence in field and wood the grass-lined roads bluebells tranquilly blossoming in the ditch snapdragons glaring at the honey bees the honeysuckled afternoon beneath a triumph of clouds the eye-like blue of the sky when all all showed him the outlines of a face now he was surrounded by faces each of which was a fragment of an enormous and ongoing burst an endless explosion that created in unnerving delicacy a destructive creation that formed ever new delights to feed its fathomless appetite. But the ugliness of humanity affronted him in the tangles of the city light a light saturated with darkness. The adjuration to seek god in the heart did little good for in his heart was only a narrow spiteful and self-pitying anger. That at times almost suffocated him. He hammered in tearful wrath at the closing walls of his cell. The past was a blinding happiness the future a blank blackness the present a shaft of dirty sunlight. He woke from dream to dream fearing he would never escape into day. They cased him in like a Russian doll. Winked closed clicking like an egg.

Yet at him inwardly they smiled.

There was an element of the ridiculous in all this gadding about. Floundering. Like the fish flapping about on the sand by the fisherman's boot. Of the fishermen no longer near.

He grew despite everything. No matter how hard he clamped himself down the shackles periodically burst and he had added bulk to his biomass and a ring of experience to what he was hardly old enough to call his past. He was growing. Alarmingly. He looked emphatically backwards because back then he had been happy so he thought. No good. He kept moving forward anyway. There was nothing he could do about it. Except hold on.

The family was starting to tear light began to appear through the seams. He held his hand rigidly across his eyes. No good either. When life wants to have a nervous breakdown it has one whenever it damn well feels like it. The winds began to gather at the four corners of the map and eyeing him began to slink inwards. Poor fellow. And he had just started to date.

Annie. Geri. Karin. Caren. Siggy. Lorraine. Barbara. Paula. Leslie. Lesly. Leslee. Ann. Roberta. Nancy. Nancy. Teresa. Kathy. Judy. Meg. Claudia. Mary. Nancy. Margie. Cindy. Linda. Maria. Anne. And more but he couldn't remember their names. The goal of the date was the kiss. The end of the date was good night. At that time. Sometimes the goal was attained. Miraculous. Interest was however difficult to sustain. Usually an hour in he was looking at the thin Swiss watch with numerous jewels his father had given him without a thought of harm in the world. Then shortly after he walked home unkissed with a sigh of disappointment and relief. Later he would learn there was more than kissing involved. I resisted the idea at the time. But it didn't help. Later still pride and resentment turned you into something like a monk. Without faith. You learned to extinguish the first spark of tenderness and to be pitilessly polite. This was the beginning of your success with women. On the verge of the end. You smiled at the end beyond the ends of their fingers. It hid for the longest time the unbearable loneliness. From you. So solitary revenge.

(You're getting ahead of yourself. You must first sink a fathom at a time into the labyrinth. And try not to get lost.)

What the maze saw. At the crooked ends of the turnoff. Toward a downtown pillaged by pain. Its eyes round with amazement.

The ubiquitousness of frustration and unhappiness everywhere parading as contented satisfaction with life's unendurable awfulness the militant aggressive stupidity of this peculiar form of denial impressed him repeatedly. The dismaying insistence on cheerfulness at all costs at the very least teeth gritted in smiles. A frank weary fatigue and sadness seemed preferable certainly more appealing and easier to sit across in the ill-lit cafe. Even angry harping bitterness was better than relentless good cheer the unfurling of the vast banners of. Triumph. Over the corpse-strewn battleground.

The rat-eaten heart of the city had this merit that of an obscene yet stimulating honesty. One could not grin it out of countenance.

But it took you a long time to discover this.

In the meantime the history of his innocence left him deaf and blind to the moral lessons hanging from every corner of the prison yard he was stuck in.

He pushed his way through the filth with a sense he had been betrayed.

As you have been.

He was hanging by the neck until he was dead. It was a highly elastic noose made of crepitantly asphyxiating bungee and could afford to take its time. Quite a bounce.

Adolescence. Etc.

The greater fool.

Partook of the ingredients on jar labels and cereal boxes. The romance copy sent him out of his mind for minutes at a time.

You were always being tripped up by your knack for believing. Skepticism was a lesson that never quite held. Till it held all. Becoming for a time a personal brand. Furious-flavored fanaticism. The torch he bore to justify his misery. And infiltrate the sty happiness of everybody else. The twerp!

He was not going to not believe again. In anything.

(This came later but its roots were as those of the weed in the rended mat of grass near his sneakers. If you did not kill the last fibre of that innocent-looking yellow-headed coin of vulgar flower it would grab and twist and grasp and throttle the entire acre. Bobbing dead white heads in a week. Choking anything that is not they. Seeding unrelenting downwind.)

As it did.

Cynical with devotion.

Meanwhile he carried his solitude with him like a badge ready to flash it at certain officious and suspiciously interested females. It was a white star on his flannel jacket.

They never did get the message.

It was a form of happiness not vouchsafed to all they must keep him at the edge of their eyes but go no further. This way his solitude became peopled without collapsing into desperate loneliness for long. Desperation being the tone of the hour a foregone conclusion between futile experiments. Stabs at being. Oneself again.

And dwelled uneasily on the image in the mirror the one he followed for decades the purest contemplation from end to end of the spectrum of his life. Odd. Not that it was a pretty face but it was yours. You were stuck to the back of it and dangled like a hidden photographer under the black cloth of an antique camera shouting at the top of your lungs "Don't move!" at the hapless model relentlessly blurring.

Funny. She remained nameless behind the whirring fan of names. Such a smile granted to few. A luxury long longed for the taste a crumb of dazzlement.

One carried it away and hoarded it and gazed at the memory for days watching it fade into a hard small crystal of promise. Perhaps today the small morning light twittered. Or tomorrow. Anything could happen. And would. And shall. Defend hope from every foe. Family. And friend.

The family swirled with false laughter around the quiet one the solitary one the child. Who missed many cues that way. Waiting far too hard.

He could only open his eyes to objects in half darkness and alone. They did not rebuff him. Yet. Or only his contemplation. The handling with its barbs would come later.

There was you see too much anger in the laughter that surrounded him. It hurt his eyes like too bright a light. The eyes winced tingling. As if from photophobia. It made him feel naked and jeered at. Ashamed of being still there.

Yet you must fight back not let your own happiness be plowed into the soil of their. For them to. Flourish.

So he inched the ice into his face. Gave nothing. Watched as their fingers slipped down the wall their eyes bewildered with frustration. Eye to eye with cold blankness. Saved the fire for the anxious core. Foolishly oh foolishly but helpless.

You had to save yourself. From them all it seemed. Or but only seemed. Which was enough.

Foolishly oh foolishly.

Not to know a better way to remove the burden he could not bear for long. Yet had to.

The monkey blinking from his shoulder in the mirror.

No way to enter adolescence. Retreating.

The memory of a clump of trees. Where you could hide. Chanting the name of a teacher.

Miss Schmeg.

Which made you think of nutmeg its sweet nutty smell.

Miss Schmeg smell of nutmeg.

He hoped her for his future. Where was she now. Nowhere but in my past. What he remembered did not exist. This was why it was remembered. It was the inflexible law. To find her again would have been intolerable.

The city thickened. What happened here did not exist what he remembered did not exist what would happen tomorrow anywhere did not exist. And nothing in between the empty points of time.

You stared from the bed at the ceiling. You stared through the branches at the sky.

In silence.

Vanishing.

Panicking

Ever?

Ever.

It wasn't exactly practical to be the way he was. But he was stubborn. Surrounded by fences (he remembered) he had sat still at the center of the grass. Breathing the cuttings.

Beyond the fences was a chaos of traffic in the angry heat of summer.

Calculation was possible given time in some cases. Of the general shape that is. Of no individual however. I took comfort from that from the incalculability of my own trajectory across the. What. Shavings of dust. Quadrille of the infra-red. Captious swirl of enormous smoke in endless rooms of gigantic night.

It was curious how when all was said and done it looked the starry night when examined through the haze of photographs gotten many years later from the infra-red and other amazing telescopes hanging and looping above the sky it looked like well an infinitely enormous drop of muddy pond water undefined and blind and turgid and snaking and filthy and brown and irritably alive. Eating itself. Anxious. Opaque. Strangely frisky. An infinite tangle of spectacularly encoiled ouroboroi each encircling its own thousand-dimensioned universe eating then spewing out all the others. In turn. Out of turn. Simultaneously. Beyond the limits of beyond the spider-ice of light.

But he did not know that then. Could not see that then. All he saw above him were the endless phalanxes of the clouds marching marching across the blueness like Romans flashing in splendor. Or hanging over you soft as a woman's skin. Smelling tartly of earth and sky. Or high in ice like vast dragonfly wings stretching between rings of the horizon. Or mackereled in tufts of snow-like drifts and pillows of whiteness. Or gray and shapeless and sombre pierced with folds of illusory light. The sun snagging in sheets of tearing fog.

Between these clouds which he could see and those clouds he could scarcely imagine he had closed his eyes (he remembered) and let the moscae wander.

There was much laughter in that household despite what has been said nor was it all anger. It would be a mistake to call it an unhappy home.

There was a kind of elegant giddiness in the air that put a sheen over contention. A sense of specialness of welcoming and open-minded exclusiveness an exclusiveness that paradoxically excluded no one but invited and entertained everyone and only felt a slight pity they couldn't stay in the magic circle where gaiety and the golden future lived and traded jokes and looked out on the world as a field where pleasures might bud berries of joy drop one at a time at perfectly gauged intervals to perfectly hungry fingers. A world self-contained yet airy and light filled with elegant furnishings good books thrilling music beautiful pictures audacious and satisfying entertainments exquisite dinners wonderful stories the prospect of exciting travels an insouciant optimism a certainty of contentment a world that opened from blossom to blossom till the entire tree dazzled like a garden filling the air with the bracing scent of happiness.

A smile for the future a smile for the past. The present a flushed leap between hope and gratitude.

There was no reason it could not continue forever. When he thought about it calmly and alone. In his room stretched out on his bed. Or walking solitary and happy under the evening.

The humiliation behind the photograph's smile.

Now.

If there ever was a then.

For there seemed to be movement. Like a python uncurling from its knot in the branches of the lamp.

A slick if slightly mangy lattice for it was shedding.

Uncurling down to your hand.

The impetus of time thus letting itself be felt against the uncalloused palm.

Seeking to wrap around the arm an affectionate or merely voracious tendril.

Around the shoulders around the rib cage and pelvis a helix linking groin through heart to head the eyes unblinking above the lined forehead the forked tongue tasting the random air.

Becoming your eyes.

(He considered this as he (as you) (as I) moved what were at one time eyes across these words just written and paused to consider the slowly darkening paper.

The scaled cord slipping across the eyes ...)

Yes there was much happiness between the troubles.

The afternoon at the river along the lightly sloping banks under the wide-spaced trees the thick layers of pebbles beneath their feet cold and sharp and giggly. Moving into the water was an adventure yes slipping here and there on the river-bottom rocks fuzzed with slime there was the thought of water mocassins between the shouts echoing across the surface and the chuff of water against the bank. Everybody was laughing at everybody else. It was charged with teasing the innocently treacherous ridicule yes the generous and exhilarating sarcasm of a fathomless security. The towel flicked back and forth in little punishments of joy. Yes aggression itself was a signature of complicity the bonding of a conspiracy against the world. It gave happiness its spine. There was nothing to lose and everything to gain. Was that the secret of childhood's happiness its sometimes desperate calm? Yes?

They crouched giggling on the long flat rock above the river daring each other off into the first plunge.

(Not yet not yet oh hold to the rock for the sun will set and the sun will set at the fall of the eyes at the edge of the hand while the waters suck you down yes ride you like a lover devour you with unforgiving desire.)

The air rushing through the car.

Brother and sister asleep beside you.

The smell of cut grass horse manure the occasional dead skunk wet earth of bark and leaves humus of the woods scented bushes whipping in through the open car windows also the smell of gasoline vinyl rust a smell of dried sweat.

The blur and rush of trees on either side of the road behind them farms and valleys streams and fields in ragged scattered sleeping herds of dairy cows and horses hen houses self-conscious and startled leaning pig sties noble nonagonal barns white-walled and field stone farmhouses all in a combination of near-view rush and farther view stately procession and farthest view near immobility at the point where hilltop became the ridge of a horizon halting the sky.

And the pale clouds reflecting the sun above them staring into endlessness like a blind and irrefutable benediction.

Sun and clouds and the brazen cars.

... and opened his eyes out of memory again and took in what he had to of the pale surround of his present.

It was fleeting furtive might have been painless had it not been for the edge of light pursuing a remorse that had no clear justification. It stabbed him periodically and at awkward moments. An inconvenient and uninformative demon. It was like a hot coal shifting in his shoe. It made him dance with feverish spastic movements and sparkling laughter from his peers.

The look in their eyes of merciless contempt and joy in their power and the white horseshoes of their grins made him wonder.

It was feeding time in the playgrounds.

His teachers stalked blind and unbending above the pint-sized mayhem indifferent and bureaucratic and booming like foghorns. They watched the bullying from the corners of their eyes with shirt-fronted satisfaction.

The only shield against mortification and despair was to sheathe the face in stone and stand in the margins of the yard unmoving and taking everything in.

The coal against the foot quietly gaining.

(6 × 7 × ... what is it now ... 45,301 ÷ ... let's see ... (2 × forever)... plus ... + 8) the whole minus infinity ... and whatever happened to the primes ...

Taking so long to learn the tables of shame.

Pass. Pass on. Pass out. Pass over. Pass away. Pass the course. Pass the buck. Just please God let me pass.

(He walked the halls of school murmuring blasphemies.)

Aloft.

Cast your eye where you've never been.

Here. Now. Nowhere.

Pencils of planes move against the clouds.

Lost in abstraction. Like the retelling.

Thinking behind the emphatic blue irresolutions of shadow.

Eyebeams from which they hang like plotting ecstatic school boys paper angels mouths alarmed with praise children in the dark whispering stories.

Spastic.

Flinching.

Resigned.

For the dead power whose fingers spin their wings.

Their fathers.

The wombs that sucked them out.

The vortices.

Up there.

Beyond this.

Not beyond this.

Surrounding and subtending it like a cord an arc of the infinite circle whose center cannot be found.

Has not been found. Yet.

Your eye.

The top starting to wobble.

The family drama skittered around the edges of historical catastrophe. Mice panicking on the imperilled vessel. Or rather sandpipers bickering in the skirts of the runoff over a few shreds of crab and worm.

When the sudden tide thrust out showing wards of kelp colonies of crustaceans hospitals of coraline monstrosity uncovered to an irrelevantly dissecting light. A bit late in the day. Kaleidoscope of seabirds. Burrowing sand crabs in a tide pool. A quiver of anxiety half hidden fingering the fletches. The fishermen looking up startled from their daydream. The smell of women on their hands. The wall of water lurching above them unscaleable bright curling down to them. A roar of ten thousand trains.

All enacted at the edges of the dining room.

Cube of light and gin and laughter.

At whose center obliqueness coded warnings. Wisecrack semaphores. Paper napkins in an origami of crushed animals. Messages tapped by silver on crystal. The reflection of a face on a butter knife. Two knuckles a bare bum on the bowl of my spoon. Ha ha. Abrupt silences. The taste of vinegar and olive oil. Of safety. Of betrayal. Of sea brine rising to the walls. The implosion within meeting the explosion without. Without passion but efficiently. The uncharitable love of Eros. Sucking the beach like a vacuum.

Standing wave about to wipe out the happy colony on the beach.

"God *damn* it over *there* I said."

Slam.

"I thought ..."

"Shit.... "

Silence then renewed clatter of utensils.

"... just put it down and get the ..."

"... wait ..."

"I have *been* waiting for the last ten years for you to figure out the fucking ..."

"... Daddy? ..."

"Watch yourself go back to your room your mother and I are ..."

"... but this one didn't we ..."

"*That* one over there *not* that one by the ..."

"But that was ..."

"Now the *rice* is burning...."

"... it seemed ..."

Slam.

"*'Seemed'?* If you'd open your eyes and shut your mouth for once you'd see what it *is*. But you never have not fucking *once!*"

Sound of breaking glass.

Alert frightened silence.

"Forget it!"

A rustle of angry steps and cloth being torn from a hook then a door slams. Then a sound of water in a sink. Then sobbing.

Like hands drawn behind his back manipulating objects in the dark to a background music of incomprehensible bitterness.

(Yet in the ring of darkness the circle of light. At the center of the light a crystal spinning. Shimmering. Seeking the level where it can come to rest. At last. The level of its flaw.)

At that time. At this time what is known reflecting back on that. Though what is known now is still uncertain. If known. Hardly believed. Guessed. Uncertainty revealed as never more than that. Again.

Impenetrable vagueness.

No relation whatever it seemed of cause and effect. Post hoc ergo propter nothing whatsoever? No comprehensible thing. Only a flickering of images in the dark. A very strange movie.

And the slipping of the blade beneath the nails.

Tell me. Tell me. *What?* Again.

Not the physical bluster only.

No the undercutting that slipped unseen from afar.

That with a single well-placed desire blew the castle to kingdom come.

Wait. Are you remembering accurately? What? How can you remember what you did not understand? Do not understand. You are inventing. True. I think. Again. To reduce it to grammar seems after all unavoidably to. It did not happen grammatically. Almost nothing was spoken until it was too late. And what was said. Inenarrable. Yes. In memory all of it happened at one time. The only time.

Once.

How describe the trust he did not know could not know he had and could not believe he had lost. Had lost. Even before he lost it. What it meant. Means. Shall mean. Picking the pieces of glass from his skin. For years. Astonished at the blood. And the unending pain. That ended. Would have ended. Caused by that? *That* that? Doubtfully. Layers of pain. Once one is broken a deeper revealed. Down and down. In. Proceed gently here. For the subject tissue is yet living. And quivers at the knick. Tell me. Again.

The betrayal happened swiftly and lasted long. A slug that kept slugging. Years and years. How much can happen at once.

The face of the father frozen in prissy triumph.

A face he had never seen behind those eyes.

I loathe you loathe he loathes she loathes we loathe you loathe they loathe.

That face had helped make him. Had been the north star during many an uncertainty. Given guidance through perfect and imperfect storms. Given value and measure against the credulities of disgust and of love. Given an example of wisdom courage devotion virtues we laugh at now you and I. Given a mold for the sand of the future. Given an image and a target for the long-breathed arrow of adulthood.

It now spat him indifferently behind.

Dared him to live. Now. Without love.

Father. Abba.

Dropped like an inconvenience into the trash of a life.

3

What ails you? The vertigo of the streets.

Like a spiderweb that sticks to your feet.

Nowhere to fly to.

As if patiently waiting to be eaten.

There was the compress of flowers in the morning. — *Will he ever be happy again.* — *Not impossibly.*

There is the setting of jaw and the grinding of teeth. Classes to wrestle with. Classmates to spar with. Wars rising from the horizon in smears of TV gray. A decade of hatred in front of him. Had he known it was to be a decade. Or had it been only a decade.

The solitary one raises his teeth in a smile for the camera.

Hold it.

Hold on.

Hold.

Educare. To exfoliate what is coiled within. To meet the blaze of the other ignite and burn. With oh what new fire. Learning! Yes.

Euclid to Einstein add carry divide Columbus to Bird Tigger to Heffalump beneath Charlotte's web to run Dick run to Caesar to Hitler monster saint genius Joan of Arc Gandhi Leonardo Voltaire Beetoven Edison Morse Bach Whitney Bell bacilli radium uranium plutonium pandemonium cotton gins telegrams telephones television the Wright brothers Goddard von Braun the air electric with signals wings rockets from the Straits of Magellan across the western Rockies beneath the beckoning moon and the dare of the stars by the Arno and Athens through Paris and London through the gates of ivory to Jefferson's quill. Rapping the seance of schooling. All those noble ghosts.

In the loose fist the scattered straws.

Rain in the schoolyard. Random shouts and orange jackets. The squeals of the swings. In pendulum the squeal of time they heard with a giggle it seemed so old who could take it seriously. Everything took place behind its back.

The squeal of the chalk against the blackboard. In fact green. The chalk yellowing the fingers of the teacher. As he frowned describing the depradations of Simon de Montfort against the *pays d'oc*. The squeals of the girls during recess. Shrinking before the invasion. From sacking to slaughter. Stakes flaring like matches at random lighting the heretics in the naked southern fields. Their screams. Resolved to teasing at the back of the class scuffle in the corridor the boring lecture waiting for the last buzzer. Homework to come. Then television.

He wonders if there will be a quiz tomorrow. Reread the last chapter. Stare at the plate of knights in armor the shield with its cross the fish-scales of chain mail. The text floats out the window. Lies down in the wraps itself in dew. Worried by a deer nibbled by a fox dragged by an officious raccoon into. Is unreadable by morning. Pawmark. In the ink of ash of starlight.

The heretics' fading cries.

Mr. Grabman gave it a look of deep puzzlement. But it survived. After all you looked so innocent.

Repeat lesson. The slippery ground of everything. Learned early learned late or learned not at all. Repeat lesson. Archetypal category of its own unambiguously labeled total ambiguity. Yes? As though a film of oil covered things. Slipped into the cracks between words. Denied contact. Except with itself. Where rest where there is no rest rest in the restlessness. The human animal was a porous sack of fatty tissue and dread. He thought at one point later. Only the slipperiness could be counted on he thought forgetting his own stubborn will. That shook but would not give. True it was a strange way to be unjust to your peers. But it became his way. He is rarely disappointed when underestimating them. Their motives. They will provide decades of amusement unless you're a victim of idealism. Unfortunately if you expect. And have the tragic flaw of having a tragic sense. Beneath the dome. In the upper tier of the amphitheater. With the cries of the vendors drifting up to you. And the backs of so many heads lined up in descending crescents from you. Toward the spectacle.

As here on the first day. Minor sideshow in the greatest etc. But his own therefore noted. Peeling into his generation which he loathed as others loathe their families. But not yet. The first day of school first day in the punishment room. First the instruments are shown. And you have no idea what they are they look like ingeniously crafted toys. Look my thumbs can go in here. They let them lie around so you get used to seeing them. Hearing the shrieks. No longer noticing or only vaguely wondering. Or congratulating your friends on having escaped. Narrowly. Everyone quite cheerful otherwise. Trading sarcasms and clueless smirks. The quiet patient efficient undercut. As the cries from the neighboring rooms pierce to you. Louder it seems than last time. But you're afraid to ask. What if they look at you and ask what screams? As they sanded the point of a more radiant shaft in the dry woody smell of shop. Shaking a head at you in pity between buffs.

Till you no longer trust your senses. And slip into the prison of their words.

Grass stains on the khakis. A kite above the swings. Thick round pencils olive and soft. Their smell. The thrill and the wall of that first day. The solitary one no longer solitary or so he thought. For a moment or perhaps longer. Till the unwelcome in the other eyes welled away to. Scum on a stagnant pond. Parrying. The quick twitch of the rapier. The touch and crumble to the floor. Ironically crass the brittle arch comments the attempts to be smart and rude. Your own timidity was no excuse your penchant for self-protective pridefulness only worsened. Silly and spiteful in your own way. The meanness a shared facility. On the first day however he saw it for the first time tacked in large black lettering on the wall. The warning. Vague and bloody-minded. There shall be war between us. Troubling the wall above the bulletin boards between photos from Life and Look and Norman Rockwell. Monsters with names and deceptively caught expressions. The delusion that this time we will not be above all you will not be fooled. The curse of the generations. As we launched grandly at our very own our unique our industriously cultivated bred and groomed our carefully dressed our meticulously coiffed our perfectly hip and extremely cool. His. Your. My. Mindlessnes. So far ahead to come. So far! As we sat at the first grade table gritting our teeth at each other. With innocent disdain.

The fisherman pulled suddenly up. Taut. Something leaping beyond the breakers furiously shaking the barb further in. Catch. The bullet ball. Rebound. The click of the rod as the fisherman ratchets the hooked fish. The plastic mange of sand. The rod nodding like a polite bird. Violent flapping in the surf. Shouts of relay between the four. Then five. Then three. Then two alone. The exhausted blue heaving in the foam the sand dragging into its gills its terrified eye's blind in the suffocating air. Lurch up into the hand the rip of the barb out and the plummet into the bucket. Got three today. Then four. Then five. Then none. You missed. The sound of the tail slashing against the side in weakening flourishes. Gone still. Softly panting. Staring at bucket bottom and sky. As the girl skitters away with a laugh.

A moment of bliss followed by years of misery. So he discovered later. Which he was then too young to imagine. The obscenity of the trick. Unless it was none. And the old wisdom was right after all. Mean but clear sighted. Do not touch the moistness outside the ring. Through the ring. On the other side of the ring. Impanelled angels yet away. Their wings shuffling in the stalls. As they listened with bored air to the testimony. Like a therapist the nattering obsessive. Whatever the question always the same answer. In the same words. The same inflections. Talismanically. Over and over. In the vaults of his inheritance. The chromosomal chains never to free at last. Curling inward to the final link.

The damned words.

Scenario taken as read.

The lesson the quiz ignored heaven the sky within the mind hell the fire between the thighs.

But truth is both hard to find and not always immediately persuasive it needs to be hammered in with a knout. Hung at the side of the blackboard. The movable one. So that it swung as the blackboard was moved from place to place at the head of the classroom. Reminding the slow among them what their heads might need. Periodic bashing. To help the little truth sink in. Like a staple through a thick wad. Convincing the stubborn among them at last. Of what had never seemed entirely plain. But an evasive deception. Ringing changes on the sadism and paranoia that together form the basis of every society whose acquaintance he would make in decades to come its culture being the pathological construction society imposes on its members as a form of intellectual and emotional regimentation sadism both its supreme entertainment and its preferred method of instruction though usually subtilized into simple dread for example of failure therefrom social even economic ostracism and its recruits among the wreckage in the streets. So they said at the time. Not said dared not say but but would one day think in a moment of startling brightly illuminated black. As they looked on the animals gathered in the snow. At the bottom of the playground. Among the dead weeds. So many beaten dogs.

But then the place was back-training in failure the best kind first fail at small things then progress to larger and more ambitious until one has mastered the skills ensuring success will not snatch you but grappled to the ground or bayoneted to the plank or tossed the grenade will ensure its immediate neutralization. Even success in such a place brings all the shame of failure as though once again you had failed at keeping yourself secret and unknown. Unhidden the eye that pins you with all its congratulations to the wall. He was shredded with approval yet all he wanted was the acknowledgment of his teachers he had soon learned to hold his peers in contempt what you could not hide was how you despised them. Not good politics. Their malice. Their ignorance. Their laziness. Their arrogance. Their moral cowardice. Which in decades to come would blossom. Discharge. Like an infected cyst. And in which you would find yourself flecked like a splinter of glass. Revealed. Not having avoided the pitfalls listed. Any of them. Thrilling to the kazoo of defeat buzz buzz. The astonishing ludicrousness of failure.

Writhing around you in the white carton with the little handles on the hook pack not far from the hipboots of the fisherman. Slippery. Irritable. The twitch of muscle riding from a spot behind the neck to the tail rolling spasm completed in a little hopeless flick you could almost hear the tiny cries. As the fisherman picked another up and smoothed it onto his hook. "It doesn't feel a thing" he said as you looked at the wet shiny inch of brown. Flail. At the end of the tackle. That he then heaved beyond the surf. Past the breakers. The line spinning. Then yanked stiff. Out of the writhing nest of fingers. Waiting.

Then woke from his daydream and stared down at the uncompleted calculation.

They irritated each other while they waited. Exposing scars lifting unhealed wounds. The rain had not let up since morning. It felt cozy and abandoned. Droplets trickled in crooked paths along the window to little pockets of water until a big one plunged to the sill. In a path that reminded you of forked lightning. Some played guessing which would be next. I had always wondered why the rain clung only to parts of the window little archipelagos unless there was an emulsion and the result was a silken sheen with long shallow swells and a filmy patchwork of refractions of rainbow the light beyond alive iridescently.

Your safety from others was thus in concentrating on objects their betrayals were innocent they might inflict a wound but didn't try to reopen it. The others ignored the rain and you ignored the others. This could go on for only so long. At the first sign of sun they barreled into the landscape as into an empty and astonished room.

Confetti falling from a great height.

Everyone enjoying the parade except the sweepers of course and even they.

The world was the more intensely bright after weather oh how it shone the air drugged on smells mud grass ditch wood oil stone. You breathed deep. Yet deep. They scattered across the wet ground no one aware of any danger. Except the tedious anxiety of the adults. Their ravenous and tyrannical guilt. Waving frantically from their corners like scarecrows in a gale. Whistling. How you pitied them. Despised them. Jeered. Ran.

In the great circle of perpetual return.

Dreaming said the famous doctor who became famous by saying it is the brain's natural state. If so how unnaturally you have lived. Jamming the mind awake with insistent questions he hadn't actually wanted answers to there was something oddly calming in the lack as though one were hovering on a jet of air and had no need no immediate need to land. It was the others who insisted on answers serving notice when the answers were of dubious provenance or irrelevant.

He was bound legally to serve them for twelve years. To answer their questions one way or another and accept their condemnation or praise as given without appeal. To dread the fell F sneer at the common C grovel and sweat for the arrogant A. It suited him despite his pretense at chafing. He loathed what made him live. It was not an unusual state. Carping was a way toward intimacy. How often friendships being based on shared hatreds. The common burdens of loathesome mathematics and famously bad-tempered teachers. The shared smirk on the playground and the innocent look above the school desk. A collective lesson hammered ever so gently home over the decades of supreme conquering delicately tempered hypocrisy. Cemented. The awkward cunning manipulations of childhood beneath the anxieties and tantrums. The craven innocence of a hungry and cruel mind.

And the uncanniness of looking back at it.

"An answered question's hell" he found scribbled in the margin of an old school notebook one vacant afternoon in his uncontrolled hand.

This dream then. Much later oh much. Collected in bouts of waking like rain in cisterns. A crowded street fair. Tiny eateries jammed with eaters. You motion down the way for a friend indicating a certain spot in the middle distance. You consider the time time for a chat time for a coffee time for a beer time to be going to take the walk in the countryside you have been promising yourself in hope to find there the solution to a problem that won't leave you alone you had almost given up but someone else engages your attention it's your father you have a miraculously pleasant talk with him as you stray by the side of the street unable to get away he is amiable and you are charming and you cannot escape and you think how soon the night will come and the problem will never be solved so be it it has been a lovely day and I have done nothing I hoped to do. And so it goes on crowded and eventful full of character and incident from end to end of its short life not quite coherent but giving the sense of a consistent if sometimes hidden narrative from beginning to end yet there is something before the beginning and there is something after the end at least that is suggested and it seems plausible doesn't it just like life itself any life it almost adds up and is certainly very interesting and almost actually makes sense. The water in the cistern being very pure here and reflecting almost perfectly if a little dimly your face and the clouds behind it. As you bend down to drink.

At the far corner of his eye she. Vanishing when he turns. Ghost at noon. Less than memory or hope. A flicker. Binge of wishful thinking hallucination of the groin. Yet he is so sure he saw. Eyes as bright as. Lips as soft as. A mind crackling with wrath and laughter sudden in rage and in tears. A body softer than tighter than. Profile sharp as. Hands that took and gave gave. Look both blunt and pure. Spell of honesty and longing. Schöne schein. Utter illusion worth every truth in the world so he you I thought at the time. Insanely thought it could be for him for anyone so willing to be made the fool. And was if he were willing to suffer. And did. And still refused to learn the lesson repeated again and again to his stubborn and hopeful mind. As he threw himself against the ice. And again.

Who could she have been?

Something like memory reborn. In the open palm. A turning leaf. Summer not quite forgotten. Though the edges curl inward and are brown. Hand to hand. Wet with dew. In hand. The heart of it yellowing and the veins. Brittlely clear. As though he could see through them. Toward spring. Behind. And the coming snow.

You have not learned your lesson. Flunk. The shock of it. He who is used to nothing less than. Even when he doesn't. And he hasn't. So foolishly certain in love's blind knowledge that he had. It. Her. Forgetting how treacherous was the calculus of affection how perverse the transforming into memory of obsession. The eel between his hands as it shook. The blank despising in her cold flat eyes.

The books. Crack them. Sink into them. Breathe them let them absorb and for the time being become you. Vanish from the scene into your paper cell. Raise the spine to her in defiance the white blind wall. The crenellated tower of words. Repeat over and over the student's hopeless mantra. Despise yourself and collect all A's. Amaze. Astonish. Astound. Allure. Avenge. Appal. Adore.

Nights of the lamp. Days of mockery. The expectant uneasiness of twilight. He tasted little despairs in that confusion of dusk hour of danger and magic when others are as poorly defined as oneself. And moves through them like a ghost into a ghost. Away however toward or in.

They were not impressed. His twisting into random knots of lyrical confusion his half-desperate flights of fancy shot from a gun of self-regard at heart targets dispersed on a diagrammatic field made them yawn at the futility of it. Snipped into topiaries of self. Never was the lecture of silence and sarcasm more pointless or fed to deafer ears. For longer. Giggles and sneers. He tried to give it up in the end. He tried to give it up in the beginning. His body was stubborn it would not give up its pride. It failed like the worm on its barb refusing to believe it was already dead. As good as. Thinking the heave toward the surf was its launch into flight.

The heart must always be broken. Again. No no no he kept shouting no. No. And the world echoed Yes.

The school was a larger safety zone shared by others. That leaked at its borders a keen sweet threatening scent flickering flamelessly in the air. The anxious daydream of an explosion. Fingering its way through the cries in the playground. Invading slowly eating in. It seemed safe at the time behind the scapular slate. Its mossy almost oleaginous mineral green. A scrim of ice over a face in a pond.

The school was a colony of the outer world setting up a freehold in his mind. The hall monitors watched over their charges with fatuous authority. They were being led into a world not theirs but to be theirs. They were being misfitted for the world outside. In this (you thought) particular school.

For the world outside was reflected here through a complex apparatus of distorting mirrors. What was shown was what was believed what was believed ought to be shown to minds still innocent and needing above all hope (you thought). Not what was believed what was believed was actually there there in the world outside (you thought). For that was barely endurable by adults. Indeed was not endurable by adults (you thought). Hence their need for fairy tales to feed their young. Half hoping they would believe them half hoping they might relieve one by one the misery they condoned or had learned to ignore with more or less set teeth and a defensive pretense at cynicism or simply could not fight or simply could not face. If (you thought). If they believed the tales. If they held on despite the hecatomb beyond the school fence. The cries of the animals and the people in the streets. The slaughter they would witness and the scars they would grow like flowers in gardens of promise. O the noble hopelessness in the sad eyes of the teachers!

There was after all still this strange belief in education. It was shared by almost everyone. It served to your mind two functions one to weed out the losers two to give everyone a chance to lose. Even when you won. Heady stuff! Though you considered it very strange. It was a field of carnage and blood beneath the waxen smile of the teacher. Children wandered lost and dazed toward the burning cities of the future. Their small hard faces were shaped with axes.

And yet beneath his eyes the glorious words flamed with hope ah such promise his heart blazed with his mind in sudden and binding recognition the towering amazement at being human shouted across the valley toward the uncanny shame. The uncanny shame. Oh the pride and the shame of being human.

They could not make you not believe. Not after giving you this taste. No matter how hard they tried.

And yet as he fingered the map of scars that already grew over his heart how could he in the end not not believe. Which was the veil which the veiled. Avail. Not avail.

When he was very young he ripped out of the book each page as he read it. As though it were the wrapping on a gift.

Here the livingroom there the wall closets a bank of wooden louvers shifting open to rows of stuffed parkas mittens dangling like amputated hands from the sleeves knit wool caps rows of boots yellow red blue for the girls black for the boys umbrellas and the rest of it while here the fireplace rarely used the rows of books half unread the silent stereo the shutters made of walnut and oblongs of translucent sheets of plastic between which pressed leaves and peacock plumes peered like ghosts the picture window looking onto the brown gravel path the small flourishing dogwood the tiny bluebells shaking in the spring the row of black green bush creating a quiet space just outside the window and beyond the bushes an outstretched plain of grass dotted with yearling trees the flat gaze of the neighbor's house in the middle distance beyond that forest and valleys and the distant rolling thunder of the hills leading to the horizon where the river defined the border of a neighboring state and the horizon the edge like the lip of a great clam between the land and the sky.

The axis between home and school was created by the route of a yellow bus.

Two cocoons. Each one breaking slowly inner outer into the splendor into the misery of the. World for lack of a better name.

The phrase "giddy disgust" would not come to him for years.

The books however made him reflect. What is this place? What am I doing here? What are we doing here? What am I supposed to be doing here? What should I do next? Who should I believe? What can I hope for? What do I know? Who am I? Where am I? Is there a God? What is God like? A person? A thing? An equation? What is the world? What is the world exactly? What is this universe above and around me? What is this thing called time that flows through me and around me at every moment whirling a kaleidoscope in a carrousel spiraling around me behind me throwing a long shadow pricked with fading brightness in front of me an even longer shadow of impenetrable darkness? What will happen to me when I am dead? What will heaven be like if there is a heaven and I go there?

The answer again came back to him heaven is the place of your greatest happiness and what is your greatest happiness. Despite what you know what you do not know. *To live my life moment by moment over again. Over again. And over again. Forever.*

Starburst. The teachers came eagerly with the news. They spread their eyes like peacock tails both proud and vaguely fatuous and did their little dance in front of the library. They were all aflutter. Diplomas stuck from their pockets in exaggerated tubes of approval. They had their favorites embalmed and placed on biers of honor in the front hall. It was all rather embarrassing how they strutted during assembly. They fanned themselves with report cards and gossiped in the cigarette-scented lounge. They were unremittingly saccharine but never forgot their sovereign power to mortify. Mrs. Booker the hateful beauty who detested her pupils and taught them the rudiments of the German language once made Bill Peters pee in his pants in class you should have gone during lunch she said clean it up. To say nothing of the constant petty humiliations of the coaches. And the math teachers. And the science teachers. Simpering sadists. They filled the funnels with grade-point averages historical dates rules of grammar diagrammed sentences multiplication tables and the names of dead presidents then jammed them down the production line of little ears. The pupils bleated the teachers smiled. The pupils regurgitated the teachers examined the half-digested residue. Tut-tut this morsel is not correctly gagged. My my this morsel is perfectly untouched ready-made from the mill of my lectures. Unalloyed with thought and expectorated pristine. Here (they passed it around to their colleagues) isn't this a pretty one. They marked their favorites for a fall and graded the radiant collapse. They slogged determinedly through the herds of little ones their faces in grimace of barely controlled fury and disillusionment hailing each other at hopeless intervals beacons of wrinkled despair towers of blindness foundering in the quicksands of relentless childhood. There was one he liked. There were several he liked. But most of them he detested. Yet he felt despite rather sorry for their plight their valiant stupid battle against the stupidity assailing them from all sides. Their look of shock behind their pretense of control impressed him increasingly as the years wore on. There was so little they could really do between the studied indifference of the parents the raving idiocy of television radio smarm the resentful laziness of their pupils the sanctimonious cretinism of the school board the political pusillanimities of the principal and the vicious laws of the marketplace for which they were preparing their charges like sheep for the slaughter of a corporation's bottom line. Baying tongues of an insolent darkness. Some of them actually believed in what they were doing they lectured pleaded tried to pass along their learning their belief in knowledge the search for truth and the importance of integrity like guttering torches in a relay across generations though it was more like a match lighting three they believed in the quest for truth and the cherishing of beauty and the absolute value of absolute good like a very dead Greek indeed but they were alive alive and they carried their little faith like a weak lantern in a gale. They were ridiculous and true. And he longed to be faithful.

For he was curiously even strangely at heart in love with authority. He wanted the people who insisted on being respected to be worthy of it. He wanted his authorities to be authoritative. Indeed he considered rebels ludicrous and pitiful. Authority stood in the shadow of his father whom once in the long ago he had worshipped like an idolater whose every word he engraved in his mind examined in little corners for subtleties nuances profundities missed at first. Even his long silences were studied in detail the timing of a frown the angle of a glance the little signals conveyed by the swiftness of a gait the hieroglyph of a gesture. His teachers were pathetic copies of the great original but nevertheless bore the essential markings even in their drab mediocrity and hopeless aspiring. Dusty plaster busts. Petrified memories of splendor.

Alone he sometimes aped his father's voice his opinions his mannerisms he looked in the mirror for hints of his father's efficient authority the calm intensity of his gaze. In despair. For there was little resemblance he could see till his mother who was not his mother but then who was his mother gone she once pointed out the little fold over the eye she claimed he shared with his father and indeed all the family on his side it comes from the Indian blood that came into the family many generations ago. He became terribly proud of that little fold of his Indianness of his fatherness. It gave his face an exotic cast that almost feminine face with its pudgy cheeks pale eyebrows cropped blond hair. What frightened him was the irritation he would suddenly see in his father's face when in order to please him he tried a brief imitation. The face froze in what it would take him many years to realize was recognition. Where did he get that phrase that expression on his face that way of turning his back on the room. What does he think he is doing. Throwing my weaknesses in my face as though they were flatteries. The little monkey pantomiming the king. In exasperatingly faithful idolatry. That would one day be so deeply betrayed.

For the father feared and loved and hated what he saw in the mirror that was his son.

And his son in baffled longing absorbed his father's fear and love and hatred and made it into the bone of what he was.

Neither could turn away from the other. For neither knew more than what he saw. And that was all reflection. Hypnotic in adoration and repulsion.

Till escape expunged the necessary little war.

But that was still to come. Now he studied bent over his books. Like his father spent many an evening or weekend afternoon bent over a book his teachers told him to study he pleased the adults by studying. Even his peers grudgingly respected the swat. Evenings were hecatombs of paper and pencils. His natural laziness was flattered by the ease with which he conquered his homework and excited his teachers with the cunning nonsense of his compositions in English and his date-perfect responses in history.

Arithmetic was more lugubrious and science a meticulous bore until one Christmas you were given a chemistry set with microscope and proceeded to kill ants for examination and blow up test tubes of intricately frothing cocktails.

Exploration and experiment these were your watchwords talismans for happiness in your hermit-like room.

Interrupted by dinner the elaborate feasts jest-fests off-the-cuff lectures quick-hand attacks of hard little truth delivered with a grin and obliquely adult chronicles of the public relations firm where your father worked and the more mysterious affairs of the household when the house breathed a kind of nocturnal existence in daylight when you were at school. Then the troop to the TV den while you increasingly kept to the chemical studious and musical haunt of your room.

For you were left alone to explore the new contents of your discoveries. To get lost as you did alone a little frightened and deeply attentive.

You turned inward like a screw and kept your joys perversely to yourself.

Not as if you had not tried to share the little flecks of opal and sapphire you found among the books and recordings of your father's choice library. But like as not their value was an acquired taste and those around you seemed to prefer more usual stuff. The insipidities of television. The brutality of sports. The radio's static crooning.

Though your parents pretended otherwise.

This was bewildering. Reality was scorned as pretense the pretense respected as reality (so he thought). It was enough to make one go mad or philosophical.

He went both.

Wrapped in silence. Furtive withdrawn watchful intense inept serious and sincere at the wrong moments sarcastically comic at impossible ones.

He made them uneasy himself above all.

Every other week he shed a skin and grew a new interest. Your eyes are bigger than your stomach mother who was not his mother told him whenever he was unable to finish his third helping.

It was as though he wanted to eat the world from different positions at the dinner table.

He was fascinated by the word understanding.

He had perfect faith it could be acquired.

It was only a question of accumulation and openness. And time that treasure chest of fire.

Adulthood would be an era of ever-deepening understanding.

To understand was to stand. At the edge of the sea on the crest of the mountain and survey earth ocean clouds and sky in a single sweep of the mind.

It was stronger than power it was deeper than knowledge it was even deeper than love.

He stood on the little hill in the piles and serenely overlooked the halted excavations and the gray hard fields the lure of the woods the little boxes of houses plunked down by the country road and the hills rolling away behind thickening screens of dimness in the far distance to the east.

It would grow only richer forever.

He was sure of that at least of that.

How it thrilled him.

That certainty.

The legacy that awaited him.

It came as something of a surprise to learn that the will was written in invisible ink. So much trickier the task of deciphering a text on a blank and tumultuous page.

The darkening halls.

At the far ends splashes of linoleum light.

Noisy crowds of shadows through which you pitch and scuttle.

Small acid comments.

The relentless cynicism of children. In the trap.

Yellow stains of light on the ceiling.

Silent teachers wading through the crowd clasping papers to their chests and looking absent.

Little notes of cheer and increasing laughter as the day wore on toward last class.

Classrooms like dusty jewelry cases with the students lined up in their disingenuous settings glinting dully toward the teacher.

The utterly secure orderliness and boredom of it fractured by the occasional menace of a test.

At the end of each year the automatic notch into the next grade.

Twelve in all divided into three.

With the thrill of college waving you on from the other side.

Then the triumph of adulthood the victorious career the woman you love the children you will teach your wisdom to all the gains you have made in your ever-deepening understanding the magnificent house the mobs of friends the enviable reputation and travels to the most exotic lands a progress of triumphs the sheer excitement of the world in your hands the world welcoming you like a lover like a potentate like a conqueror it would all come as naturally as breathing.

You remember a time in early childhood you snatch eggs from under a gaggle of chickens and place them in your basket braving the defiant squawks and indignant pecking and then waddle back to the kitchen under the white load heavy and fragile feeling very proud of yourself the smiles and cheers on every side as you raise the basket in the brilliant kitchen and walk up to the table now one more step and totter to the oh look at him edge grinning yourself now totter up to the edge again oh look of the tabletop in the totter to the smiling with one more time totter up to the victory look at him then

oh no down they go!

(and all that scalding laughter!)

But this sums nothing up.

Katy's hot pink nipples in the white of her skin bathed in the light through her blouse her fingers holding the neck of it open she laughs giddily into your ear your vague feeling of disappointment for they looked so like your own only pinker there was nothing particularly special about them why was everyone including you so excited about seeing them? The boys had gathered at the edge of the woods at the edge of the playground whispering among themselves "Katy's going to show her titties." It seemed very exciting at first many of them never having seen a girl's naked chest before. You had seen your sister's naked dumpling torso with its little nipples and smooth cloven groin and thought nothing much of it also your mother who was not your mother which seemed more formidable and troubling pasty lunar globes massive florid aureoles and a wilderness of black between her thighs also your great aunt once great wrinkled sagging dugs and brush of graying fur between her legs disgusting and vaguely terrifying her breasts were bigger than your head. Nudity was neither flaunted nor hidden in your household it happened without coyness between bedroom and bath you often shared a pee with your father in the john glancing timidly at the monstrous shaggy penis next to your shoulder and jiggling your own petite hairless willy in mock imitation. So why the silly excitement over Katy yet it was so. The anticipation as always everything a setup for disappointment it would not be the last time you were disappointed in a woman. When the boys giggled knowingly about something they called screwing you were not taken in it was too preposterous. You could not imagine your father and mother who was not your mother in such a silly position. Although you had been masturbating since early childhood you couldn't imagine doing it in any sense with a partner. You would be too embarrassed. For the rest of your life. As it turned out. You always to be happier or if not that more content alone than with any other human being. Lecturing the ceiling. Whispering stories to the pillow. Daubing the air with fairy tales. Delivering angry and eloquent speeches to the hushed and silent walls. A helix twisiting madly in a pure crystal cube. Turning your room into a universe. You both darkness and sun and the terrifying embrace of the stars. Oh that vast gale. As you nursed your body and mind with ever-faithful tenderness. Your own lover. Loyal beast in the palace. Pacing the corridors trying door after locked door. The candle going out in a draft before the turn in the mirror. In which for a moment you saw. The only faithful one.

Schooled to a hard and useless edge. At that time. For a time. Against females! Their uncanniness. He thought a fake beauty that hid alkaline smells a mucoid formlessness hysteria of uncertain identity boundaryless entanglement with the air a constant threat of dissolution like jellyfish though less symmetrical wedding themselves to totems of Beauty and slipping away like pools of mercury he was made uneasy by (he thought) their lack of definition a certain shapelessness hungry attachment yet didn't know how much they troubled him he was being shoved into nature's trap and the gaudy circuitry of sex the trap was being laid inside him in the arcana of his torso at the base of the abomination swinging from his belly he was being sucked down a drain bored out behind his navel girls were becoming less vials of pride and irritation and more probing and manipulative egg reservoirs of epidermal magnetism organs of dark vacuum with wet holes between their legs the objects of a deathly longing the tools of nature's perpetual self-creation and destruction tyrants of desire. In their eyes he thought he could see they were aware of this it seemed to them their natural right and any rebel against it invited torture and execution it was enough to make him declare war against them. At that time. Like the long arms of the man-o'-war they enfolded him in a stinging clasp blindly caressing and absently murderous. Fear and anger were his only weapons fear kept him apart anger startled awake their fear. So they ran away to their opposite and opposing universes passing annihilating glares between them. Nothing formed. There was nothing to attach to in that slippery blindness however hectic and overwrought. The hormones provided their own antidote in aimless panic. It was horrifyingly funny yet so close to the bone it was infinitely remote. Imagine wrestling with a rabid dog made of honey and phlegm. Every so often one would peel off from the pack and pursue him. Bacchante of the playgrounds. For nothing he could recall he had ever done. Or intended. Abruptly surrounding him a suddenness of girl. Scampering frock and mary janes. Giggles and screams and frank goggle eyes. Conferences of skirt behind the jungle gym followed by the ignominy of a sneak attack. He turns to see a grin in a corolla of flying hair and a flash of bobby sock beneath a shriek. Vague bewilderment and prepubescent disgust. A slipping over his shoulder makes him turn to see the parting lips of the cootie catcher showing tick-like dots dancing in revulsion and the gaping mouth of one of his buddies laughing. His third-grade misogyny will never quite die it will haunt the stillborn romances of his future.

Take as read.

But this was all country folk. Before the expulsion and fall. A memory. The school in the city was a different world.

The labyrinth of cement and fury surrounded it in a hard tender squeeze. Like a nest of stone snakes. Breathing.

The snide flair of his peers here had a sharper cutting edge. The teachers were colder and angrier their bafflement part of a grand strategy of preemptive vendetta. Let them sink or swim promote the strong punish the weak then move on to the next relentless batch.

It was a factory of children and they were laborers hammering and riveting raw ingots into quality-controlled machines.

He was fed through the belts each day a well-behaved and slightly strange boy intelligent on paper but without obvious gifts. Respected more than liked. Moody and a bit withdrawn. Attentive absorbent and unassertive. Quiet in class. Few friends.

Their hands skimmed over him plucking at the overachieving and the obstinate. Over their heads they would pause irritably shake their heads and pass on.

They held him up for inspection like an egg to a candle then perfunctorily laid him aside.

He'll do well enough the impatient pre-emptive assessment.

Survive if just barely. The vomitting into life.

So he read in their sighing eyes in the pause between the pupil ahead and the pupil behind.

Only his father was angry that he did not get all A's.

A different world yet the same merely surrounded by other battles.

The faces on the girls were growing hard. He would find himself despite all his vows and denunciations daydreaming about one of these smooth cold faces making it break into laughter or tears at his wish. The harder and colder the face the deeper the intensity and fascination of his longing. They filled his thoughts with their held secrets their carefully reserved splendors. He dreamed of their bodies beneath the prim frock or the crisp sun dress imagining the small breasts the ripening hips the dark moist sleeves within the loins. He imagined the feel of his skin against their skin the molding of his hands around the hollows of their bodies long journeys through the forests of their hair. Their bodies were continents of wilderness and he was their discoverer exploring jungle and mountain and deep path of river and fertile estuary the long barrier islands off the coast and the wind-blown interior. He gazed into new-born universes expanding in their eyes the swarming of galaxies the birth and perishing of stars. He breathed in the dark perfumes that followed them. He listened to their voices as to an uncanny music the shifting of their clothes was an afternoon serenade. He lost himself in daydreams about their hair. He grew stupid and shiftless with desire and could not mutter hello in the halls without losing heart. The heart that hammered loud enough for everybody to hear. He couldn't meet their eyes. His own ineptitude drove him to despair. As they sailed out of his sight signalling messages to each other and trading indecipherable laughter.

Throughout his life he retained the scars from the searing.

For the break was abrupt and savage. One day indifference and self-sufficient disgust the next a collapse into longing. Timidity and desperation replaced the robust self-assurances of childhood detachment. A hovering duplicitousness the brutal frankness. A regimen of self-deception the ready glance in the mirror. Arcane manipulations the off-hand turning of the knob.

He could not keep his hand out of the viper's nest. Where his own desires bit and poisoned.

Oh it was thrilling the first descent into the masochism of desire. The despised gender suddenly transformed into sleek idols of beauty of lust in niches of worship.

He was entranced by the emptiness between them.

The solitary one idled in the nave dreaming and gazing imagining dialogs he would never have counting their charms in memory repeating to himself the ambiguous words of greeting they couldn't always avoid. Building hope on illusion.

He collected Playboys found in the trash hid them under his bed examined them minutely before masturbating happily on the bed cover he had no guilt thank god about that. He sacrificed his flesh regularly to the altar of the pinup. But this happened later. In fact he had discovered the wild if limited pleasure his penis could give him in early childhood while watching television a middle-aged bare-chested man bound in a chain that crossed his nipples a chain he by expanding his chest was at last able to burst. Like Zampano in *La Strada* though he was too young to know this at the time. Watching this so excited him he got his first hardon then fell to the floor and humped the carpet until he came finishing just in time to see the chain snap.

He felt no shame or guilt just pure gonadal thrill. And the obscure certainty he mustn't be seen embarrassment similar to being caught on the toilet. He was three at the time and surprized to realize later he was thought sexually precocious by some he who in decades to come would be thought so backward.

The practice became regular. The tugging thought the sight of a man's bare chest a woman's bare breasts striking him as obscenely huge. Which for one who was roughly two feet tall they of course were. To say nothing of the fact that women's conversation drove him even then to distraction with boredom. Which would continue throughout much of his life causing a cramp of ambivalence craven lust for the glories of their bodies and ache of tedium at their preoccupations. Ah. The exquisite joy of tonguing their skin of fondling their now perfectly sized breasts of lying between their legs ensheathed by their vaginas was more than made up for by the rambling torture of their talk. They would nibble him into a stupor with words. Oh. So he ran away. Then lust would make him forget his boredom and drive him back. So he thought. Not knowing yet that beneath the boredom and desire was the scald of the first betrayal the one that would not heal. But this comes later we are anticipating. We are always anticipating the disaster that must come. Yet never actually arrives.

For what excited him in his boyhood was boys. It would be always the masculine that gave him the supreme thrill though the gonads shifted their interest. He identified with the boy the boy was both invader and invaded in his fantasies where he was roped to a stake at the far end of the bathroom facing a firing squad his little chest bared to the guns heaved out in defiance the muskets would shoot or the arrows fly he was a fan of Robin Hood and the Swamp Fox freelance hero of the revolution and he would collapse writhing in agony to the floor imagining the blank astonished faces of his heroes gazing down at him or away in a distant stare as he excitedly humped the bathroom mat. After taking his bath for the hot water relaxed and aroused him. In the far children's wing of the house where he was alone with his solitary ecstasy the rest of the family upstairs watching TV. He was caught only once and warned but it was too late he was far too accustomed to his play. So much so he was deeply shocked to learn later that sex was something two people could do together. Which he never became entirely used to a partner always seeming an unnecessary intrusion into the fantasy.

In the meantime. His first infatuation was for a reckless half-delinquent who led the pack in the fifth grade a year ahead of him. Pale skin wild-eyed dark shutter of bang over his forehead a crazy happy look on his face a mischievous glitter following him a curiously feminine face retailing boy-man outrages he shouted through the playground raced leading his pack down the field had a bullying streak was often in trouble then shrugged it off and with an aimless laugh ran back into the air. He never knew his last name only Bobby. He spent most of recess in search of Bobby generally fruitless. For Bobby was a furtive brat only appearing then vanishing into the wilderness of the solitary one's imagination. Any solitary one's imagination. For he was an image of bravado only and at the end of a single year disappeared.

Except in the solitary executions beside Robin and Fox of the bathroom.

The cold sleek ravishing face with the withdrawn luminous eyes blurs after a dim pause into a cold and gorgeous girl with the ambiguous name of Geri. She sits behind you in the next row in English and history smiling vaguely and ignoring you as she ignores everyone except the fat ugly girl her best friend who serves her as a perfect foil. Her face is smiling or expressionless she never laughs nor scowls. This gives her an aura of almost frightening power. Perfectly dressed at all times. You suspect make-up but cannot prove it. You corkscrew in your chair at every opportunity trying to catch her eye when the teacher throws out a question. You show off your little bookish learning. Triumphantly tickle the class into laughter. Make smart remarks that prove your ignorance like a theorem. And in an entire year catch her eye perhaps twice. It must have been more often than that. It is laughing each time it skims over you. In barely acknowledged contempt.

In no other eyes but your own do you exist was the lesson begun now and to be repeated ad nauseam until you mastered it. Of the nightmare that was beginning called love. It was serenely cold and even rather kind. At first. A gentle quizzing foreshadowing more brutal rites. No knowing of course that the student would prove so slow. So dense. So deservingly failed.

The agonies of those years unbearable yet bearable and unfatal and silly. A form of torture without the dignity of killing you merely spitting you out into the world a spastic wreck shamed inadequate despised by the one inescapable authority yourself put through the paces of the genes stumbling rebelliously obedient despite yourself as you performed each night to the bored crowd in the sideshow hoosegow of

Where you were convict prison guard clown
In the absurd torture chamber you
In the prison of circling shadows you
Became
Were
Must be
Wobbling like a calf in your head a ridiculous grandeur.

No.

No. Too soon to tell.

Somewhere back there the fork and the turning.

The building up then the tearing down.

Somewhere in the principle of the building up the principle of the tearing down.

The lump of gold of the melted crown mixed according to plan in the rubble.

The ranks in to assembly a scum bouquet those tousled heads
a rhubarb murmur clouds of arms mobs of legs row on row aimless
spitballs targeted whistles insults weak as jokes but inadvertently
crippling the simmer of hormones in ranks of laps thrumming knees
in nervous leery paradiddles little male titters at the flumed bouffants
of that never-so-innocent era monitors stalking the side aisles heads
bobbing like marionettes elbows in the ribs dominoing down half a
row the ever-lookout for objects of scorn what one learns about the
psychology of a crowd one need look no further than an assembly of
teenagers lashed into nervous order by the gazes of their defied and
obeyed teachers.

He sits cold and alone at the end of his row pretending to
look over his notes not one of them never to be one of them proud
scornful despising them in despair.

How do they do it how do they live so easily in the heavy light
how can they breathe what makes them so calm and cheerful as
they butcher each other with blows of breath in preparation for the
bloodbath of adulthood?

Yet he too is at ease even cheerful in his scorn as he calmly
condemns them from his niche high in the shadow of the nave.
Knowing no better. Sometimes even suspecting he knows no better.

But not here. Not yet. Not now.

As the rhubarb climaxes to the sound of the bell.

As the ridiculous prinicipal the principle of the ridiculous calls
the principle of anarchy to order.

Beyond the confines of the days' routines the scheduling of classes the ranking of curriculum examination promotion the grid of grades and the false measure the click and shove of hour and term the petty rebellions and petty punishments the little triumphs and little defeats the looking forward to Christmas vacation in the fall the looking forward to summer vacation in the spring the hope for snow and the disillusion of Monday mornings the gradual light and darkness of a world beyond the terrors and boredom of this little bootcamp for the mind they gathered in a crowd against the classroom window it lolled its tongue at you like an idiot.

It was all fantasy what you dreamed beyond the schoolyard fence. You built little towers without compensation piling sand on sand of exuberant hope romantic disaster. Yes! A catastrophe would be exciting. So you taught yourself a loathing of security. You despised safety though careful not to actually endanger your own. For the most part. How eloquently you soared heroic and unwary when completely alone in your room or at the edge of a field hidden in the shade. How nervous withdrawing stuttering in the presence of any other person at all. The distance between the mask and the face grew daily. Sailed toward opposite horizons between them a baffled sea and a radiant sun. But which is the mask which is the face? Am I what I think I am or what others think I am? And which others? Or am I neither but something else entirely? Then what am I? A confused and morbid preadolescent came the most convincing and unbearable answer. From which you ran. Toward your dream of the world.

Which one day broke you. And scattered you like salt over the cuts on your hands.

But not yet. Let's stay a while longer cooped in the boring safety of school intrigues and routines. The games of dominance and submission the exercises in triumph and failure the comparisons the trade-offs the contests the betrayals the pricking sarcasms the pen-knife victories that would seem meaningless in the years to come. But I am anticipating as always an author's prerogative. Because after all I survived or I wouldn't be sitting here writing this for you. Am I sitting here writing this for you. Something wrong there but I can't think what. Anyway I didn't sink like a stone as he did. Almost did. Did I? Am I? In fact my hand extended toward him and my eyes watched him as he sank. Amazed and horrified and pleading and contemptuous. Loving and hating. Before coldly turning back toward safety. The little victory to come time and leisure and just enough money and a talent for indolence and ordering memories into dazzling little patterns to please the slightly inflated ego. Surviving as I said.

Didn't I?

4

Then on a certain day at a certain hour the catastrophe began.
Not all at once.
Something slipped.
It was terrible at the time yet it seemed alone.
Later they would go on with their lives.
Unbearable things happen then we go on. To other unbearable
things.
No? You deny this? You mean it is not true?
It is not true. It is not true. It is not true.

Autumn. Sooty plastic bags belly like medical gloves decorative sneakers on telephone wire detritus littering the street's methodical crosses of sky. Tiny yellow leaves scatter like hands at the foot of the ginkgo tree. The light outside the house is heavier the streets cleaner than summer's. An underlayer of damp skitters up the flank. Just enough to tickle your skin. Hah ah. A hollowing of bottles somewhere up an alley. Where are we going. Somewhere anywhere. Out of this world. A snap in the air wakes you up. At every corner. Snap! On the beach in the field in the street. Snap! And in the wetness there is the smell of burning leaves.

The dew on the doorknob makes it cold to the touch. There are shouts to stop the bus. Hey! *Hey!* Its yellow flashing back lumbers to a halt by the bank of mailboxes. One red flag is raised in a cavalier wave.

But now it is the jam of muff and scarf and parka hood in a diesel-scented 25¢ morning. You demur to the sarcasms of the bus driver hidden behind his charity. *You look like a little old man!* The smell of diesel and spilled gasoline of tar and whiffs of doughnuts bacon coffee and the scum smell of whisky mash from the river. And underneath the persistent smell of stale bread that dominates the early-morning city. A mush of leaves rotting in the gutter. Filthy pigeons fretting on the sidewalks. The cold fitful angry blurring of the hastening goal-driven crowds.

It was moving to a climax something that would explode into crystals of hysteria the massive collision the bolt of power the clash with the avatars of a strident unbegun and unending.

War.

Pinwheel fireworks at first spinning in a corbelled heaven that aim to blind and blow off the fingers of the rocketers themselves. And every innocent and guilty thing around them. Innocently nevertheless for the only drive was need. Perceived need. Imagined need. Feeling of need. The fluctuating mirror locked in the middle of the iris. Imprisoned everywhere in projections. Of me. Of you. Of him. Where there is no other. What was not given was anything beyond the self something to call a world only trash and a bright commercial try this and go to heaven fail to try this and go to the hell you so richly. The spinning flak on all sides a chaotic baby god gleefully rips its toys apart then tosses the pieces in the air look look glitter glitter chortling at all that panic. When the bullets tear through the skull in the car it stops a smile shocked on its face.

As he cradles it and sinks into the brightness of its eyes.

A historical memory. A chapter in an unread book. A website visited with increasing rareness.

A savage brightness. As if a curtain had been torn open revealing the madness of the day. In the melodramatics of Marxist discourse the superstructure sheered off the base like the peeled face from a clown. Doing his bit for the paying audience eating his dead.

He turns to the camera inspired by a brilliantly bad pun. Or rather palindrome. (A clown speaking in palindromes!) Babbles on for a moment unheard a prattler of bliss in this darwin morning. Then returns like a jaguar to his feed.

Unimaginable evil. What is that.

A hollow in time continuity slackening in a slowly unravelling weave. The texture of events grew quicker as if. So many shearings through a fabric of petroleum and compound interest. Asegai in chips. A cicatrice designed in enamel and disgust but disgust would become passé moral numbness splintered in sarcasms to the east perforated with grins elsewhere the preferred response on the talk shows. But we are anticipating for everyone will have the moral sensitiveness beaten out of him out of her taught the acrobatics of self-interest strategies of suspicion tactics of fear the adroit calibrated hermeneutics of self-aggrandizement. For each their own and grammar be damned. And what better method for this than the display of the horror of man against man. Against woman against woman against man. Enchanting. Informative. Educational. And fun. Switch channels in the rapids of changelessness. Before even the remote was invented whirlpool of cement flecked with body fluid and tissue. This you he I write down in school notebooks in preference to the banalities of his teachers. And achieve many A's. And think I must be on to something.

For from that afternoon everything spins away. Of course not that the received wisdom always suspect. Yet another time is inaugurated. He is no longer he but riots of they a heterodox otherness in invasion. Besides his genes the world that squeezes at him through the television is a mobbed shattering signaling like a mirror flashing his eyes to the sun the designs of hysteria inside him. His shout is a hollow wrenching that sounds in small blind acts of self-defeat. Calmly. It is the only power he knows or it recognizes. As it slowly veers toward you. Not to be resisted master mister sir buddy guy or denied.

(So fold up like a wallet or a fetus. Flick open in random acts of fury like a switch blade. Gash the accommodating hand. Fold back in with a click. Snarl. Shake gently in the corner before pouring. Cultivate indignation. Be determined to live.)

Euthanasia was impractical at the time so one might as well live.

Water stains the carpet before the front door.

An animal moves outside brushing its flank against the walls.

The house has become permeable or rather static massing for a strike.

What had always been out there is now out there no longer. The small faces inside the television set are biting into little worlds. The walls are beginning to merge with the air. There were no masks left to fit on our faces our faces were damaged masks. The solitary one is solitary no longer he cannot find solitude he walks the city and finds a crowd of eyes. Home post-father is a brusque gale of facetious malice and electronic nattering. He blares his stereo and wedges himself into the gutter of a book. There seems to be no private world left and it will not leave him alone. Shall not leave you alone. Cannot leave the alone alone.

Avoidance maneuvres leading toward the cliff.

Into a finger of the sea.

Or no. A thumb. Splay from the hand insignia of obstinacy said the fortune teller. Plucking at it clucking when it springs back to its prehensile jut. Mother of tempests. Wilding annihilating gray. Where the fishermen stand with their long nodding rods and pull in fish or just wait. Patient. Hip deep in the gnash of the surf.

You will not give in. And you will pay.

So the private linked to the public in a spasm at once absolutely detached and resolutely intimate the eyes gaze like fish in a bowl and the groin thrashes. In loss. Feeding the starved eyes. The absolute impotence of absolute awareness the chains of light that seal you to your chair. As the riptide of your family sucks the sand around you. Threatening the rock where you sit caught between the kaleidoscope of the sun and the corruscations of the sea. Eyes of chaos and chaos. A starfish flicking a prickled arm in a spit cup of foam. In the livingroom. Between the stairs and the antique glass. And the bickering on the upper floors. A silence that throbs constantly like an omen. The whisper of moving sheets.

There was a plan for order in all this so many aims goals limited purposes over-riding interests etc. Magnanimous or miserly gestures toward organization generally willful and sanctimonious military in style coercive in nature good-hearted loving and tough. Brutal goodness. The point will be to shove him into being. Whether he wants to go or not. It is the right thing to do. At the right time in the right way. There being no other. Only one. Only once. Or you will destroy not yourself alone but all of us with you.

Everywhere he looks there is a hammer raised above a nail.

The perspective is closed and global. A face pressed against a screen. Background then as now in process of elimination.

There is no telling where you are. You are everywhere you are nowhere. Always. Never. Now.

As the flames began gathering in the city.

It will not do not to admit they repelled and fascinated you their shadowy oily skin not black at all but many shades of brown the odors of their bodies their harsh dry hair their big-mouthed laughter their anger their unrelenting poverty. They disgusted frightened mocked you challenged the doctrine of kindness in you. Of truth and kindness gazing with suspicion at each other within you. Dared you to look them in the face. Beyond the sentimentalism of the victim. After the last blackmail has been paid. Their misery everywhere like an oil that slicked the shafts. The hopelessness and filth of the neighborhoods where they lived. That went to the horizon on moorlands of homes in ruins strafed from the skies interrupted demolition. The constant fear walking their streets fear of them the fear from them. The blank tired druggy look bloodshot gaping scattering shriek murderous following stare. Angry laughter from knots of kids resentful laugh vicious little sharp laugh of lying victory scornful flamboyant theatrical laugh laugh to show one is not crying not beaten or crushed crushed beaten weeping laugh. The tone gave the city the richly gray sheen of misery frustration and shame. It infiltrated the curtains soured the clothes hanging in the closet. Sour bitter filth like the stench from rotting wharves.

You walked the streets in revulsion and fear among them and watched in pity and shame as the television flickered in the livingroom. Flickered with the lambent fury of hope in the comfortable precarious livingroom. ("Luxurious poverty" as his mother not his mother laughed with strained triumph. It was a hidden little home post-father in the labyrinth of alleys at the center of the city.) Watched with fascination and a detached admiration for them as they braved the vicious white. (Kitchen clatter and comeback lent a domestic background music.) It was so easy to be virtuous before the helpless chattering box with the submissive buttons and the pleading face. (The bantering bickering lent a charm to the melodramatics of the evening news.) The efflux of whirling banalities and immediate demand seemed petty when compared to the marching of the thousands and the display of a historical revolt the epic of the revolution. (The angry hysterias seethed around him across him on a rock above the rush of waters. The intensity of his attention to the shadow play in the box kept his would-be interrupters at bay.) As he ignored the dramas of the house and rose in ineffable sanctimony to dizzying self-righteous heights. He drank in virtue like a poison.

> High-pitched.
> Rhythmic.
> Coming from where one knows not.
> Out there.
> Outside.
> Mechanical.
> Little sharp stabs of sound.
> From elsewhere.
> Pulsing.
> Penetrating.
> Only the human could have created the inhuman city.
> It kept you awake.
> It wove stitches into your sleep.
> And then on the other side of the mechanism the distant human

cry.

His childhood split open like a seam. Suddenly he was all buttocks.

He was collapsing he was growing. He assaulted the air in uncontrollable fits of self-assertion. People looked at him as if he had just farted in their faces. Which in a sense he had.

The cracking voice the shortening cuffs. The callow gawkiness the zits in the mirror. The quick blush the ready stutter the false moves that sent crockery flying. The nervous tic that moved like a mole from one part of his body to the other. The grotesque dental braces the vile glasses. The touchy agonizing ridiculous pride. The laughable despair.

Of course he was self-absorbed. What else could be more interesting? Except the revolution of course. But was there any difference?

The chaotic armies after all not only engulfed they erupted within him. The world's anarchy had its fifth columns or was it rather the reverse the genetic misery ordered its sympathetic agents to infiltrate the world.

However it seemed the solitary one became his own crowd.

Rioting in the mirror of the television. Spying on his dreams.

You were not innocent but overwhelmed.

You became vague and frozen and dreamed of fire.

Of heading marches into the city of leading mobs through the capitals of the world of swaying masses by your eloquence of conducting great orchestras to mighty climaxes while your unknowing flame of the week listened in hushed and reverent silence from a box near the stage. He laid down his baton to the thunderous ovation and turned modestly and reverently to his lady bowing to her in esteem and megalomaniacal ecstasy.

Then woke on the coverlet to a call to early dinner.

And burned to the shame of the ordinary real the world as it is which he would not which he would never entirely accept. Even if it killed him which it would in any case would it not? No! he shouted to himself. Never.

Then went outside for endless and aimless hectic walks across the city.

The air was sharp and tense in winter clammy and suffocating in summer. The city seemed orderly on the surface it was only the expressions on the faces and the barking frustration in the sounds of the voices that showed what seethed beneath.

Knotted hemp of shrill.

He ran he tried to run away but there was nowhere to run away to so he pulled back at the edge of his limits and ran ran ran. In ever. More. Tightening. Circles.

Listened. It was on the corner of a park beneath tall trees. Flickering patches of shadow and sun. Rattle of glass bottles hum of cars distant vanishing siren horn beep dog bark shouting kids in a farther corner the shift of leaves above in a little breezy swell. Had stopped unthinking on the way elsewhere. And for a moment dissolved in the moment. And for a moment knew something almost like happiness. Is that the word? Something almost like tranquility. Breathed in the smell of. Exhaust fume wet soil falling leaves. Yes. A whiff of coffee grounds and rotting fruit. Yes. A thread of cigarette smoke the sweet acid smell of diesel. A trace of perfume. Layers of grime shoe leather wool. A sour dog turd. Yes! The mucid smell within his own nostrils. And breathed and listened and forgot who he was and what and felt something almost like peace. Yes? And what should I do? And where shall I go? And what should I be?

And then the moment passed and he was once again alone in the light.

The crowds folded hands and formed a circle dance through the weave of sidewalk train subway transit bus and around again. Moto perpetuo in an endlessness of dancing. A restlessness of endless dancing. A cheerlessness of endless dancing. Since no one began what no one could stop. Looping and frozen. Except for those cast out staring at the side of the falls dazed and wondering before turning inward triangulating bridges of revenge. Join the rush or join the rage maybe he could sit on a rock at the edge between them and not be swept away. Entirely. This was an unlikely hope. To be sure. If only to be sure. Birdsong piercing the thunder of water.

Crusts of light and towers of shadow spangled and glittering above the glamorous and threatening streets.

And and and.

Yet you must live even between the peaks. Or try.

The marbled maze both within and without the impelling dance music toward danger and thrill. The tactile sensation of crime and the longing for punishment. In a single beat of the band that played on every radio on every station at every hour. The hour of the young which was every hour at that time.

Bacchantes in bobby socks and penny loafers. About to shed into purer madness.

Alarm.

The youthful barbarians demanding entrance to the city.

In phalanxes of desire and futurity. Their cars flashing in the sun.

A cold and unrelenting rapture.

So come he thought. Come.

And they came.

In waves. Tides. A sea.

The moon pulled them in a vast wash across the continental shelf.

You wondered at all the shadows and mirrors parading through the streets.

Youth in its strength. Yourself writ large in the crowd.

The sledge smashes the column of glass and the delicate structure of memory and words falls at his feet. Where he must tread on what he is and who he was. Looking for traces of him between flints of reflection needles of sky the bright opaque eyes of his peers. A blank wall where letters were beginning to form.

A wave a tide a sea of crashing glass.

Crossing the sandbar the heads bob across the gully like little cheerful beachballs ribbons of giggling and commentary rise from their mouths. On the sandbar a line of swimmers the arms of the women raised demurely hieratically the hands of the men dipping and scooping the wash the swimmers leaping gingerly as each wave crashes around them the faces of the swimmers are turned toward the horizon and the cresting troops of the waves. Shrieks. Whoops. Yells. Guffaws. Sunlight skims the surface like a stone. Or in long curling cylinders flashing. Or in a shimmer like an enormous rippling tablecloth of silver blinding to look at lashing as if alive with great shoals of fish. The joy of enfolding the body between vast sea and vaster sky. As if cupped in the hands of someone kneeling. Suspended in the air. That gift from the thrilling shore. That warning. That promise. That happiness.

Something to daydream in the afternoon bed between the windows that overlooked the trash-strewn alleys. The light tipped in glowed and bowed away in disenchanted whiteness. The bricks stood exposed like betrayed couples. And the alley leaned back toward the west with a tired and nearly forgotten indifference. There were still long hours of quiet then when nothing seemed about to happen. A bicycle clattered past or was that another decade. No matter. His thoughts hummed or vanished into a single hovering sensation. Then a dry trebly music buzzed up a nearby airshaft and tapped at the window with a reminder of time.

Only. Only one. Only once. Now.

And flicked its dry nail against the glass.

Smiled.

Danced.

Skimmed mockingly outside his window dancing on a column of air.

And you turned to look distrustfully remembering only the dreams.

Always. Always everything. Always ever. Then.

No said the mocker as it slowly raised the pane. Till the sun had scoured the room of rememberance.

From the house on the hill with the view down the valleys toward the heralding sun under noon and its half-turn west toward the bow of the twilight to the pinched defensive white-walled apartment a block and a half from the slums. Was a loss of family luck no one faced but bravely denied you less bravely stung by the shame of it even the shame of being ashamed of it of the loss of caste in a world where there was supposed to be no caste we are all equal here are we not we are not. A society agglutinated putatively from individual particles and kept together solely by virtue of. Of what you wanted to know. Particular purposes to which each individual member agreed. Which resulted in fact in. The only answer that occurred to you disgusted you mightily. It could not be true after all it was too simple it was simplisitic it had the terrible simplicity of truth. Money could not be it could not be enough. Of course it was not. And the family slipped like a house badly anchored on a hill that once the heavy rains began starts to slip down the hillside. Slowly at first. The porch sheers off and the windows pop the rain gutters dangle before the eyeless windows the frame twists the roof caves and buckles. Then more quickly. As the house turns into a ship rocking over seas of mud on a journey toward disintegration. So you rode toward the valley of the sea and the shoals of humankind.

Devouring memory.

One afternoon alone in the apartment you stand in front of the mirror in the gold octagonal frame and stare long at your reflection. You try as long as you can not to blink. And after a few moments the image in the mirror begins to shift into patches of blank color yellow azure magenta green fading in and around the eyes then the face transforms into a mask suddenly very old very young vast expanding to fill the infinite space of the mirror's world then imploding to two hard points and a shapeless mouth monster ghoul clown flailing on the stage behind the glass curtain. Yet you never lose your sense of clearly delimited even mildly condescending self despite all the mirror's attempts to erase it. At one point you smile and the mask grins back at you immediately collapsing back to the prim familiar form you are used to seeing in the mornings above the bathroom sink.

It is when you walk away that you feel suddenly as if you might disappear and turn back abruptly to catch the shocked gaze of the spectre in the mirror.

Susurrus. The blind scratches the edge of the sash. A breath crosses a young maple. A memory of sheets bellying and falling in sways of air. Vanishing in the gale of a traffic that never ceases.

Though it creates its own mysteries layers of sough of bus and car groan ratcheting growl of motorcycle plangent sirens each one differing for police ambulance fire. They wove and wove. A web of comb that called out to him calls of enticement and warning. Suggestions of the whirlwind called by some reality or history or the modern age the free world the murderous dance of survival last best hope of earth. It sat on its claws and waited visions of the future flickering in its eyes. Its smile seemed far larger than it was. Like the Milky Way one no longer saw but imagined across the night. Beyond the flecking chips of visible stars. Oh it had to be there still. Everyone told you so. The city however powerful and great could not rub out the stars. Or become them.

Could it.

Must it.

Shall it.

He asked he was only asking.

Are the stars only the city tagging the night. Is there nothing then not stained with the human. Nothing not touched by the hungry stare fingering dismantlement denaturing manipulation. He wanted to live innocently believing that was possible and not corrupt the things or living things or people among which he lived. Above all to do no harm. Precautionary principle what a lark. He lived tenderly toward the world believing that tenderness therefore would be returned. Must be in just compensation. Ignorant yet how careless the world was as to justice. As to tenderness. As to everything. He would think at a later time. But how am I to be sure I have grown so much wiser? Perhaps the world cares deeply for everything cares far too deeply for everything. And in so caring grows confused and incompetent and makes everything in it unhappy. Like an old woman in the wreckage of her life providing hordes of ceaselessly multiplying cats. Poisoning her world with her own generosity.

Or perhaps it is something much simpler.

There was in him the wisdom of a foolish hope nonetheless it gave him a brightness in the morning between the trash and shadows of the city. A brightness that could not entirely believe in anything impenetrably dark. And despised those who whispered to you light's secrets. Ah yes you were one arrogant son in all your wished for humility. It was the light that most impressed him the stars throwing their frail bridges across the vastness the moon's perishing and renewing tenderness the sun's command of the earth. So call him an egomaniacal sentimentalist and be done with it he thought he didn't mind. I am a romantic I will live and die a romantic. What can they do only starve me let them try! He was not yet afraid of the light. He basked in it like an opening flower or a new-fledged deer. Perhaps he was overly gentle with himself and overly hard on the world he had insufficient respect for the values of aggression and power he gave himself lectures on the subject he was not entirely unaware of his weaknesses. But at such times the city was less nightmare than challenge the generous eye of the camera would capture the celebrations of his victories. He dreamed of his heroic acts as he lay in reverie on his bed the respect of his elders admiration of his peers the love of a beautiful woman. Nature and God celebrated his youth he was certain of his destiny. The world held him in the palm of its open hand. The ecstatic grace of every moment was available at every breath. The world loved him as he loved the world at every moment in every part from its smallest tendril and opening leaf to its glittering mass of summer forest to its farthest peak and hidden secret of distant rushing star. At times he felt he was being stubbornly ridiculous and mocked his own pretensions but he pretended in the end (I am free I will do what I like) not to care.

For the unarguable fact of being human the absolute miracle of
being human in the world thrilled your modesty and pride. Modesty
(you fully realized you were a minor member of the order) and pride
(look what humanity can do but can it?). Yes there were shadows but
they seemed to form a frame for the center of light. Yes there was vast
and petty evil conscious and unconscious cruelty the willful malign
and cheerful destruction of goodness there were the massacres and
death camps but could this be only to make greater the final victory
of good you thought it possible. At least possible. Perhaps the hand of
the divine shaped the world into the harmonies of an eternal music.
If we would listen. Behind the silence and noisings. The sound of a
perpetual singing. All the world taking part the vast and unknown
universe taking part each little voice having its music then choruses
gathering here and there building together into masses of sound
vast Olympian symphonies an eternal mighty and infinite fugue yet
gentle and sweet without bombast but with true and graceful strength
nobility and grandeur oh the perfect truth of the perfect artist of
which every human artist is a hopelessly incompetent imitator.
Perhaps the human artist partook more directly than others of the
divine order behind the world's random destructiveness. This your
privilege your shame the knowledge of your own inescapable failure.
But the privilege looked brighter as everything looked brighter at
that fluid time. And what was needed then was a direction out of
possibility into something like being. So the decision by the solitary
one to look fate in the mirror and dare it to keep him from becoming
an artist. His only certain audience his conscience and his god. His

hope was to learn the key to unlock his solitude. In moments of ecstatic abandon. Communion momentarily overwhelming. Flashing vanishings of grace.

Such the love that blinded him with joy the joy that blinded him with love.

Or so he thought at the time. Go gently. Down. So he hoped to think to hold the thought that would not be held or stay.

Outward.

Away.

Toward one more unconvincing certainty.

For all certainties dissolved in the acid of the world as you witnessed it. All was tenuous and not to be seized only by time and handed over to dissolution. A divine order was a hope and a longing art music poetry crystals in the flux vanishing even as you admired them frost flowers on a country window melting in the morning sun. Bits of wreckage in the waters sinking beneath your weight as you touched them.

And you fell away lurching from one piece to the other fighting to keep your head above water.

You could not accept this at the time. Perhaps at any time. It seemed too senseless too brutal to be the full truth about the human condition (you were old enough to think in such terms) too crude to be ultimately real an excuse for failure the residue of a lifetime of defeats.

You would not be defeated. You balled your mind into a fist and dared the world to take you. At the very least you would fall fighting. Punching and kicking at the dust that you yourself had raised. Your hands strangling the neck of your shadow.

And the world which notices nothing would notice nothing.

The sounds coming through the wall. A reminder of the presence of others. Beating their lives into shape. Molding. Weaving. The staccato rejoinder. The sarcastic comeback. The grunt. The pause to consider the work. The shrug. The sigh. The curse. The occasional dying moan. The weeping. And the endless shuttlecock of the tread.

He did not yet know strangers beyond what he heard through the wall or saw through television's disingenuous eyes. They were a murmur of random knocks and tatters of unintelligible speech. He wondered and wondered yet more. What could be going on on the other side of the wall? At times. As when in the country darkness he wondered what was happening around the far speck of light across the valley on the distant side of a hill. At other times cringed at knowing it could only be more acting out of hope where there was no hope cheerless people putting on cheer and insisting he join them forcing him to smile and look at the smiles pasted on their faces like badly fitting masks. Laughing with false laughter and forcing him to laugh. Until all you longed for was to run away. Into your room but you no longer had a room of your own you shared with your laughing brother. Out of the house and down the road but there was no house and there were no roads there were only the streets in an infinite and pitiless grid the city that lay like a vast prison around you of noise and filth and badly lit forms hurrying beneath yellow streetlights. So you stayed and put on the mask and heartily laughed a cursed laugh and no longer wondered what went on on the other side of the wall or around the starred light.

One day he caught himself in the act of making a grotesquely unfair judgment about someone he knew.

It lay there before him a sickly mean child of his mind a little lump of wailing injustice complaining bitterly about injustice.

He pulled back in shame how could he have been so mean-spirited? willfully unfair cruel? He hadn't yet given it voice it had kept inside his mind sneering and bellowing only when alone had he let it hop out and squat on the table in front of him. It could happen again an eruptive scarf of bilious meanness. He would have to watch more closely the thoughts in his mind where they simmered and leapt into contortions of meaning he had thought beyond him beneath him mocking prodding daring him to embrace them and fly to the conclusions they pointed to.

A force sat somewhere behind his eyes. It was something both within him and behind him and it inflicted its judgments suddenly and without mercy on himself and all he knew. It had the gift of irrefutable argument and universal condemnation. He had to marshal all his forces of debate to dispute it haul it back to moderation reasonableness something like contentment.

Which it hated like a vampire the sun.

Then the world would pitch into another spin of random cruelty and justify seem to justify the demon.

Who would snicker knowingly in a corner of his mind and lick the air with its fiery tongues.

Playfully dividing.

Playfully urging each other on.

Into rollicking laughter at his innocence.
His hopeless pretense at goodness.

Adolescent. A brand a name an accusation an excuse. The enforced idiocy of a certain form of youthfulness. The curse of the no-longer child not allowed to be an adult. Lying in a trough of unidentity for a decade. With the world looking down at you from the rim with changing fashions of sneer on its face the contempt for the well-meaning calf the fear of the possible delinquent the resentment of the generational replacement the irritation with the idealistic rebel the worry that you might not after all want to join the heterosexual country club.

Your skin was loosening and tightening as the long bones shot up and the joints knobbed and angled and the voice cracked up and down the octaves and the clothes crept up your shins and wrists. You got your first pair of glasses and turned into an instant dork. Your chin and cheeks mortified you with little parties of black heads that turned into white heads that turned into boils that turned into scars. You sent glasses half-full of soda pop flying across the room when you forgot how long your arms were. You found it hard to get used to seeing your parents on the same level as your nose. The girls in class began to grow breasts and you longed to see touch kiss suck their nipples lick their bodies penetrate deeply their various entrances with the penis that burned and hardened between your thighs and your desire drew you to them but did not draw them to you on the contrary they found you repulsive so your desire ended by frightening you it set you up for humiliating defeats therefore you ran from girls so their forms would not trouble you ran away within into the dark palace where you could not be humiliated and began your collection of photographs of naked women offering you the sight of their breasts and bellies and thighs and learned to use your hands to bring you a pleasure you did not know how to ask for yet or indeed ever from a woman. You cheated yourself in a way. In your cowardice stole your own happiness. Safe and alone in your palace. Your obscure and shadowy kingdom. Drowning in the sea of shadows of your mind.

The tight hard thrill of the loins was no new occasion only its direction became a burden. The itch in his groin he had learned to relieve through mounting beds and rugs and towels around the house clumps of grass piles of leaves in the woods boscage thickets snow. Fantasy and solitude enflamed his mind excited his little sex. Just as the presence of others tamed him into the good grandson he was so proud to be never quite understanding why others despised it. His politeness rose around him like a cage cutting him off with a mortifying gentlemanliness. He was a prig in the livingroom and a satyr in the woods. He wanted to be whole and was broken. He was paralyzed with shame and desire. His pride condemned his loins and his loins took revenge by killing his pride's joy. Until unhappiness became the hallmark of his pride. The stimulation of the hand became a necessity of hygiene like brushing one's teeth at the end of the day. Eventually. Partnered sex a humiliation continually deferred. Though longed for now. Longed for. Longed for. Almost like love itself.

He parsed desire into its components mild attraction strong attraction affection fondness admiration liking lusting love in like in love interest crush infatuation passion delirium suicidal ecstasy etc. He measured his feelings by this gauge occasionally extending it to the left using such marks as dislike disgust fear hatred disdain repellence revulsion contempt loathing and the like only uncertain where to place indifference should it be at the zero point of interest or was it not in fact a hostile note did it not begin the left-ward extension whose ultimate term was the desire to murder just as the ultimate term of desire was the wish to merge and become one with the beloved? Unless in a sense they were the same. He debated this question with himself but never brought it up with others. What troubled him was a sense of the destructive power of this thing quaintly and misleadingly called love. It was a thing inside him that could overwhelm him a thing that regularly and unambiguously informed him that he was in control neither of his life nor indeed of himself a small omnipotent god by turns magnanimous and cruel that lived at the center of his mind. Small flashes of eruption swelled now and again across him. On the horizon of his body there was distant thunder and clouds began to mass at the back of his eyes. The photographs of the women took the edge off his body's appetites but his heart remained hungry and ached and gnashed at its solitude. At the ferocious bars of his pride. His silence grew. It circled him like a wall covered him like a shield. No one would know that within him there was constant weeping raging fear and singing.

His peers jammed the high school halls with touchy sneer too-quick comeback defensive face merciless putdown body-language of the tough guy cocky walls of uncommunication. The breezy smirk the preferred mask.

The halls echoed with shouts talk laughter the loping click of the late-to-class the midterm mutter of the disgruntled shuffle. The halls were lit in yellow and brown and sounds echoed down them like shouts in a hangar in an abandoned airfield the crowds filled them with foam till they shattered and the foam hissed among the fragments on the laboratory linoleum.

The shouts and whistles filled the air above the embankments outside. Invisible. Yet comfortingly certain they were there.

For he could only stand his peers at a distance much as he needed them so many mirrors to help imagine him into being.

And they met his blank beseeching look with puzzlement and suspicion.

As though they could not believe he was not and could not be what they couldn't help but choose to have been. The missing parts so much outweighing the common. Because there was no way he could wedge himself into that compact mass. The terms for admission were too strict strange. And unexplained. One fumbled in a lightless room until one found the keyhole and the key. And withered in the shrieks of laughter that followed one's every plunge at the wrong guess. Until one gave up and stood there frozen and blind with raised empty hand pointing vaguely in the direction of an eternally locked door. And the audience bored at the disappointing performance drifted out leaving behind a silence more withering than any heckle.

Yet it was not much more in the end than boyish clowning. The measurement of young rapidly growing bodies against kitchen door jambs strength in the school yard quickness of wit in the classroom wrestling matches at recess fights to be king of the hill in the fields verbal matches of putdown and charm to show who was funniest and therefore master the weak laughed the strong made you laugh. The constant jockeying for dominiance stood around him like a wall. Every boy invents his own method to be king. It took him some time to discover his own. Years. Decades. Although he had always had one in secret unknown even to him. Hidden in the crannies of his mind. Like a message from his remote past. Sent to his distant future. A page of simple instructions. A code. A promise. A secret. A name. That he must never divulge. Or risk losing everything.

He paused on the threshold as he had often heard described. Yet nothing resulted that would not have resulted otherwise or so he imagined. The rows of school desks that leaned toward the back of the room. The wall of glare from the high windows advanced hot or indifferent. The bodies between made no more commotion than absolutely necessary. A hand scratched chalk over a slate board. A poorly modulated voice droned opaque explanations. A hand shot up with a clever question. Another shot up with an even cleverer answer. The room tittered with compulsory and unconvincing laughter. Nevertheless he was impressed by the question and not impressed by the answer. So that is the point it hit him as he walked down the grassy hill away from the building in the light of the fading day. The readiness of answers is not the point. The knick in the flesh of a question is. And the deepest knick is the question that has no answer. There is the goad of a lifetime he thought as he descended the stairs to the filth of the subway ...

... which loomed ahead in smudges of yellow light phalanxes of girder and pylon webs of wire loops and hammocks of electrical cord flashing of unreadable signs niches of incandescent light wells of dimly filtered sun cold stale air rushing in through half-closed windows the clarmorous rattling the rush through the darkness the fluttering of the ties the glints on rails ahead. The aqua green of the inner walls. The crush of bodies. The smell of decades of crud and grunge ionized dust and other discharges from the third rail the smell of half-asleep bodies crammed into the cars and waiting dispersed on the gloomy platforms smell of urine oil chewing gum ozone. The roar of the impending train. All settled in a sense the future a rail into darkness hazy with a light from precariously nested lamps spaced at rigid intervals like border guards. Rushing by into an unilluminated past. The light a dull gleam between mockery and pity....

Time. Even then he had been dazzled blinded by the idea of it the idea of a sensation that immediately divided betwen the dubious reports of memory and the delusive compulsions of anticipation. That sketchbook of constantly rejected drafts. The past which held an intimate and charged world of ghosts thronging in vastness. The present which filled the immediate with startling brightness and immediately vanished. The future which was a complexity of infinite possibilities that resolved into an ever-renewed blankness. And he and everything flashed between these three mirrors of time from which there was no escape except in some impossible time outside of time but must there be an escape perhaps eternity was the ability to see all of time in the completeness and orderliness of the past the overwhelming immediacy of the present the unresolvable suspense of the future. In lieu of which one had he felt more than anything else the past for the present was a chaos and the future a darkness but in the past he found calm and an orderliness that revealed a meaning for events that had seemed senseless when they occurred and patterns of events that had something like grace the past was time's palace the present the scrubby construction site. The past was the place of that understanding for which he longed this would be the principal joy of being old the ability to understand one's past and era and life. So he thought. As incommunicable as that must be nevertheless one had the solitary contentment of understanding what one could not say or have understood. One was alone with one's thoughts. He thought. One could share them with a god if there was a god with none other. If there was no god then one was alone absolutely and forever the thought frightened him and he turned away from it. He turned away from it back to time. Back to the natural forms of the world. Back to the moment as it rolled across the sky. Where flashes of splendor and memory and hope above all of the memory of hope kept counsel in signs of what is either divinity or an indecipherable emptiness. Of a darkness not perfectly dark a brightness not perfectly clear. A question that held him between hands of despair and joy.

The banality of it don't forget that. One recalls most vividly the peaks and valleys of the motley haphazardness of one's life but not in every case immediately the long tracks of shiftless weasel-eyed boredom the unmeaning dullness. Or even more the absence of a sense of the uniqueness of one's destiny. That which in no way strokes one's pride or throws an interesting shadow across one's fate. The little failures of imagination cunning and will that result in years of aching frustration a daily imbibing of shame. Or not even so high a drama. Merely the absence of luck of any kind. As though one had been locked in an enormous room in which nothing was allowed to happen. One stewed off in a corner while the better stories happened elsewhere outside earshot or camera range and one worked on math problems of an intricate uninterestingness embedded in anxiety and boredom. Beware. You are trying to make it sound interesting again. Ever the danger of writing it down. The desire to excite envy through the displaying of your wounds.

One day he discovered a patch of woods at the back of the high-school playground on the lower slope of the south lawn. He entered the woods with a tense and happy watchfulness holding his breath as he looked and listened halting just inside the border of trees. A small meadow of tall grasses flickered in the sunlight insects weaving beads of light above them. A light wind passed through the upper tiers of branches the leaves. A bird whistled in the shadows. He walked deeper into the woodland passing a stump and a large fallen tree rotting in a patch of light. When he was beyond the sounds of shouting and traffic he stopped again. And watched again. And listened. In the green quiet. And for the first time in many years felt both alone and comforted. He had often felt alone and comforted in the past when he lived in the country it was perhaps of his experiences the most common. Then because it was nearing the end of recess he turned and went back a little afraid of being seen leaving the woods alone. They might think he was taking drugs or masturbating. As he walked up the slope toward school he heard a volley of piercing chirps from the grass near his feet. He bent down and saw a young bird little older than a chick dragging a broken wing through the grass. He cupped the bird in his hand where it stared toward him or seemed to in what looked like terror and chirped even louder if louder it could be said to chirp since it had been chirping in terror. Unsure what to do he carried the bird inside the school building its cries of distress unrelenting even rather embarrassing and left the bird in his locker with a vague plan to decide what to do with it at the end of the school day. After the day's classes were over he opened the locker. The bird writhed like a live knot against the locker door its neck swollen head bent back eyes half-closed and white wings jerking and jerking it had broken its neck in its attempts to escape the lightless foul-smelling locker. The cruelty of his blind kindness.

Misjudgment. Ignorance. Folly. The blindspot behind the blind-spot the one you can never factor in because you are never aware of it — your own yes and not for the last time. The enemy against which you are perfectly defenseless. How often have you recounted to yourself the humiliations caused by that little flaw. A flaw that changes shape and position like a puncture in a pudding so that eventually it seemed to be a central function an identifying mark of your existence. My Stupidity as you call it. Your only truly faithful consistently affectionate blindly loyal lover. She sticks to you like your shadow. Your dominatrix how she loves to see you fall. And fall. And fall again. How she loves to wound you and then kiss the wound. How she loves you down. Yet you aren't deemed a particularly stupid man. Generally you are qualified as intelligent even highly intelligent and you have no patience with stupidity in others. You do not suffer fools gladly you chew them up spit them out and trample them under foot. Verbally. So that your own instances of stupidity when they occur are first of all stunning sometimes even spectacular displays of flamboyant folly based on some tiny grotesque error of judgment that no schoolboy would have committed and that leave you writhing in shame and bewildered mortifying impotent fury at — yourself! No one else would have committed that gross misjudgment you were the only one there. No one else could have come close to ruining everything with so sure a blow. No one else only you only him only I. And out of that comes a most perverse pride. He holds in his hands the rubble of his life. Well some of it. But is it not true that he himself made what he himself destroyed

— his playground and his trash dump his wreckage and his throne? Or isn't it?

He carried the bird outside and left it under a bush. It writhed in his hands still not finished dying as he carried it.

The cities burned in the gray shadows of the television as you watched in pity and bafflement safe pity protected anguish. Of which I was starting to be aware. Around him stood a layer of glass that revealed and protected he could rub the surface of the glass but feel nothing of what he saw the wind didn't touch him. You found your protection irritating then infuriating you hit at the glass though never quite hard enough to break it. He longed to test his heroic theories about himself or rather thought he longed for it was easier to daydream them into being. And paid the price of dreamers created my own uncertainty. You hit the wall of glass with lessening frequency and then altogether stopped. Until one day furious at myself for my indolence and pusillanimity I attacked the glass with all my might and shattered it. And startled and dismayed bathed in the wind of an absolutely terrifying freedom.

Yet don't forget the exhilaration of it. Yes. Yes. The hard bone chill of the cold bare slap the seizure of the air shook him awake from the sleep of childhood in a suddenness without mourning and a fever of self-assertion that gave him a reputation for an arrogance that was only an over-reaction to his timidity. He was like a young bird soaring beyond the sky startled when his wings cupped nothing and gravity which had made him after all possible embraced him back to stone. Having lost one chain he thought he could lose them all having escaped a cage felt he could live best without any shielding at all. These bones are a nuisance let's live all flesh and music. This frame is a wall between me and light let's burn it down and become one with brightness. He was crazy with nightmare and ecstasy. He hated reality and longed for truth. He was noble and ludicrous and hopeful and foolish and dragged between mortifications like a saint in training. He was afraid to believe in God. Any god. Ever. Yet his body's surge toward the future defied him. It would believe in nature it would believe in life it would believe in the divinity he could not name. And charged faith to him. How could he not be proud.

Then one day the war took over the city. It had been burning on the television screens for months. It seemed like many wars yet also like a single battle between demons who claimed to be angels. It burned like a black rose in the sun. What was demanded in anger with threat of reprisal was the immediate choosing of sides. Ambiguity was not allowed it was the mask of the enemy. The day was a rolling debate between hardening sides nothing else was allowed to matter moral intoxication became a habitual indulgence then a need then chronic then an addiction. Then an imperative. Finally a strategy. And those who did not join vociferously and with enthusiasm were agents of the enemy or worse waverers. Those who vanished when you turned in need to them. Phantoms of. Ghosts of. Faithfulness. There was marching down the grid of the city streets and the city became grand in the face of the crowd. There were rallies of thousands in park and mall windless campus windy plaza. For an hour for a day the city rang with a human cry. For pity. For love. For a moment's compassion of the masters. It could not last but it could be repeated. Until it faded like the echo of its own futility. Ringing down canyons of that other city the city that lies behind the city. Phantasmal city. Eternal city. City of time and the dead. To think of all that brightness and clamoring and joy and anger and the euphoria of purity and anguish of innocence and certainty of hope in the future. Except in that magic box of tricks he called with boundless trust his memories.

Yet it was and it was there and it was there in its fullness and clamor. Repeat it. Over and over if need be. The tens of thousands filled the streets fists raised in defiance banners rippling pickets held in angry mocking the air a spindling of confetti and carnival a festival of grinning revolutionaries the megaphones blaring indecipherable slogans and the chants that followed taken up by thousands in the snake dance of the marches. Then there were the hours of bad rock and roll and then the hours of garbled speeches and the whoops and laughter and scattered applause in the eddies and tides and swells and calms of the sea-like crowd where you lost and found yourself again and again. Leafleteers passed through the crowd spreading broadsides bringing word of some new miscarriage of justice some hideous atrocity mimeographed descriptions of the vectors of power that dictated the direction and guaranteed the injustice of the nation heated prose depicting in tortuous detail the abominable crimes of wealth leaflets urging the reader to join a political party a steering committee a forthcoming march or rally in New York in Boston in Washington a new or old leftwing political party and at last bring down the state. Tables were set up selling books by or about Trotsky or Mao or Che or Gramsci or Muste or Cleaver or Malcolm and the sellers refused to speak to each other except in the slippery argot of hip. A middle-aged Communist was left with his booth of Stalinist literature to pine alone. Girls dressed like peasants or in flak jackets and facepaint or like flowers shedding their petals in the sun. They twisted and bent eyes closed and smiling to the music dancing around dreams of themselves. Or raged in pity and fury at the news of the latest carnage the rumor of injustice the fist of bigotry that clenched even them by the throat. The boys tossed their hair about shouldering the girls back to their private cars the girls hiding their exquisitely painful desire to please behind a sometimes brutal independence. Groups eddied into larger groups then broke down into individuals that lashed more easily into the largeness of the crowd. Was there any sweeter and strangely serene joy than this joy of the crowd of being part of a vastness that reflected you back to yourself and that called you to call back to it? With eyes of recognition and tongue of acknowledgment. Yet within the euphoria there was the fear that at any moment the joy would break into a panic that was the obverse side of its innocence its anger. Or be provoked to revenge by the blue-shirted providers of order. And did.

For the waves spread from a point at the edge of the crowd where a wedge of the defenders of order pierced or down along one edge or from two edges at once parallel and contracting toward the center and the waves broke from them and swelled across the crowd waves of panic swirling into a turbulence as the crowd tried to stampede away and broke over the city streets like. But there was no like. And so the air was filled with screams and breaking glass and smoke from burning trash cans and smashed car windows and megaphone shouts for calm and surges of the crowd as though it were a beast with its own obscure seizures and panics and what you sensed in this was a little fear yes but even more alertness and thrill and a kind of giddy righteousness and sense of being in the right place at the right time on the right side in the baptism of historical grace as you moved with the sea in its wash of tides and found a focus for your contempt for the current order for you were the natural anarchist and socialist of youth blind to overly forgiving of the blatant contradiction. A wave broke over him and passed down the street. A young woman stood over a man in the gutter shouting in rage as three policemen descended on her with sticks flashing in the half light. A siren screamed around a corner and lights strobed across his eyes. A dozen marchers were dragged down the street by police who struck them with night sticks and pulled them into a white van flashing red spinning light on its roof. A phalanx of police in riot gear with transparent shields raised marched toward them. An old woman using a picket sign like a cane walked past him with a hard angry look. There were pocking sounds and then streaming cloud formations of gas that burned his eyes making them tear. The crowd broke up into clutches and clusters and fragments without aim or pattern choking back tears and hiding their faces in handkerchiefs in the confines set by intersection alley building entrance sidewalk overturned car police van the advancing pincers of the police lines. Like a gigantic hand pushing ants off a table top the line moved up and pushed the mob over the edge down a cross street into the next avenue. And the crowd sluiced away to the other side and became a mere scattering of individuals in rout melting into the faceless nameless crowds of the city. As the pincers met and fell behind on the last defenders.

He fled with the rest obscurely sensing his guilt. As though he should have stayed and been arrested with the true believers. But he was not a true believer. He was at best a sympathetic fellow traveler and to have taken the martyr's prerogative would have been grotesque. He had gone as a spectator a contemplative of rebellion who wished all well and everyone well and was appalled at the destruction caused by riot because the price would be the defeat of whatever cause however fine the intent sublime or beautiful the form. The impatience of violence only provoked greater violence and in the battle of fire only one side could win the side of power and fear it would brook no defiance it would annihilate them. And thus the war invaded him as he fled the site of battle.

It was no longer outside peering in the windows or through the television's gray on gray. The fisherman's hook cast over the waves and fell near the mouth of the hungry blue. And in the brilliant forenoon the fisherman reeled.

It was not what it had been or at least had seemed to be. Not quite. He learned to dance to the pistol of the day's meannesses. Not that they were aimed at him far from it his legs merely happened to be in the way. But he did learn to dance.

What is the limit of responsibility? Your own your family's neighborhood's city's nation's humankind's. Where did it begin where did it end did it ever end was this gesture made in this way forever provoking the future to move in the direction its motion seemed to ordain? Was the burden of the world on the shoulders of each whether old or middle-aged or young? Was it a ball in the hands of a child? Or was it parcelled out in little boxes so none need sink beneath the entire weight? Beneath the world's entire weight. As you felt yourself sinking beneath the weight. The thought of the entire weight.

He struggled up. It was imaginary after all. You found you could make it disappear by closing the mind's eye. But as soon as he opened it again the weight reappeared it grew on his shoulders like a great boulder-like mushroom. And he felt he must see. You were not allowed to turn away. For not only was the world a burden on you you were a burden on the world.

The reach of responsibility was power. And the sense of responsibility reached as far as awareness took it. And a blind child played in the mud building and smashing worlds with a shrug and without pity.

For the power of the human was slowly being revealed. Immense. Terrible. Godlike. Attached to a clever frightened well-meaning and good-hearted runt that could not endure its own mortality. Something no one had suspected would be this final usurpation of the titans and the gods. So you felt with flashes of pride and something like horror. The furtive glance in the mirror failed however to show the beast. That could break into any moment. Caked with saliva and blood and smeared with acknowledgment. Or the god it goes without saying. The dazzling blade of passing light. It only showed the uncertain shape of a young man's face an expresssion as blank as the bathroom wall behind him. Peering into the labyrinth of the future. Flickering with lightning and ghosts. Between glory and shame.

But all of this is getting rather solemn. We have not dealt with the ludicrous self-importance of this person have we. Although we have suggested it by the cartload. He mistook himself not for the center of the universe but for having unique access to it. His trust in his own judgment was absolute despite the regular kick in the shins given by his ever faithful Stupidity. So was his contempt for the supposed idiots he was condemned to live among. His self-regard knew no limits and amounted to a minor religion. The gods spoke to him on the borderlines of sleep. His sense of self regularly pumped up to fabulous size and then as regularly collapsed into a sink hole of self-loathing though he had yet done nothing to recommend so hard a justice. He would lie for an afternoon dreaming what kind of genius he wanted to be when he grew up. And the next day moped about convinced he would never have another friend and die poor and despised. Then even more grimly he would imagine a life of neither greatness nor desititution merely ordinary without masterpiece or crime to crown it a mediocre life sweet gray endlessly dull. And it was at such moments that he was most in danger. At such moments the devil that lived inside him and always gave him his best thoughts and his worst impulses came alive with a jerk and proposed some lively thrust at triumph and self-destruction.

His judgment was not always poor. He was generally good at catching himself before making himself a fool in too gaudy a light. And the result was a small intense war with himself between caution and desire his longing for the intensity of self-assertion and the realization that such assertion would seed his future with enemies every ego more or less resenting every other ego. But as time moved on the devil became harder to dissuade and prudence began to look like pusillanimity judgment and care like milk-toast fence-sitting like refined self-centeredness. And this was a time when frank self-centeredness was not yet in fashion. It was a time when the best were infatuated with a kind of political virtue and evil was seen with a ruthless eye and hated with a passionate hatred. It is difficult to recall now as everything is difficult to recall in a time that can no longer imagine what the past was so upset about after all we survived didn't we and that's all that matters. Isn't it. The ego's natural moral obtuseness was loathed in others and in a few fine beings loathed also in the self. Though it was easier when one could see its face. And morality required judging oneself no less coolly or strictly than others. Against which all were pitiless. For when self is all all selves are others. Including eventually oneself.

But he believed he was not yet what he would become he was netted in the certainty he too would become sharp and hard tightly outlined perdurable as stone yet that you were not a stone but more like unmolded jelly exasperated then outraged you the total ambiguity at the heart of your being frightened you for it made everything possible and nothing certain it took away what it offered with complete indifference you felt yourself sinking into a kind of quicksand of time each moment offered a sensation in the present the hint of a memory a suggestion for the future then vanished leaving nothing behind another moment appeared unrelated to any other moment a handful of beads falling to the floor without connecting string you smashed the beads together in your hands trying to force a connection but they fell in a bright scattering to the floor nothing took hold he tried to force the nameless impulses attacking his body mind heart psyche into a single mold and they writhed in his hands like snakes wrapping biting him poisoning his nights with his unfulfilled days there was no direction he could not endure not taking he was helpless before the torrent pulled between fear anger ambition desire there was nothing that he was yet also nothing he was not he recognized nothing inside him saw nothing he knew yet it rose inside him clamoring with fury to escape you were afraid more of yourself than of the world saw within you an enemy that knew no limits that included everything within and beyond your world a chaos that promised no rest except in its own destruction. So you fled though there was nowhere to flee carried the dancing star within you and it would not leave you for it loved you. Loved you. Or so you thought not yet knowing that it was you. Narcissus of fire.

The repetition of music and the spell of words helped organize the chaotic emptiness of his days. He read for hours though does one call reading the blank racing through pages in search of an almost molten thrill. And listened to music over and again thrilling to the ecstatic climax the despairing cadence the shifting of key without warning and tender as love itself. As love itself. You sought tenderness its sign in a sigh of foliage or in the tinge of evening the unravelling of a cloud into blueness the purling of a stream as you remembered under the shadow of a brief country bridge but there was little tenderness where you were most of it seemed harsh resentful unforgiving the only sign of gentleness a flower nodding in a crack in cement or a cloud eclipsed by an office tower. It was partly the absence of tenderness or what you thought was tenderness that drove you toward despair. And yet you didn't despair or not wholly. Toward hatred of the city the modern age your country society at large humanity in general the triumphantly mediocre tasteless stupidity of the humanly created world the name changed but the hatred remained for the hunger for gentleness remained. Yet the world at the edges of its harshness offered a thralldom of grace art itself a supreme goddess who offered her body in signs of beauty radiance intensity happiness darkness that simply deepened beauty pain that simply deepened joy the image of love of the redemption of hope of the transformation of earth into yes don't be afraid of the word into a soul through creation out of oblivion into oblivion again endlessly or so it seemed. And there you turned to worship between nature and art the patterning of the hope of a god of the search for something to redeem this life your life such as it was art a kind of song made both from the search and for the search the little heaven of the little god in his attempt to wrest hold in his heart of creation's yes call it that its glory. Glory in art was the touch of the robe of a god a few stormy aristocrats of being distilled the eternal into a liquid palatable to any who opened themselves to its offering. And you wept with happiness oh with joy such joy in your night bed at the thought and prayed one day you might deserve the privilege of such being such knowing such godlike you called it godlike creation. And thus he began in his mind to play with the stones of destruction building them into kingdoms of a moment by the seaside under the nightfall. And the night fell and the sea rose and sleep drowned kingdom and king.

The tutorial in illusions was a demanding one. The teacher was hard and mocking you do not believe enough what will not disappoint you? You must believe again even longer deeper harder. Where is your faithlessness give it to me again so I can redden it with my deep pencil. He grew at last into a virtuoso of self-deception but only after much hard labor. And your motto my motto! was truth.

Then one spring in his delirious age an easy woman and a hard book took the measure of him and pulled him between them until he split. The year the year of revolution. The time the time of plucking the green fruit and spitting the pulp in disgust into the wind. Then shovelling down for more seed.

In his dreams he flew.

5

She turns. Turns to look. Turns to look at you. To look at you in a way no one has ever looked at you before. The eyes wide. Opaque. Shining. The lips parted as if in surprise. The mole you notice only now near the lips the eyes shining above the mole near the lips the lips parted as if for breath. In surprise. She turns away her hair turns toward you its black and shining wall. Turns away then back. Away then back in surprise. Then back to you then turns away. Away then back to you. Away then back. Then back. To look. At you. Until you're forced to turn to her you think you're forced to turn to look and in the shining eyes the parted lips the delicate dark mole near the lips in its dramatic frame of black and shining hair in the tremble you detect in the air between you you see a wavering like the heat above a summer road a mirror shimmering in the splendor. Of what you strangely sense lies open and revealed in your own face. Joy. Hope. Wonder. Desire. Fear.

The car driven by the boyfriend jostles with the bends in the road. Voices in the back chatter and giggle. He hears nothing of what they say. Something is taking place. A softness opens at the base of his belly. Above his groin yes there a sense of giving way. All calm. Strange. He ought to be shaking though why. He wants to sag down and in to fold to give up to give way to. To what.

The young girl you met in the morning hunched beside for an hour on a white flat stone in a creek. She talks about her father the betrayer you nod your mouth grim you have a common theme. She talks about her family the misery another. Listening to the creek and the birds and admiring the pixie prettiness of the nose and cheeks and eyebrows demonic little eyebrows the strange shining beauty of the long black hair. But it's fall. And the air is full of a smell of dead leaves and damp mulch mold and rot a sweet sour smell of the happiest and saddest of seasons to you. Where the year is harvested in death and rejoices subdued and contented in the quiet. Calling more freshly than spring to love.

.

He glows for days over the copy in curlicues of her phone number lying like an abandoned leaf on his desk. A flurry of noisings from the floor below this time almost comforting. Nothing is there for years and years and now between his elbows beneath his eyes there lies the phone number of a pretty girl. Inscribed with a childlike neatness. Exact. He tries to recall her face but all he can remember is the mole and the wings of the brows and the long black fall of hair. And the disconcerting stare. What is he to do? Call her up. Naturally. Once he has overcome his paralysis. So what are you so afraid of? Failure. Defeat. Rejection. Scorn. Humiliation. Self-hatred and contempt. But look what you might gain.

What might that be?

The mind goes blank. The pleasure of sex with a girl must be in some way an extension of solo sexual pleasures the rest is hazy. What is more to the point is the almost unbearable joy of having an infatuation returned. For you are already practiced in infatuation. You've had several a year see above though none have any place outside the gauzy spider-tongued kingdom of your mind. For the first time you focus try to focus but can you focus can anyone focus on the absolute existence of a being absolutely other? Value thrust beyond these suddenly narrow walls. Your own value suddenly crushed and glorified by and through the simple unavoidable existence of this other dazzling being. Through *her*. Her appearance bright and sharp as a knife her smile or frown sudden generosities acute sarcasms. Her ability to flatter or insult with the cock of an eyebrow to build or destroy your confidence. How believe in the overwhelming radiance that you see. Or the overwhelming darkness. No. Feel. Believe you feel. Want to believe you feel. And plan your life accordingly. With at the heart of it in the wooded valley in the courtyard of the palace in the nest and herd of the mountains the hallucinated goddess who reigned over your world. Your mind awash with hosannas the clouds staggering to the sun with hosts and regiments of angels thrones dominions. Though you cannot lift your eyes to meet her eyes nor utter a single word. Thus you refashioned her in your heart's image in tossing hours of dream. Your dream. Her dream. So many thus had taken over your dreams in the past.

.

But here was something more approachable. Ah it had approached him. Unexpectedly that fall. His own callowness was delicately cruel in its delicate and exquisite clarity it whispered its ridicule and giggled in all the desks behind him. The mirror winked and laughed. All he had to do was pick up the receiver and dial. But which receiver both family phones were exposed someone might break into his scene of shame at any moment ask what he was doing no lie could hide him. Suddenly the receiver was nailed to the cradle the cradle nailed to the table the cradle and table were made of marble cored with sand cased in lead anyway the digits on the paper had become indecipherable runes.

Would my voice shrink to a gag at the moment a voice calmly answered at the end of the infinitely long wire? Sweat slick my hands and sting the skin under my arms? My undependable mind go blank? A stutter flutter my damned muttering tongue?

But this had been before for one simple reason he had known he wasn't wanted by the girl he had wanted this was different wasn't it this girl offered hope in her small pointed fingers. For what exactly. And your mind went blank again. Then you remembered the pretty pixie face smiling knowingly into your eyes. Knowing what. As if she knew. As if she were hiding a secret she was only waiting to share. Or held a gift for you behind her back. He remembered her voice. Just a little shrill aggressive loud but with that sly look around the eyes and a wicked mouth a wicked mouth inside it a sharp tongue eager for action. Eager for action. A pretty little sarcastic tongue that cut away reputations like soap. Leaving nothing but a bubble behind. And promising the heat of action. Maybe that was it. To come.

A challenge waving to you across a bright summer field. Something like a dare to your young and hungry mind. Your body in its perilous innocence.

He flushed where he sat staring at the phone number. All he had to do was place his finger in the circles die-cut from the circle and dial. Of course he was betraying a friend. A friend? The boyfriend who had been his friend who had invited him to the picnic because he felt sorry for him in his loneliness. The heat of the body hardly noticed this. It did not seem to care who it wounded on its way to. What? A possibility he dared not even think of. Yet. Though he must pretend to. Or seem even callower than he knew himself to be. And to hell with minor scrupling against pain.

Picked up the phone. Put it down again.

Absolute clarity of the moment.

What after all if she were seeing someone at this very moment? You might lose your chance forever. Of course not rebukes common sense. But I'm in no mood for common sense. He tries to remember her voice. With patchy success. Her eyes are easier they grin at him as her mouth opens and flashes. He keeps remembering her writing down her phone number and giving it to him the same gestures the same wondering look on her darkly shining face. Over and over.

He dials six numbers and hangs up.

It's too good to be true. She can't really want me to call it was a passing whim she now regrets she hardly knows me we sat and talked for half an hour and she did most of the talking. I was the good listener slowly pummelled into senselessness by my own good manners. Not senselessness in this case of course no a keen waking to sense such as he had rarely known before. Only when listening to certain pieces of music. The pretty girl with the sad tale who sat beside on the rock the rush of the stream around them the cool autumn sky above them the flickering of falling leaves the calls of the migrating birds the smell of the mossy water and the moldy earth of the creek bank. The smell of the light. And the quiet profile nodding and weaving its spell over him. Weaving its spell over him. Over him weaving its spell.

He walks away from the phone promising himself he will call tomorrow. Yes. For sure. Tomorrow.

Orion stands above him.

The white door with the glass panes of the row house looms sullenly above him. He no longer itches in his jacket and tie as he had an hour earlier. The bouquet of baby's breath he had brought with him in the early evening is now he knows though he can't see it clearly pinned on the front of the girl standing before him smiling up at him in the darkness. One did such things then. The hand does not remember pressing the buzzer but a swim of simpering faces had glowed suddenly up out of the dimness behind the glass and the door had swayed inward suddenly open.

The face he remembered hadn't been among them. Out of the early evening brightness he had moved uneasily in with a vacantly polite smile. Then down the stairs came a voice familiar already and then a movement of a form in a pretty slightly formal dress a flickering of ankles a hand on the banister then the smiling pixie face the mole near the mouth the shining blackness of the hair.

The walk through the industrious-looking working class neighborhood to the trolley. The trip downtown. The dinner at the restaurant with the Polynesian theme. The moment he debonairly flipped a basket of rolls onto the floor while trying to make a point in philosophy or politics. Her trilled excited laughter. The movie with the saccharine and tragic subject eased with the firm serenity of Mozart. The hands held for one held hands at that time on the awkward armrest. Her thumb tickling the palm of his hand in a gently roving circle. The walk back to the trolley stop. The trip back on the trolley to her neighborhood. The walk beneath the night to her stoop.

Orion stands above him.

He remembers the moon-like smiling face floating up to him in the darkness and the kiss as the mouths open and the tongues leap over each other in the little caves of their mouths his tongue touched her teeth and slid along her palate and then suddenly she sucked hard on his tongue and then her tongue was inside his mouth fencing with his tongue and squirming like a snake. He had no idea what he was doing he followed her lead and his own dreamlike thrusts and feints it was like dreaming standing up in the darkness. He pecked her face with kisses dotting her cheeks her chin her forehead her brows he drew a line with his tongue from her forehead along her cheeks down to her throat past her throat to the seam of her dress above the valley between her breasts then up again to her ear which he tongued and gently bit. She pulled down toward her his head and covered his ear with her mouth and sucked in and blew out and he quivered. They laced their bodies together and rubbed their loins through their clothes. He slipped a finger beneath her bra until he reached a sensation of nipple and flicked the nipple with the end of his finger and listened to her sigh.

Suddenly she withdrew and smiled at him in the streetlight and kissed him one last time and suddenly disappeared up into a sullen doorway into the dark whiteness of the house.

He threw his face to the sky.

Then walked down the nightside street. And hailed Orion raising his sword to the west.

.

He told no one. Many years will pass before he learns how unusual it is for the young male roiled in his natural insecurities not to spill into the nearest ear news of his conquests of the night. And how shocked had he known how the female naturally blabbed in agonies of fleshly detail. And might have for years to come remained therefore a virgin. Out of pride if nothing more. Until curiosity and hormones conquered pride. But this is speculation. It is all speculation nothing here is sure or true.

He told no one. None of his friends (he had none). None of his family (his family was a dramatic stranger). Hardly told himself. He held the memory like a shattering of joy in his hands so fragile and perilous it seemed so delicate and dangerous. A butterfly that might explode. At any moment. Not killing you. Merely destroying you.

He told no one. He turned it over in his mind like a jewel flashing in the dusty black of velvet and memory. Often at school at home he would disappear into the blank day staring out a window into a gray tangle of trees at the suddenly blank page of his book into busily empty space loomed with shadows and thinking of nothing feel an echo of what he had felt at that moment the touch of skin against skin and sigh whose bits and liquid fragments he tried to piece together weave and run together but never quite could memory never exact enough it failed him he could not live it again try as he might. Try as he might. Try as he might. Try as he might. Try. As he might.

Then it hit him. A staggering shock of light as sharp as glass and he was there again under the night filling his eyes and his mouth with her skin her flesh her body yet not her body the promise of her body and he knew such hope as he felt he had never known before he did not know for what just hope hope hope and the world in its eternal round of disappointment and disillusion seemed right and beautiful and good. And true. And he believed.

.

For a time. At that time.

.

Oh to hover on the threshold and not enter in. To linger in hope and ignorance there and see passing couples appear suddenly in the light holding discourse with each other and their shadows to overhear occasional mysterious passages floating up suggesting worlds of meaning beyond your possible understanding and yet beckoning you onward to learn and join and master and conquer to dream of all of this at the edge of the crowd and wait a long a longer moment before you plunge in counting the peaks of joy in advance and imagining the future as a weaving of your life between the hands of grace. To stay and watch and wonder and not move into the waters. To stay where you are and let yourself only imagine. And wince and cringe at the couple whispering in the corner at the dancers giddy with happiness and flush at the smug local celebrity of the hour the talented poet the brilliant scholar the grinning lover the hasty contemptuous young executive the dazzling lights against the obscure background and finally be impelled into action pinched into the fray because of the envy you feel at the appearance of other people's happiness. And are you going to miss that happiness love conquest? Now is your chance. Take it. Plunge. Enter the garden.

Plunge into the sea. Hold nothing back. Grab as best you can the rewards of your assertion. Find the dream wither into the always slightly seedy slightly faded vaguely disappointing reality of the here and now. Which for endless years you will reject believing the dream to be around the next corner. This cannot be real. This cannot be true. It makes no sense. *That* must be true *that* must be real. What I see so clearly in my mind's eye. And I will accept nothing less. And onward plunge into the vast shrug of indolently laughing darkness. Seeking the source of that laughter. Imagining the mouth of the woman from which it must be coming. Imagining yourself mastering your fear and covering her mouth with your own.

·

She stopped your mouth for a moment and told you to stay where you were. You were standing in the small glassed-in porch of her family's house in a western district of the city. The darkness watched through the windows. A television babbled in the room beyond the wall her brother and sister were staring from the couch into the flickering box. She disappeared into the house and you were left alone to think imagine consider but you did not think or imagine or consider all you did was stand vacantly in your blazer and tie and stare toward the dimness of the television room from which insincere laughter cascaded from a sit-com then in progress and a few minutes later she reappeared having changed her clothes from the rather stiff discount frills of a formal date between poor but genteel teenagers at the time to weekend wear denim cutoffs a loose shirt and bare feet and she dragged you by the hand back to the porch and pulling you to her thrust your hand beneath her shirt and gazed into your eyes with you amazed as you felt your hand smooth up her warm chest to the tender warm softness of her breast its nipple beneath the ends of your fingers and she whispered you're touching me and your hand moved to her left breast brushing the valley between them and she whispered you're touching me and you felt your penis stiffen against her belly and you reached down and pulled up the panel of her shirt and bent and looked at the small mound of her breast in the light from the TV room beyond the door and then closed your mouth over her breast around the nipple and instinctively began to suck tickling the end of her nipple with your tongue. And her hand stroked your hair and played with your ear. And you released her breast and tracing with your tongue the skin of her valley along the line of its passage moved to her other breast and nibbled and bit and sucked and tongued and fluttered the tip of her nipple with your tongue and bit testing the tenderness here and there and she playfully hit you and said ouch not so hard and wondered am I giving you as much pleasure as I am sure I am receiving was he I must see. So you suddenly rose to look at her face and you covered her wounded frightened happy face with kisses and dotted her eyelids with your lips and trailed your tongue from her ear to her eyebrow down her cheek to her neck then up her neck to her other ear to her eyebrow there wonderful she has two of everything and she bent her head forward a little and shivered a little and sighed. Yes. Was that yes. It was yes. And she took your hand and pulled it into her pants your fingers tickled the edge of her pubic hair. No. Yes. No. If I do that I'll take you right here and right now. And you pulled out your hand. We mustn't. All right. We mustn't. All right all right. With a sound of disappointment yet satisfaction. Not yet. That's all right. And kissed from mouth to mouth from mouth to mouth. Until you both looked away for a moment and heard the silence. The television was no longer on. Only a single dim light was lit in the livingroom behind you both. You kissed. You both had not realized how many hours had passed. You kissed and you made to leave. And you kissed and you made to go. And you kissed. Then you had to leave. But you kissed. It's late I have to go and she let him go then pulled him back and you licked her skin and tasted her hair and tongued the labyrinth of each ear. You were silent she did the talking or most whispering do that don't do that don't bite yes there harder softer there there and you whispered only a single word over and over against her skin against her eyes against her ear against her hair her name. Her name. I'm sorry I'm so small she whispered. You're not small you whispered back you're fine you're perfect. You're fine. And you stooped to kiss them again. And then you both cleaved into a single shadow on the lightless porch in the silent house. And your mind went blank. Then you heard yourself speaking I have to go. And you made to leave and she pulled you in for a last kiss and her tongue filled you mouth and turned in a flickering spiral. Then she opened the glass door and you descended still holding her hand and you looked up and in the darkness he could see her smiling smiling him away conspiratorially into the dark.

•

… Where am I. Alone in a room far from them from there. Across generation and continent. So what is time or space then to them what memory compared to them what are they compared to memory? Who are they on the porch in the city night do I know them would they know me? Would they consider me an intruder would they hide their games in embarrassment it is only me come to help you consummate the game. I hear you whispering and I want to listen to help you reply what you didn't know how to say then I know even less now. No. Maybe we can help one another you soft and warm with youth and passion and all that generous ignorance and courage and me wan and cautious and dry with middle-age clarity apathy and civil controlled disgust.

But how can I help you who are dead?

Our ears are loud with the sound of our blood too loud to hear such distant shouts such distant whispering across so much of time it roars like the roaring of the sea.

.

He went home. His skin felt as though it were made of eyes.

.

Days. Dazed. But the telephone meets your hand more easily now. When are you coming over? Soon. Soon.

You lie on your bed in the bleak dark and imagine the parting of the thighs the soft cushioning of the breasts the delicious mouthfuls of skin the sighs against your ear the vacant distant expression then the burning eyes as you fumble with your cock.

You do not dare yet imagine the next act.

How unfold it? Too much happens to recall too little to recount.

He visits her family home they sit on the couch before the television fumbling with each other's bodies. Often.

They meet on the barren sidewalk outside a high school devoted to girls. Where a crowd of others meet. What has passed between them is their secret yet the air pierced with light seems to shout it to everybody. Yet what is there to tell. They don't speak of it except with their eyes. She burrows her pixie smile into him. He can't imagine what appears on his face.

There is as always a certain amount of more or less impatient waiting.

He wasn't sure he hadn't already reached an acme of happiness with her he wondered what exactly might happen next. As if it were not clear and of course it was not. And frightened him into claiming ignorance as much as it excited even exalted him. To enter a woman what heaven. Being the passive type he had to wait to see what she would do next being the active type she would not keep him waiting long. He knew he suspected wondered hoped. Worried as he tried with increasing inefficiency to study for school. As said above she knew how to draw it out. And being easy knew how to be hard.

.

Late one night in the kitchen of her house. She had pulled him there from the TV couch where they had been raking each other's fire. They tongued each other's mouths before the fridge humming in parallel to their moans. He was never sure he was doing the right thing felt self-conscious odd and slightly ridiculous was too embarrassed to ask outright to seem not to know what he was doing he was glad she took the initiative it would ruin him for decades to come. He fondled and sucked her breasts she fondled and frigged his cock from behind her stretched denim he stroked her flanks and caressed her loins in their half-bared cutoffs he felt the spiky hairs on her thighs and fingered the muscle behind her knee. Then she shoved his hand down her pants between her thighs. And he felt a moist fissure aimed up and fingered the loose purse of lips and slowly pushed his long finger in. She gasped near his ear. Acting on instinct he worked the edge of her clittoris rhythmically as if cleaning the edge of a pipe and listened carefully to the sounds of pleasure so similar to the moans of a wounded animal he had heard often in the country sounds coming more intensely until after several minutes of twisting and lifting his finger in her cunt her body stiffened in a spasm her mouth gaping her eyes closed her voice a rattle and a stifled choke. She stopped moving no stiffened quivering. Then with a moaning sigh melted back to softness. And silently grinning up at him she pulled his hand from its place between her thighs. Which glinted with flecks and scales of gold and covered in purple half-dried blood.

He stared in horror as he raised his bloody hand in the air its central finger raised in a demonic salute.

With a smile she pulled him dumbly to the sink with a smile washed his hand with a smile embraced him in the kitchen light with a smile sent him home.

And the winter buried the air with cold.

Blood begins vomiting in his dreams.

A dusting of snow as the phrase has it. Wind devils of white powder no hardly so tall. Spirals of white on the stained gray walk. At his feet near his shoes. Parting as he walks or stands surrounding him he guesses though he has yet to grow eyes on his heels. And the creases of ice in the gutter. He finds the cold exhilarating it makes him feel alive. The hands of winter held your face in its palms. And gently breathed upon it. Expecting what a cloud. Foul weather one was forced to call it. Handsomely beautifully foul. And you rejoiced. Not for you the carnival of summer with its hard brilliant sun and its too brief night not then at any rate the sun would come later in your self-regarding mythology. No now it was the winter night the suspension in the void of cold and dark walking across the field of snow glittering under the moon. A punctuated equilibrium where you were the sole glow no one small glow calling to others distant lights each to the others made more bright and more distant by the cold and dark between them. And wrapped in a warmth of daydream deeper than all of summer's noons. And above you above them the absolute farness silence and cold of the cold far silent stars. What joy to look out the icy window across the night. Staring not at any star but rather at the darkness yet not yet absolutely dark between a spattering of them staring at the wall of the cosmos so to speak the impenetrable infinite backdrop. Or so he thought at the time. Having not much else but your own eyes to go on. And extravagant books of astronomy.

Torques of brilliant and vast chaos suspended like microbes in an endless globule of thick viscous shadow. The photographs you carried from the broken-spined paperback in your mind's eye. The thought was terrifying you were reading Pascal for French class but the view was glorious glorious. The view that the thought remained. You could not quite forget except for long intervals what the blue sky like a theater flat secreted. The blank sky. The mottled sky. Unspeaking sky. With its invading never quite conquering armies of heavy cloud. Air cloud azure moon sun star black.

And all between cold. Ah.

Yes she said. Yes. Yes.

Nervous deep moist whisper on the couch before the giggling TV.

Yes. Yes.

She pulls him up where he lay on her kissing her face and ears and hair and takes him by the hand to the kitchen again. He dreads the possibility of blood again but not enough to make him even vaguely rebellious. No. She has said yes. That is all that matters. Is all that. All. He thinks he is ready for happiness at least for this happiness at least for. Wrong he doesn't think anything. He follows in the wake of his cock which follows in the wake of his girl. Marvelling at his good fortune. He thinks. No. Again he doesn't think anything. He is on automatic pilot. He is mindlessly. What is the word. Glad? No. Excited? No. He is mindless. He is all body. He has become his body. He is id. Is it. There is almost no you in him at all. He is in a trance like that which precedes his masturbation sessions. But this time it is with another person.

Down to her breasts and nipples in the kitchen light and the short sighs and the longing stare from his frightened excited girl. Must we go into it? We must. As he mushes his nose against her chest he feels her suddenly undo and lower her pants and a light pressure on the top of his head and he moves downward though with mild reluctance wondering what is coming next and thinking of the blood he is slightly appalled at what this is probably signalling my god she wants me to kiss her there? He has heard neither of the concept nor of the word cunnilingus. It had never tickled his fantasies. He dutifully licked her torso tummy navel and traced a line of saliva downwards past the line of the pelvis its mirror symmetry of smooth protruberance of bones and turned inwards to the top crest of her pubic hair. Here he stopped a moment and licked the skin lightly actually he was appalled at the smell steaming up to him from the crotch a few inches away like stale catfood with a light undertone of urine. God what if there's blood again. Please please she whispered exerting a light pressure on his head. Resigned and slightly sickened he bent lower and was confronted with an upside down triangle of black matted curly hair dank and odorous clustered atop a little bony hill the mons veneris he knew it was called and leading to a pair of spungiform lips he would one day know were called labia traceable like a pair of long serpent mounds in the thicket of hair and a tiny triangular space between the thighs at the vertex of the pubis. And the rich scent of her crotch suddenly filled him with a desire to bury his tongue there. He gently applied his tongue lightly to the surface of the hair. Use your tongue she whispered from above please please. Having placed his finger in her vagina more than once he knew more or less where he should place his tongue. And he pushed his way down and up and in there in a slit of moist flesh bunched on each side and giving the tongue little purchase he slid his tongue back and forth as rhythmically as he could he suspected even then that rhythm and stamina would supply the trick. His chin must have reached as far back as her arms he tried to scotch that thought by opening his eyes. They looked straight up and met in a blaze her own staring down at him caverned in her hair watching him between her breasts and the unbuckled bra that rode them and the foreshortened torso belly navel boulevard of pelvis and the imperial wedge of her pudendum stuck in his mouth like a feeder. And he worked his tongue fascinated and repulsed and hungry and desiring. And getting a crick in his neck. And she murmuring please please.

Too bad he had never heard of fellatio either. Never occurred to him he might reverse the position. At least not at that time.

At last she drew him back up to her face he reversed the direction of his licks and they french-kissed passing her tastes between them and he finished off with his hand between her thighs.

Then she pulled up her pants and took him back docilely to the television room.

.

DO — YOU — KNOW — WHAT TIME IT IS?

His mother who is not his mother stands red-faced in curlers in the corridor at home her voice a shriek.

IT'S 2 — O' CLOCK INTHEMORNING.

One light is on. The corridor light. He tries to stare into it.

YOU'RE JUST SCREWING THAT WHORE.

She is shaking.

YOU'RE JUST *SCREWING* THAT WHORE!

He stands staring exhausted ashamed.

YOU'RE — JUST — *SCREWING* — *THAT* — *WHORE!*

Nothing. He is paralyzed. She knows how to paralyze him. All women do though none seems ever to realize it. He cannot move until she breaks the spell.

GO TO BED! *GO TO BED!*

He skitters up the stairs hearing a door slam behind him and thinking at least I wasn't hit not as in the old days when his father was there who would have struck him again and again and again and again and broken him and left him whimpering on the floor like a dog. And he would never have touched a woman again.

.

They met daily on the bleak sidewalk outside the high school dedicated to girls.

She was loud and brassy and embarrassed him and he sometimes longed to look away when her look of a voluptuous pixie would draw him back and her dropping of words of promise in his ear would weld his ear to her mouth tender him on hooks of fantasy of what was yet to come the fantasy and fumbling and self-administration dedicated to the redemption of flesh. By flesh. By other flesh. By the other's flesh. Have we mentioned she belonged to a church the truly sensual often do in the heart of the soul of their loins. Or have done when the loins long dormant ignited. The church was called Pillar of Fire. No kidding. Advancing before them in the perpetual night. Strange name for a sect whose name he cannot now remember if he ever knew one more mob of low-church Protestants with which the country has always been rife. Giving it its eternal good conscience. Cursing it with holiness and triumph. She gave him a long hard hungry and demanding stare across the packed subway car. Then her strident voice bellowed freezing him with desire and shame. She was so short she came up only to his chin it gave him fits of paralysis. That he was free to go elsewhere made him feel like a traitor already. Not that he was so free. Walking away from an available body is not something one does at that age. Sweetly lubricious. And yet to stay by the side of this rabbit-fur coat hurling insults at the world was not possible either. For long. But he stuck it out with the stubbornness of an assuaged cock. Hoping for the best. Thinking of the feeling of her nipple against his tongue yes that was the obsessive memory. The feel and the bite and the taste. And the look. The look of her torso bared to him. And her whispering. And with the glow of longing came the mind on fire the testes shaking cock raised thickened hardened the blood surging like an invading army the head both clear and dazed the groin a city in ecstatic revolt and pillaring flames.

·

But blood began vomiting in his dreams.

·

The day after the first contact had been the setoff of the dark implosion to come. Its long and lingering fuse.

It was not that sex was death for the rickety jerry-built ego confronting it it was more it was less it was otherwise it was it was …
… engulfing annihilation erasure of even memory of having been replacement of a spare part with a hole a demonic descent into a …
… kaldera.

(In your pleasure is my death. Was. Will be. Will have always been. No. Casing that pleasure. Enfolding it. That joy. Ecstatic squalor. If only one could have died. If only one. Could die. Might. Might die. Would. Will. Watching oneself die again and again. Without the comfort of ending. No comfort. No ending. The flesh peeled from the mind. Over again like an egg. Charred at the edge and bleeding at the heart. In immortal hell. No. Not even that. Not immortal yet never ending. Pitched into bliss. Tortured into the body's heaven the mind's hell. The soul shuttered against the cement torso. The soft body's wall. The scream locked behind the teeth. The mouth quivering with happiness.)

Though there is still here no She. No She? No one by that name could be said to be here. No one other than he. Yet. Yet it was the impinging on him of her otherness so to speak that brought him to himself in tight sharp unappealing focus. A nightmare of clarity. Of being. No longer a reflection in a tarn. No? Yet it was he thinks he thought at the time. A face brought face to face with a face. Not to be escaped. As he was. Not as he daydreamed on his bed on his walks while staring into his book while fantasizing on his back beneath a bray of Wagner. Or Tchaikovsky's mischievous laments. Etc. The romantic canards. No. It will not be fancied away fancy that. So fancy harder. Not the maladresse not the irrelevant rejoinders not the weak jests not the hysterically strangled conviction. And surely not the manifestations of excruciating insecurity. They flash back at him from the look on her tongue. And the cheerful sarcasms in her eyes. Thus she all she any she pillories him on what he is. Half finished and half effaced. A kind of puddle of inadequacies. Crippled with pusillanimity and pride. Or so he condemned himself in later years but who is to know not I.

How place the other there there. One asks. Like the billiard in its pocket it is at once inhumed in the word. Speak the other and the other becomes an expression of me. Of me. Only me. Now if this were a play we might be able to get somewhere. But it is not it is but it is not. Play that is. A play on play. Laboriously pursued. A dream of words not a dream a pretense of a dream of words half fantasy half manipulation. That doesn't sound right either. Whatever happened to our free association? It seems to have gotten lost among the adolescent shambles. You were trying to be something. You were trying to pull the pieces of yourself into a form or a pattern or an object into a knot yes that's it from a not into a knot anything but this vague lethargic anarchy this cloud in siege of cloud this woozy fogbound permanent revolution you feel yourself and the world the world to be to be to be. You think you would rather be dead. Yes. Stated simply. Sometimes you think you are dead. At others merely paralyzed. In a frozen delirium of fear. An anguish without cause or hope. A spectre and its own haunting. Then you stop thinking try to stop thinking for all thought seems a horror and let the hollowness around you invade.

Ungrateful wimp your first genuine sexual encounters should have made you overjoyed why are you suddenly cringing with misery anquish (that again) confusion bewilderment shame guilt (that again). Enormous guilt. Well rather large guilt. You liked grand intensives in those days. Absolute crushing incredible ineluctable thank you Stephen etc. It was an expression of the weakness of your feelings. No. Of your nonexistent and even if existing in that trough unavailing judgment.

It was as though the membrane between you and the world had broken and you had to work full time nonstop to seal the mucilaginous break. The world was hemmorrhaging into you you were hemmorrhaging into the world the silt of either mixed in the liquid of the other there was no telling the difference between them that hotel was your anxiety your anxiety was a hotel for business travelers and lost conventioneers. You were being annihilated without even dying you were dying without being annihilated you became where you were but only as long as you were there. Then you were gone. And the world bobbed around you like a life jacket like to drown you. Reviving you for the next assault. Kissing your body as if it loved it. Loved it! Well after all it was still possible at that time. And the proof of her love was she tortured you.

She again. Waves of heat peaked in writhy fingery tonguing and writhy tonguey fingering and tonguey fingery writhing on the sofa in the kitchen on the porch in the bedroom in the garage in the rec room and elsewhere but mostly in the kitchen. Ah what bliss of membrane and flame! The dissolution of the self into moments of unmemoried bliss. Yet to come. For he is technically still a virgin is he not. Though she is clearly working hard to remand the sweet shame. And we are circling for the kill.

For blood vomited in his dreams.

Torture. That was the word. We may not kill the thing we love but how we make them pay. Finger the nerve until it is raw. Watch with fascination the flinch and cringe and squirm. Listen for the gutteral choke in the throat the gurgle in the larynx shallow pant the quivering diaphragm. Measure the touch that triggers the spasm watch the spasm with an amazed and religious awe. Examine the face control its uncontrollable rage. Watch it seethe. Watch it sink into the twilight flecked with the lightning of its bewildered anger. Watch its head suddenly surge toward the surface of the sea. And at the last moment tongue into an astonishment of joy.

Yes.

.

Visiting friends in a remote part of the city. How remote? Near its furthest end. The girl left her family to live with her boyfriend. They are now only shadows in the cave of memory. The fire is low but warm in its way. The four have finished eating a dinner that has long been forgotten and are chattering away about nothing everything nothing. The air is static with suggestion. A series of signs pass between the other three that he cannot read at first then abruptly understands. The two friends giggle and abandon the room closing the door with more giggles his girl friend pulls down the murphy bed tosses a blanket on it switches off the light turns her back to him peels away her cutoffs and shirt he sees her entirely naked for the first time she turns in the half light and pulls him beneath the blanket toward her sweet and terrifying body.

Now that no body is terrifying to you or sweet.

Now that no body is to your body a body at all only a sack of hide behind which impotent furious eyes twitch like those of a harassed hen.

Oh the wonder of that joy of that wonder. He lies atop her feeling like a sack of potatoes on a living settle. A curious wondering amazed anxious and exceedingly excited sack of potatoes. Her legs are parted beneath him her face averted in the darkness his face buried in the hair at the side of her head he can feel her ear against his nose he draws an imaginary line with his finger from her ear down her throat down her shoulder past her flattened breast along her torso across her hip down her opened thigh past the crooked knee to the mid-calf and back again past the knee up the thigh over the pelvis up the torso across the flattened breast past the shoulder along the throat up to her little ear his fingers tingling with his mind's joy. She is whispering through the haze of his virgin thrill. He can feel his eyes open as wide as coffee cups. All instinct he unzips and pulls out his stiffened penis he can feel it rhythmically spasm. I'm scared I'm scared she whispers. He nudges his penis forward uncertain where it should go exactly how far he dares go in. He fumbles maladroitly against a hairy obstacle fearing with some repulsion he might be trying to penetrate her urinary tract or loathesome thought her anus when suddenly a moist unresisting softness takes the head of his penis in. He halts unsure what to do next. Go all the way in she whispers into his ear go all the way in. And he does so. Suddenly he feels his penis lipped in and surrounded by soft moist warmth and he thinks this is where it belongs. Again he halts and lingers over the sensation the sweet soft feeling of this penis in this vagina ah. Then abruptly starts frantically humping. Go slow go slow she whispers. So he does he is a docile pupil. And then she begins to respond to his thrust and release with thrust and release of her own. It's tricky he has to concentrate. Now is the delicate question of timing. Clearly there ought to be a mutually maintained and acknowledged rhythm. But should he thrust when she releases and release when she thrusts or on the contrary should he thrust when she thrusts and release when she releases? There are problems and pleasures both ways. Though mostly problems. The idea of talking about this never enters his head there are things you can do but not discuss. The only communication for him above the neck is his gasping and heavy breathing through the black mass of invisible air into her invisible ear. Sweetly turned against his lips. A fleshy shell. A flower petal. Her ear. She sighs rhythmically in his ear too with an occasional ecstatic rhythmic gasp. Gasp to gasp while they adjust to their rhythms to something that is close to mutually satisfactory. Or disregarded. Or happy. Do they know which. Though the problem described above is not resolved and they go back and forth between the two dispositions of thrust and release release and thrust taking the satisfactions of each other's bodies where they might no where they can.

It requires more physical dexterity than he is used to having all his life detested and despised sports the pathetic jock. Being a bookworm with grand intellectual pretensions. Immensely pleased himself over the bricklike tomes he carries under his skinny arms to school each day some of which he actually yes reads but not now exactly though perhaps yes but in an immensely different way. Now miracle of miracle he is all body sunk in body surrounded by and surrounding flesh and skin a sudden worshipper of glands and the moisture of the loins and an intoxication of eyes lips breasts thighs throat tongue hair. A pagan worshipper of the heaven of matter sex an act of the divine. Yes ah yes. Sailing above and into her body flying across the plain of her into her across her above her the wind of his blood pulling him ahead pushing him winding him into her into him losing the skin between them until there is only one skin and that the one between them in the dark and the moist of sweat and the breaths short sharp in her ear in his ear the tickling of her tongue in his ear the feel of her arms crossing his back clutching his shoulders the feel of the flesh of her ear in his mouth his lips lipping the edge of her ear his teeth biting the mass of her hair his mouth mouthing her hair and the sailing sailing into the night into the dark into the night the sailing and the motionlessness the divine movement that was no movement but a spinning without rest into stillness yes ah yes.

How long did this last not long. Time has almost ceased for him even as its speed increases. Maybe a quarter of an hour maybe less maybe more who knows. He has not come though he was close and could less and less control his tendency to gallop between her legs when she whispered with sudden officiousness in his ear you better get out now I don't want to get pregnant.

And with a strange grateful docility he does. He hasn't heard of the female orgasm so doesn't know of the female orgasm so doesn't know that she hasn't had one in this particular instance. Nor thankfully has she.

The light goes back on. The clothes return to their respective bodies. Then he and she in her white rabbit coat leave their friends who have returned giggling from their orgy in the next room waving them out the screamingly bright door and they walk hand in hand in the streetlamp darkness to the trolley she asking him are you happy he replying abstractedly yes not knowing if he is or what he is feeling he feels hollowed out and vacated though he has no words for it at the time so he says somewhat distantly yes he can barely remember what has just happened and then they stop and suddenly clutch each other in the stinging winter air. Reassuring each other. Murmurously. Almost loving.

How sublime how ludicrous how sublime. One falls to one's knees before the mystery in painful embarrassed laughter remember your first time? Noted decades hence. At the time you were too dazed to either think or feel. The bulkhead had collapsed and a wave of light sound touch taste smell billowed up and overwhelmed and flooded and drowned the small vacant island.

·

One day soon after you sit in the audience listening to the girl singing in a chorus staring at her face among the other faces hers brilliant amidst the well-meant banalities of the music. And you almost break into tears. I have desecrated her he thinks with monotonous fervor. I have desecrated her body I am a barbarian a monster. I deserve to be destroyed.

When the one with the desecrated body runs up to you with pixieish smile afterwards you mutter monosyllables of encouragement an excuse have to go home and study have a test to fail then vacates in panic anguish and lament. You do not notice the expression on her face.

•

He walks about mechanically not knowing what has hit him a pustule surrounded by a bruise. Delicate. A breath scorches him. His mother who was not his mother glares at him as at a faithless lover. He argues with himself: what have I done but taken the body in the body isn't it natural to rejoice in the body why this punishment on all sides and inside me who have I betrayed?

Your mind goes silent or babbles like a baby. Or floods with inflations of orchestral grandeur. Or whispers almost silent. Or obsesses on a song. Flashing the sight of her skin in the darkness. The feel of her body against yours. The canticles in extremis of. Love? Neurotic attack psychotic break? Sharpening on the end of your finger the raw nail. Or rather not rather a balloon sagging out toward the delusion of his stars. Where hitting a snag in its expansion it must seize up in a sudden ludicrous pucker. Deflation abrupt. Imploding. Sucking in all his pride and the collapsible city of his ego. Into a lithe tornado of guilt. A fear of annihilation. Yes it happened the thing you yearned for dreamed about masturbated to the thought for years alone in your bed dreaded. For it has power over you. The engulfing uterus the sucking tube of the cunt. After the pleasure of half an hour a world of confusion where nothing any longer is sure not even the bastioned edges of the self not even the calm of the mind what the eyes present to see the ears to hear the scents backing up in the nostrils the hot tastes of the tongue. Even the hours have turned molten and ooze in slow surge from the clock like lava. And all comes from the slow shrill torso of his girl.

As the blood vomited in his dreams.

.

Demented by a disharmony of hormones he is lucid enough to think one of many one of all ashamed mortified tormented by self-contempt. In daydream a hero saving the world from a fate worse than what in nightmare a whelp whimpering in a corner his tail curled between his legs in appearance calm to the point of phlegm my he's mature for his years he vows to find the first opportunity to correct them it is torture to be praised for what does not belong to him but what is he in reality what indeed does belong to him? But that he does not know.

Not that. Not that. Not that. Not that.

A voice whispers to him you can be whatever you can imagine.

But whatever you can imagine you are not that.

He reels between so many exploded contentions. And his girl stares at him coolly as if waiting for reply to a question he has not heard.

.

The attorney turns with a smile. He furtively blinks, his eyes askant away, then one shoulder thrusts with a swagger up while the other vulnerably sags.

"Did you," the attorney says, looking demurely into his eyes, "did you, Mr. Renard, say what you so clearly said on that occasion with the intention you so clearly had? To insult, to wound, to mortify, to offend? And did you realize, at the end of your little speech, just how you had succeeded? How well you had failed? How genuinely you deserved the punishment which you so obstreperously demanded?"

He takes a quick step back and gazes at him, full face. The court is a pale of wounds. Or perhaps the magnifying glass is adjusting to the focus that will burst the beetle into flame.

You want but are unable to shout No! Because it is not so it is true every particular on the bill of particulars you deserve ejection from the herd the stamp of your guilt between your eyes the rest of your days in solitude without friends family or succour in your hour of need exile at last until your last hour. And even beyond that why not ignominy disgrace your body dismembered for the edification of first-year medical students your belongings and personal abortions stuff to caulk cracks in a landfill for your name oblivion for your soul hell. An evacuation accompanied by puckering sarcasm and snickers of contemptuous laughter.

Thus the banshee whispers into your private ear shrieks wild across the fields of the air of the cold of the night of your mind.

·

It hit. A sound of distant collapsing. The outermost walls of the ruined city streets spanned with debris alleys warrens of shattered brick cracked jamb split lintel scoured with tilted beams of shadow in sunlight and rubble noon spectres of dust. Penetrating inward toward the center toward the hall and the plaza and the cathedral and the tower. Toward the heart of the city its dead center its hidden cell where lurks in frenzied exhortations to the silent walls its chaotic inner tyrant. Secret demolition crews on call sneaking in at night and tearing down a neighborhood a block of shops a desolate region of factories chipping at cornices slaying drywall sweeping out the forgetfulness of lives into the dusty brooding of the street at dead of night between a dead and a killing sun. All fall down in hecatombs of dust and jungles of ruin the dust of clouds dancing with choirs of flitters and bits and a crumbling of splinters and deep long rasps and sighs of falling groans of reluctant crumbling dry heaves of final fall slowly slowly collapsing in the bitter light of the moon slow enough for those just in earshot to shake their heads for their neighbors and thank God they have been spared as they huddle behind their curtains basking in the safety of their TVs. Still thanking God when the ball pokes its great black head jeeringly through their wall.

.

She is still only a shadow against the exposed retina. The old problem how make a series of threads of words become in the listener's or reader's eye a living presence vital engaging sharply cut out of the air and shadow of memory unmistakable something one would recognize on a summer's day yes beyond all text and the pale redactor weave blend into become a piece of the world within the world. Puzzling. For does anything have such independence is there anything inside words that is outside words as well? Strange question with an even stranger answer if the academic mountebanks are to be believed but who can confute the jester when his buttocks hides the throne? The writer's sleight of hand. Slipping even before the senility. Not really any lawyer will tell you so. Unless the delusion is tacitly shared. Axioms unquestioned postulates definitions by good breeding unchallenged. She. He. You. I. All of us of doubtful provenance the dried pulp of the dictionary and the private lexicon of idiolect.

Let's try again.

Must I.

.

You no longer knows which way is up. Unless your raised penis obedient to the compass rose is meant to tell you. This way is up hails the shining glans and this down tug the sullen testes. This way you cannot become confused. But it requires frequent and on-call erections. They are fortunately frequent but unfortunately never on call. Willy having a mind or rather mindlessness of his own. Never planning further ahead than the next possible climax.

She shrills in another part of the house.

She seems to like to cry your name viva voce and at high decibels frequently and for small cause but enough. You go to her in baffled obedience her allowing you to toy with her anatomy has given her certain rights it seems. It seems. It seems. You feel attached by a steel thread to her womb tied by a musty smelling thread to the clasp of ocean and bay brine between her thighs held by a magnet coiled within her groin. Groin to groin with the current on humming at the back of their minds. The payment you have made for entry is severe and at all times at immediate demand. You are no longer the master of your own body. And your mind lives shoved in a crack between her inanely nattering television set and her smooth plain of belly and her delicate crest of face and her saliva-flecked breasts and her pearl-smooth shoulders and her fairy's ears and her black-winged brows and wind-black hair and the hairy mouth of her vagina. Dreaming there of its fish-scented darkness.

His grades are failing.

He has not studied in weeks in weeks no he has made midnight lamps burn late with his devoted swatting of the curves of her skin the softness of her flesh the smell of the caverns of her body. He has opened only the book of her body and devoured it. He has immersed only in the wild sea and wind of words of the smell and sound of her body's breathing hungry panting rhythmic and soft and hard by turns into his dazzled ear he has only studied the texture of her flesh in his night's dream has only crammed on what he has never known as though for a test he must pass and will forever fail. He knows her body by heart the anger in her mind always escapes him. He tries to penetrate her soul by way of her body through her flesh he aims for the impregnable heart. That will not give way. Not yet. That targets his fleshly weakness his young vulnerability with its own hard consequence giving only as much as must needs but never more not like the man fool giving all in the sudden single rush of despairing attack. The way he comes in a spike narrow sudden and soon over like a child gasping into the air behind her ear then knocking out into sleep on her shoulder. He sees himself how stupid he must seem indeed is. So he must study harder practice burning inside her learn to bear the soft darkness into hard joy. Must pass the ordeal must but in some sense already begins unable to hear he must to grind against the wall. Of a softness that is only there between the thighs hardness thrilling the air. The hardness of her mind. Of her woman's lucid shining mind that only knows demand. He will learn. Though it horrifies him to see. It. Flaming in cold splendor. There. All high ice and fire of the tongue and demand. Demand. In love no doubt. But of what. Of steel shafted in desire like a stone. How the legend grew illumined. The cock cemented in cunt. However lovingly invited. No. It cannot be. That bad. He is not looking close enough all he sees is haze. Her shrill tones still calling. Down the hall to the end of the garden. Lustily belling into the twilight. The mouth a grand O. And he all in love with the skin around the hollow of her flesh. Must go. Now. For to come. Slightly feverish in anticipation at times almost morose with concentration on what may happen again never certain she never promises anything and even then. And she noticing nothing but the flattering cravenness of his hunger for her. It seemed. What now the chains are soft and bind. And hold. And hold. And bind.

A voice at the far back of your mind is beginning to shout though you hardly hear.

When you walk into the room one day the air sucks from your lungs.

.

And this is supposed to be ... what? what again? He wonders strange and uneasy at it is it happiness is it joy? It holds him beyond happiness beyond joy. What is it then? Is it fulfillment? fulfillment of what then — of body and mind and soul? The end toward which this body has been ever moving? The great goal of being alive being human of life? Of life! Is it love? Is it love! Is it only the chain of the body? Body! Chain! Only!

Another stumble on the high road to sainthood as someone says nodding over the dinner table with a leer. Someone imagined or in some other way profaned. Abrupt focus out of half-witted stare. A face cagey deferential and mocking attached insecurely to a neck. It floats in noodling figure eights and holds him in a pincer of eyes. *You'll make it fools always do they stagger blindly across the abyss. It's simple. Really. You just have to hold on. Hardly knowing it hardly wanting hardly aware of the delicate fly caught in your clammy barely conscious clasp. So. Lightly. But lightly! Don't crush it in the fist of your desire.* The tongue lolls out. *Yet!*

The hand of mail slowly closes over the head of a rose.

.

Have we progressed? We look at each other in ill-timed dismay. It hardly seems possible. The black marks however trail back into the whiteness behind. So perhaps against all odds we have. Dimpling the snow with our waste our exonerative sign. Our dead or dying spoor. Out of the vagueness a smear of light sucks inward to a simple blinding crystal. Shocking out in a sudden noiseless shattering. Shattering skewing light in the thousand directions of the compass out into the great darkness abroad. Ahead. Beyond. Pointing the way. Into the blankness. Everywhere.

A stamp embosses the chrome. In quick hard sequence in the shop behind the shrunken house on the alley. So many irredeemable florets peeling to the stained floor of the garage. Everyone shouting at once. Not hysterically but to show that they are still alive.

Yes. No. Maybe.

.

Her smile was now more likely to be a frown. The pixieish eyes detached and dim. A weighing gaze. Without shine and most often blank. Watching for a sign. Askance. What can the bitch possibly want now. It will take years before this thought is allowed to break the crust of his uncandor. Though he grumbles clearly enough now to the air.

Her laugh strident now with malicious victory goes still. Into rich silence.

I need to keep her jabbering only then is she happy though I never remember a thing she says. I strain my bored mind to show a face tense with curiosity. Like on the rock in that stream so many months ago! I bend and screw my body into the semblance of fascination and concern I dodge my head in response as from a blow I do not want her to see the depth of my indifference. I fear the revenge of those who bore us and who guess you may be bored now but we will see the serene complacence of your yawn as I lingeringly remove each layer of your skin from the layer beneath until I reach the fat and the muscle and the funny little organs and then at long last the bone sweetie honey lover darling am I boring you now?

Her body is becoming eloquent with the tricks of the embarrassment of waning desire.

They play with each other in more dangerous arenas. In the porch off the livingroom while her family is watching TV a wall and a shadow away until her father barks suspiciously his daughter's legendary name. "Deena!" In the upstairs back room between commercials while her sister and brother romp up and down the rowhouse stairs pretending to notice nothing in the quick sharp sigh the abrupt turn from the door the motley press and rumple of clothes. In the midst of family and friends asleep on the floor of a house rented by the sea on the brine and Pepsi-scented Jersey shore threatening to wake them between gingerly thrashing and barely controlled moans. In the parental bed for the first time in all nakedness playing with marks of tongue and lip on the soft page of the body slapping sweaty bellies in the silence grunting with bliss playing out the revenge fantasy against the parental crime the crime of the parents in having brought forth these bodies now playing with the fire of generation on the pyre of their bed lapping lunging burning as if nothing would be the consequence and yet everything might indeed everything must they lunge again and again. They venture forth into the wrack of the body past the sea's edge into the open ocean they curl beyond the riptide and defy the tide to swallow them they play the edge of defiance and capture sally and withdrawal invasion and rout to keep appetite fresh and deep and pared to the bone and hot. The salt sharp and dry and quivering and hard. And they succeed for a time. As in a dream. As if flying over the earth in their dream.

He tells the story badly. He's making it up like a bad liar in a desperate spot. At this rate nobody will nobody can nobody should take seriously it or him or even you. Even you! Hear me? After all who are these people and why should I care. Who were they and why should I care. They were not me.

Lapped in the irresponsibility of oblivion ah.

But someone won't be able to resist the temptation to prove even that wrong. Short-sighted deluded arrogant and fatuous. To rub your nose triumphantly in your own trash.

Text for midrash.

Either way I risk defeat. Either way victory.

So play in the mud as long as you are able. And wave your dirty hand at the sun.

What you take for the sun.

What you have always taken for the sun.

6

… and a hard book that made abrupt and inescapable demands on the curious unguarded unsuspecting reader who raised its pages with the innocence of a child expecting to disappear into another world instead found a harsh and glittering mirror where he saw his own face framed in wreckage the precise definition of his own past the little heap of failures the small change of defeat grotesque allurements of guilt supple mnemonics of accusation rehearsed in a backroom before a sadistic taskmaster and then paraded on the naked page for all to see and applaud or heckle and humiliate at will. It was as though the book had been written with you in mind tracing your glazed stare above the pages the furrowing of your brow the parting of your lips as they muttered selected phrases in the orthography of its letters the austerity of its font the barbs at the ends of its serifs gibbet Ts jeering Qs goose-stepping heil-saluting Ks locked in double-bind Zs. All books faced you with their own faces bearing down on your own all books had grown on their shoulders this authority and power. You had waded as a child into the sea of books with humble and trembling joy your eyes scanning the shelves of your father's library with anxiety and desire your fingers plucking down the random spine your hands opening the cloth boards and weighing the book's lightness against a sense of the riches opening beneath your eyes the smell of the binding glue rising to you so you bent and touched your nose to the book's gutter and breathed deep the sweetish chemical smell the smooth off-white of the pages the soft matte glow of the paper the little ridges on the backing of the laced quires the dimpling of the pages near the gutter and their gentle rise and fall from the gutter to the far edge of the how you loved that a book's pages were called leaves like the leaves of an oak or a maple which you so loved and the coloring along the tops of the pages of some books red or blue or oil-polychrome and the torn-looking outer edges of the pages and then the look of the letters on the pages all lined up like little toy soldiers all spic and span small and solid and awaiting command and the comfortable margins and the quiet field of paper around the words and the lightness of the weight in your hand as you stood with your head bent above that lucid tangle of ink as small as a bird's nest a labyrinth of reflected light and dark shifting like a kaleidoscope focussing the light of the world in bright and shifting shapes as seen intensely and intensely known through another pair of eyes another soul another mind if you believed in soul and mind. You waded into that world with hope and a little fear but more of hope and an almost militant trust. The hours you spent propped up in bed like a puppet made of nothing but elbows and knees and eyes absorbed and racing through that maze of straight lines that is a book vanished away in a haze scored with lightning a scroll of luminous images fading into a wash of murmurs a rocking tide a silent room awash with a net of sea light glimmering against the ceiling like the shape of thoughts within the mind the only sound the sigh of turning pages shifting leaves. Always there had been books as far back as you could remember sometimes accompanied by an adult though not always. Not always. Yet you had needed adults to break down the wall of barbs and thorns that stood between you and the temple's sanctum of illumination. The mystery of words on a page would haunt your waking hours like an unresolved dream and you would need those guides from above to help you carry the dream into the day. Always. For in these small treasure chests with their deceptively innocent faces and infinite false bottoms there was no end to the locks in need of keys. Out of the resolutions of one question flowered a thousand others in the quiet eyes of an answer glittered an enigmatic star. Yet always it allured onward the quest to the end of the page which opened like a gate to a new path in the garden a new arm of an enchanted labyrinth. You were taken with the spell of the storyteller who organized the anarchy and endless suspense of the present into splendid decision and heroic order who took your obscure sense of confusion and vagueness and stamped it with clarity and resolution. To read was to dream with open eyes to stand shoulder to shoulder with the splendid hero and share his burdens confusion and determination the vertigo of fate the mischievousness of accident the near disasters and the flirtations with catastrophe the games of destiny the seductions of defeat the rush of final victory. It was to live through the dream of another to multiply one's life into a host of shadowy figures on a perpetually shifting stage to become everything one saw looking back at one like an audience in a theater divided in half for each half the other was the stage for each half the other half was the audience they were forever fluctuating back and forth between the dramatic pose and applause. And the murmurous whispering of the words held it all in meaning and music. And all of this was reflected inside you as in a mirror. You became not only the audience but the players as well even the theater itself. You became the theater that was the world.

You were all but the author of the spectacle.

The essential mystery and the unlocking of the mystery which together held the secret power of all books enthralled and carried him in its shining cage like a seller of birds to the market but books offered as well other and rarer delectations more complex chambers and harrowing labyrinths. He found. He found and learned. Less penetrable and more enigmatic yet still partaking of the essence of following a thread into a maze at the heart of which lay as on a couch supine with sleepy wonder or stood like a totem of stone and blood the casting of a mystery's shroud a mystery's revelation. A mystery's revelation. The promise of its revelation. A glimpse into the eyes of the god. A book was a forest in which one wandered in absolute trust. At that time. Before one learned otherwise learned that even books are suspect. But at that time there was no otherwise. The book was close to nature one that unfolded within the human world flowered in the mind like a garden under one's hands. Even when the book most proudly defended its proudly defended humanity's proudly and vainly defended man's apartness even when it raised a wall as black as the words within it austere as the margins of its pages white with blankness and hostility and pride even then the book was part more of the natural world than of the world imposed by man or so you obscurely felt but were you not right to think so? You wanted this to be so and therefore it was so that was the logic your dreams demanded. For the book's softness its simplicity its ease were in stark and radiant contrast to the brutality of the concrete glass and metal world that he had come to equate with the unforgiving world of the human. Though you also felt and resisted as you felt it the subtle connection between them the metallic though almost invisible thread that connected the dream over the open pages to the fist that grasped the warm and pulsing earth in its grip teneo te terra mea. But not all books and not the book in essence for some of them and these held you in their joy some of them warned of the fist and lamented the fist and presented an alternative to the fist and gave you the very thoughts with which you learned to open the fist and make it release you into the air. If you listened. If you watched. If you remembered in time.

Other books challenged him they did not make things easy for him as the storytellers had those seducers of time. They built columns raised walls of imbricated prose or deafened him with obscure music or deepened the maze of meaning beyond the capacity of his thought to unravel it and silently laughed at his hopeless attempts to encompass them with the small hands of his mind. At first he was perplexed by these books all thorn and barbed wire and threw himself at them with a wild and exasperated will. Some opened their secrets at the second or third assault some grew coy and withdrew even further into the glittering forest shadows of a frustrating promise some opened not at all but gaped at him with the saturnine blankness of a vault forever closing but never perfectly sealed. His little schoolboy pride grew infuriated though his humility told him to wait and in the obscurity of his room he dreamed of the day when he would be able to grapple as adroitly with the speculations of Leibniz and the categories of Kant as he now could with Verne's marvelous voyages the flagrant satires of Swift the liana-like adventures of Kipling. In the meantime he collected even books he could not read in a mirror image of his father's serene library. You built your own little tower of Babel and prepared without impatience for your eventual assault on the heavens. With the overweening pride of youth the intolerable confidence unbearable hope. Stacked the books to the clouds like a ladder. For you were convinced that a path to Ultimate Reality was to be found. There among those papers unfurling in the breeze coming in through the window the Secret with its pout of mystery waited on the next page enlaced in knots of words hidden and revealed in the same startling lines. All you need do all he need all I need do is attend faithfully. For the Secret had been known and forgotten countless times and repeated and forgotten and heard and forgotten and spoken and revealed and forgotten. Until you will find it. And not forget it but hold it and keep it and savor it and rejoice until you become it no until it becomes you enfolded in its white-hot rose.

And what is the secret after all? It speaks to you one day. It rises from its couch of sea and snow and stands on the carpet before you and speaks. And its lips murmur a silent spell you watch carefully to read. What does it say? What? And just as you think you have caught it caught it the mystery of its awakening from its silent and flickering lips it vanishes in the sunlit temple of the day.

He pondered it long that secret what he had guessed of it a secret he could only guess. The secret contained in the books the secret of the

mystery they revealed. And proposed to himself to put it into practice
for it was not only a revelation it was an imperative. At a guess. And
you sat at the small table in your room overlooking the grass of the yard
as it grayed and shadowed in the evening. And drew before you a sheet
of blank paper from the pile at your elbow set aside for the scratched
and frustrated calculations of homework. And took a pencil the same
you had used to take down notes at school and doodle obscurely in the
margins of your notebooks. And leaned over the paper with pencil in
hand. And waited patiently as you now wait patiently for a word. For
a word to come. For a word to come of a kind you had not yet known.
A word like the ones you read in stories but reversed. A word with
an imaginary meaning. A word that did not grope or gesture or wave
vaguely toward its meanings. But rather drew them out of itself like the
spider the filaments of its web. Magicked them into the light. Conjured
them. Dreamed them into being. And hung them as if magically in the
air held by their almost invisible strands.

·

But books were both duty and hope liberation and chore obligation
and dream. Not all caught him in a spell the speeding days could not
shake off. Not a few times a book would sink him into a marsh of
unfathomable obscurity boundless reach and he would slog through it
in dazed bewilderment condemned by his delicate reader's conscience
to finish reading whatever book he had begun. Not yet having read
the good Doctor's scornful admonition. Sailing in a fog between the
margins of its inland sea. Hoping against hope not to land among the
rocks. Sometimes stranded for hours if not days on the shoals of an
impenetrable chapter. Idealist and blockhead that he was.

Reading was a means of disappearance a way of being in a room
yet vanishing a warning to others to respectfully ignore the reader

don't interrupt him he is reading as though he were in intimate conversation a deep communion that must not be broken sleepwalking immured in the holiness of a spell. It was also like wearing a mask the open book a face between one's hands the prospective face of one's future a mask without eyeholes or ones that only looked within a hideaway in open daylight a rehearsal for a future death. There was the pridefulness of the very young in the way you strutted about the school corridors showing off the cover of your new book. Yet it was not pride alone it was a wistful dream a defiant shy unfurling of the banner of what he hoped he would become one day a move a grasp a plan then an attack on fate a proposed meaning brave and nervous and unsure a beckoning past the shoulders of his teachers and peers toward the future threatening and hopeful. He tried on destinies like costumes each book offered him a different kind of fate a nexus of possibilities an opening onto the wonders and terrors of the *adventure of human life* there seemed no end to possibility even though each life must end in having been only itself and no other limited defined explained cataloged and dismissed at last. And yet to keep oneself open to the fact of possibility to the presence of the infinite wealth of the might be and the could hovering like great flocks of birds just over the horizon seemed to him of all things the most precious it was madness to cut oneself off from this root of fertility life existence itself it seemed foolish and self-defeating to hole oneself in the confines of a cranny in a corner of the universe when the universe itself seemed to call. The word both sheltered and released him rooted him in the orders of meaning of communion with the world and with others in the world and liberated him to touch the world with the innocence of tongue and eye. The book was a cabin in a shadow of the woods and pinions that shot him into the sky.

Yet you didn't always read the books you bought. You acquired early the bad habit of buying half a dozen books at once reading one or two of them then succumbing to the temptation of another book-buying spree (ah how I loved the subtle thrill of browsing through volumes in a bookstore weighing each book in hand flipping through its small tightly set pages smoothing my fingers over the bad slightly crusty paper smelling the glue reading the hyperbolic blurbs lingering over the design weighing the pros and cons of purchasing this legendary masterpiece against that spanking new volume by a famous contemporary name) you had an almost physical sensation of appetite of a desire to gluttonize and engorge yourself with books whenever you entered a bookstore you felt tentacles emerging from you to ingest this combination of excitement profundity and orderliness this generous gift of the world's greatest minds its most abundant spirits you could suck in through the pores of your skin as much as through your eyes you wanted to make these words part not only of your spirit and mind but of your body as well. Every bookstore had its own smell yet like that of all other bookstores. You would stand briefly inside the doorway and breathe in deep looking around you with round dazzled greedy and happy eyes. You hardly saw the people there hardly noticed them at all the girl in a winter overcoat the counterclerk looking harassed and bored no they were merely decor you already felt alone with your beloved. Then you would walk quietly with gentle tread and perfect trust to the sleepy row of bookracks. First you would visit authors you already knew fingering the spines or just grazing the covers with your eyes. You would pull out an old favorite and flip through the pages thoughtfully. Then you would move on to the much greater crowd of authors whose names were becoming familiar to you ringing down the years decades centuries (there was magic in the idea of a book that was *a hundred years old* like the great oak that stood across the road from your old home in the country ancient yet intimate obstinately pure and nobly enduring against time and its harvest of grass) and he would repeat to himself in an undertone under his breath the author's name or the names of the titles of their books like words of magic that could ward off evil shame change ignorance uncertainty loss and death. Or so he thought reasoned dreamed because after all they had lasted the books remained when all else kingships countries cities empires had failed faltered fallen vanished and now were merely names marks of ink to be found solely on the pages to be found at last only between the covers of books. And who were the masters of books? Authors! Authors who collected hecatombs of praise from the finest minds of the time! He loved the praise on the cover of the book almost as much as he loved the book and thought of history itself as a long arched hall flickering with firelight in a winter night echoing with wonder and praise. And he would count his money surreptitiously and take down one book and then another agonizing over which one he would buy could afford to buy and it was always too little for what he wanted. For he wanted more than he even then knew he had time or even stomach to read. But desire was not cautious and the hunger for books not altogether wise so he would spend all his allowance on two or three or even four books with a sigh saying farewell to the books he had to leave behind promising himself he would purchase them with his next allowance. And he would pile the books on the counter and give the money to the dubious clerk who thought the books far beyond your reading level and he was right of course and walk home with the books in a paper bag under your arm and walk upstairs at home with them and slip them out of the bag and arrange them in a carefully disposed tower on your bed table next to last week's unread books and curl up with the most intriguing cover and open to the first chapter and disappear into an afternoon of reading.

You remember the fishermen standing solitary yet together at long intervals down the shoreline their long heavy black poles held in pockets belted around their waists hanging from their groins the poles shooting toward the sky the fishline leaning out from the tips of the poles toward the dashing and scattering of the waves. The grumble and hush of the waves. And the fishermen waiting patiently stubbornly a little stupidly in the feet of the water frowning vacantly at the ancient tumult and framed with unearned majesty by the wheeling and raving of gulls.

Clouds piled pink and silent in the evening. Seen through the wind racing into the back window of a car fresh and tangy with the smell of earth and damp and leaves and grass. The onward rush of the car toward home the smell of fields and wilds of farms and woods the serene bank of cloud basking in the falling shadow of the sun.

The sough of the traffic outside your window shifts with the wind now crisp now diffuse changes with the size of the clusters of vehicles the kinds sedan coupé station wagon pickup truck bus jitney semi the size of car from dreadnaught Olds to minimalist Beetle the heft of police car the harmless ridiculous practicality of bread truck the buglike backhoe the confused tractor the formidable embarrassed and dementedly assertive steamroller crushing everything in its path into a smooth roadbed for itself. Like the world. The sound of traffic passed over him there where he read like a dream from which he emerged occasionally to listen to it and to the dim soft sound of shouting and laughter on the beach delicious and tender and distant and sad and joyful and unreachably far.

For it was by the ocean in the lazy yet strangely bracing summers that books poured out their treasures like chests from sunken pirate ships. So that there was a struggle between the paradise of books and the paradise of sea and sun and sky a war for the young boy's attention for your young and callow soul. These black gems flung out on the modest paper drew your head down and your thoughts inward while at the same time on all sides of you wheeled and crashed and soared the seabirds upswelling crests of waves the sun forever ascending through courts of palace of wind-sheered cloud and whirlwind-colored sky. The world in a seizure of universe called you to join its splendor its festival of inconsequence its riot and rule and revolt and restoration of all the tyrannies of light a crowd of faces smiling you out of yourself into their hands and arms a net of promise and prickle and thorn basking you into a gold of storm and the perils of a spinning joy and the soul's hushed world whispered through your eyes promising what what what the stillness of the reflection of a star quivering at the bottom of the well of an eye the tracing of a line through the tangle and labyrinth of circumstance of an arc across the leaping fire of the world's blaze out to the serene and calm out to the charged tranquility of the spirit enthroned at the heart of its gaze.

Where you would know the bliss of rule having held the world weighed it in the hands of your mind overruled it mastered it transformed its treacheries into invitations its betrayals into welcomes its thunder into the snapping of a winter chimney fire its autocrats into shadows thrown against a bedroom wall its dragons into unicorns its monsters into clouds its chimeras into dancers turning at the edge of sleep.

It was the other half of your life the half you discussed with no one. You held the key and shared it with none it was yours alone this world revealed in books that scaled the walls of your room as if they towered to the sky. That slipped in through cracks in the air like the root of a flower a slice a pinpoint of light opening to the tumult and blaze of a distant city filling half the sky with a cope of radiance. Books made you aware of these breaks in space and time for books revealed the only reality the reality of the slippage of the break between aspect and aspect of the world the shaft of light down an alleyway against a garage wall beckoned like the hand of an angel the shift and hush of a breeze through a glade of weed and tree seen briefly from a passing car that seemed to speak to whoever listened called to whoever saw the line of a crack across a threshold the shape of a stone the stance of a tree on a bank above a road bend the pattern of a bird's flight across the evening sky the dissolution of a cloud into ever more mysterious shapes of the world faces ever more droll acute sapient and admonitory until they all vanished into the shapeless blue grayness of twilight cloud these moments pulled you out of yourself into the clarity of the day the opacity of being fell from you you were completely transparent a lens through which the light of day passed intensifying and unifying as it went. You were a gathering of darkness and light shepherd of chiaroscuro and clarity collector of shafts of shadow and brilliance philatelist of tiny stamps of luminosity numismatist of revelations. And the clarity of the book despite all the thorns of meaning you had to cut through lay there at its center at the book's center patiently glowing and ungraspably munificent. For why should it give so much and why should it give it to you? No reason. No reason at all. Its generosity was an aspect of its being the words spilled their treasures despite themselves even when especially when their first intention was to hide to sequester their gold in a loose-lipped fog of ink an intimidating density a militant snarling of syntax. No. Not here. Not now. Ever. For initiates only. Only to those who already know will we succumb. Only to those who do not require us will we divulge our mysteries. Like the young sure of their beauty and power. Like Amazons of exegesis and interpretation who disdained the simple as facile the immediate as naive the small modest word as obscurantist and disingenuous. And who were all too often correct. For what did this word mean but another and that other yet another and that other still another in a long labor of replacements beyond which there was nothing final or certain? It was all a guess at certainty a stab in the dark many stabs at many shadows in an obscure and flickering twilight. Just when you thought you had grasped it grasped the antler of a white-tailed deer as it brushed past you in the graying wood it changed into an oak branch the body of a snake a fish tail the wing of a hawk and slipped out of your fingers away thrumming switching beating through the shadows and foliage of the night. The flight into obscurity of this glimmering and beauty a distant and seductive echo of its beauty. And you gave chase long after into the brambles stumbling ahead falling into the mud panting breathless determined and hopeless all at once feeling foolish and ecstatic and eager and lost yet feeling when you stopped and listened to the bracing air the breath of the fleeing doe the scattering of dry leaves on the path ahead the sudden stillness as though of waiting the flirtatious challenge to drive home the perilous attack and take your beloved in one final desperate all-consuming assault.

Then you woke.

From the deep dream of a long-dead author murmuring quietly into your ear of a world now no more than a litter of signs and images reflected from paper to the perplexed charities of the mind to the bright dream of the broad and present insistent and obstinate day. You would blink briefly disoriented at first the change was so abrupt. Enough dreaming now you must do something. The blood tingled in the veins the muscles ached from the fatigue of rest the doors hung open and the air outside like emptiness called for your presence to fill it. Now. Or never. It was a command and almost a fear this call to take your pleasure at once in the stark bright day. Kingly day. All light and brilliant eyes and soft embrace of hair and skin and breath and bone. Of voices beyond the threshold of your room.

So you emerged all chatter and laughter and chaff and counter chaff for the Others the jokes and asides the gripes and promises the gossip the aspersions the gaudy complaints and homely jests the crying on of games on the summer beach (hear them? do you hear the distant shouts drawing you toward them? you wonder at what is happening now drawing you to them like a magnet toward its own peculiar star) down the steps to the cement yard across the yard through the gate in the fence across the alley into the dunes across the dunes tufted with grass to the plain of the beach under disintegrating clouds through the cooling sand (it is nearly evening) plodding your way through the heavy white luxuriance of sand to where your friends played on the firm brown ground wet with ocean water leaking higher than the day's highest tide. And you joined them in their cries and their shrill laughter. Why not? The air was crisp with the crashing surf the brine thrilled your nostrils the wind flicked your face with quick sharp caress and you were off adding your cries to the distance. Hey! Whoop! Aaahheee!

The football soared up like a rocket. You rammed down the beach with all your might your small arms raised like a blessing over your head your head twisted half back over your shoulder. Run! Your heart pounds in time to your legs. You see it peak in its arc and curve the curious six-panelled pod-shaped ball and descend toward a point far no it's just ahead if you can just run hard fast long enough you'll catch it you'll catch you'll. And down the nubbed leather nose shoots right at you and your empty arms stretch out no they aren't going to make it oh no yes they are no they can't it just when they are smacked hard by the bright wet snout of leather and you almost stagger down stagger tumultuously ahead one step two then trip and splatter to the ground your arms hugging the ball to your thin pale chest. Then proud and sand-smeared and harmlessly skinned you jump to your feet and wave the prize aloft to your cheering and whistling friends.

Curl of crashing. Loughing shirts. Reeling gulls. Or just a crumb and randomness of gulls puling and squealing over the trash on the beach above the comfortable cool of the sand their veiled eyes pealed and distrustful their black heads their orange beaks open in shrill complaint and warning their graceful wings half cocked for flight even as they tear at the plastic sacking the roll crusts the banana peals and peach stones. And the toil over the sand again to the sound of your name calling down the land breeze suddenly warm and mildly stuffy and smelling of marsh grass gray and pink crushed clams mouldering ivory crabs and gully water thick with algae and impetigo the sound of your name calling you to dinner your mother not your mother or your half-sister calling and you could see her standing on the porch dim in the shuffling evening the sun gone the sky a marbled swirl of blue and yellow and pink and high pale grays banking into bright white and a massed choir of cumulus drifting like a defeated flotilla out to sea in dignified retreat into the night taking with it the fading echo of your name. And you called back and waved imagining how you must look from the porch a little stick of sun-tanned legs and white T-shirt and flickering arms and ambiguous cry to reassure them you are on your way. And turning to your friends already disappearing in the gathering dust at the bottom of the twilight trading cries of farewell till tomorrow and whoops and cries and you think how strange we look like ghosts of ourselves our voices strangely sharp and distinct though our forms have almost vanished in the dark. And one more whoop and another cry and another cry tag hey you're it and a laugh over a joke you didn't hear a joke from someone who seems so close by voice but seems so far away by the far trace of their shape and then a murmur and a skittering of back and forth and you almost wanted to go back and catch what's so funny what're they talking what's up but it's getting late and you had to go they're waiting for you for dinner. And suddenly you are off the beach and the sound of the waves shuts behind you like a door and you are out of the sound and the shadows and the cries and the murmuring and you are alone.

Pleasantly alone for everything is pleasant now whether alone or with your friends or with your family it always seems pleasant and happy and calm at heart all varieties of something unquestionably good. Unquestionably good. Happiness is given all you need do is open your hands to receive it all you need do is stop and listen and look. It requires nothing it demands nothing or so little it feels like nothing. To be there. That is all. To be. Just to be. And to accept the gift held out to you with such careless casual hands.

For the world is being offered to you. Life itself gathered in a ball like a ball of yarn is being offered to you. To trace your way as deep into the labyrinth as you may or must go. To knot and unravel the darkness there. To trace your passage into the maze of time and fate and crippling chance and duplicitous opportunity. To switch you back and forth like a cat's tail between folly and folly. To trail behind you faithfully like a memory that will not let you go. To follow you a line of dimming gray in a thickening maze of darkness. With its promise to lead you when you can or dare back into the abysses of light back out into the flowering morning of the sun pealing like a bell. To thrum like a guitar string at the moment you confront the great bull's head the snorting stinking beast. Such a thread. Such a gift if you knew how to use it. Such the promised kingdom rising stone by stone at the invisible heart of the labyrinth.

Yet how easy to drop the thread and wander blind and lost in the labyrinth. For years on bitter years. Lost. Blind. Alone. Decades. For the rest of a life. Having lost the gift which was merely acceptance of the gift. Staggering into walls that merely threw you back into the embrace of the maze.

You walked up the stairs to the apartment at the head. They were there waiting for you though they did not appear to be waiting they did not let it appear so plain. But they were you knew it the call of your name still lingered in the room the call from the porch outside the french doors. A little irritable wave of impatience swelled across the dinner table at your entrance as you hastened to your seat half breathless and embarrassed and a little defiant carrying a little stream behind you of the cheerful darkness of the beach. The plates were still full an impatient sound of tapping fork interrupted only by the usual hectic rush of words from his half sister half brother tangling good-naturedly in a spat invented for the sake of the moment's entertainment. The mother pretended to be appalled between laughing attack and retort. The little drama and comedy boiled up and simmered down all play and feigning ambush farce of battle amiable insult. He rarely joined these frays but sat quietly eating meditative smiling laughing mildly at the strongest jokes feeling vaguely ill at ease. As though despite the requirement of his presence he did not perfectly belong in that magic circle made up of mother and sister and brother to be precise stepmother and half sister and half brother however often they reminded him that he was perfectly welcome among them and equally valued and loved. The words hovered in the air before him. Equally valued and loved. His father was often not there. To be precise his father. Not this summer evening or many another work demanding his absence. The one to whom he indubitably belonged no reassurance required. As he had always known. Thought. Thought he had known. You. Thought you had known. The one idea to which you clung. Hiddenly clung. That sustained you among the uncertainties elsewhere and everywhere was elsewhere. Your little pride. His little pride. Drawn up like a proud little horse on parade. Irritating foolish childishly pompous and prideful the link to this one absolute love. To the earth that had given him birth. To the chain of time that linked him now to the deepest hollow of his past. To the one brightness in the unravelling dark. Yet not dark bright in its way and warm and kind and generous oh how kind they were how generous yes and yet in the end not his as he could never be entirely theirs. Never. He never felt entirely theirs though he loved them. Only to his father did he belong. Laugh or condemn who may. Or laugh and condemn. Among whom he was a stranger.

So it played out yet again on this evening as on others the cramp as he sat partially ignored a witness and audience to the happiness and the love of the others. Locked out by their bond. And oh how anguishing the more because so clearly unintended. How the look once in a while of one of them to you burned with its welcome come join us you're one of us too which said so clearly you are not one of us and never can be but we will share our happiness with you we will share with you our love. Here. Take it. It is yours as well. Whereas the real bond never speaks so never thinks so never regards itself as anything but what it is inevitable unspeakable inescapable the small change in fate's iron hand.

And so he left wrapped in warmth while he chilled in solitude alone. Bewildered into silence. Reprieved yes but only because he was in reality guilty. Of what? Of what? Of what? *He asked the sky and asked the sun and moon and the clouds and stars and the fields and woods and the sea and the serene wall of spines still and erect and faithful as sentinels of his books.* He could not ask the faces that shone in the box of leaves and snake skulls and the litter of dead flowers and ashes of incense the dust of small talk and the silence of hours that marked the limits and boundaries of his home.

And yet this was love.

Perhaps the answer will be found in this book.

Or the next one.

Or the next.

Or the next.

For it was as if this too were part of the dream you had merely interrupted on your bed. There where reality raised to you between your open hands its wounded and flowering eyes. And gazed at you. In wonder so like your own. The world a child gazing at you and mouthing whispering on the other side of a wire fence on which its fingers were hooked. Oh what was it saying? No matter how hard you listened no matter how hard you gazed. The meaning paled and disappeared into the white stillness. Like fish in a pond. Rising to nibble the surface then falling back into darkness. You wanted to fall into it and melt into its waters. Its perpetual murmur and gaze. The pond and eyes of the witness and the listening. This child.

And yet not all. Some swept all before them. Intransigent. Demanding. Seductively intense like a warm finger on your elbow. Almost frighteningly sure yet inviting even welcoming to their worlds of passionate alarm and impossible promise baleful threat and paradisal allure of intricate darkness unfurling in explosions of a brief all-illuminating light. Those voices. Passionate and low yet turning into shouts inside you so arousing they left behind no coherent thought only the wind and thunder of a tempest of words. A fugue of voices a mob of passionate cries filling the theaters of his mind till they rang with echoes for days weeks months on end. Pulling him in a thousand directions demanding his allegiance to a thousand conflicting causes. Out. Away. Beyond. Toward every point of the compass. Away from where he was away from who he was. From who he was there was liberation but also danger. He was swept up in directions not his but to which he submitted trustingly even happily even with relief. And the rush that clasped and smuggled him away pulled him back in time to the past a past peopled with richly garbed presences eyes flashing with invitation and peril a shoulder turning a back eloquently still a hand raised in mute beckoning a hat cocked up in genial mockery a rush of beards and glinting spectacles a crowd of eloquent dead men and women pressed into his mind with clearer and more persistent shape than anything he saw in his own world more so even than the moving face the magic carpet of television offered its ability to show the world from any point within it. But compared to what the book offered him all the screen presented were bloodless puppets uttering dismal inanities without eloquence or power or truth or music the screen had no inwardness and knew no nobility its light was a fog of ions rushing at the apex of a cone of babbling vacancy its words disemboweled of meaning its time no time a shallow rootedness in the empty now a scum on the pool of the present a continuous self-erasure there was no time on television because there was no past its vividness was a mockery of its emptiness its purpose to destroy meaning and purpose except to bend the spectator to seduce you to its will. Which was to watch obediently and purchase the wares it extolled. Whereas the book gave its reader sovereign freedom along with its gift of the past of time frozen into an immensely complex and graceful shape its words almost too rich in meaning its ever deepening of the present with the echoes of the never-yielding past. The past which stood against the present like a martyr before a vulgarian petty criminal and fool for whom the martyr had died leaving his ashes and the memory of his words as a testament. The past whose death was life just as the life of the present was the incarnation of death. And so he sank gradually at first and then completely into a hopeless and futile worship of the past and contempt for the present that subtly undermined him without his realizing it forced as he was to pursue his life in a time he came one day to condemn as inescapably worthless.

By definition. In effect.

For it was the very presentness of the present pressing its sloppy muzzle to your face screaming petulantly into your ear snagging your shirt in its dirty fists and bellowing at you demanding everything immediately at once and never satisfied with anything that was offered shrieking in the wind against your door and rattling the closed window it was the totality and endlessness of its demand that made you close and lock a private and internal door against it close your eyes and ears to it and curl into a dream enclosed in the castle of your mind drawn up in a throne room enriched with the furnishings and decor of the deep and dead past. Its ghosts living once again within you rank on rank of phantom at your beck and call. Servants of your imagination and will. While the present howled futile and hapless in idle possession of the world but annulled in its search for your soul the conquest of your mind its nails slipping off the glass you turned to it its teeth chipping on the lock.

Until one day …

It was not one day. It grew over days. It grew over years. It insinuated itself into you got under your skin like a chigger buried its eggs in you at last like a wasp in the body of a caterpillar. It came to feed on you for you were its nourishment. Then one day it opened your belly and filled the air around you with the harpy wings of its children.

The present. Medusa of now.

The periphery curled up at its edges first showed signs of strangeness a wilting that was also the crisping of the nob at the end of a stem a flair of danger and dare in the eyes of classmates a restless angry flippancy a hungry strangely lustful optimism seeded the air like heavy dew on a late spring morning. Something under the skin of light that covered the air like cellophane was stirring. Awake almost but not quite. About to open its eyes then open the day like a drunken surgeon. Dangerous and necessary and brutally young. Stupid and sharp and cruel. Hollow with a hunger for time. Exacting. Libertine. Monstrous. Inhuman as only the human can be.

6

But only lurking as yet in the lunchrooms and playgrounds and absent after-school corridors of the schools he knew that bored with stubborn and monotonous regularity a nattering insistence on their own shadowy and hectoring inconsequence. Nullity raised to a chant twelve years long. Droning at the head of the class. While the barbarians fletched their arrows and tongued poison to the barbs. Pygmy-like. Snickering among themselves in the bush. Itchy. Yet patiently waiting. For the world to fall like an over-ripe plum into their hot little laps.

The coming of reality. That was it. It was not to be denied but only avoided as long as possible. Until it was no longer possible. Until it surrounded you and paraded you through the rioting streets of the city face to face with the fury of your peers.

.

Rumors of war. They rose on every side at that time. The daydream of annihilation occupied regular afternoons civilization's burial under a hammerhead cloud. It was hard not to live without a taste of nerves in the mouth and a doubt about any possible future. Futile as that despair turned out to be. Hope itself was a marker of the child one could not soon enough leave behind. Physical comfort was nightmare's bed. Money was the short change of oblivion an obscene and humiliating joke. The past was prolog to a shout of grief and sweeping devastation.

It was becoming increasingly difficult to hide find a quiet dark corner in which to weave his fantasies of delight. The light was spectral and lurid the music raucous and vulgar. Silence was canceled in a mob of furious shouts and imperious futile demands. The adults shrugged and sneered or panicked with baffled righteousness. They were the ones you honored sometimes pitied despite their foolishness even now. Not the nihilists who harrowed the schoolyards with their bullying mockery and all-destroying innocence. The sneering rictus of their fear.

There were those who softened and waited with an almost complicitous patience a generous openness that let small anarchic whirlwinds score the dirt and blind the air with the moment's accusations. Moments of clarity insinuated between hours of dust storm. A smile a joke a sigh. A patient ear. A friend here and there crystallized out of the smoke and static and reflected back a yes to your yes a no to your no a comfort that you were not wholly alone in the desert brilliant jungle dark. Yes even here even now the void does not gnash everything into its inscrutable plain of waste. Or not yet.

Steve Adams for one. Quiet patient smiling wise a friend. A friend. That mysterious term no one can quite comprehend the how of. He cocked an eye beneath his heavy dark brows and smiled his kind ironic smile shrugged easily but without malice traded bits of lunch at the outside lunch table traded school gossip with a light heart and a skeptical eye slipped away from confrontation with a laugh that stopped in his mouth. Olive-complected. Serene. Much alone but never hungrily lonely. You bandied between you jokes about your loftily bewildered elders those fools of owlish learning and frazzled responsibility those others you were both headed outward toward becoming. Resignedly. Whose power and folly could make your life a little finely calibrated hell. At the flick of a misunderstanding. Or even something more banal. Something akin to malice. Or incomprehensibly and thus more terrible still. Envy.

We saw it in the glistening white triangles at the corners of their eyes. We saw it but had no name for it and so we made up brutal jokes to defend ourselves from its cloying and malignant thrust. We slaughtered their dignity in little ritual murders of shame covered them with disgrace parried envy with contempt into their hatred buried our fear.

Because we could not even begin to fight our peers. Which is where our terrors really began. Adulthood was a caricature of life so far from us we couldn't take it seriously. Not entirely seriously. Our parents lived in a pantomime and noisy silence our teachers were humbugs and bullies adults were nightmares and therefore as spectral as they were awful. Great cloudy ghosts threatening us with a distant future. They held our lives in their hands as it were abstractly. A bomb. A nuclear bomb. A herald of universal destruction utterly unreal. Whereas the other little boys and girls around us had all the pathetic inescapability of a small dull pen knife squeaky with corrosion.

No we could not face them. So we hid. And shot ineffectual barbs at the leprous titans our masters.

We were allies. Yes that was it. Around us we built a rough fort of wattled fencing and staves and inside it we crouched hidden from the grosser stupidities of the world. The insults of adults and fellows. The humiliations of matter and man. The offense of everything that was not ourselves. And we warmed with an indefinable happiness.

For a time. A time. A lovely time. But only a time. Only the time they inhabited the space and time they shared.

For the fort made as it was of shared glances and the relay of words that dovetailed with a neatness he had never known in family or school collapsed as soon as they were outside each other's range and he was once again buffeted by impatience and incomprehension the rude blank look of the human.

.

Somewhere back there. But where. There. Somewhere ...

.

... most easily found between the covers of certain. Books.

Them again. The change of color between two dark-bellied clouds. The moment daily hourly yearly when the world changed outside the possibilities of the human. Went from vast gray to an enormous greenness to motley gorgeousness to white and ghostlike triumphs cold pressed out of the raging heat. Books or the strange glory of music. Not now. But if not now when? Oh music music! It is too much now. That vast country. Those overpowering nights. That august grandeur of an inconceivable joy. Yes. Not conceivable. That ecstasy greater than the meeting of bodies. The debauchery of the mind making that of the body seem childish and frail a prelude and shadow to this to this the kiss of. For one was meeting. For one was facing. Melting into. Becoming. Losing self and mortality in. What? Call it what? That immemorial and inadequate syllable? Call it the divine call it the sacred the godhead call it God? Hopeless? Or call it nothing at all all these words a hopeless substitute for the name that cannot be found? It would take you too far! But it would take you far. For only it was the book's rival. The word beyond the word the voice of the depth of the sky that cradled the world in its arms. And it would remain so. At war in his mind. Another empire another allegiance. Oh far!

Unspeakable. That is what makes it a danger the danger. There never were the words for it. Enough or remotely the kind. All that could not be spoken was encompassed in its black radiance. His mouth fell at the thought of it. He grew stupid at the first whisper of that choir.

Yes.

No!

Yes you must. Sometime. When? Then. Then. Sometime.

... can't this wait? No. The majesty of the mortal imagination its gift to the hour of something outside the hour the gift of the savoring of untime was partly glimpsed in the formal disarrays and crystalline gentleness sublimities and exhaustions of an intricate progression a melody a modulation gallop vivace the lingering of an adagio or the gouge of a stinger the subito pause before the rush into a coda and the hammering single detached chords hammering the final cadence home. The thrill and call of tonic and dominant haunted his mind played weft to the bus growl on his way to school. The mysteries of the sixth chord the sweet dischord of the seventh the squabblings between major and minor the melting of boundaries of chords augmented diminished the diabolical pretensions of the tritone juggled in his mind with the plangent mourning of English horn pearly breathiness of flute piano seductions tympanic spine-tingling abruptness the magniloquence of brass the strings' drunken velvet. He felt seduced and martyred to the beauty of sound his spirit grew drunk and danced alone in the stillness just as books seduced him to the beauty of dream that opened worlds to him even as he lay quiet and unmoving on his bed. He was taken into another world of splendor and sign of intensities scuffed with meaning far beyond the everyday world he knew yet part of it one to which he had access almost at will. It was as though in the ordinary world there were doors that opened to the infinite. Through doors marked Beethoven Schubert Mahler Mozart Bach Wagner. He could not stay there long he always had to return before he was ready had to return to spend the bulk of his hours in the banal tough little scrimps and tweaks of everyday life potholes of dullness and scrambling. But the doors though closed were not locked were indeed always ajar and bits of radiance leaked around the edges reminding him if only just enough to set him dreaming. The warmth filtered through the blank brightness of ordinary day.

It leaked in elsewhere he found. He had always known it in the rustling of the life of the world beyond the human only here first in music and books did he find it in the human as well focussed to a point framed as in a theater where it could be dwelled on enjoyed wondered at questioned the mystery at the edges of life revealed in peril and hope played out in inhuman worlds of sound and story tone and phrase unleashed to their own provocations. It was like nature itself small and fragile and intricately fertile of shape and color and form of life willing to bring more of itself always into a world vast as the sky grand as the night dense as marble and blinding as the eye of the sun. All of this in small and large reflected in music and books and later on in paintings photographs movies wait and here he paused confused unsure only in certain books in certain music in the occasional painting he found reproduced in a book photograph found in a magazine the rare movie in fact so rare that when he saw one that echoed back to him his own feeling for what he called the mystery he sensed behind the world it shocked him and changed his mind about movies for good. And this distinction between works of art that expressed and revealed that mystery that hung like a backdrop behind the natural world and glimmered deep in people's eyes beyond even their own knowing the mystery of being itself and as he discovered to his surprise those that do not alarmed and intrigued him. Because not only was there a distinction between them there was even a hostility a refusal to respect the other's truths a refusal to understand one another a mutual distrust and disdain. There was art that let the mystery in and left it alone unanswered unanswerable and art that denied it would not leave it alone goaded and prodded it into an answer it would never give or worse denied any mystery flashed it away in a wave of cheerful steely-eyed contempt. Critics. Of a kind. The professional suspicion of mystery. You loved the first but the second perplexed you you could not understand the violence of its rejection its fear of and need to remove all trace of the unanswerable all shadow all smear across its window of the unknowable the ungraspable its angry and hurt mistrust its insistence on itself its naked and exasperated egotism. Yet you were drawn to it despite. What drew you was its dry hurt gaze the wound behind the intolerable mask.

And so you were pulled and drawn between the poles of your love and your perplexity annointing the perplexity with your love stinging your love with bafflement. Did the crown of beauty circle a mind of evil? Did evil's fist hold within it beauty's cry? Did evil and suffering shape beauty's clay into the spirit's delight? Did beauty hide evil's face behind a betraying mask? Or or or …

And his mind began to turn like an eddy disturbing the surface of a pool in the fall woods.

These then enclosed him opened worlds within him gave him the same sense of safety and adventure beyond what even friendship did. Love promised. Dangerously close to the living glance the quick shared sigh. Until they became more human more world more embedded and glowing in the real than anything merely human flesh and blood stumbling through syntax and time. They made it almost too easy to be free.

But you didn't care. Here was joy indeed daily hourly in great armloads who would have been weak-spirited enough to deny it to walk away to the virtuous drudgery of the merely physical and mortal? Arrogant? Foolish? Self-destructive? Self-defeating? Yes. Childishly sublime. A burnished and burning mirage of heroism more desired than its sweaty and bruised reality. That grew into the determination and despair of the over-weaning would-be. Young fool. Dreamer. Wool-gatherer. Fabulist. Megalomaniac. Conqueror. Artist. A word he could intone solemnly to himself without a trace of ironic detachment.

Until he applied it to himself. Then the skittering of gnashing sarcasm teethed his tender ego until it stung his mouth with gall. And he shouted to himself spitting out the word he had sucked on before so indulgently.

You? An artist?

Fool. Idiot.

The war deepened. He felt it become the hidden agenda of every conversation. It poisoned the air at school tarnished the air at home provoked disputes and skirmishes without any of the participants realizing what had been the underlying cause. It strained and broke friendships created enemies and lovers heightened tensions between the generations sealed the distrust between sons and fathers. An air of hysteria insinuated itself into the streets never far from the surface waiting for a chance to discharge like lightning building in the hot darkening air. And not alone the war abroad. There was the war at home the war between black and white between young and old between man and woman between left and right between future and past between the anarchy of sexual expression and the hierarchies of sexual control between freedom and form chaos and order destruction and creation desire and death. Hope pooled forces with anger into a torrent of moral delirium in the streets marched bannered to the echoing rallies denouncing with all the blindness of innocence and the drugged ecstasies of righteousness the country's follies the nation's crimes the criminal tolerance of anarchy the ferocious denial of freedom the mutual oppression refusal of justice. The police became the armies of the enemy the young the barbarian hordes.

The air reeked of gasoline and poetry.

And you were hungry to take part in the tidal sea you felt rising around you terrible as a hurricane sea pushing everything before it sweeping you and your peers what they called a generation up over the coastal islands and across the inlets and harbors and coves up and over and across the cities of the plain.

It was impossible for you to stand detached and removed to remain the spectator observe and study take your intellectual and spiritual treasure and depart. Though this is what you pretended even to yourself at the time. At the time.

He started to attend marches and rallies to join picket lines to sit huddled at spontaneous meetings at lectures and seminars where theories of the war were expounded and theories of revolu-tion insinuated eyebrows cocked fists raised in favorite salutes blood-thirstiness encouraged even as it was denounced. Anger called to anger down the canyons of the hour.

Rage became one of his favorite words.

Yet it was a riot of shadows and ghosts a mob of shapes without substance wraiths of void and fierce eyes their mouths jabbering incomprehensibly into the clotted air. It was a vast and furious dream a nightmare of the herd stampeding a plain with no direction but the hard vector of flight.

Despite the rhetoric of the hour. Despite the apocalyptic hope. Despite the drugged promises and the dionysiac air. At the edge of the plain the earth dropped and the herd poured into space like a river down a fall.

This was that river this was that fall. But none knew that the sensation of flight was the pleasure of collapse. Or that the sensation of collapse was the promise of flight.

He did not either but shook with joy and terror by turns like everyone else at that carnival of bliss and destruction.

He burrowed even more deeply into music and books music to escape the moment books to lift him above it he hungered for insight and reassurance if not harmony and light at least dominance and escape. The world shouted a demand in the darkness a cry that was both command and plea a code of warning and promise that he was trying to decipher it lay beneath his hands and he could not meet it or thrust it away but the shout of pain and anger still rang in his ears. He was tempted to run away and he did when the shout became unendurable he ran to the furthest reaches of his mind and curled up in sunny nostalgia sighing for the lost fields and woods of his childhood. It grew harder to bear after his father left the family near collapse the support reduced to one an atmosphere of subdued panic filled the house and the hysteria of the world penetrated and lashed the rooms. His only haven was his room propped up on his bed a book against his knees a single star penetrating the window above his head. The crisp sound of the stylus as it found a record's groove lovely antique sound. The familiar sound of dust and the held breath before the first tone. Or the resonating silence after the victorious crashing chord.

His soul curled up inside him like the overly tightened spring of a watch. The falling of a leaf made him twitch. A feather's touch made him seize and spring. He carried a ticking bomb in the pocket of his mind.

Then one day he opened a book as hard as stone.

There were books that flattered and absolved. There were books that amused and books that seduced books that thrilled and books that terrified books that bowed and scraped the reader to the very end and books that stood aloof and impenetrable watching the reader with a sullen implausible detachment and a strangely thirsty disdain. It seemed to him now that most put the reader at the center of the book and in this way fascinated and conquered. Not that he thought of this at the time he simply took full advantage of the author's need to be read listened to followed briefly and enthroned for an hour in the reader's mind. To trade identities with the reader to be brought briefly to life again then returned unceremoniously to the graveyard of the shelf. (For authors were by definition dead.) He had not met an author whose attitude toward the reader was not one of the highest if not deepest respect. He had not met an author whose main intention was to wrestle with the reader force him to look and dare him to act knock him to the ground conquer him and challenge him to fight back. A living author who would not pretend to be dead.

One day he opened a book. It was as though an arm rose from the pages and seized him by the throat and a voice angry learned and terribly clear said look hear listen act. Who are you. What do you know. What do you believe. What have you done. What will you do. What will your life have been worth.

A book that nailed him to the dock of his own judgment. A whirlwind of precise condemnation. A book dedicated to the chisel of the word no. Not this. Not that. Not that. Every answer responded to with condemnation.

A voice like his father's.

Remember then now. The small thick book with the nondescript cover. A scholarly book with a mildly defiant tone in its title a hint of challenge whisper of brimstone. You bought it on impulse for no reason but the shadowy lark of the moment. Pressed the crisp bag containing it under your arm and walked briskly through the cool spring afternoon home. Shyly proud. Of what? Of the names dropped there like drops of rain on a parched tongue. Names to conjure the hour with. Names in your private hierarchy of angels and heroes. Demonic names secret names. Almost forgotten names. That peopled the pantheon of your imagination with the sweet and demanding hopes of your future. Like promises. Like commands. Like an awe-inspiring welcome. Such was your private childlike and trembling romance. You would live if only to join them in the heaven they defined of the past. The past! So you dreamt of your future. As of a past already unfolded and only to be found and worn like a cloak. The past! The names! The noble tomorrow you rose toward like a dream.

So what was your shock when the words that rose to meet you ungentle but not unkind faced you with a past as unsettled as now as undefined and suspended in eternal unknowing as any uncertain future. Hard and austere and unknown and fiercely exhilarating. In a voice that spoke across to you not as to a reader a child a boy as you were still but as to an adult to a man. That did not rest you in its flattering arms but put you on the spot and demanded of you. Tested you. Demanded. Decide. Soon. Decide now. How shall you live.

It was like no book you had ever read. There was no page no line no word in it that invited you to rest. Each sentence sparkled clear and hard with a strange toughness with edges that cut even as they shone with unsmoothed corners and stiletto-like points with hard and unanswered questions. The voice was uncompromising unsettlingly clear and sharp truculent at times irritable at others at no time obscuring its questions or softening the brightness of its unconsoling light. It hit hard and unrelenting with as much heat as light though on topics abstract academic obscure in a voice that never hid its human demand. Its impatient and angry dissatisfaction. Its hunger. You flew through the book in alarm and dismay and thrill. You had never been spoken to so clearly. No. With such driven honesty such hard sharp truthfulness. About the names! Making them live again the mighty dead as they had not yet lived for you and they were the most living things you knew. Outside the woods. The ocean. Clouds. The sun.

What names? What matter. Enough to know that they lived. Across the dead hollow of time across the decades the centuries across millennia. Millennia. Those great dead ghosts that will not die.

Your head spun. Never before had a book had such an effect on you. You felt dumbstruck assaulted dizzied by the panorama shown you swept up and giddied with a cold clear thrill the exhilaration of a sovereign clarity of mind. No one would be allowed to get away with anything again. The tale-tellers and frauds the charlatans the phony pabulum masters would be nailed to the wall with their own hammers. You felt a strange rarefied intoxication as though you had been granted second sight. You might almost become able you thought to lift a corner of the mask. To see. To see through. To see through the here and now. To see through to the other side however terrifying it might prove to be. To see through the cynicism and despair of the world that surrounded you. To see through yourself.

And it was at that realization that the sense of thrill skidded into a kind of panicky desperation. Salvation depended on catching yourself before you were caught in a trap from which you might never escape yet how could you being you ever hope to catch yourself ever know yourself thoroughly clearly and deeply enough bend a mind blinded and a will-power weak to the point of frailty bring it to a light you could not see or to a strength you had never known? You knew you felt you knew you thrashed between a despairing certainty and a muted hope that you would never be able to rise to the hard bright pinnacle of those words never rise to the occasion be able to open your eyes so unpityingly and follow the brief sharp demand for action never meet the steady level gaze with your own or answer word for word. And you threw the book down and left the house irritated and anxious.

Always again to return. For the voice was seductive. And the demand profoundly flattering. He felt hounded and battered and assaulted and watched. Sternly thrillingly exultantly. Put on the spot at the end of an accusing finger. Made to feel both guilty and essential required in the working out of a destiny. Not a throw away. Not a redundancy. Not meaningless. At least for as long as he submitted to the dry tart-tongued fascination of that book. That feast of goads and questions. The sneer and scowl and lashing out. The ridicule that hid the scalded disappointment. The glare and exaltation of those words.

In the end the book confused and bewildered him. For all its brightness and clarity he felt himself wandering blind and wounded in a wilderness of implications lost in a stinging swarm of contradictory demands. What the book called for was a ruthless penetrating and detailed honesty one that was so exacting even painful the young reader could not focus it clearly. Yet the legitimacy of the demand was not in question. Once heard it could only be followed however reluctantly. It swept away all other values like a moral hurricane.

After laying aside the volume he felt a great and terrible calm come over him and the sense of sitting in a cool room filled with a steady light. The conflicts that had ruled his mind and life fell away the teasing delusions mocking pleasures suspect joys tedious angers fears regrets envies. What was left was the transparent hour and a brightness amid the shadows of time. What was left was a finger pointing to a simple demand.

Yet not so simple. For something testy and irritable ran down the back of the time something that made him wonder how if ever he might join the occasion evoked by the book. Its challenge. Its dare.

Thus under the calm hour there grew a new but focussed uncertainty. Whether he might meet it. Now or ever. And on the other side a subtler struggle. Whether he should. And the combat within him grew wings of definition. His mind became a battleground between a desire for truth and a despair of truth. A field of skirmishes and ambush. A war with only brief victories and many defeats. For either side. A war without end. As he would learn. Eternal war. Between the intoxication of the dream and truth's flat clarities. Reality's reassuring banality and illusion's mocking happiness. The promise of the one poisoned by the provocations of the other. The crippling and the shipwreck and the treachery. The delirium of a hope endlessly repeated and endlessly deferred. The two worlds locked in each other's arms in hatred and desire unspeakable longing unbearable demand intolerable pride infinite sweetness.

He closed the book with a slam and walked outside for hours.

7

The hook lunges across the air above the waves out out beyond the foam then down in a splash and little crown of seawater and gulls flutter up on askant wings puling in alarm at the treacherous arrival. A blue flops heavily at the bottom of a metal bucket its gills lift swell puff retract as it slowly drowns in the air. At the triumphant feet of the. Fisherman. The sun signs the air with its finger.

The village sleeps. Although the morning has not advanced beyond the net of sighs the lingering of flocks stunned and deaf despite the wintry lapses the corraled hopes. It sleeps. Midnight has come and gone without a sound obscurity broods on its defeats. Fail fail the bell tolls and the silence pricks up its ears. In the rural outback between the switchback roads a cunning of foxes meets a loyalty of wolves. The fur bristles on the shy hides. Bare and plotting the moon slinks through fistfuls of branches and abandoned leaves to the secret heart of a stucco room snared in the web of a dream. She whispers his future into his ear.

.

Between the woman and the book a war began. Unknown to you its extent and depth its life-long implications. For the woman begat other women and the book begat other books. They unfolded out from each other like fans the wings of toy angels the span of a dragonfly across a farm pond. Between them they held you up carried you carried you over the field of battle enjoined that year. Your little war inside the larger one. The larger one that swelled and overwhelmed the little one like a wave. Like a midnight sea. Like light itself. Sharp-edged hard-fisted nervous light. That would not leave the darkness alone. That bullied and pummeled the darkness into a bruise of mortified exposure.

Here. See this? Take more.

It was not as though life were not a series of carpets being pulled from under him at every turn. Not yet. He was still spared the indignity of annihilation as farce the pathetic wrenching and sapping of personal drama flitters and dregs of one's own little soap opera no what he was granted with a generosity he was still too young to appreciate was the ritual grandeur of a national tragedy that left a generation a moral wreck. Not for the first time in his bloody gaudy century or so as he learned from the books and not for the last as he learned from the women. A continuous one seeming to play out in different arenas for the benefit of different audiences here brushing a corner a ruined family wondering what appalled mistake had taken it out and down there entertaining the global village with the operatic carnage of world war a nonstop tape of ludic gore complete with sidesplitting mortifications public shamings and a laugh track of ridicule punctuated by sarcastic outpourings of liberal piety and horrified scorn the mill of blame grinding slow. Grinding fine. Distant outbursts of laughter. Appalling silences. Irritated coughs. Occasional sneezes. Stifled yawns. Even slaughter growing tiresome in the end. The rack of heads surrounding the century glaring gape-mouthed in all directions.

And the barbarians were now descending to the valleys from

which you had been withdrawn and the citadel of darkness and squalor to which you had been sentenced. The age seemed to be in the jaws of several wars at once each trying by and for itself alone to tear its prey to pieces. But the prey glared its fangs and savaged back leaning over the mirror of hatred and succumbing to its unconquerable power. Oh love? What was that? It forgot what it loved in the delirium of the taste for blood no not that. Worse than that. For blood honors the enemy. Contempt. And lost love in the same shrug that lost all of awe.

Whirlwinds descending across the land.

From every point of the compass dust devils slip and stutter into funnels of tornado and dance drunkenly across the plains. The desert opens at the feet of the mountains. O daughter mine in the bed of cactus and dry arroyo. The loudspeakers wail like sirens. A cacophony closing on a jeremiad. And laughter. Such laughter!

Or so it seemed nothing else or less. Sold. Down the pike. Genially raped. Violated not to put too fine a point on it. Imperially as was fit. Properly dead and no mistake. Good fellow!

Torn between three jaws or three thousand. What rose to meet him out there. Where he ran to escape the book. Or the woman. The woman! The book! A war is on.

.

How describe the battles that took place almost entirely offstage thus all the more. Terrible. Terrible and unreal. It hooked beneath his skin and slowly pulled him inside out. Like a sock. So that his internal organs lay like large soft medals hanging on the outside of his torso. And he holding back his cry because if he started he would not be able to stop. Until he dissolved into one loud unbearably long shout like a violin made of spine and gristle that split apart in a final soaring scream.

Silent. Frozen. Invisible. He did not dissolve or disappear. He remained watching lusting with his eyes what he denied with his hands listening with his touch tasting with his mind denying and devouring penetrating and vomiting murdering what he could not ingest ingesting what he could not conquer assassinating time with blind will. Until it tasted touched lusted conquered murdered denied devoured. Him.

That year he knocked skulls with the future. Any future. Yours. Ours. Imagine a colony of ants exasperated to fury by the pokings of a young boy stirring their nest with a burning stick. They belch into the empy lot in their hundreds. Increase the size of the ants then the size of the colony. A thousand fold. Ten million fold. Imagine them swarming a continent in their raging.

Another man is killed one afternoon in a southern city. Another leader vaguely admired by him as more sharply by many others more significant than he would ever be. It jolts him awake as the previous killing had jolted him asleep seemed too horrible to dwell on and unravel its conclusions. Something sharp cold and clear falls then from his eyes like two cracked shells. And his eyes bathe in the hard white light. As before they had crawled back into his skull like two mice. From that other death. The death that opened the chasm at his feet. Or no that first knocked on the bottom of his feet announcing the frailty of mother earth and all that inhabited it.

Crack of a rifle. A small bullet falls from a window in a southern city. It spirals through the air in a slightly depressed arc at an angle several degrees below the horizon moving as it does so a fraction out of alignment due to a flaw in its manufacture. It moves resolutely for an inanimate yet forcefully projected object toward its goal. Toward the shootist's goal. The rifleman's loving and much beloved target. For is there anything more beloved than a target by its bullet or its gunner? One longs for it as a believer longs for his god lover for beloved body for body sex for sex soul for soul. And nothing satisfies till it smashes into it for a moment becomes it for a moment becomes. In a flash of darkness blotting out the abysses of light. A moment of ecstatic disappearance. Transcendent. So the bullet moves with amazing speed across the southern sun above the heads of the crowd watching the motorcade then over the grass of the lawns and the cement of the roadway down and across too fast to see a shadow or one that so flickered and was gone it hardly grazed the surface of macadam then soared over the tailend of the limousine black in the shining light then seemed to pause lovingly over the young leader's hair blowing slightly in the convertible's backwind a little colic upgrown at the crown of his handsome head then threw itself into the skull shattering the skull's plate and sinking into the gray tissue of brain too sudden for the mind that had the brain to conceive what this sudden darkness was and where it had come from and what had smashed its head in as it twisted did it twist? into abrupt and absolute (but after all is there no) I was just waving at that young couple (after?) termination.

You had seen the young leader before he assumed his mantle. Once in the artificial light and darkness of a television studio where your father sneaked you in you saw the candidate in the glow of his smile talking to his aides after a broadcast then turn and look your way. Turn and look your way. Where the young boy stood dressed formally in jacket and tie a large campaign button pinned to his handkerchief pocket his own face smiling fit to burst he could feel it. With bright shy joy. The young leader about to be about to come over to him perhaps shake his small hand he could hear the voice with the already immediately recognizable accent say something charming and witty and slightly patronizing but well-meant and glowing over him radiantly for a moment then turn away to the next appointment on the pressing schedule of a presidential campaign but instead just as he knows instinctively the young candidate is about to approach his young supporter you are yanked out of the studio into a corridor all flat gray light pulled along it to an office where an agitated man talks angrily to someone on the phone then to your father the phone slams into its cradle the voice is testy then your father who says nothing abruptly leaves with his son who suddenly feels ridiculous and small and in the way as they walk to the parking lot get into his father's small car and drive home with few words. Not sure if you should be proud or ashamed of your adventure you breathe a word of it to no one. But you remember it as a kind of happy secret you share with your father. And feel a kind of proprietary pride in the young leader when a few weeks later you sit up watching the election returns as late as your parents will let you and learn next morning that during your hours of dream your hero of the hour was elected the country's president. A strange victory that depended entirely on the approbation of others somehow tainted and obscurely unsatisfying dependent and cloying a cleft victory a triumph that could be questioned yet victory still and sweet despite. And the young boy felt vindicated even smug since his position had been a minority one at school though not in the country the knowledge of which dented his smugness only a little. And he followed the progress of the new president as he took control of office as he had been more obscurely but trustingly aware of the previous one an affable grandfatherly figure he knew to have been a great war hero though without any of the obvious vices or graces one would expect from such neither splendor nor arrogance just a muteness as of a mothballed battleship. And began to read the news magazines received regularly at his family home and to acquaint himself with the political and social issues of the time.

The drama of which thrilled and alarmed you. The enormity of it. The danger a danger of annihilation not fable or myth but present like a cloud encroaching on the sun. The wing of a massive bird approaching across the sky.

The possibility of it iced the steps of the day when you looked up its coldness iced the news with an unease clouded with permanent anxiety the headlines always pointing elsewhere as if to avoid it every incident rippling outward toward yet fleeing unthinkable possibilities.

That must be thought. Or fled. And thought. Then fled. But thought. Both thought and fled in a kind of controlled hysteria. Sirens howled in the distance and you had obediently knelt beneath your desk. Feeling frightened and obscurely foolish. And now the war of words sank its fangs into your mind trying to frighten you into concession and obedience deeper than prayer in a suburban bedroom into assertive even militant participation. A side must be chosen. You were being asked to join but what was it exactly? And who exactly were the enemies the holders of destruction in their fat blackened arms? Grinning with triumph as they volatilized into dust and fire.

A childish patriotism swept him up. The flag bannered in his mind the anthem chanted thrillingly the idea of his country enchanted him he gave in to the instinctive desire to trust his leaders even as he trusted blindly as he felt he had no choice but to trust his parents his teachers his doctor the police the school principal. His parents. His teachers. His doctor. The police. The school principal. His leaders. He followed it was easier that way demurred assumed their truthfulness their good will he felt he had no choice what did he know? They controlled what information there was he was unarmed except for an ability to question still callow timid easily discouraged and a small growing library of books. Which swept him out of the range of perilous inquiry. You were vulnerable to your desire to believe that indolent desire to trust and the ease with which you dreamed yourself into small vague paradises shot through with gossamer and glamour where you were always hero and your wishes were sacred as laws. He wished to climb into his dream and stay there folded in its warmth whereas the world kept pinching and kicking insisting on its inconvenient existence its sovereign exasperating rights it kept clawing him back into loathed and humiliating reality.

Yet reality presented him with comforting options as well symbols bannering in the blue air of foam and gold and blood starred beckoning plausibly ennobling a temptation a promise. Were symbols reality then? The thought quivered within him. Or an access to reality of which daily experience was merely its opaque other side symbols that had failed drafts sketches defeats of reality as they were defeats of dream? And quivered more. Was physical reality precisely what was not real the grand illusion that played us for fools and pretended to offer what it forever withheld? Or was the physical world the path the royal road to reality a part of it but not all reality itself a city to which this road led the city of the whole and we were forever getting stuck in back alleys and confusing those alleys with the world our corner with the cosmos our unkempt room with the universe? For wasn't the world wasn't reality all of it and what we called the physical world merely our sensations of the small part of it that we knew? If so were we therefore in a sense condemned to ignorance as long as we remained locked in being reduced to the small jail cell of ourselves? But was there any avoiding that was there any way to transcend ourselves escape that jail which our very existence seemed to entail so that we could indeed know reality surpass our limitations the limitations of being see know grasp hold *understand* the whole? Understand. A whole that included ourselves. Yet might this require *becoming ourselves first?* Must the physical world be fully materialized before it could be spiritualized? Did not the divine after all only speak to the I? Was the divine then reflected most deeply in the I? Might the I be a kind of compacted crystal refracting and reflecting back the shifting yet changeless scintillations of the divine?

These questions that sometimes conveniently answered themselves on the other side of the years' anxieties hovered before him on his edifying walks by the sea each summer. At first however he stumbled on two simple emblems of his search emblems that nearly stunted and froze him on his way.

You became a believer. Such belief! And yet behind that belief what faith? The flag the anthem each morning's pledge of allegiance each morning's prayer at school brought a chill shivering you into pleasure a thrill of determination though determination for what? Slightly aggressive an eager desire to strike out to hit something display one's little power enforce respect subdue press into the face of others a few a crowd of one loved one a willing look of awe. Your blood rolled like a sea. Your mind flared with luminous storms. The wind whispered at your ear. And before you marched the bannered blue and white and red around you stood the ghosts of the founders the revolutionists as you thought of them of the year of the origin the spirits of liberty and of victory in war images of the recent war on another continent in another sea and more terrifying images of possible war without victory but only universal destruction against the enemy colossus across the pole.

The other the more tenacious symbol walked ahead of him in the air two lengths of wood joined bearing between them the invisible body of a young bearded man dying or dead around it a nimbus burned and a distant singing as of a chorus hovered in a dusk of cloud. And a moral teaching spoke to him and a spiritual promise consoled him. Like a child. And the teaching spoke of love and the promise spoke of hope. And the only requirement made was to believe.

And how not believe when so much had been promised when so little had been asked when so much had been given when so little had been expected when so much sweetness had been killed with so little pity? The drama and beauty of the story swept him up. And he asked himself if so many had believed in it for so many centuries how could it not have some truth much truth how could it not be true? If only be the have the speak the truth of an offer of food to an inescapable hunger? Would we feel hunger if there were nothing to satisfy it? And if we find something to satisfy it is that not therefore valuable indeed valid indeed is it not true?

No said the shadow walking beside him on the beach. Not necessarily.

And he argued with his shadow as he walked along the shore the sound of falling breakers crashing in his ears.

.

And both symbols worked on you coming from the world around you symbols you picked up from television the flag waving to the strains of the national anthem or on parade or at sporting events the cross appearing on Christmas specials on movies broadcast at Easter or implied by the prayers given each morning at school and the bells rining every Sunday morning over the woods and farm fields. They roused a tension an unstable feeling of exaltation that easily turned into belligerence a tense belief prickled with doubt a defensive desire to believe that was not altogether convinced. And he fluctuated between intolerance (why should untruth ever be tolerated?) and tolerance (after all the truth will inevitably prevail) as his moods shifted from denied doubt parched for belief to brief certainty afraid of its own confidence to renewed doubt to new certainties based on new evidence or arguments always quickly undermined by new doubts once again in an unending spiral that seemed to drive ever inward and lock him in the end behind a wall of unanswerable questions.

But this would happen in years to come and leave him exhausted in doubt ripening into a crossroads that would tempt in many directions rebellion capitulation careerism the flimsy shelter of the quotidian the doubtful transcendence of flesh or words the passiveness of despair in the meantime he groped to hold to these symbols and what he saw was the truth each one contained assuming both their compatibility and their adequacy to the task of answering the questions he was asking what is the sense of life and what should I do with mine? Do with mine. Mine.

America. Christ. Liberty. Love. Victory. Paradise.

Dazzlingly simple and clear.

The bullet the size of a pebble dislodged an avalanche that would bury many others of his generation at that time.

He took a step outside himself turned on his heel and observed. A dangerous exercise he had not yet learned the full danger of. Yet that is where he had essentially been all this time. He had only recently been doing the reverse stepping inside himself and observing the world his world with all the authority of his own eyes. Which were limited and which he knew to be limited. So he guessed at the dangers there. And needing certainty at the very least a basis for certainty he stepped outside himself again and turned to look back at himself. Since here his authority mattered. He believed. And here he knew the grades of his motives the chain of causes that led him to act or fail to act and how in any given circumstance. He believed. If not he who? God who swam in silence was the hopeless answer. And therefore he must take his own soul in his hands. And knead it into shape. And burn it in the kiln. And enamel it with a shining enamel.

Yet it was not so easily done. First he must cut the tendrils that joined him to his family that desperate but still comparatively comfortable prison that kept him from seeing either himself or the world. And by so doing he might clip the umbilicus of his being and bleed to death on the stones the scissors cocked in his hand. And he might not know till it was too late which tendril was the vital one. Yet sever it he must or suffocate and drown in a rich blank terrible selflessness.

You began the cold hacking by looking hard and long in the mirror telling yourself what you saw there in dispassionate and unflattering tones thus feeling both your humility and your pride.

You came away with a rush of exhilaration a charged sense of importance a strange feeling of power the sense of standing on a pinnacle looking across the world as if from a giant height seeing its proportions its details its bones its denizens its peculiar moment calmly turning through the hours everything you had ever seen or known reflected with tranquil exactness within yourself. And if you listened you could hear music at the edge of the silence music that beckoned you on more deeply into it into the silence at the edge of the world the horizon's rim as far from you as you could ever be forever retreating as you advanced toward it forever to be out of reach since you your position your existence itself defined it.

At which point you became aware of the essential limitations that existence imposes the odd prison of being through whose loopholes you he I longingly stare. And I placed my angry hands on the bars of the cage and shook them.

His people now that his prophylatically relentless father had gone preached *acceptance of reality* a passive capitulation before the necessities of economics and power anything else was condemned as avoidance and escape you can't fight city hall. Yet a rebellious voice at the back of his mind rose in revolt exacting its own obedience demanding that *he take reality in his own hands* insisting that *reality was not to be accepted but changed that reality was the clay with which one built a life* and *if a prison one from which one had the obligation to oneself if to no one else to try by every means possible fair or foul to escape.*

Yet the essence of reality was materiality the only escape from which was into the ideal the dream of the real it could be changed into an image a word an idea of itself the idea infinitely manipulable in the royal courts of the mind in art poetry philosophy music other workings of mind pure contemplation forms of communion with the universe's unknown creator in the scientist's curiosity the mystic's vision the saint's love in certain passionate moments of outraged collective political will all of which organized reality into meaningful terms returned meaning and purpose to reality all of which were humankind's answer always inadequate but ever striving to nature's enigmatically loving challenge a challenge so vast no human expression had ever adequately portrayed it it required you to drop the book leave the theater flee your home stop and raise your naked and undefended face to the sky.

Only then did one realize what was left to answer for and to. And the effects of the human shrank to perhaps well-meaning perhaps ill-intended gestures of an ultimate insignificance human accomplishment and human power human riches human grandeur its cities and arts and temples and armies its terrible glories its glittering toys civilizations annihilating weapons crowing of triumph vacant tragedy reduced to the boasts of a miles gloriosus the whining of a bully on a remote childhood playground his voice barely audible in the shifting wind.

(Yet firmly take in hand the hard earth until it yields happiness and home teneo te terra mea.)

Yet yet yet reality though not reality rather the delusion that human beings called reality and that seemed merely the collective obsession and self-deception of the hour would claw him back to its bony chest with every announcement of the day's news. Pity the great corrupter as he would learn from the asperities of the contemptuous German poisoned the insight he was on the verge of having and he was pulled back into the maelstrom of suffering and anger righteous assault on evil battle that both liberated and blinded of the day's implacable necessity. Of course you despised those who valued their souls more than winning this war on society's evils the self-indulgent self-absorption of it yet still you were haunted by the question that balanced world and soul and found the world wanting. What if the war was won only by losing the point of it? What was victory worth in and of itself? Nothing perhaps? Was every victory in a sense only temporary only a warding off of eventual annihilation? Was victory a kind of delusion and every battle a meeting of madmen killing each other in the name of nothing whatsoever? And what of defeat? What of loss what of giving up? Might that open the door to what one had always wanted to the knowledge of the spiritual possession of a kind of unquestionable worth a good beyond any conceivable value a look between the eyelids of the divine?

.

You stumble through a labyrinth of clouds illuminated with soundless flashes of lightning. The walls shift.

The village sleeps.

The fishermen stand in the morning light light gleams from the rising cavern of a swell as it curves into a breaker gleams and is gone the wave collapsing into a roar and hiss of foam.

The leader's murder drove a crack into the world the foundations shifted just enough to reveal the fragility of what you had taken for granted the riddling of cracks in the concrete flooring the delicate balance of the rafters the thinness of the walls and swaying of the columns. You felt dizzy contemplating it the collapse of trust the folding of the banner its tucking into a pocket soaked in gasoline the cigarette offered to your lips. Distant thunder rumors of earthquakes magazine spreads on hurricanes. Then the stark rap against the door. Bringing it home. The eyes meeting above the table. Comforting and treacherous.

The walls caved out into winter. Yes that was how it seemed. Was that how it seemed? The ice invaded his bed. The television roared like a crazed aunt paranoid self-righteous terrified furious screaming at the top of her lungs at people who would not listen to her. Yet people listened for they had no other choice. It spat horrors into the livingroom and they watched with dead mute stares. No one discussed it.

His classmates were stirring in ways he had not seen gathering in small knots in the cafeteria on the grounds after school debating political topics exhilarated angry laughing tart-tongued hard-headed unforgiving. The ones he most respected were the angriest fact-dropping totting figures shoving alarming assertions into each other's faces assailing the complacent know-nothings ones easily frightened by the rhetoric of their elders teachers fathers. The ones who scowled and smirked through class who were quick to answer and quicker to question the ones for whom doubt came as naturally as sneering not the most likable gratuitously offensive yet throwing a slap into the bumbling policeman's face questioning power's extravagant edicts digging at the edges of its authority ridiculing its loyalties condemning its ideals shadowing the air with inconvenient questions to which there were no quick sharp and gratifying replies shifting the grounds of the debate until it was no longer possible to locate them.

And woke to the appearance of a hard-edged otherness around him the existence of personalities that set an absolute limit to his own identity with a shock of finality. Once again. And it turned you inward in a chase after certainty a search with sweat on your palms for a stone to clutch a bough to cling to for bedrock a foundation reality. Lost as soon as found.

For his relations with others shifted and fluxed his first reaction as above had been to reject the doubters out of hand to trust the government's pronouncements spurn the questioners as presumptuous and arrogant after all where had they gotten their information how could they be sure it was more credible and complete than the information supplied to of all people the president a new one now the young leader was dead the idea was ludicrous a favorite word of the time. But then a small crack of doubt would appear on the surface of the government's case a little contradiction hastily patched over a small incoherence an obscure but patent lie and the doubters no longer seemed so reckless but for all their insolence and hideous address prescient rude and offensive prophets who might indeed have a clue to further incongruities or insight into the madness of authority a shaft of light into the darkness behind the blinding light of power.

Every rock crumbled at the first tendril of a question. The more he examined the less certainty he found. The bedrock melted into tectonics perpetually moving continents mountains merely swells of matter on the verge of cresting the world a jenny at any moment about to spin out of control the universe a stormy sea even the words in his mouth were porous and malleable melting like candy even the ideas behind the words fluctuated and pulsed with their own shadows the only constants were the rising and setting of the moon and stars and sun the alternations of blue and black that held like a scrim against the sky's background the continued milling of the clouds dissolving and re-emerging the four corners of the seasons blocking out the sun's walk across the sky. That nature beyond nature that defined the frame within which the human hydra writhed that alone provided the constancy he craved and he would walk beneath its canopy for hours.

War moved from the television to the streets. The angry parades began. Mobs in passion met the misery of authority bloodied night-sticks the flickering gray fires of the screen displayed floods of white as blacks were hosed in attack he watched enthralled by pity. Murders began the shots of assassination had only been the crack of the beginning opening a season on murder. The determination was to win or kill or die but never back down compromise was not allowed better death than the enemy's victory. Fever seized the air. The leaders were spellbound their ashen faces nodding between commercials and clashing mobs. Arguments rang over the dining room table at the passing of a word or a silence. The common misunderstanding became menacing people began expecting to understand and be understood the result was panic and fury. Everyone's private code became an object of suspicion. Contempt for leaders and contempt for law joined in a chain of paranoia it seemed anyone might be a spy informer narc. And the combination of suspicion and anger of war fever and war hatred of mobs in the streets and the assassinations of kings was laced with new drugs that bent the mind into shapes beyond its vastest possibilities heretofore known the age shape-shifted into a bestiary of universes beyond the farthest shape and shame of thought's nightmare and marvel. Anarchy invaded even the thought of anarchy. Insanity and brutality took on reality's face. He woke to find his world becoming an armed asylum and himself locked unable to escape or face it.

Whirlwinds descending into the streets.

He joined marches and rallies protests pickets attended meetings listened to speeches lectures was swayed repelled by turns joined the backwash of anger of offended moral purity until it lifted and fell in broken waves across the crowds echoing off the highrises scarped above the street marchers like canyon walls washing in swelling tides of chants a swarm of bodies and voices raised in a strangely cheerful resentment of innocence furious and oddly whimsical picket signs decked out with flowers marchers in facepaint a ragged dandyism ornamenting the protesters their signs too endearingly silly to offend the one sign of the actual seriousness of the cause the massiveness of the demonstrations tens of thousands sluicing through the streets into the parks where the mobs rallied a hundred thousand marching at the feet of the office towers the police lined in riot gear along the side streets the sidewalks peppered with hecklers angry frightened by the carnival of protest the clowns of revolution the festival of revolt that was intent on burying them under a pile of revolutionary rhetoric as cheerfully grotesque as a cartoon.

He wasn't sure if he was a participant or a spectator of the crowds he joined always a solitary one in the midst of them watchful cautiously threading through the mob eyeing the others with fascination with skepticism bemused irritated appalled at this generation of grotesques indignant fanatically complacent unplagued by self-doubt drugged on spectral selves bearers of apocalypse dancing in a brew of indulgence questioning everything but the questioner marching marching with blank-eyed zeal into a future they reduced to the inversion of a drugged fantasy a trip without any conceivable destination but its own infinite regression an imploding mise en abime. Yet surrounding it in the margins and corners of the screen was an earnestness born of moral horror an outrage not feigned but a gift of that sense of endless power and life of the young (so you thought) that out of the moral generosity that thus resulted is horrified by the world's evil and refuses to accept it a kind of naive nobility of spirit a proud innocence a stubborn and unyielding sense of the good and of what the good simply clearly requires. Not harming other people. Not speaking in lies. And finding themselves alive in a time when lies and death fed one another like lovers. Or seemed to. Or seemed to do so more openly than at other times though how could they judge they had only just been born.

Only just been born.

And into their young and unscathed lives poured the howling of the suffering of the unjustly humiliated the sufferings of the innocent the torture and death of the blameless villages burning at the torch of a lighter brains blown out on a television screen mobs attacked by hoses and dogs a war at home and a war abroad sheriffs blanking out doorways with their stars soldiers cutting machine guns through the jungle and swamp airborne bombers unleashing tons of explosives over forests and villages in scattering lines of small gray clouds the sense that the world had become on every level possible to it a zone of ineradicable war like a disease at home a new war between the generations a huge bulge of the young like a boar in the belly of a python taken with a kind of rage of power despising their elders and flaunting their enormous energy and hunger the young became for the young a horror tale and a mystery what would they do next how would it all come out amidst blood and television radio and rock the bullhorns of riot and the whisper of the nightstick and not much later the veil and smell of tear gas.

And so they took the war to the streets the war they now carried permanently within them a war between them and the world and between themselves and one another and between their need to join the bitter world of adulthood and their need to hold on to their past their childhood not to be shattered on the rock of the world. And these wars joined the public wars and were magnified by them until the country rang only with the cries of the young their shouts of indignation their angry speeches their outraged protests their furious denials their great refusal spoken in one voice in tongues of fire as the chemical fires in a land far off ate their way through the miles of field and jungle reducing villages to ashes and scarring mountains with craters. The world had become an echo chamber of the angry and the mad the violent and the innocent until it drove the innocent to violence forced them to take on the mantle of guilt the irremediable obligation the madness of the hour. And they paused just long enough to look at each other with a blank gaze hesitant appalled filthy with the mire the bloodied mud of the present then plunged where they were forced into the garbage and tears of the inescapable now.

In a single year the war increased its inane and nattering fury the dead piled on jungle floors in the villages in their footpaths between fields and at home two leaders of hope and promise murdered at the edges of the continent. The young at their schools took the universities in their dubious hands and shook them like salt shakers. And the rest of the country sank into the carnival of a presidential campaign.

Toward one city in the middle of the country the forces of the hour converged. And reckless for once in an uncharacteristic hour of courage driven from his ingrown lethargy and grasping at phantoms and straws feeling reality for one time converge into a solid mossy ball and play into his willing hands he determined to go to the tall cold city and join the angry and the hopeful ones in their spasm of righteous fury their spell of bewitchment at their own purity demanding an end to what perhaps could not end in a way that might only prolong it for now was the time to sign the air with the ideal before reality swept it up like the leaves of autumn after the green glittering of summer. Wherever it might lead.

And the heat of that summer deepened. Tanks rolled through the streets of a foreign city and crushed a youthful rebellion of clover and straw. Sweat dripped from the air-conditioners. He hung out with cynical friends and a black girl who shimmered in his presence. The streets whitened daily in the sun.

A flash of white shirt leaping from a police truck a stick in its raised hand.

The eye of a girl seen panicking over the flanneled shoulder of a young man.

A line of military jeeps with metal netting raised along their grills.

A night stick raised and falling. Repeat. Repeat.

Clouds of tear gas roll through a park running with scattering crowds.

A woman's scream how near or far or for what exact reason unknown.

A man with a bullhorn telling the crowds to walk don't run for reasons he cannot know guessing what he cannot know describing what he cannot see.

A wall of white shirts riot helmets glazed masks clubs resting in restless hands.

An elderly woman standing on a curb looking bewilderedly at the crowd as it cascades like a river down the avenue. The crowd is strangely silent except for the sound of scuffling feet and an occasional random shout. The woman stares after them her mouth gaping her eyes shocked and frightened.

In a park at night in the near distance a crowd rallying with great banners of an enemy country waving above it and a chant exhorting the enemy to victory rising from many voices. It is theater a pageant carnival and trial a children's party in a torture chamber a circus and a shaming a festival an execution. Clowns dressed as terrorists

terrorists dressed as clowns mock the cops. Then a roar and a battalion of motorcycles springs from the trees and the crowd surges screaming away out of the illegal park into the streets scattering into the tony neighborhoods the flags dipping and bannering and falling and the signs scattering in the streets as the police gun their engines toward them and force them to flee evaporating within minutes to the wails of sirens and the flashing of beacons. Until the park lies silent in its fragile light and sweeping plain of trash.

A line of ambulances parked at the edge of the street nurses waiting smoking chatting watchful with pained sympathetic eyes.

A line of national guards in green uniforms standing in formation beneath a painlessly blue sky their gray and brown rifles held in readiness across their chests their eyes staring ahead like the eyes of dolls.

A young man shimmies up a flagpole to the shouts and whistles of a crowd of thousands he tears the national flag from the line and hauls it down to the ground. And around the base of the pole a riot erupts.

A rain of bottles pours over a police car a police car smashing its windows crusting it with a glitter of shattering its tires slashed its hood battered its side doors caved in its signal light shattered and broken. The crowd taunts the police the police stare back after withdrawing watching the car's ritual destruction. Between them is a sparkling plain of glass.

You wander through this mutating polymorphous labyrinth of bodies made up of demonstrators quaint name rioters students the young like yourself cheerfully jeering angrily mocking insistent violent demanding furious pleading marching running wedged between police lines vanishing down alleys choking in the smoke of burning barricades thrown up from trash cans and newspaper boxes and the gutted bodies of burnt cars or in a fog of tear gas erupting from a line of guardsmen moving jeeps up the packed avenue the crowd running screaming weeping in the haze of gas soaking handkerchiefs in public pools water fountains then covering their eyes noses mouths as they run from the billowing gray-white clouds. And you run with them following their lead in the shadows of the carbon arc street lights of evening and the absently flashing neon lights of bars and restaurants and the flat fluorescence of office interiors leaking weakly into the street. Or just walk quickly alert to the appearance of the police though there are plain-clothesmen in the crowd two confronted you at one point accusing you of being the youth who climbed the flagpole and tore down the flag two angry middle-aged men wearing light summer outfits and sunglasses one a sporty straw hat and stormed at you hatred buckling the lower half of his face the memory is strangely silent like that of a silent movie or a film with a sound track deliberately unsynchronized with the picture you frightened of what might happen to you if you cannot convince them of their mistake and deny deny deny shaking and trembling until they turn and vanish into the crowd in contempt or in hunt for the real perpetrator or content to have frightened and shamed you.

You are surrounded by tens of thousands of people roughly your own age and you find this fascinating and find them fascinating there is a mild air of intoxication and a sense of strange power a flippant insolence in the air a contact high of pride slipping into arrogance the young men look cold and cocky when they aren't leading a chant a march with raised fists and exposed teeth the young women look evanescent and dreamy in faded jeans or wisps of ankle-length dresses that nearly trip in the stampedes up the avenues outside the hotels where the politicians are gathered then there are the older men with the bullhorns who direct and sway the crowd when it is not panicking who soothe and cajole or rile it as need be or try to seem to exercise the appearance of the possiblity of the hope of the trust in an eventual and ostensible control haha. And there is the occasional couple some young some old some very old wandering among the amorphous ever-changing clusters of the young clouds dissolving into one another the middle-aged academic with a look of cheerful overbearingness the tight-lipped Irish girl raging against the

girl behind her eyes the baffled businessman standing at the curb in
his clean suit with his briefcase his eyes boring two exasperated holes
into the ragged mob the construction workers trading insults with
the crowd from their perches on the rust orange girders the busload
of young conservatives staring down at the motley children's crusade
with angry disapproval holding the young radicals up to inspection
as in a pair of tweezers painful stinging yet peculiarly gratifying the
scowls and stares and frowns a measure of the accuracy of the blows.

For all the excitement he yet felt strangely detached slightly
withdrawn as if between him and what he saw a thin layer of glass
protected him from what it revealed. He slipped through the city like
a watchful ghost intrigued by the strangeness of the living their anger
and grief and wiliness and mischief their detailed and lumbering
lunacy. He both understood and did not understand felt for and felt
nothing for joined in sympathy and rejected completely the rioters
and their adversaries the foes of the young and the young themselves
the enemies of the hour and the hour's tolling alarm. The result was
a fascinated paralysis flickering like a reflection between the mirrors
in a barber shop or in the mirrored walls of an elevator trailing on
all sides to infinity freezing judgment and action in a single self-
regarding arc. He had come to join the demonstrators to seal his bond
with his peers but the bond would not take it slipped from the grasp
of fury and an oily violent fire into a kind of weariness and disgust
the carnival of sanctimony and theatrical anger the histrionics of
outrage and the indignant pose playing false to a genuine pleasure in
mayhem and abuse insulting the self-contained the easily mortified
however honoring and honored however admirable and noble the
hard compelling cause. That cause through these means was itself
betrayed and abandoned. It was a mortification of the springs of
that honor to excuse the misery that followed. And the dishonoring
fed dishonor until the evils of violence and counterviolence met and
wedded on the city's streets beneath the cold gray eye of television's
messenger. He found himself detesting the system that met opposite

with violence and despising his peers for their willful provocations each side committed to a lunatic proposal that willed its opposite to destruction. Defeat was not enough humiliation was not enough merely winning one's point was not enough only paraded defeat shame erasure and oblivion however unlikely or misguided.

He saw two enemies bound like lovers feeding off each other's lust their moist hate and anger grown great and greater still in each other's obsessive need.

And yet he joined the mayhem with a gusto that surprised him. Being an agent of chaos gave an irresistible thrill the excitement of those days blossomed in euphoria inflated one's sense of importance the sense of nudging if not moving history possibly of stopping it in its tracks hence its bloody frustration its screaming panicky bludgeoning the mobs commanded the streets for three nights running each night angrier than the last the festival of scorn scaled paroxysms of rage in the chants of thousands whistles and shouts single and massed signs and banners waving in the cold stiff breeze off the sea-broad lake. The city was a theater for the performance an enormous walled stage for the acting out of the indignant mob a studio for a modern epic being broadcast to tens of millions in their sedate homes ripe for being scared stiff into denying every assertion or demand or plea the self-wounding rioters made. If ever theatrical event was designed to close the very week it opened this was it. But he though dimly aware of this and repulsed as any who watched from outside still he let himself be swept up in the riptide of the event for the mob was like an ocean sluicing the streets in a hurricane flood it obeyed the same laws as difficult to stanch no impossible it must rage on until the winds played out and the waters drew back of their own accord leaving wreckage and marveling in the leached sands hugging the flotsam of broken ships wedged in the girders of office towers like splinters in rows of broken teeth. There was a thrill in being part of that flood even if for a day or an hour alone he felt himself expand to meet and mingle but more to become briefly everyone in that mob and hence all the smiles that were traded even during the moments of greatest crisis even especially at those moments such peaks of joy such certainties with so little basis but the irresistible forces that shaped the hour and so rode them despite his doubts despite his certainties despite what conscience and lucidity whispered into his ear in the midst of the chanting shouting cries.

Until the last night when the word was passed that a curfew having been set we were to try to get as close to the target as we had ever gotten and that through a ploy an invitation by one of the hosts of the rebellion to visit his home for a little party in his backyard which was itself within blocks of the goal. And a trickle moved down the avenues south and the trickle gained in size till it became a stream and then a river and then a tide of bodies until it met a wall of nets and jeeps and camouflage and uniforms decked with gas masks and rifles cocked toward the air and the tide flung itself against the metal and netted wall in exasperation like a trapped rat all teeth and squeal and the wall did not yield and the chant rose as the television trucks with their well-known logos appeared until a contingent of the mass began rocking one of the trucks (he was watching from a second story apartment he had found almost by accident as he approached the crowd where it massed impacted and stuck at an intersection in the southern part of the city) rocking it back and forth till it shook out its riders and driver who disappeared into the crowd and more joined in rocking it as though it were the enemy or a surrogate a powerless effigy of power on which the crowd could expend its fury since it could not against the cocked rifles and the netted jeeps without the fear of an overwhelming response and they rocked and shouted and chanted and rocked until the truck canted over on its side and a pause as the crowd seemed to suck in its breath and a shout uncoiled as the truck fell over and the shout uncurled like a vortex a verbal spout from the crowd now a mob as even those who were too far from the truck to have seen it fall joined the barbed web of voices and at that moment or just after in the full cry of exultation the truck looking ridiculous like a small elephant on its side two wheels cocked above the gutter as an explosion of gas whitened the air along the wall of nets and the cry of triumph swelled and turned like the turning wind from the sea to land as the evening turns toward night along the oceanshore which he had seen and felt along his skin so often in his childhood from the cry of triumph it turned into a cry of panic choking on tears and gagging on the wall of smoke and the mob peeled back from the wall of the green army and crushed in panic the piling and unknown bodies behind it toward the north until in waves the cause was communicated to the back masses of the mob it was like the rush and confusion of currents in a hurricane cove how the forces pulled and shoved one another the confused and frightened mass of bodies until the entire mass moved chaotically terrified and choking on air back the way it had come. And the wall of nets silently followed pushing north.

He left his post by the window and retreated to the streets moving along the crowd's route up a parallel street until he reached the site of the previous night's riot at the foot of a great sphinxlike hotel then walked one block over to find a scene as close to war as he was ever to know.

The street at this point opened out to a park pocked with trees and fountains and backed with a walled railroad cutting. Into this park fanned the panicking mob vague in a billowing fog of tear gas that followed it from the launchers the mouths of the advancing troops. The rioters were no longer a crowd or a mob but a disintegrating mass of frightened children acrid tears stinging and straining from their eyes as they ran some with the presence of mind to soak handkerchiefs or strips of shirt and blouse in the fountains and apply them to their faces others just running from the stinging smoke some not sure even to do that crying rumors that they were surrounded that there was no escape that they were shooting that they were being rounded up and arrested that they would be killed. The settled roar of the crowd had disintegrated and dissolved into solitary shouts and screams above the terrified hush of running feet and straining lungs and gasping of runners and sighs. Until the word was passed that an alleyway was open unguarded and free for escape and his eyes tearing under a soaking handkerchief he followed a trickle of runners into the escape route and emerged a block later in the blue light of evening and the traffic of a seemingly oblivious shopping day. A few people watched the tear-stained escapees with alarm but most gave a disapproving or sympathetic glance before moving on to their own unavoidable tasks.

He escaped to the home of the old-time radicals where he was staying and watched the news that evening the tapes of the riots from the vantage of the impassive camera that eye without panic invulnerably perched above the swirling crowd like a bird above a swirl of autumn leaves and he wondering at the sense of combined deja vu and disconnect an eerie sense that his experience was being hijacked by the television networks stolen by the collective memory and filed into an irrelevance of cliché misguided commentary and political silence. He saw how the last few rioters who had not known or spurned the available escape route were surrounded by soldiers and police and bludgeoned by police as the soldiers prevented escape and dragged limply by legs arms shoulders hair into police vans until the vans were full and they were transported to local sports arenas arraigned en masse for disturbing the peace and inciting to riot and vandalism and resisting arrest until the arenas were full and the streets were empty of any but soldiers and police.

The kaleidoscope twists between thumb and forefinger another crystal falls with a light chink into place and transforms the design from one perfect symmetry dazzling from no apparent necessity to another perfect symmetry dazzling from no apparent necessity. Chaos facing its reflection in a mirror becoming symmetry and order. Pierced with insight's almost unendurable light.

Over the next year he tread lightly on the earth convinced that at any moment it might crack open and the sky fill with butterflies and roses thick enough to blank out the sun. Revolution was the word that belonged to the hour that blazoned across the day yet also hindering the hour obscuring the horizon with a wild and indefinable hope an enflamed appeal to the imagination an awe-inspiring sense of immense possibility and unmitigated promise bliss was it in that dawn to be alive. But to be young. To be young. It felt both impossible and absolutely real life was about to turn into a poem and soar off its dowdy foundations into an empyrean of its own wondrous invention. Love and triumph would be the order of the day as was only natural. Power was about to shift from the dusty halls of the old and the frustrated grip of the middle-aged to the hot arms of the young their eager eyes and hungry lips their tempests of imagination the flames of their mouths their geysers of righteous anger their indignation at that feeble bugbear reality of their absurd and sweet and self-defeating ideals. The world was beginning anew like a bud never seen before beneath a virgin sky in spring about to burst from its calyx into the first light and no one knew where it would go or how it would end for this flower was a new being under the sun. Under the sun.

He soaked up the sense of change and danger and possibility and risk that rose all around him. The riots had not seemed a defeat rather a clarion call to greater efforts the vanguard of a revolution that could erupt at any moment a drunkenness a high a trip that swept up the generation and promised more than the world to reshape the very possibilities of human life the foundations of the possibility of being the gods and all their rules.

He laughed at the thought gently at first then over the years with ever deepening scorn but even as he laughed he drank in inhaled the wild promise that hung in the air like smoke or fog seductive and beautiful and beckoning. A beloved betrayer he knew it no he did not know it but he was certain against his own desires a detestable certainty that he must test and what better way to test it than by believing the thought he wished to believe in even though he suspected it would cripple him if he trusted it. So believing it he allowed himself to close his eyes and step into the extravagant air.

At that time worldwide an entire generation was erupting in anger preparing a hecatomb of the political the streets of Paris and Tokyo and New York were torn and burning with riot it seemed only a matter of weeks or months before governments would fall before the nonnegotiable demands of a new race of young revolutionists. And if the crackdown against them was severe it only suggested the idea and the hope that the forces being cracked down were of a far greater power far more ominous threat than even their most faithful supporters could know that these skirmishes were merely the opening rounds of a greater war not the closing battles of a brief slave rebellion. The result was an incorrigible hope a sublime if lunatic optimism (he saw he thought he knew) a crazy sense of promise in tomorrow's brief spectacular radiance of a soon-dying dawn.

The war had just begun. The war against society against America against the world against the universe and the hour. A war without end except in victory or annihilation. A war of what? Of hope. By itself. Alone. Against the despair and desperation of reality's locked door.

And he joined this war with all his heart. The only war worth fighting. The war against reality.

He began reading Ortega. Marx. Sartre. Kierkegaard. Shelley. Unamuno. Nietzsche. Authors and poets of left and right who sought less to explain the world than to change it root and branch from the magma to the firmament from the foundations to the rooftops from the iron foundations bolted to the rock to the glass and iron towers scraping the clouds. If need be by blowing it up burning it down sweeping it away. Like outgrown toys from a table.

8

Exterior. Day. Sun.

Autumn. Sound of trees in a mild wind.

Across a city university campus on a winding concrete path beneath trees, their leaves yellow, brown, red, walks a young couple in their late teens, leaning sometimes out, sometimes in toward one another, concentrating on a spot a few feet ahead of them, a spot they never seem to reach; they are immersed in talk, oblivious to the looks they get from passing students, professors, utility men, campus police — his gestures are a little melodramatic, he has a laugh that is too quick, and a nervous, staccato voice; her gestures are reserved, ironic, her arms tightly crossed over her torso; her eyes watch him from the side, curious, not quite believing. Is it that? Doubtful, but maybe.

He is a thin, bony, nervous, intense young man, in gold-rimmed spectacles, his hair sandy blond, thick, trailing his collar, in faded dungarees and wearing a used corduroy jacket, its collar raised, and shoes of scuffed suede; thick-nosed, weak-chinned, with small, nervous eyes and abrupt movements. He talks too fast and too loud. She seems self-contained, cool, with dark long hair and a long hourglass figure, in a dark sweater and slacks, with sunglasses propped on her forehead, her movements focussed and controlled yet graceful, somewhat self-conscious. He seems shaggy and sudden, anxious, compared with her, she a little prim, watching him with a piercing, laughing interest.

The shot picks them up in the middle distance and follows them, pulling back slightly, down the campus walk until they turn at the vine-covered side of Stowe Hall (its name is engraved in the wall by the entrance) and vanish around the building's corner.

Note: Throughout the following sequences the faces of the couple are not seen fully, either full face or in profile, until specifically mentioned. This will not be the last time he sees his life as a movie.

Cut to a close-up of her mouth, thin, bright, pale lips pressed firmly shut in a dubious smile. The two of them are standing near the Hall entrance.

He, with wildly overemphatic gestures that can be heard rather than seen (hold on the young woman's mouth): Not only is *such a change possible*, it is *absolutely necessary*, American society, *world* society, but particularly *American* society cannot, it *must not* go on like this, it will *im*plode if it doesn't *ex*plode, it has gone to seed, it's a rotten *nut*, it must cave in, a child's hand would be enough to *destroy* it, but he must know enough to pick it up and *squeeze*.

Close-up of his hand, closing in a fist.

Cut to her smile: it broadens with quick irony, then resets.

Insert of his arm, casting aside the "crushed nut" and waving off toward the side.

Shot of his hair, shaking as he gestures.

Cut to her cheek and the edge of her lips, grinning.

Sound of him bursting out with a laugh.

She: You have a colorful way of speaking!

She speaks with a light and uncertainly identifiable Central European accent.

He, still laughing: But I mean *every word* I say!

She: I don't doubt it!

More laughter from both.

They have only recently met and there is a tentative joy in their reactions to each other.

Inserts of close-ups of his arms, hands, torso, the back of his head, his eyes, mouth, neck, etc., and of parts of her face, hair, ears, shoulders, etc, are mixed into the dialog that follows. They both carry school books.

He: Crunch!

She: Do you really think people can change?

He: Oh, people change all the time, they can't help it, I've already changed *three times* this morning …

She: Only three times, oh!

He: (Or maybe it was *four!*) but it's without their *knowing* it or *facing* it or, here it is, *controlling* it, that's the important point. Anyway, they must change, *we* must change.

She: Or what?

He: Or, or we'll be stuck with … *this*. Ah!

His free arm gestures sweepingly toward the "world" — a ragged urban university crowd with individuals and groups standing out: a couple locking lips on the grass, a jock running past carrying a duffel bag, an officious-looking teacher treading self-importantly toward class, a couple of hippies giggling under a tree, an angry-looking young black man glaring at the camera as he stalks past, a nerd hobbling to the library, grasping his briefcase helplessly to his chest, a homeless drunk being escorted down the campus walk by a cop. The sunlight is intense.

She (off camera): Some people would consider this a paradise.

He shrugs: the camera focuses on the nape of his neck.

He: Or the *reverse*.

Close-up of her lips, half smiling.

She: You don't really believe that.

He, suddenly collapsing, giggling: No! But then maybe I'm just too optimistic.

She: Or naive.

He: Or stubborn.

She: Or credulous!

He: Or defiant.

She: Or just in denial.

He: I deny that!

She: Point for me.

He: To deny I'm in denial hardly means I am! Quoth the Cretan.

She, laughing: Help! — She pauses. — You're blushing! But I have to go.

He: You're no fun.

She: Aesthetics wait for no one.

He: *Politics* waits for no one!

There is the sound of her retreating steps as the camera focuses on the back of his jacket.

He, calling out: Aesthetics is humble, she's endlessly patient, aesthetics will wait forever!

Distant laughing call: But maybe *not* for *you*!

The back of his jacket doesn't move.

Cut to two young laps, male and female, squatting squarely across from each other in the grass, with lunch things between them — sandwich, salad, coke, paper cup of tea, two brown bags, clear-plastic wrapping, napkins half crumpled. The hands rise out of and back into the shot as the two finish eating and talk. It is the couple we have just left, on another day. Though their clothing is otherwise different, he wears his eternal corduroy.

He, overemphatically: No, I don't!

She: I think you do. Or did.

He: I don't now and I didn't then.

She, teasingly: Somehow I don't quite believe you.

He: This isn't getting us anywhere.

She: But we're here now, aren't we?

He: If *here* can be called somewhere!

She: Everywhere is a here, and isn't here what counts?

He: Perhaps.

She: And anyway it would be if you weren't precisely "here."

He, exasperatedly: Now what does *that* mean!

She: If you were in Soweto, if you were in Uganda, if you were in Warsaw, longing to escape. "Here" might be the only somewhere that counts.

He: Touché.

Her hand dips down to catch a napkin blowing away in the breeze. The shot follows her hand as it takes the napkin up to her mouth, wiping it briefly, and lingers there.

Her voice (an exact repetition of the words just spoken): … *if you weren't precisely here.*

Cut to her eyes.

She dared you to set her boundaries. She lashed according to absolute moments.

He: But I *am* "precisely here," and that makes all the difference.

Cut to his shoulder, then pan down to his elbow, then down his forearm to his hand.

He: Though the Buddhists might not agree with me on that point!

Hold on his hand. They have finished eating and he fiddles lazily with the grass, the edge of his shoe, his knee.

She: Oh?

He: How can I be *anywhere* if I "am" not at all?

She: So what about me? Do I exist? Am I here?

In our mouth dwelled early warnings of the disease.

He: Oh, *you* exist! *You* are here, there's no doubt of that! Nagarjuna has a lot of explaining to do. But it does make all the difference.

She: How sincere you sound.

Cut to her eyes, mocking.

He, strangely upset: I am *always* sincere.

She: You are *always* this and you *never* do that. Did you ever notice how you always speak in extremes?

He pauses then barks out: *Always!*

She throws a crumpled napkin at him: shot of the napkin catapulting from her hand, then cut to it hitting his face (it is too quick for us to see his face clearly) — crunching his face up and guffawing, he lunges at her. She falls back giggling in the grass, weakly defending herself with pretend calls for help. They wrestle. He straddles her, pressing her hands into the grass, his long hair falling around his face. Cut to her point-of-view: looking up at his shadowy face against the sun directly behind his head, dazzling. Then to his point of view, but very briefly: looking down at her, her face in exaggeratedly deep shadow against the grass, her face dimly smiling, dazed. Her eyes are open a little too wide, like a doe's in headlights. Swift zoom down to her face, to her eyes, swiftly losing focus and darkening. Her eyes in the darkness. They do not close as the shot zooms in.

Cut to a profile close-up of the grass, with a single wild flower twitching among the blades, blowing in a breeze, out-of-focus forms of people walking past in the distance.

Her voice, whispering: Yes, you did…. *Confess*….

A pause. Hold on grass.

Her voice: Confess!

A sound of bodies moving in the grass. Wind.

He, whispering: *Never*.

A cold spring day — pedestrians wear overcoats, scarves, gloves, but bright yellow founts of fuschia sprout, crocuses blossom in mud patches along the streetside, and a light mist of green confuses the gray parks. Random shots of this old eastern city neighborhood: the young man's point of view as he walks down the morning street. He looks up: high cirrus clouds slowly shifting against a metallic blue. The following dialog is heard against this background sky.

Her voice: I don't know what you want. What do you want? I'm not sure who you are. Who are you?

Cut to a canopy of green oak leaves against a brighter, softer blue sky. Bird whistles.

His voice, evasively: I'm not sure. Of either.

Cut to fishermen standing in the surf on a blindingly bright summer morning, seagulls puling above. Sound of crashing surf.

Cut back to the leaves. Silence, breeze.

His voice, in a different space from that of the previous shot; whispering, as if to himself alone, in a small room: I want to live like the sky, I want to live a charmed life, I want to live a poem.

Cut to the previous cirrus clouds, beginning to shred in the high wind of the distant sky.

Cut back to the leaves.

His voice: Do you always know what you want.

Sound of him turning in the grass to look at her.

Her voice: Sometimes. Isn't that the most important thing?

His voice: Is it? Sometimes all I want is to *live*.

Her voice: And what does *that* mean?

The sound of his shrug.

His voice: To feel. Breathe. Without obstructions!

Her voice: Utopian!

His voice: Maybe. A believer in Nowhere.

Her voice: You're unreal, I can tell you that.

His voice: Ah, reality! A highly overrated concept.

Her voice: Except by those who want to survive it.

His voice: Sometimes survival is dishonorable, some circumstances it would be immoral to survive.

Her voice: *And* a romantic!

His voice, dryly: Guilty. As charged.

Her voice: And crazy!

His voice: As well as being facile, glib, and hopelessly pretentious. Brief silence.

His voice: You tease with an ice pick. It's what I deserve as I sit here failing to think up witty comebacks.

Her voice: But not to get in the last word.

His voice: One should never try doing that with a woman!

Her voice: Chauvinist! Sexist!

His voice: Filthy peeg! I am a filthy peeg! But also I am right! Oink oink.

Her voice: Whatever happened to the revolutionary?

His voice: Ah! I bleed! I'm dead!

Her voice: Without even being wounded.

His voice: Merely erased.

Her voice: You should be so lucky.

His voice: *You* should be so lucky.

Her voice: Now we're both regressing.

His voice: You took the words right out of my mouth.

Shot of the faintly cirrus sky, now almost dispersed.

His voice, whispering; she doesn't hear it: *And you, who are you, you who are so beautiful?*

Pan down from the cirrus sky to the spring street as he continues walking.

Cut to her eyes.

Her voice: I don't know what you want.

Cut to the street. Pan down to the pavement. He stops and stares at his shadow on the sidewalk.

Her voice: I'm not sure who you are. Who are you?

Cut to a dirty bathroom mirror: the left half of his face alone is visible, his neck, part of his exposed torso, skinny, pale; behind it, a stretch of wall traversed by a strip of light from an unseen window; he stares at himself searchingly, seeking a crack that might help him reveal and explain him to himself. He fascinates and appalls himself: it isn't simply vanity, though there is much of that. There is an element of preening, but also a certain distrust; a little intrigue, a little disgust, pride and disdain, harshness and compassion; above all, a question, and a large number of partial and unsatisfying answers. He doesn't know who or what he is; suspects he may never know.

The sound of a homeless man shouting in the distance in the afternoon outside.

Hold.

Cut to her face, dimly visible in tree shadow, rising to meet his gaze. Her lips are serious, but her eyes smile as they search his face.

Repeat.

Repeat.

Cut to the bathroom mirror. Hold.

Cut to her face, closer.

Cut to her eyes.

Cut to the bathroom mirror, which now shows only the bathroom's back wall above the tub, crossed by the strip of light from the unseen window, which has stretched slightly since the scene began as the sun moved across the sky. Sound of bathroom door quietly creaking. A cloud crosses the sun, darkening the room. Another shout, more distant, from the homeless man.

Hold.

Exterior. Night. He is sitting with her on a stoop on a narrow, tree-lined street near the center of the same large eastern city. They are in the middle of an animated conversation. The camera shifts back and forth between them, never lingering on their faces shadowy in the weak light of the sodium street lamps.

At first their voices sound faint, the words undistinguishable, as though they were speaking in the next room, though their faces are seen close-up in the darkness. Individual words become audible: "party," "rally," "teacher," "class"; phrases such as "next boy," "my neighbor who," "march downtown," "moves to the left," "symbolic action"; and the sentence "I went out of my way to get there, and still couldn't find it."

He, his words for the first time clear and crisp; spoken with an almost ironic mildness: Burn, baby, burn.

Silence.

She: But you don't really believe that.

He: Why wouldn't I, this country needs to be brought to its knees, humbled and reduced, at the end of every speech in old Rome, Cato would end, however irrelevantly: "Et Cartago delenda est." "We must eliminate the salt tax! And Carthage must be destroyed." Well, I say, "Et America delenda est"!

She, slightly appalled: You really hate your country so much?

He: I hate it, I detest it, I despise it, I despise its so-called "culture," its so-called "society," its sanctimousnes, its arrogance, its lack of respect for everything in the world but its own self-interest, it represents the modern world, it's the scourge of the earth, I say, bring it down or it will bring all and everything down.

She: And how would you replace it?

He: Does it need to be "replaced" at all, why not simply *replace it* with *what it replaced* — forest and meadow and river and plain, mountain and canyon and wilderness and desert, "from sea to shining to sea?"

She: And Apache and Seminole and Navajo and Hopi and Leni Lenape.

He: Naturally, yes, why not, they didn't pursue "creative destruction." What a phrase! Any society that believes in *that* deserves whatever it gets.

She: Are you sure that we do?

He: Capitalism is our religion and the dollar our god whatever church they *think* they go to, why do people come here, to be free, yes, but free for what, to get rich, it's only a matter of time before the destruction overwhelms the creation, everybody *knows* this, but we're betting it won't happen in *our* lifetime, baby, let our *kids* deal with it. Down with the Reds and down with the Greenbacks, if the Soviets collapse, all we'll need is a neat excision of the American tumor to save the world another three generations of wasted time, but people won't — they want to believe they too can become filthy rich, it's insane, and it needs morons to prop it up, the existence of our society depends on people deluding themselves, if people woke up and behaved intelligently, the whole thing would immediately collapse, it's the biggest scam the world has ever seen, east or west. A plague on all their houses.

She: You are *very* American.

He is silent.

She: You couldn't live anywhere but here. Anywhere else would simply eliminate you. Here you can froth and foam and no one will notice you.

He: And that is precisely the problem! It's castrating — you're defeated before you've even tried. At least elsewhere you're taken seriously enough to be shot at.

She: But if they took you seriously they'd "excise" *you!*

He: The problem isn't just America, it's summed up here, in our "way of life," our chaotic, hopeless, murderous "innocence," our moral vacancy we call "freedom," the real problem is the modern world, the desacralization of everything, life, the dehumanization of even the *human*, in the name of the only "god" left, the last illusion of them all ...

She: Well, I'm listening, now you have me on the edge of my seat. What is the "last illusion of them all"?

He: You can't guess?

She: Money?

He: Ah!

She: Fame?

H: Cold!

She: Sex?

He: Is a bad joke! Nature's greatest trick to keep us stuck here ...

She: ... Love?

He: If only ... !

An appraising silence.

She: Ego, like yours!

He shakes his head, a little smugly.

She: What then.

He leans over and softly whispers into her ear: Power.

He pauses, then leans back. She smiles.

She: But isn't that just what is real?

He: Just what *isn't*. Power *seems* real, we've never had so much *power*, we have the capacity to destroy the world, before now, what was the morbid dream of a psychopath is a functioning political option! Yet in fact power is the biggest, the most seduction illusion of them all: no matter how much *power* we have, it will never be enough to protect us from our ultimate enemies: our limitations, mortality, randomness, the rule of unexpected consequences, simple mutability, we'll always be in danger of being overwhelmed by a natural force greater than we are, a meteor from space, another ice age (we're already past due), a mutating bacterium, an insane idea that deludes an entire society, to say nothing of the danger we *human beings* pose for each other: the most powerful person in the world will always find somebody who has power over him: his bodyguard, his chef, his wife! He is always at somebody else's mercy — to have power is to search for it forever, and never, ever, to achieve it. The search for power, that entertaining pastime with bloody consequences, is at bottom a futile and ridiculous search for a secular Holy Grail, though we haven't grasped that yet, *and yet our entire culture is predicated on it.* We're no better than the Middle Ages, our civilization is *also* based on a shared delusion, a golden lie, a faith in salvation, in safety, protection, eternal life!

She: A delusion that *you* have managed to avoid.

He: I've got my delusions, I just don't know what they are! I have a "pious hope" that just maybe *that* insight, if it really is an insight and not just another delusion, might spare me the worst punishment of living in such a time and such a place as *this* one!

She: How noble of you!

He: Yes! Damn it, *how noble!* Because I do think that I — and not just me, *any* human being is better than … well, than *that!*

She: An "idealist egomaniac." I now know what to call you.

He: Correction: a *romantic* idealist egomaniac.

Silence.

She: Be careful about that.

He: Why.

She: It makes for the very best fascists.

He, irritably: Oh, that's true of anything with a little passion. Why is it when anybody *believes* in anything and doesn't play the universal cynic card, he is *immediately* accused of being a fascist? As if nihilism were the only morally respectable idea!

She: I had an uncle in the SS. I've had some experience of the perils of a passionate faith.

Silence.

She: He was denazified after the war. He lives in Graz. Alone. He used to run a ski lodge.

Pause.

He: Did he ever …

She: I don't think so, he wouldn't have been cleared so easily. If it *was* easy …

Pause.

He: Sorry to hear it.

She: Don't be. It doesn't mean *I'm* a Nazi. My best friend is Jewish, and she knows.

He: I've always thought the equation of romanticism with …, well, the distortion of an idea shouldn't be equated with the idea, or every act made in the name of a faith could be set down as caused by that faith. Which is crazy. Look at Christianity. I can never accept *that*.

She: Never! Ever!

He: Absolutely! Always!

She: Even if it were proven true?

He: But an equation like that can't be proven either way: any idea can be used to justify any action in the minds of those who believe in it. I'll bet you this: liberalism itself could be used to justify the assassination of a right-wing fanatic who looked like he might seize power or merely be elected. In fact, it might even impose an obligation to kill him. Marcuse makes that point in his "Critique of Tolerance." For example: *someone should have killed …*

He pauses, flustered.

She: Your American manners are showing. It's okay, say it. "Hitler."

He: Someone should have assassinated *Hitler*. That would have been an example of extreme moral and political courage: someone who had taken *Mein Kampf* seriously, as seriously as Hitler did himself. Such a person would have gone down in history as a despicable terrorist, a madman, a pathetic fanatic because no one would have known what he was sparing the world — a saviour indeed! And, being an actor rather than a martyr, he wouldn't even have a cult surrounding him, yet his act of love for the world — yes, *of love* — that act of sacrifice, of self, life, honor, reputation, everything but his sense of moral rightness, would have been total, the *ultimate* act of self-sacrifice. It's for such sacrifices, beyond any human capacity to understand and reward, beyond any mathematician's calculation or scientist's ability to test, that we need a God to recognize and reward, because they are utterly beyond mankind to judge, recognize, even *know.*

She: Maybe not, though.

He: Yes, maybe not! You know, sometimes I think that we, that the human race in a weird way, *has* grown in moral sense along with all our wealth and our power, we may not be so utterly hopeless after all.

She: But do we still need a God?

He: As long we as we don't *know* everything, and I doubt if we can, *pace* the physicists, and as long as we can't *do* everything — and of that I'm as sure as I am of my own name — as long as we need more than we can ever possibly have, as long as we're limited and weak and changeable, untrustworthy, mortal …

She: As long as we sit on midnight stoops, pontificating on the human condition!

He (whispering; it is uncertain whether he says this out loud or merely thinks it): *And as long as I love you.*

His point of view as he takes her face and leans toward her: close-up of her eyes as they close, in the dark; of her face, of her cheek, her ear, her hair. The sound of their kiss as their tongues fence inside her mouth, the sound of their hands, of their clothes rustling, of passing traffic and pedestrians pretending not to notice them.

Ah, so I can love….

Cut to black.

Dazzling.

Between every pair of stars.

The border guards like torches of pitch.

The screen goes blank with beauty it was so great a joy we vanished.

Cut to a close-up of the bottom legs of an iron railing on the stoop where they sit. It is still night.

Her voice, muffled, whispering: I have to go home.

His voice: Don't. Not yet.

Cut to his hands holding hers as they remain sitting on the stoop, leaning back slightly from each other with heads forward.

She: Really. I have to go.

They remain.

Sound of traffic and passing pedestrians suddenly intensifies. There is a sound of rain, though no sign, as their hands tighten. Hold.

Cut to an overhead shot of a park's brick path, lined with grass, of passing black umbrellas, with one or two in violently bright colors, shining with wet in the downpour; continuing sound of rain, distant sound of one or two young people laughing. The shot follows one black umbrella covering a couple as they walk off. Cut to him, watching from an upper apartment window — his profile: he withdraws inside and shuts the half-open window.

Cut to view of window from deeper inside the room. A slow zoom back. The final movement of Bruckner's Ninth symphony is playing at low volume on the stereo. Distant sound of rain against the window in the pauses. Cut to a cat staring vacantly on a small green armchair. The room is echoy, as if underfurnished, and too bright. A sound of kitchen clatter.

Cast about the room are books, papers, notebooks, records, postcards of Renaissance artwork, on the wall a poster of a stormy Turner seascape, etc.

Various close-ups — some so close the object cannot be immediately identified — of objects in the room, *though not of the objects described in the following except when explicitly called for*, cover the following sequence. The phone rings: a shattering sound. The clatter in the kitchen pauses. The ring repeats several times, then stops. A moment of silence. The room light goes off. The phone starts ringing again, this time half a dozen times or more before stopping. Close-up of phone: an old-fashioned, heavy, black rotary phone, undusted. Cut to the record, which has finished: the sound of the needle riding the inner groove; a sharper sound of rain gusting against the window. Cut to brief shot of the window, spidery with rain.

Cut to a fast zoom from the room's middle distance to the closing crack between the apartment's front door and the jamb as the door slams shut.

Cut to the startled eyes of the cat.

Interior. An office in the university's Student Union. He sits around a plywood table with several fellow undergrad and grad students, talking. Papers, notebooks, well-thumbed books on Marxism and by such authors as Erich Fromm, Herbert Marcuse, Régis Debray, and the like lay on the table.

First Male Undergrad: But it's better to at least get the minister's permission, otherwise the police will haul us in …

First Female Undergrad: I'm not sure, there's something a little dicey about getting permission first, it's like … like …

Second Male Undergrad: … being co-opted.

Female Undergrad: Yeah.

Male Grad Student, leader of the group: But if we don't, we may have to face jail time, even if it's only overnight, and are we willing to do that?

Second Female Undergrad: It would get us publicity.

He, in an archly artificial tone: One headline, one night in jail, termination of our state support, and all of us suspended, if not expelled! We'd go down in history!

Laughter from the group. Close-up of him, looking pleased with himself.

Cut back to apartment: empty, sound of cat meowing in next room.

Interior. Night. Close-up of a pillow splay with a woman's hair. The only light comes from a street lamp through the room's single window. A sound of movement against the sheets, the hair moves slightly then goes still.

His voice (soft, almost inaudible, somewhat artificial, as though he is acting), speaking in an open space as if outside (perhaps a distant but not readily identifiable sound of wind in trees): I don't know.

Room silence.

Her voice (the same as for his voice): What?

His voice: [inaudible for several words] don't know … what to say.

Room silence. During the shots of the room and sleeping woman, the silence is of the room and the night. When the two speak, however, the sound space is not the room's but of an unknown exterior.

Cut to window: distant moon, glare from unseen street lamp.

Her voice: Do you have to say anything?

Close-up of her eyes, opening in the bed in the room, staring past the camera.

He: Yes. I have to [inaudible] what I have to say, and then [inaudible].

Her voice, whispering: You talk too much already.

Cut to her hair on the pillow: it slides quickly off screen.

Her voice, whispering: You talk too much already.

Long hold on pillow. Sounds of kissing, sighing, rustling sheets.

Cut to previous shot of door closing. Cut to startled eyes of cat. The phone rings once.

Cut to close-up of her eyes.

Her voice, whispering : You talk too much already.

Cut to hair on pillow: it slides quickly of screen.

She sailed like an angel into the sea.

Zoom back to show that this is a film he is watching in an auditorium with other students. Cut to the back of his head against the screen. Sound of couple on screen embracing, making love.

Cut to his hand holding a small popcorn container: he slowly crushes it. In background is the sound of the screen actors speaking, now in their own voices.

Hand-held camera: his point of view as he walks across the campus accompanied by the sound of his breathing, rushed. His hair is longer, shaggier, his jeans are frayed, the jacket a little dirtier than before. The camera movements are erratic, nervous. He ducks and weaves through a small demonstration, briefly joins it, looks through the crowd for someone, moves on. Insert shots of students, hippies, radicals, picket signs ("U.S. out of America!" among them); incomprehensible bellowing from a small bullhorn.

Cut to a brightly lit spread from Ortega y Gasset's book *The Revolt of the Masses* describing and condemning the "mass man." At one point, the reader — he — wipes the open page with his hand as though sweeping away a fly. He turns a page urgently, pens a notation in the margin, reads on.

Cut to his point of view, running down his apartment stairs.

Cut to phone, silent.

Cut to teach-in: anticapitalist lecturer is discussing the history of the early 20th century.

Lecturer, a wiry old man with a Hungarian accent and a tendency to grin at odd moments: ... common imperialist strategies in the Middle East, in the pursuit of oil even then, including Anglo-American control of petroleum reserves in Saudi Arabia and present-day Iraq and Iran, the liberal movement in China under Sun Yat Sen, a conveniently forgotten figure for today's regime, and the political education of expatriate intellectuals like Ho Chi Minh and Chou En Lai in such places as Paris and London ...

Cut to students, including him, seen from three-quarters behind, listening intently, taking notes. Documentary style: grainy stock, hand-held camera, jumpy, over-exposed videotape, a certain flatness of light. Several students ask questions: both questions and answers are largely inaudible. Near the doorway, she is standing, a little detached, cautiously watchful, curious. She catches sight of him, looks away, looks back, watches him, intrigued, skeptical. A certain coldness comes over her gaze as it flickers between the lecturer, who is still answering questions, and him, who simply watches.

Cut to the campus outside: the teach-in is breaking up, he walks toward a lunch truck; she is seen from the back, carrying a book bag, walking away with a soft lilt to her step. The camera stops: he notices, and hastens to catch up with her; they face each other and talk in the distance, forms of students and teachers passing across the screen as they speak. Their voices at first seem almost as far away as their images.

He: Hello.

She: Oh. Hello.

He: Were you there.

She: Curiosity drove me in.

He: You came to jeer but did you stay ...

She: Not quite! The lecturer ...

Voices are suddenly close-up; shot very slowly begins to zoom in.

He: The Stalinists hate him, they say he's a "Trotskyite."

She: They all sound the same to me. Have you read any Solzhenitsyn?

He: Of course.

She, sarcastically: Of course! Well, how can you take any of them seriously!

He: And you take *our* masters seriously, at least these people offer something *else* however *imperfect*, they don't just weave a spell, lock all the exits, and call it "freedom"!

She: No, they call theirs a "people's democracy," or something like that.

He: And we should be *grateful* we're not shot just because we're *allowed* to starve!

She: It's your choice.

He: It's not a choice, no more than it is there, we are *perfecting* totalitarianism.

She: Are we indeed.

Zoom is now completed: they stand face to face, both seen in profile, dominating the shot. As he speaks, she watches warily.

He: We've convinced ourselves, thanks to the propaganda system funded by the corporations, the wealthy, and the rest of us through the weaknesses tickled by *consumption*, that our system is the best there can possibly be in this the best of all *possible* worlds, it's a horrible nightmare so get over it, we can't even *imagine* changing it. We've locked all the doors and thrown away the keys: there's no way out, this is as good as it gets. And we've done it to *ourselves*, what dictator could have dreamt up a more effective organization of concentration camps than ones built, funded, administered, and worked by the internees themselves, it's absolutely brilliant.

Silence.

He: There we go again, we never meet but we immediately start arguing over politics, did you ever notice that?

She. Yes. I did.

He: Stupid comment, sor-ree!

She: You're excused. Maybe!

He: Dahnke shane!

She: *Bitte.*

He: Bitter bitter!

She raises her hand not carrying books in a clawlike gesture, grinning gaily.

He: Let's start over.

He walks backwards five or six paces, then walks back up to her as if seeing her for the first time.

Cut to their shadows in the grass as they meet and after their greetings, walk slowly over the grass.

He: Hel-lo!

She: Hello.

He: Well. God's in his heaven, and all's right with the world.

She: You just say that to all the girls.

He: Only to the angels I know among then.

She: Which can't mean me!

He: Then you must be a devil, but devils are fallen angels, before they fell, they were the fairest of them all.

She: And the proudest.

He: And the brightest.

She: But what if I meant, not that I'm a devil, but merely human?

He: Then I'd have to say you're as close as one can come, fair as an angel, smart as a devil, mysterious as a spirit, sexy as a ... hm!

She: Some people have called me too masculine.

He: You're all woman to me me me!

The shadows stop and face each other, then she bows her head and walks away. He watches her a moment before following her. Their bodies cross the screen in a blur, and the camera focuses for a moment on the bright green grass.

Cut to a gray patch of outdoor wall.

She: I have to go.

He: Not now. Stay.

She: I have an appointment. I have to.

He: Break it.

She: No. I have to go.

He: When will I see you.

She: You know where to find me.

He: No, in fact I don't.

Sound of retreating steps.

Under his breath: Damn ... damn, damn ...

Cut to the university library, a shelf of books in French: visible are spines of books by and about Balzac, Gautier, Stendhal, Baudelaire, Rimbaud, Mallarmé, Huysmans, Sade, etc. His hand brushes the spines, stops at Balzac's *Peau de chagrin*, pulls it out and pages through the opening chapters. Cut to overhead shot down at the flipping pages back to front: stop at the opening page with its epigraphic doodle from Sterne. Close-up of the enigmatic squiggle. He closes the book, slips it into his jacket, under his armpit, and sneaks out of the library.

Cut to him walking hastily across the green campus, in a light rain, hunched over, clutching the hidden book. He careens vulnerably down the walk.

Blurry shots of an empty corner of his room in the apartment seen previously — books on a shelf, a lamp, lit (it is evening), a desk corner, a sneaker, a surrealist landscape taped to the wall, an umbrella lying on the floor, etc. all viewed from floor level. End with a wide-angle shot of the room from a corner across from the door to the kitchen. The sound of a clock ticking. The occasional sound of a book page being turned, of a pen rapidly tracing a word, scratching it out, writing again, a sniff, a body moving in a chair. The cat seen before meows offscreen. Suddenly the cat's head appears, dark and blurry, sniffing the camera curiously and staring into the lens. It meows again.

His voice (offscreen; gently): Hungry? Hmm?

The cat looks up from the lens and meows.

The sound of the reader as he gets up, goes to the kitchen, the cat running after him, takes a can of catfood from the fridge, with the sound of a spoon scraping the can, of tapping of a food bowl, of the bowl being placed on the linoleum floor, of the cat meowing, of the fridge door again opened and closed; then the reader returns to his chair. Sound of scratching wood against wood. He gets up, passes over several squeaky floorboards, sits down. In the background, through the kitchen entrance, the cat's tail can be seen moving as she eats. Throughout the sequence the shot does not change from the wide-angle shot last described.

The sound of flipping book pages, of snort and sniff, as if the reader has a cold. Suddenly he gets up again and walks swiftly across the room; kicks the camera inadvertently and it whirls to the left and goes black.

Cut to his point of view, looking down: a large art book — he flips through it, stopping at romantic landscapes by Ruisdael, Constable, Turner, the Barbizon school (on the record player is the opening of the opening movement of Mahler's Titan symphony, played at low volume): close-up of details of stormy skies and distant mountain peaks. Insert brief shots, in black-and-white, of actual hill country, distant woods seen through a moving car window, sky, clouds: his memories (silent sound track for the inserts). Return to the richly colored paintings and bucolic music. Close-ups of the pictures sometimes resolve into abstracts of brushtrokes, smears of color. Then, cutting to the outburst at the opening of the final movement, he turns a page to a portrait by Van Dyke of a beautiful young woman staring at the observer gravely and haughtily, like a challenge. Hold. Close-up of her face. Hold. Close-up of her eyes. The music cuts off: silence. Close-up of his eyes, music continuing. He stares for a time, then bends down, closes the book, walks away. The shot lingers on the book's closed cover as the music continues tempestuously.

Cut to view of his open window from outside, ground level. Night. Silence.

Reverse point of view, from the window: silence, darkness. Is anyone there? Uncertain. Slight zoom back and down, from the window frame, into the room's half-lit interior, revealing the frame. Silence. While this slow zoom is in progress:

Cut to: much later, same view, with gray light and snow falling outside window. The window is closed. Silence. Zoom continues into the room, dimly lit.

Flash: Her face, for the first time seen clearly, close up. She looks a bit like the Van Dyke: narrow, severe, handsome, proud. It is outdoors, spring, in natural light, with sounds of birds and muted traffic. Her expression is somber and hungry.

Snow. Silence. Repeat the immediately previous zoom back.

Flash: His face, also seen clearly for the first time, close up: not a handsome face, but "interesting," intense, blue-eyed, sandy blond, his hair longer and shaggier still, his eyes small, with an epicanthal fold, his mouth fleshy but shapeless, his expression blank. It is indoors, in artificial light, with muted but reverberant sounds of students scattering and chatting. He looks distrustful and anxious.

Snow. Silence. Zoom continues, longer.

Cut to lintel above his apartment bathroom: across it his hand writes, in pen, in awkward block letters, "Nihil humani alien …"

Cut away from his head while still writing to: snow, swirling. The sound of wind rattling the window. Zoom continues then stops.

Cut to spread from Nietzsche's *Gay Science*, on "the Madman." Sound: a recording of "Brown Shoes," by Frank Zappa and the

Mothers of Invention, on his record player. After a moment, his hand turns the page, then turns it back again as he reads and rereads the passage. Close-up of the opening sentence of the section: "Have you not heard of that madman who lit a lantern in the bright morning hours, ran to the market place, and cried incessantly, 'I seek God, I seek God!'"

Close-up of these last words.

Cut to view through his apartment window of a snowstorm. Last winter light before the dark. Long hold.

The blare of an organ is suddenly heard over this shot. Then:

Cut to church interior, Sunday service, Episcopal therefore a "high" service. Inserts of early parts of service, from the introit to various hymns to the offertory and collection. As the collection ends, there is a shout at the back (it could be "I seek God! I seek God!" but the reverberant space of the church makes the words uncertain), parishioners turn nervously, and a small band of young people, the same seen in the Student Union earlier, including him, but all wearing blank white masks and costumed as poor modern peasants, charge into the nave.

First and Second Man's Voice: Halt! Stop this blasphemy!

First Woman's Voice: Children are dying, women are weeping!

Second Man's Voice: Bombs are falling on our villages!

Second Woman's Voice: Napalm burns the flesh from our bodies.

First Man (at center back; the others stand at the backs of the church aisles): Halt this blasphemy, stop it now!

Third Man: Our villages are dying in a rain of fire.

Third Woman: Bombers roar like terrible angels across the sky.

Second Woman (running down an aisle she suddenly collapses midway and wails): Aiyeeee! Where is my child? She went to get water at the village well, then I heard the roar of the planes, then I heard the falling bombs, then I fell in a dark pit under our house that stank with filth as the bombs crashed around our house. How long have I been there? I've lost track of time. Where is my child? She should be back by now.

Fourth Man runs to the altar and throws himself to the floor. He is dressed in a long blue shawl partly covering his face — he is thin, pale, bearded, with intense, groping eyes and frightened gestures: the blue robe gives him an Old Testament look; he is shirtless beneath it, his feet bare.

Voice of God (from behind the altar): Jeremiah!

Fourth Man looks up wildly.

Cut to a student lounge, he is talking to her. They sit at opposite ends of a small divan, facing each other; they appear in profile throughout.

He: ... and you wouldn't believe the reaction in the church. They thought they were actually being raided by a bunch of terrorists, Weathermen or something, it was amazing, the looks on their faces.

She: I'm sure you loved playing God.

He: It was the high point in my short, happy life in guerrilla theater. "Jeremiah! Before I found thee in the belly, I knew thee, and I ordained thee a prophet unto the nations."

Heads bob up, curious, annoyed, from books around the lounge.

He: What we get away with. The "Merry Pranksters" of the Rust Belt! No apologies to Ken Kesey. Who would believe a work-study program would be training revolutionaries!

Pause.

She: You know you're not serious.

He: What do you mean by that.

She: For you this is a game. It's all very jolly, raiding churches, raising consciousness, thumbing your nose at authority — but only as long as authority lets you, as long as it isn't inconvenienced by it, even requests it, to smooth its conscience, even reinforce it — as long as it pays the bill. But what if it *fought* you? Seriously.

He: You fight back.

She: Without a salary? You'd move on to another work-study program, and the "guerrillas" would vanish like mist.

He: Well yes. I guess! But that's the test — not to be co-opted exactly when it's most convenient. I can't say I know I'd pass it.

She: But isn't the biggest cop-out *pretending* to rebel when in fact you don't pay any price for it, when rebellion is even rewarded? A titillation of rebellion that threatens nothing.

He, sarcastically: You're starting to sound like a revolutionary!

She: I'm not. I'm just asking if *you* are.

He: Me! I don't know! I'm talking about *them* …

Pause. He stares hard into her eyes.

He: And it *has* fought me, I was almost drafted, why do you think I'm here of all places? I applied as a conscientious objector last summer, I couldn't play crazy the way some of my friends did, that was just too, too hypocritical, I don't know, and I'm not even sure I *am* a conscientious objector, I spent hours with counsellors at the American Friends Service Committee, the Quakers, but am I a Quaker?, anyway they rejected *that* and gave me my "4-Q," ready for service at the next draft call. I applied here and got in — a 2-S, student exemption, thank you very much! So they tried and they almost got me. So maybe I haven't been tested. Sure, what we, they are doing looks easy, they're "Merry Pranksters," East-Coast style, harmless and charming, nice kids with good hearts, dedicated to symbolic action because the real thing is just a little too hot to handle. We're young, we're stupid by definition. But we're *students*, for God's sake, and doesn't that give us the right to be a little irresponsible? It's part of our education.

She: A pretty soft "education." A Romper Room for revolutionaries.

He: Maybe, maybe not. They, we might be co-opting them as much as they're co-opting us, insinuating ideas that imply the denial of their authority, the collapse of their power, oh I don't know.…
She: That's very idealistic. If not wishful thinking!

He: Ideas have power, look at this fucking country, it's founded on a bunch of highly questionable ideas. Equality. Freedom. The pursuit of happiness! Does anybody think about what those things mean? Really? So somebody tries to plant the seeds of a bad conscience in the powerful so they'll become their own worst enemies: they know their own weak points better than anyone else, and a bad conscience is its own destroyer. No? (satisfied by his own phrasing) I like that!

She: It sounds good but it could backfire.

He: No!

She: If you expose your hand to those dedicated to destroying you and your ideas. (She looks hard at him.) After all, they have ideas too. Which ideas will undermine which?

He: They're not necessarily my ideas. I certainly don't know! But that's for the future.

She: The last election doesn't hold much promise.

He: Maybe we need to go beyond elections.

Pause.

She: Would you ever let yourself be drafted? If the law changed and …

He: There's always Canada to run away to. Or Sweden.

She: Or you could go underground!

He: I already am. I'm ignored!

She: Must be a depressing thought for a revolutionary.

He (with disgust): I'm not a revolutionary. A person can carry on a Revolution of One in his own world, in his own time, on his own terms: a revolution of the mind, of the spirit, without that, any other revolution has to fail anyway, like every single one has since *ours*. A *social* and *political* revolution is inevitable — maybe it is (The ideal surprises him, as if this were the first time he had seriously considered it), maybe it is! — *but* it can only succeed if there's a *spiritual* revolution at the same time, a *change of the human soul*, and that can happen only for one individual at a time.

She: Bravo! Though it's bad Marxist-Leninism. But how, o noble leader?

He: The hell with Marx and Lenin! By each person staring at himself in the mirror and telling himself what he knows and hates to admit: *"You are mortal"* and *"You aren't good enough."* And then changing *himself* while he still has time.

She: What if you can't. What if no one can.

He: There's always something you can change — be brutally honest with yourself, never stop bending yourself to your will, your will to your ideal, your ideal to your understanding of perfection.

She: How very hippie.

He: I hate hippies! "Do your own thing!" So I can be a hippie the rest of the world better not be or I'll starve, their minds are insipid from too much pot, give me a revolutionary any day, at least you can talk to them.

She: Actually, your ideal sounds more like Eternal Reform than Revolution.

He: Unless you believe in permanent revolution, like Trotsky! hell, even Jefferson thought there ought to be a revolution every twenty years.

She: I thought you didn't like Trotskyists.

He: I don't, I don't like "ists" or "ics" or "tians."

She goes cold, then gropes for a cigarette in her bag. He, aware he has offended, fumbles for a match and, after two failed matches, finally lights her cigarette.

She: Thank you. I think I know what you mean about "ists" and "ics" and "tians."

He: Epigones!

She: Followers. But we can't all be leaders....

He: Why not?

She: There'll be no-one left to lead.

He: We can lead ourselves.

She smokes her cigarette silently for a time, not looking at him but staring into space, then suddenly crushes it out in an ashtray.

She, pertly, without looking at him: I must lead myself to my Spenser class.

She gets up, takes her bookbag, turns and gives him a little wave.

She: Don't burn down the library while I'm away.

He: Beware the Bower of Bliss!

She walks off, turns to give him an ironic look, then continues without looking back.

His point of view: her retreating back. Hold.

Cut to the exterior of the church in the earlier scene; its largest bell tolls once. Hold — wait for reverberation to diminish to silence.

Sound of waves crashing and beach noises over darkness, of family chatter nearby, distant calls and laughter, a barking dog, sea gulls, lifeguard whistles, etc. Light leaks in from the sides of the screen, and it's soon clear the camera is wrapped in a towel carried by someone: after a few steps, the towel twitches from the lens, and the view is a bobbing, jiggling one of a summer beach.

He, unseen: This seems good, how about here?

She, unseen (she's the one holding the camera): Looks safe enough.

He: When all's said and done, a house in the suburbs and a blanket in the sand might just be the best formula for happiness.

She: So it's about being happy now! We're converting you.

The camera looks off away down the beach for a moment, then swings from her arm as the couple spread the beach towel between them.

He, squinting at her: Unless, of course …

She: What?

He: … it's quicksand.

The towel is lowered to the sand.

She: We'll soon find out, won't we.

She places the camera on a corner of the towel: exaggerated view of the two of them from very low, wildly distorted, as two giants in bathing suits, facing each other. She sits first, he watching her; then he crouches down by her side.

She: Afraid you'll sink in?

He grins. They glance up and down the beach.

He: Let's go for a swim, the ocean's less ambiguous than we are!

She: Is it.

They both stand and walk toward the water. The camera does not move until they have left the shot a few moments.

Cut to their feet as they step into the surf wash and foam, the gray wet sand pocked with air holes from sand crabs, curls of seaweed, broken clam shells, a trace of jellyfish. Roar of waves, cries of gulls, whoops and hollers of waders and swimmers. Life guard whistles.

He, shouting: It's not that cold!

She, also shouting: You go in …

He: Then you join me …

Her point of view: he wades in to his knees, looking back, grinning and waving to her, then dives in over a wave. He swims out to a sandbar, walks across it and dives in to the waves on the other side, turning back briefly to wave toward her, showing off. Camera divides between her point of view — watching him, glancing at the other waders, the lifeguards, the seaweed in the wash, jellyfish, etc. — and his, as he dives, swims, body surfs, looking at her standing timidly at the water's edge, watching him with a big grin, at fellow swimmers, or out past the swells toward the horizon, which is claustrophobically close in, given his low elevation above the water. After he swims past the farthest swimmers, there is a peculiar sense of being closed in in the midst of the ocean. The view takes in nearby waves, rolling, glimmering, toward him, and a gull dips down and settles on the sea surface not far from him. It seems to appraise him. Flip point of view between seagull and him: close-up of his eyes just above the water, then a close-up of the sea gull's single eye. Hold.

A lifeguard suddenly whistles: he looks back toward the beach. She stands unmoving a few yards from the lifeguard stand, staring out toward him: the distance between him and the water's edge is startlingly large, maybe 200 or 300 feet: a half dozen other bathers also watch him curiously.

What had been imposed melted away like snow in summer. There was nowhere to stand where she drowned. Flailing between knots of driftwood. The sand loosening between her fingers.

The lifeguard stridently blasts his whistle and imperiously motions him to swim closer to the beach. He continues resting and floating, looking casually at the beach and then over at the sea gull. The lifeguard blasts again. Finally, after this goes on for several minutes, after giving the gull one last glance, he swims leisurely back toward the sandbar.

Cut to the gull beating its wings up into the air: follow it as it flies farther up and away.

Cut to him throwing himself into a falling wave and riding it in to the sandbar. Long hold on him riding the wave.

Calm as he used to as a child.

Cut to him rising from the wave, standing. He walks slowly across the bar, then more slowly through the gully to the beach, in a straight march, almost solemnly, aimed directly at her.

Calm.

The sand loosening between her fingers.

As he pulls his legs across the gully, flip the point of view between hers and his, she watching him advance out of the sea toward her, he watching her grow in size as he approaches. The alternating of the shots speeds up as he walks out of the waves.

Cut to profile shot of both as they approach one another.

She, gaily shouting above the sound of the waves: We thought we were about to lose you!

He shakes his head sombrely. He stops a few feet from her.

He: I'm not so easy to lose.

They both look at a dead horseshoe crab, lying upside down nearby, its shell looking like a war helmet, its long bone tail whisking in the surf wash, its dead legs bristlely and slippery.

He: Darwin, Darwin on the wall, who's the fittest of them all? They survived the dinosaurs and they're likely to survive us!

Close-up of the crab's black green belly.

Cut to them lying on the beach towel. Shot from straight above: he on his belly, she on her back. His face is invisible, pressed against the towel; she wears large sunglasses, with one knee bent. The effect is as if they were moving unwittingly in opposite directions. Hold. Sound of waves, laughter. They don't move.

Cut to view of her Volkswagen as they drive, still in their swim suits, in the afternoon light through flat stunted woodland white with sand. Views of passing trees, brush, roadside, vehicles, of details of the interior of the car, of details of the bodies of the two passengers. They are silent; every so often, a view of his eyes watching her. She stares straight ahead, driving.

Cut to the darkened interior of her parents' house, a view of the front door dead center: sound of it being unlocked, the door opens to bright light, and they enter, carrying beach things, etc. Views of them walking through the first floor, living and dining rooms, hallways, kitchen. After depositing the beach bags and towels in the utility room beside the kitchen, she goes to the living room and turns on the radio to a jazz station. It is early evening.

She: I'm going to take a shower.

He, with an odd look away: Okay.

He watches her leave.

Cut to him listening to the radio; the sound of the shower starts, and he turns his head. Close-up of his eyes.

Insert flash from previous scene:

He: Unless, of course …

She: What?

He: … it's quicksand.

Cut to him listening to the radio a few minutes later; the sound of the shower stops; he doesn't budge, but his face becomes tense. He sucks in his lips nervously.

Hold on his face. Music continues. Sound of bathroom door opening and closing, of feet treading the floor, then more quietly on carpet, and a shadow crosses his face: he looks up.

Cut to her, from his point of view, wrapped in a towel with her hair swathed in another: she lies down on the carpet not far from him, her eyes closed. The music continues.

Cut to close-up of his eyes, watching her.

Cut to his point of view of her face: slow zoom down her body wrapped in the towel, to her feet.

Return to close-up of his eyes, staring at her face.

Cut to complete silence and a close-up of his hand: slowly his hand reaches for her cheek and strokes it with a finger; his finger traces the line of her chin, then moves gently down her throat to her chest, then down to her cleavage just visible above the wrapped towel. She sighs and suddenly turns to him. The radio remains silent throughout this and the following sequence; the only sound the sound of their breathing.

He pulls the towel from her breasts and the two of them embrace, then grapple. The two towels unwrap from her body. Views as they make love, not speaking but making small animal-like sounds. She comes with a moan, then he too shortly thereafter, and they sink back to the carpet, embracing. Hold as their breathing slowly calms. He gently strokes her forehead, her cheeks, her chin and neck.

He stops and stares into her eyes, she staring up toward the ceiling: close-up of their faces, dim in the living room half light, uncannily invisible to each other. The only sound is still of their breathing.

She suddenly sits up: her face leaves the frame, his eyes following her as she pulls herself to her feet. Cut to his point of view as she walks around the room, gathering the towels. She suddenly turns to him, in a full frontal shot of her, naked, from hair to her feet, and she stares at him, opaquely.

Cut to him, lying on his elbow, naked, in front of her, staring as opaquely at her. Hold.

Cut to the speaker of the radio, heard again, picking up the jazz number exactly where it broke off.

Cut to silence, with her lying on the floor, as before, still folded in her towels. Her eyes open slowly, watching him, and she breaks into laughter, without sound.

Cut to a continuation of the jazz, very loud, and his eyes, staring blankly at the radio.

Cut to the jazz continuing, but as though far away, in the next room, and to her as before, swathed in the two towels, lying with eyes closed, on the carpet: she opens her eyes and looks at him, quizzical and vaguely hurt. Cut to his face, which refuses to acknowledge hers. Cut to her face. Suddenly she gets up and leaves the room. Cut to him staring stonily at the radio. Sound of bathroom door closing hard.

Hold.

Exterior. Day. The platform of a train station. He stands, nervously glancing around him, with his fellow guerrilla-theater actors seen earlier in the church scene, the so-called "Merry Pranksters": some of them carry shoulder bags with odd things sticking out — long eagle feathers, arrow fletches, a child's bow, etc., their clothing Wild West hippie: leather fringe tops, gypsy kerchiefs, high collars half hiding their faces; several wear Indian war-paint; he wears a red handkerchief around his neck, a dented cowboy hat, loose pants, a bulky shirt. They are surrounded by homeward-bound commuters. It's a hot, muggy day.

A train comes in, the actors glance at each other as commuters pile in — the group's leader shakes his head; the train doors close, the train leaves. Another train comes in, the leader nods, and the actors enter the train with the commuters past a conductor, into a central car.

Interior of the jammed train car. Some of the passengers look over the actor hippies superciliously; the latter nervously return the sneer, trying to "act naturally" and overdoing it. He stands staring into space with a withdrawn expression beneath an advertisement for a Volkswagen.

The train comes into another station: the doors open, passengers leave, enter. The leader looks furtively for his actors as the car becomes packed in a nearly immovable mass of tight-lipped suburban business suits. Cut to view of exit door, standing passengers squeezing away from the doorways, would-be passengers lined up looking wistfully up the train steps, and the doors stay open longer than expected — camera dwells on opening — then suddenly close as a conductor sings out, "All aboard." The train lurches ahead, nearly throwing over a knot of more stolid standees. One of the actors grins as a plump businessman resumes his scowl, his dignity, and his Wall Street Journal.

One of the actors, singing under her breath: "And they all lived in houses made of ticky-tacky …"

Inserts of passengers in the crush and passing ghetto neighborhoods, abandoned factories, burnt-out warehouses, a phalanx of modest homes, backyards, seen through the train windows and the crush of standing passengers, a blur of passing rails — of speed and claustrophobia.

From the end of the car comes the conductor's voice: "Tickets, tickets," over the rumble of the train.

Lead Cowboy, after one last check of his actors; shouting: All ri-ight!

The actors pull out their props — don Indian headdresses and wave bows and arrows, yell and whoop like attacking Indians; others, the "cowboys," start shooting cap pistols, cover their lower faces with handkerchiefs like Wild West robbers (he hurriedly puts on a Lone Ranger mask), and start shouting: "Stick your hands up! This is a holdup, we're taking over this train!" Bedlam breaks out: passengers scream and try to scramble around the car, though barely able to move in the crush: the result is more squeeze in the crowd and a brief panic. War whoops and cap pistol shots. People try to duck. The only people able to move, curiously, are the guerrillas, of which there are no more than six or seven, scurrying through the crowd, squeezing through legs, clambering over seatbacks, crawling on overhang shelves, climbing up poles, etc., behaving like impish monkeys, gaily "terrorizing" the crowd, aiming cap pistols and rubber suction-cup arrows at executive secretaries and file clerks, office managers and junior vice presidents, stock brokers and advertising account managers; twitting the conductor, doing no harm but raising Cain along the city sleepers. Sounds of cap pistols, war whoops, wraiths of smoke from the caps. The silver-haired conductor continues trying to collect tickets through the melee. Suddenly he confronts an "Indian" who stands with mocking snarl under an advertisement for Coppertone sunlotion showing a little dog pulling down the bathing suit of an abashed young girl, her white bottom displayed against her copper-toned back.

Conductor, shouting: Hand me your ticket!

Indian: Me only *scalp* ticket, Kemo sabe! Yeehah!

Conductor: Hand me your ticket right now. If you don't have a ticket, you have to get off this train.

Second Cowboy: We don't need no ticket, podner, we're taking over this train and you're gettin' a permanent vacation!

He shoots his cap pistol.

Conductor: Hand me *your* ticket or I'll have you thrown off this train!

The Indians ululate, in chorus.

Lead Cowboy: We're throwing all of *you* off this train, we're giving it back to *the people!*

As he continues, the Indians whoop and yell, the cowboys cheer and shoot, the commuters watch in disbelief, some in mockery, some in bewilderment, flinching at the reports of the pistols, uncertain whether to panic, laugh, or fulminate.

Lead Cowboy, climbing to the back of a seat and addressing the crushed and sweaty crowd, waving his pistol: We hereby liberate the East Chestnut Hill Local of the Penn Central Railroad, in the name of people of color from around the world, the white man has oppressed and exploited the people of the world with his unbridled greed and desire for power, and we hereby take back the cities he has ruined, the souls he has destroyed, and the world he is despoiling. (War whoops. Pistol cracks.) We hereby take back our autonomy and our dignity and our pride. (Pistol cracks. War whoops.) We here take back our world!

Conductor: It's none of my business what you are liberating or where you are liberating or for what persons you are liberating. I am here to collect tickets and you will hand over your ticket or you will get off this train!

Commuters cheer the conductor.

Well-dressed, middle-aged woman to a guerrilla "Indian": You should be ashamed of yourself!

Guerrilla Indian whoops in her face.

The train slows down as it approaches a station.

Lead cowboy to the crowd: "We are [inaudible under Indian ululation]."

Woman: … ashamed! You all need to grow up!

Conductor: Get off this train! Get off!

Train stops at station.

Conductor: Get off get off! If you don't have a ticket …

Woman: Even if you *do* have a ticket!

The guerrillas jump down the steps to the platform.

Lead Cowboy: We're off but not forgotten! Watch your wallets! Watch your tickets! Watch your houses of ticky tacky!

Cut to Conductor's point of view: they stand, looking defeated — abashed and suddenly chagrined — on the station platform.

Conductor: Now just look at yourselves! It's all very well to liberate the world, but the next time you try to hijack a train, don't forget to first …

Second Cowboy: … fuck the conductor!

Another conductor, down the platform: All aboard!

View of first conductor as the train pulls out and the would-be guerrillas ululate at his purple enraged face. Cut to point of view of departing train: the Indians do a little victory dance on the platform, dancing in a circle and whooping, unheard over the train's rumbling; the cowboys brandish their weapons and get off a few last cap shots. Hold till platform, Indians, and cowboys disappear around a bend.

Cut to his point of view, as one of the cowboys on the platform, of the train as it turns the bend. Sound of ululating from his fellows as they remove their costumes and put back their bows and arrows, pistols, etc., into their satchels, etc. Several platform standees watch them bemusedly.

Indian: Dig *that!*

Second Cowboy, unattendingly: Out-ta-sight.

Indian Woman, matter-of-factly: That was even weirder than I thought it'd be.

Miscellaneous shots of the group on the station platform.

He removes the Lone Ranger mask from his face and deposits his cap pistol in his shirt.

A train, coming from the opposite direction, stops at the opposite platform: the guerrilla actors scramble through the station tunnel to the other side and docilely get into the train.

Conductor: All aboard!

Point of view of station: the train leaves. Hold as train shrinks in distance against the background of the city's downtown skyline.

Cut to interior of his apartment, late at night: low view of windows, a chair, books lined up on the floor beneath the window, an unlit lamp. The room is dark except for light coming from a single lamp, off camera. Music from the record player: the opening of Siegfried's Rhine Journey, played very low on a scratchy LP, in the next room. Hold this view over the following: The sound of writing: a hurried, jerky scratching. The writer (he) occasionally speaks to himself in a whisper. The chair creaks as he changes position. He sighs. At one point he gets up and walks across the room, still unseen by the camera, then a little later walks back and sits down again. Continued sound of scratching. The cat meows, also unseen.

His voice, whispering: There, there …

He strokes the cat, unseen.

His voice, still whispering: There, there …

Sound of purring as if close to the camera.

His voice, same: There, there … there, there …

Sound of purring. Hold.

Cut to same view, with streaks of early dawn visible through the windows, which offer an unobstructed view, except for the tops of one or two trees near the sill, of the sky. Sound of stylus stuck in a record groove.

Cut to same view, but from a point several feet from the floor, centering the right-hand window: a distant urban horizon is visible. Hold, over silence, with three regular jump zooms in at slow intervals as the sun slowly rises, a pink-red flat disk of flaming radiance advancing, like a vast egg of light, into the richly polychrome sea of the dawn sky, in the end dissolving the screen in a blinding corona at the moment the sun parts from the horizon. Quiet, with early morning birdsong.

Cut to desk with unfinished manuscript — he sits staring into the sun with a blank expression. He suddenly shakes his head, dazed, blinded. Cut to white screen. Sound (only) of birds suddenly taking off in a great flock, a long eruption of sound of wings and shrill cries that slowly fades away to quiet as they fly into an unseen distance.

Dazzling.

Exterior. Day. He is walking the campus, an intensely happy yet puzzled look on his face: he has discovered something in himself, though he isn't sure precisely what it is or what it is worth — he only knows it holds some importance for him. His clothing is more bedraggled than before, his hair even shaggier. He wears the same corduroy jacket but it looks uncleaned and wrinkled as if slept in. His gold-rimmed glasses lean precariously on his nose and his jeans have a tear near the cuff.

He sits in the grass under a shade tree, takes out several scraps of paper from his bookbag and reads them over; takes out a pen and makes several changes and reads them over.

Over the shoulder shot of the manuscript: it is a poem, hastily written in sloppy handwriting. Cut to close-up of the title: "The Sun," with "Hymn to" crossed out, then of the poem's first words, "I woke within the winter," then shot slides across the rest of the line "'s night within my winter's mind"; then to the opening of the following line, "within a dark, within a cold," then the rest of the line, "silent, deaf, dumb, blind." Then the same for the following line: "I had no mind, I had no heart …"

He, whispering: … I had no eyes, no thing was mine.

Cut to view of entire poem, nearly illegible from revisions, with his shadow falling across it.

He, still whispering: "Except a memory, a dream, a word, a sound, a note, a line

To which I held. And then a line of dimness dimmed the gray upon

And something rose and greeted me, dazzled me and, clenched in one,

Crowded into the empty sky and showed the Earth, and was the Sun."

Cut to middle distance shot of him sitting in grass, staring at the poem: his expression suddenly becomes skeptical; he crosses it out, begins to crush it, then stops, uncrushes, folds it up, and puts it back into his jacket pocket.

He sits frowning into space, looking as though he is trying to remember something in detail. Cut to middle distance shot of him sitting in the grass. He looks homeless.

Cut to inside the darkened front door of his parents' house (mimicking the symmetry of the similar shot at her house, earlier): the sound of the resonance of the doorbell just after it has rung. Hold: the camera remains stationary throughout the following sequence.

He, cleaned up now though not too much, goes to the door and opens it to reveal her, standing on the stoop in a glare of sunlight, dressed in a light jacket and a white summer dress with large black polka dots and smiling nervously. She is barely seen, in a bright sliver along his flank and almost hidden behind the dark shadow of his back.

She: Hi …

He, shyly but cheerfully: Just in time!

She steps inside and is immediately engulfed by the exaggerated darkness inside the house. He closes the door and they both leave the frame. Hold on door.

Sound of rustling as she removes her jacket and he takes it.

He, off camera: How was parking.

She, same: I took the train in.

Cut to dining room table, lit by a low-hanging lamp, a Haydn piano trio on the record player; he brings in two dinner plates; she sits, smiling at him. A window looks out on a narrow city backyard, with wrought-iron table and bench, surrounded by plank fencing above which the upper stories of low brick houses can be seen; already in shadow, it gradually darkens as the scene progresses. Shot through window: a bird lights on the ground and picks at the gravel.

She: Oh look.

They both look out the window.

Close-up of bird: a blue jay, with flexing crest. It pecks and pecks, oblivious to its audience. Close look at the jay — its iridescent black wings, flexing tail, its yellow black eye, its black beak — as it pecks and pecks. Hold.

Reverse point-of-view shot of him and her, through the slightly dirty window; watching. Hold.

He brings in a serving platter, sits pours the wine.

She: Smells wonderful.

He: We'll see if it tastes half as good.

He looks back out window — the bird is gone, the yard is in dusk.

As they eat, he is oddly silent, appears awkward, unsure of himself, concentrating on his meal; she watches him with curious, diffident glances, but mostly studying her plate. He doesn't look her in the eye.

He, abruptly, excessively polite: More wine?

She: Thank you …

He pours.

Various close-ups of wine, food, utensils, mouths, eyes, hair — increasingly focussed details, out of context and obsessively exact. The sound of cutlery on porcelain plateware becomes more pronounced.

Suddenly he wipes his mouth after the last mouthful. The Haydn ends.

He, smiling: Well?

She: You were very absorbed.

He: Was I? Sorry.

She: But eating is sacred.

He: Well! There weren't many ideas shared by Greek philosophers and Benedictine monks, but I hear that was one. Sacred or not, did it taste any good?

She: Have no fear, Mr. Monk, Philosopher, Chef …

He: Oh, I always fear.

She: Always!

He: Always!

They smile at each other.

Cut to view of backyard through window: it is dark. Slowly zoom in toward the glass. The dining table with remains of meal can be seen reflected, and the hands on the table of the couple facing each other.

His voice: Coffee?

Hold.

Cut to living room: a recording by Joni Mitchell on the stereo. They sit on a couch in a pool of light from a side lamp. She watches him, her elbow on the sofa back, her cheek in her hand, her legs drawn up; he sits forward, turned slightly away, intent on his thought.

He: ... but is it *real*, is for me always the question. For example, is time real?

She: Time?

He: Past, present, future — are *they* real? Or is it all just a repeated, relentless *now*? I often have the feeling that only the past is real, the present is a tiny window through which the darkness of the future rushes wildly into the past, suddenly frozen in all its splendor, with shape and form and detail and, in fact, *existence*, paradoxically — that the *dead*, in a way, is all that *lives*.

She, gesturing to the room: Then all *this* has no existence for you.

He: *This* is already past the moment you point it out, the moment you are even aware of it. Like music! Hear? (They listen for a moment.) So maybe time has no existence, the future has not yet happened, the present is ungraspable, and the past is no more than a hallucination called memory.

She: And space?

He: Relativity saves the day, or pretends to. If time is continuous with space, yet time has no existence outside the moment, the "now," how can space survive, is space also a hallucination, something created by, say, bifocal vision ...

She: The fly's world would be a hallucination with a thousand dimensions.

He: God wouldn't be so cruel.

She: So you believe in God after all.

He almost laughs, then pauses.

He: ... No! ... Yes ... It depends.

She: It depends.

He: A world without a god of some kind makes no sense: just look at it! And yet a world with a god also makes no sense, just look at it... .

She: Morally ...

He: ... aesthetically, politically, economically, philosophically. If there's a god he's a Supreme Idiot Savant with severe mood swings.

She: Unless He is a She ...

He: Especially so in that case!

She: But you are the one who said "it depends."

He: Oh well — on my mood! The quality of my hope versus the quality of my uncertainty.

She: Not despair then.

He: Not yet.... I still feel sure I, *we*, can have it.

She: What.

He pauses, less at a loss then in embarrassment.

She chaffs him: Come, spit it out.

He: An explanation.

She: An explanation!

He: That makes sense. Moral sense.

She: Of what.

He: Of everything. The world, if you want. Existence. Reality. Truth, with a capital "t." I haven't given up on that.

She: But what if you have to?

He: Have to what?

She: Give up the hope you can find it by yourself. By yourself alone.

He: Have you?

She suddenly withdraws far from him.

Pause.

He: I'd throw myself out the nearest window.

She: No, you wouldn't. You would put one foot in front of the other, and walk on ahead. As you have for years before.

He: Maybe so. But a little bitter!

She: About not being right?

He: No.

She looks at him skeptically.

She: I think you would.

He: Maybe I would!

Pause.

She: You don't seem terribly curious.

He: About what?

She: About what keeps people like me going.

He: So! What keeps people like you going?

She I'm not sure we know each other well enough yet to tell you!

He: Now you're being cruel.

She: How can you say that.

She pretends to slap him across the lips several times.

He is about to grapple her but seems to think better of it and pulls back. She notices and the glitter of expectancy in her eyes dims to disappointment; she lowers her eyes with a desolate look.

They both freeze, looking away from each other.

After a painfully long moment, he breaks the paralysis by withdrawing a pack of cigarettes, and lights one up. He offers her one; she takes one from the pack and he lights hers with the tip of his own.

He leans back, smoking. Through the deepening cloud of smoke around his head, he speaks.

He: I guess you mean Jesus Christ.

She: Maybe.

He: I find *him* the least believable of them all. I had a brief, intense moment of Jesus worship when I was a kid. Then I realized it was a hoax, the Christian promise. Anyway, better worship a rock in a tree grove or a mirror in a plywood box than a mean-spirited divinity that saves by formula, plays emotional blackmail, demands the sacrifice of your brain, to say nothing of your body, and condemns the great mass of humanity from the beginning of time to eternal torment for *premature birth,* all the while proclaiming that "God is love."

She: Nevertheless …

He: Nevertheless!

Silence.

He: Anything that requires me to give up what little intelligence I've got, and my conscience as well, can never have my allegiance. Why is it the religion of love that knows so well how to hate?

She: Not intelligence, just the arrogance that goes with it, the self-defeating certainty that gnaws away at itself because it knows it can never truly know anything. And it only hates evil …

He: By beating it at its own game. Is there anything more relentlessly evil than burning people to death who happen to disagree with you? We'd make a lovely bonfire for each other, right here.

She: The death camps?

He: Where did they learn the wisdom of slaughtering those who won't, who *can't* "convert," if only because that can't change what they are? Most Catholic Spain taught Germany *that* trick.

She: I can't defend the Middle Ages …

He: But that was your best chance. If Christianity could bring peace and happiness on earth, there was its chance: then and then only …

She: That was never the point. Happiness was never the point.

He: What is the "*point*"?

She: You don't want to hear it so you won't hear it. Why should I bother?

He: If you know something it's only a kindness to divulge it to a poor, lost sinner.

She: You're trying to laugh, like everyone who protests too much.

He, angrily: Protest too much! Pretty soon you'll be accusing me of being a secret would-be *believer*.

The music has stopped.

She: Aren't you?

He, after a stung pause: You still haven't told me the *point*.

She: If you were, it might be worth telling you.

He: Try me.

She, teasingly: You don't seem desperate enough

He: Try me!

Pause.

He, with mock, and yet true, desperation: Try me!

Long pause.

He, very quietly: Try me …

Long pause: she watches him with eyes that deepen with sadness.

She: I think you already know.

She is silent.

He, whispering (it is uncertain whether he actually says this or only thinks it): Sphinx. Sibyl. Oracle. Priest. Fake.

She gets up.

She: I have to go.

He: Don't …

He grabs her, stares in her eyes, then pulls her to the floor.

They kiss, embrace, tussling across the floor, but suddenly, after a long wrestle, while he is fiddling with the zipper at the back of the neck of her dress, she pulls his hands from her and, grabbing them, pulls them above her head. He doesn't resist.

She, whispering: I have to go.

She releases his hands, gets up from the floor and gathers her things. He watches from the floor, then reluctantly stands.

He: Don't go.

She: I have to …

He: Stay.

She: I have to go. I'm going. I'm going now.

She walks to the front door and stops, staring at it. Cut to same view as when she entered. She stands staring at the closed door.

Sound of a closet door opening and closing, of cloth against cloth, of his footsteps. He enters the shot with her jacket, helps her into it, and opens the door for her; she leaves and he follows, closing the door behind him.

Cut to a hot, dark city street as they walk. There are few passersby and little traffic. They walk side by side, rigid, a little pale, barely acknowledging each other's presence. The sound of their footsteps on the sidewalk seems far away, resonant. They pass lamp posts, storefronts, parked cars, traffic lights, neon signs lit and unlit, parking meters and signs, stop signs, metal trash cans, a newspaper box with a headline "Massacre Revealed," a grocery store, drug store, a deli with gaudy front, a bar, restaurant, stoops, other pedestrians, a darkened church with a sermon marquee asking "Where Are You Going After This?" They cross driveways, alleys, an intersection, cross a gutter, a section of cobblestone street, cross the light filtering through leaf shadows of a sodium street light glowing yellow and dim. They cross an empty, poorly lit park with a small, ludicrously splashing fountain, cross another street, come upon a set of stairs leading beneath the city street and descend them.

In the broad, desolate, dimly lit walkway, they pass barred cages on either side of them, some with revolving gates made of spokes of wood and metal, looking like the tines of rakes, painted green. They reach the station entrance; she fetches her ticket from her bag and passes through the turnstile and down a set of stairs to the landing below. He watches her blankly from the turnstile. Close-up of her glancing up at him with a frightened look as she begins her descent.

He, coldly: I will see you again.

He turns on his heel and strides angrily away.

Suddenly he turns on his heel and walks back, staring at her in painful longing.

She, unseen: What is vital is to choose. And hold to your choice.

Cut to him in the middle distance, walking away: did he just do this, did she just say that? It isn't certain, nor, if they did neither of these things, whether it was he or she who imagined it.

The section between her frightened look, his angry words, each time shortened, and his walking away is played over, repeated, several times, each with more exposure time until the scene solarizes into indistinguishable light.

Her voice: What is vital is to choose. And hold to your choice.

Cut to previous view from his apartment window over the park crosswalk. It is winter, early evening; beginning to snow. Silence in the apartment. Occasional passersby. Several pools of light flick on beneath the walk lights.

Cut to reverse point of view: from the crosswalk, looking up at the lit window. The cat sits in the window, staring down. Hold.

Cut to view of him sitting at his desk, studying, silence in the apartment: the focal point is a patch of plaster wall, onetime cream white flecked with dust, over his right shoulder, above the desk; slightly chipped, some of the paint having broken from old moisture blisters. The camera zooms slowly in toward the patch of wall. Sound of him scratching notes on a pad, breathing, coughing once or twice, turning the pages of a book. The desk lamp, the room's sole light, throws a strong shadow over the edge of the desk, a hyperbola of light against the wall. The camera's zoom ends when all that can be seen is the patch of wall, the texture of the plaster, of the paint behind the chipped sections: a very pale, eggshell blue.

Cut to his face: he is staring into space at the wall, perhaps at the same patch, with a look of vacancy, uncertainty, pain.

Flashback of him and her tussling on the floor near the couch.

Cut to his stare.

Cut to the two of them. She suddenly thrusts his hands above her head.

Cut to his face. Hold.

Cut to a view of him on his telephone in the apartment, listening tensely. Pause.

Her voice, on the phone: Please don't call me here. It causes awkward questions.

Cut to his face, staring at wall. Sound of receiver returning to its cradle.

A flickering image of the tussling.

His face.

Cut to phone: It causes awkward questions …

Her face, mouthing the words.

8

Phone: … awkward questions …

His face.

Sound of receiver returning to its cradle.

His voice, speaking into phone, blank: All right.

Cut to close up of cat's face, with sound of ticking of alarm clock.

Cut to view of snowy crosswalk, the walk lights dimming in the swirling snow. The window sash rattles in the wind. Hold. Fading darkness, to complete black.

Cut to same view, spring morning: sun, trees in leaf, grass low and green. A single bird sings unsparingly. Hold. He appears, seen from above, walking across the park in late-winter gear, carrying under his arm books and a three-ring binder. The camera follows him after catching him and lingers on him as he shrinks in the distance, through the park's trees.

Cut to a concrete bridge spanning a river. He is walking across it in a kind of forced march, still carrying his books. A high wind blows down the river. The road traffic is fairly heavy, but there are no other pedestrians on the bridge. He leans into the wind — he looks haggard, gaunt, unhealthy, suddenly he catches sight of his shadow before him against the cement sidewalk: he watches it with a kind of appalled fascination as he walks, leaning against the cross wind. Cut to this point of view: his shadow shows an almost skeletal figure with long hair and a long coat flapping grotesquely in the wind. Hold this shot, following the shadow, as he continues across the bridge.

He suddenly stops and looks down the river, out of the wind. Cut to his point of view: a river with its banks dominated by parkland and old residential buildings on one hand, a row of sculling boat houses on the other; in the distance, a bend in the river and the square dome of a ceremonial structure dominating a thickly forested hill on the horizon. The wind increases in force.

Cut to his shadow on the pavement, now in profile, the wind blowing his hair across his face, the overcoat whipping his legs. Sound of passing traffic, of the wind blowing harder. Hold.

Cut to classroom: a graying European professor in a black suit dusted with chalk holds forth at the front end of the class, standing before a blackboard marked with half-erased words in chalk, perhaps from a previous class:

"It is not a place where one can live, it is without the safety of words and concepts, it is without a name ... But it is moving in the depths ..."

Professor: ... in this way, myth and history were brought together in a tangled skein from which we have yet to emerge. Or a better image might be a chrysalis made of bafflement and bloody-mindedness that has justified any brutality in the name of a noble cause, the future of man, the purity of the soul, "national security." Christianity, Romanticism, existentialism, the salvation of the soul, the imposition of the ego, the world-conquest of man, on the one hand; on the other, the Roman imperium, the Enlightenment, the Communist experiment — the health of the City, of society, the polis; the sublimation of desire to reason; the suppressing of the individual before the *liberation* of man. Yes? And woman too!

He smiles broadly, pointing to a waving hand.

Student: How does the United States fit into history then?

The professor frowns.

Professor: The United States of America is the greatest country in the world. That is the whole point of its history. If it has one. And it's not sure it does!

Silence. The professor smiles puckishly.

Professor: The United States of America. (He sighs.) "The last best hope of earth," quoth the bard. The United States of America, for all its current problems, and heaven knows it has more than its fair share of them, the United States of America has always represented itself as an exception, the great exception to history, a society of individuals, a society of saints and pilgrims who are rewarded by God for doing the Right Thing, who get along by going along, who do well by doing right — Rome in love with righteousness, what Nietzsche himself called for: "a Caesar with Christ's soul." Yet, if we look closely we find that the United States of America is only an apparent anomaly. Under the cloak of respect for the "individual," the Roman imperative of "the city first" has triumphed in an unusally transparent way. And how has this happened? Through the doctrine of freedom, which ultimately rewards the rich and powerful, and equates their cause with that of society at large, with society itself, with society "as such," as a German philosopher might have put it. "L'etat, c'est moi," said Louis XIV. "What's good for General Motors is good for America," says a more recent form of royalty, without the Sun King's conciseness. America is the rich, according to the rich; everyone has a chance to belong. Not everyone can belong, of course, without the entire edifice collapsing. Imagine a society of millionaires! Who would collect the trash? But we in the United States of America blind ourselves to this by our belief, reiterated by every new president, at four and eight-year intervals for the past century and three-quarters, that "Today is a new day," that the past has ceased to apply and has no repercussions in the present that we need respect. But there is no new day. It is only the same day, with a different mask on the same face repeated endlessly since the Constitutional Convention of 1787. (He smiles, beaming.) Do I sound so terribly seditious?

Cut to his face, at the back of the classroom; he suddenly grins from ear to ear and raises his hand.

Professor: Yes?

He: Maybe we should burn both the Bible and the Constitution?

General, though nervous, laughter.

Professor: It *would* stir things up. And isn't that precisely what the United States of America, the greatest country in the world, needs, if it is to remain the greatest country in the world, or merely a great country, or merely a country one can live in? But, before burning them, let us *question* them. After all, are they sacred documents, beyond the pale of criticism? The Bible claims to be, and the Constitution would like to be — and constitutionalists pretend that it already is! Or are they, on the other hand, merely fallible records, however noble in places, of human aspiration? Is the individual — are you — of infinite value? Whatever you think, that is! Are *you* the only absolute, the only basis of knowledge and value? And if so, does that give *you* the right to tyrannize over others if you get the chance? And if not, *why* not? — after all, you can't even be sure that *they* even exist, in the way that *you* exist, with all your feelings, thoughts, memories, and hopes, let alone have any worth. If *you* are of infinite value, by what right do other people limit *your* actions? If they are of infinite value, by what right do *you* limit theirs? Or is it indeed, to use a very old-fashioned phrase, just "a war of all against all," without end or resolution, victory or victor? You will recall that phrase came during the long fight, still being fought by some, over evolution and natural selection, that amusing entertainment in which the roles of king and jester combine. *Did you ever notice how Darwin's face looks like that of a clown?* Yes, very amusing! Though if survival only goes to the fittest, then the fittest might just be the amoeba, since it outlasted the dinosaurs and will probably outlast us! And where will that leave our Bible and Constitution?

Cut to his face, flickering between fascination, a grin at the enormous joke of what he has just heard, and a dawning sense of moral horror.

Professor, seen in a slightly uncanny blur, as though he were hallucinating these words: *Well? What do you think? You are the one who must choose, you know.*

Cut to a medley of shots in black and white of student riots at night in a city street, in silence, followed by the sound of a body turning in bed sheets. The shots include those of running crowds of students and young adults, police in plastic riot masks and helmets, wielding batons, several cars burning at the sides of the streets, one or two trashcans on fire, police cars and trucks and ambulances with rotating emergency lights; these images are caught in a series of rapid and broken zooms and rapid-fire panning shots so that the whole sequence is as incomprehensible as it is violent. Suddenly the violence increases, there is a close-up of a young girl stopping and staring, angry and frightened, toward a spot behind the viewer; cut to another young girl screaming at the top of her lungs (all still silent); cut to a close-up of the face of a young man washed in his own blood — he is unconscious, pulled by his hair by a policeman toward a police van. Cut to closeup of the face of a riot cop, raising his truncheon — the look on his face, frightened, angry, determined, yet impersonal, clearly visible through the plastic mask as he swings down toward the camera.

He wakes abruptly, with a sharp intake of breath. Cut to a view of the room window facing a brick wall, dawn light dim in the room. A shaft of sunrise light streaks the wall. Color has returned. The distant sound of a passing car, of an even more distant siren, of the song of a single bird. Hold. The sound of a sigh.

Cut to his point of view as he walks across campus in mid-afternoon, in spring. He passes other students, teachers, custodians, etc., surreptitiously darting looks at the people around him. The camera follows his looks: mostly of men, lingering on them, then returning to him: he momentarily takes that pose, tries on that expression, mimics that walk. The shots pass nervously over the women, curiously, distrustfully, longingly, dismissively, then return, fascinated, to the men. When a man catches him looking, he pulls into himself with a disdainful expression and glares in another direction.

Cut to distance shot of him merging into the crowd.

Cut to reverse point of view: it's she, catching sight of him; hestitant. After considering a moment, she follows after him: the camera remains where she stood and watches her walk toward the crowd.

Cut to him, sorting through his books under his arm: he has forgotten something in his last class and turns around sharply. He looks gaunt, unwell, tired, unslept. He looks up, catching sight of her; she is walking cautiously toward him, hesititating only a moment after his abrupt turnaround. The camera weaves around her face: facing her directly, shooting off anxiously, and returning, unable to focus her at its center; focussing anywhere but on her eyes. The camera remains tensely on her face throughout the following dialog, as the crowd disperses and they are left alone on the campus, beneath trees, near a sunny lawn.

She: Hello.

His voice: Hi.

She: I haven't seen you in such a long time.

His voice: No.

She: I thought you might have dropped out.

His voice, with a nervous laugh: Not yet.

Pause. She prepares herself for what she is about to say.

She: I'm getting married.

Cut to his face, which clenches.

He, strained: Congratulations.

Pause. The camera remains on his face.

Her voice: I hope we can still be friends.

Pause.

He: I don't think so.

Her voice: I wish you weren't so hard.

Close-up of his mouth.

He: Me?

Close-up of her mouth.

She: You.

Cut to profile shot of both facing each other. They are in bright sun, with a sunny stretch of campus lawn behind them.

He suddenly breaks into laughter, which as abruptly breaks off. While he is laughing, her face breaks into a charmed smile, which lingers a moment after he stops.

He: You're the one hard as nails, I'm a sponge you can squeeze dry with one hand.

She: I never understand your metaphors.

He: They aren't metaphors. Who's the lucky fellow.

She: It's not relevant. An old friend. He proposed to me once before.

He: So why did you turn him down?

She: I didn't. I asked him to wait. I was a child.

He: And now you're grown up and the waiting's over.

She: One thing I do know about him.

Pause.

She: He'll never hurt me.

Silence.

Cut to his point of view: her face, yearning.

Cut to her point of view: his face, cold.

Cut to profile shot: neither face could be called either cold or yearning — he face is resigned, matter-of-fact, disappointed; his face is angry and defeated.

Hold; a cloud passes over them, the line of its shadow moves away from them across the vacant, sunny grass behind them. They notice nothing of this.

Cut to a time somewhat later; they are sitting on a bench nearby, not speaking, not looking at each other. It is twilight, darkening.

She: It's getting late. Will you walk me to my car?

He: Of course.

While walking (she cannot refrain from teasing, even now):

She: Why "of course"? It's terribly polite sounding.

He: I was badly brought up.

A moment later, the campus walk lights suddenly switch on.

He, bowing to her: Fiat lux.

She: Just for me!

They walk on. She stops and looks at him.

She: You're so *strange*.

He, despairingly: I'm only what I can be. I'm sometimes not even that.

They walk on.

She: I suppose I shouldn't be surprised. After all, the world is strange enough.

He: Our mistake is to expect it to be otherwise.

She: Is that as profound as you want it to sound?

He considers.

He: Actually, I think it's a lot more so!

She: No one could accuse you of false modesty. Or having a weak ego!

He: Don't know about that. Did you ever notice that people

with "strong egos" never threaten other people's self-esteem?

She: Your meaning?

He: They never do anything at all.

She, groaning: Oh, let's not get philosophical again!

He: Too late, without that, you and I wouldn't exist. (He gestures vaguely toward the camera and seems to address the "world") *Would* we? (He turns back to her.) People are waiting for us to supply the answers.

She, groaning: Oh, let's not get philosophical again!

He: Too late, without that, you and I wouldn't *have* existed at all.

They walk into deep shadow.

She: It's strange.

He: What is?

Silence.

She, apropos of nothing, almost angrily: I would have waited for you if you had asked me to!

He: I waited for you without asking at all.

Silence.

She, despairingly: Why can't we just be frank with each other.

Silence.

She: Hunh. There's a puddle.

He: Watch it....

They move back into the light, she glancing over her shoulder toward where she misstepped.

They walk ahead silently, as if they have exhausted everything to tell each other. They stare ahead, although it's clear their attention is riveted on each other. The sounds are abnormally clear — there slowly emerges the internal body sounds of one of them; of breathing, swallowing, the clearing of a throat, and underneath it, growing in presence, of the beating of a heart.

She stops and turns to him — they have reached her car, which stands in a nearly empty parking lot. The sound of the beating heart continues over the following short scene. Cut to his point of view: her face, as she looks into his, has a sweetness it has never shown before. Hold. Her eyes are dazzling in the darkness. She reaches up to the camera and after a moment pulls it toward her. The shot is buried in her hair. Hold.

Cut to near-distance shot of the two, in shadow, next to her car, embracing. They almost seem to be wrestling. Throughout, the sounds of their bodies and clothes, of mouth against mouth, hair, skin; their sighs, gasps, grunts and, this time, both their racing hearts. Continue. The glittering of light through leaves crosses the couple.

Cut to a farther distance shot, with night sounds (distant street sounds, traffic, a passing bus). After a time, they slowly separate and stand staring silently at each other. Suddenly, she gets into her car and drives away, leaving him standing alone, staring after the car. At a certain point only the tail lights are seen, then in the distance they make a turn and disappear. Long hold. At last he turns, with a limp, and walks weakly into the shadows. Same point of view: a single long take between the break from the embrace and his disappearance into the shadows. Hold. Street sounds. The lights from traffic in the distance. A distant siren, slowly fading.

9

I stand at the edge of the Forum in Rome, appreciating the ruins. I am not sure how I got here. I may have always been here, waiting. Or I may have been brought here, by vehicle, by litter, for instance. Out of the dark, through the dark, into the dark. Who can say. Can you? Do you know how you got here, without question or doubt. I thought so. Neither do I. Without question or doubt. I may have been brought by hand. Yes, that may be how I was brought. In a palm of seed, out of an envelope, between rows of beans. Questionable, but possible. I am here, nevertheless, as much as anyone can be, and I contain memories, like fossils.

I remember the village, spread or clustered among trees, near the woods, by the creek, across from the church and its compost heap of graves. Gray graves, headstones undiminished by time, as of yet, though heading thitherwards. An odd, archaic word, but I like it, so it stays. It was a pleasant village, with a grocery store, where we shopped for small items, milk, a loaf of bread, a pack of cigarettes. I was too young to smoke but both my parents smoked. Oh, them! No, they have since quit, in perpetuity, so they say. Dead? Not at all.

And of course the shed. I remember it, where I hid, when I wanted to hide, though never for long, since the spiders frightened me. And its musty gloom. The smell of damp and of dust and the gloom and the spider silk my face broke through it sticking to my face as I walked between the joists. No one thought to seek me there, in the shed, they all thought I feared it there, and I did, which was why I knew it was safe, I was safe in my fear, in a sense, safe from a greater fear, the fear of being found.

And the gulls, flying above the beach. They turn and turn, shrill, and turn. Ugly voiced, not pretty to see, demanding, scavengers, yet incised on the ocean air like fleshly boomerangs. And like fleshly boomerangs that come, ever, back to me. They fill my mind on autumn nights, their summer sun is always crisp with the chill of coming fall.

I am surrounded by ruins of empire, brightly lit marbles of the Forum at the base of the Palatine hill, a stone's throw from the Capitol, among low walls no higher than graves, not far from the temples of Amor and Roma, mystic palindrome engraved on history's archway, in English the bad pun of a precocious child. The arches of the Basilica Nova provide a nice frame for the empty lots that once were temples of Julius Caesar, Fortunus, Bellona, Moneta, of Magna Mater Lupercal, the great mother herself, alas, of Apollo, of Hercules, of Happiness itself, the Rostra of Augustus, the Column of Phocas … What is it you said, what do I think of it? To which I glibly responded, "Read Gibbon!" I may as well have said read Livy, or the Beards, or this morning's Times. My own history is as shrouded as my future, despite the glimmering of shells in the schist. A bone fragment for you, and you, and you. From much less one can deduce a man, a brachiosaur, a language, a kingdom. A kingdom? Half the title I thought to call my memoirs, once — "Ruins: A Kingdom"! But what would the colon signify? From these ruins how evoke what kingdom? What dream of a kingdom.

Three surviving columns, as tight as fingers, rise down the walk between shaved faces of paving stone in the dirt.

There had been several possibilities (let's call them that for lack of a more exacting phrase) open at that time, and they could be arranged, if we wanted to, by name. Morgan, Yuri, Gabriel, Earl, Sohrab, Alan.

Or others! it makes little difference. What names revealed they also hid, secreted in the folds of their syllables, the shadows of their sounds. What could not bear communion. Unless you surrendered completely to them. And then the sounds were like silence.

Shoots out the lead beyond the waves from the fishermen in their shiny nor'westers and macintoshes and black long boots, shiny by the shimmering sea, their great poles stuck in pouches at the groin, a bucket or two slapping with dead or dying fish nearby. The fishermen are silent. The sea crashes and roars. The line is taut from the high pole out to where it disappears beyond the breakers into the sea. The water blinds with flashing.

Let's say "Morgan," then. Let's say "one day." Let's say one day Morgan meets someone, say a "runner" for a certain nameless organization. Like the one he had belonged to, with its church sieges and its train hijackings! But shades more serious — an illicit, if not expressly illegal, organization, with real ties, not to the state via a work-study program monitored rather too loosely by its parent university, but to a militant, disaffected, dissaffiliated branch of the Communist Party. It is itself partly, or on the verge of being, or wishfully hoping to be, "underground," a word, an idea, with a certain magic at the time.

Where did he meet the "runner"? At a *steering committee meeting*. They were the coming thing, steering committee meetings, they were "*happening*." They sounded clinically rational, dissociatively detached, and as subversive as they sometimes managed to be.

When? Hm, a few months after a major *mobilization* (another of those words!) during one of those endless — seemingly endless, oh would they had been so — springs drugged with fury and hope, and dex, hashish, amphetamines, cannabis.

Maybe he has gone because a friend of his mentions it, is himself going, call him Robert, an old, nearly-forgotten friend, with whom he had shared many a rambling, philosophical walk down his childhood summers, now of earnest, grinning mien, shaggy and ragged in a student of religion sort of way, remarkably appearing one morning on the campus walk outside the student union, with whom he had shared in the guerrilla group's shenanigans — he had been Jeremiah at the church raids.

But why does Morgan go? Because he's at a loose end that evening, because he knows no better, because he's in a bleakly nihilistic mood after *she* left him, because he's disgusted with his "Merry Pranksters" at school and their hopelessly naive theatrics playing at "revolution," because he wants to explore what really lies behind the curtain of the demonstrations, to try his hand at having a starker effect than waving cap pistols at power, beyond what he has up to now thought, claimed, and done, of fashioning it to his will beyond his curiously self-limiting questioning, though he thinks that he is trying to fashion his will to its (but he is not even at the edge of being aware of this), or because he is losing patience with his so-called education, that droning of irrelevancies by balding mediocrities, prior to being given the parchment key to a social order he despises, who have the power to demote, degrade, and deny the keys to one's plausible future; because he is weary of an ineffectual life, waiting in the student halls of impotence till he has been gelded and allowed out on the leash of social permission, he is harassed by a sense that he is wasting his time, he is sick of his loneliness since *she*, his critic and goad, left him, sick of having no one to argue with, hound and be hounded by, demanded of, goaded to rebuke and proof. Something is happening, is taking place, and he longs to take part in it, drag himself into it, wants to become part of a larger whole because he is not whole, he is torn into a thousand pieces none of which match, he was whole once, whole as the sun thrusting its gold into his eyes, but he can hardly remember it, he distrusts it, the experience or his memory of it, yet can't bear this feeling of splintering, the fork kniving down the middle of his soul, and yet doesn't know how it would feel now if he ever felt whole again; is not even sure what it is that is missing. He is starving but he does not know what for.

Robert seems trusted by this "runner" fellow, which is how he's known though not how he's introduced: introductions provide a first name only, sometimes not even that — he is a pale, intense, suspicious youth with long, kinky red hair, yes, pale blue eyes that lock on his own as though sizing him up, weighing, on the verge, finally, of dismissing him. But they don't. Strangely. When Rob introduces him, the first thing Morgan says, out of nervousness, is, *It's time to tear it down!* The other stares at him opaquely. *Tear what down.* And Morgan replies, with an extravagance he does not actually feel: *The whole place! Root it out and pull it down. It's all a lie.*

Andrei, as the "runner" is improbably named, looks as though he were imagining a use for him as they start to talk deeper sedition in those overexcited voices of very young men and share a group joint after the meeting (who else is there? it's dim, I can't see anyone else clearly but those three, it's an apartment, an argument between a black couple sounds up the airshaft), Andrei tells him to call him, just before leaving the meeting, tight-lipped, morosely smiling — doesn't ask, assumes the summons will spark a response. Is he queer? But Morgan isn't the type to ask himself that question, nor explore his own ambiguous sexuality. Morgan's quiet, intensely religious friend with that look of dazzlement in his eyes and innocent, despairing grin, must have vouched for him: "He's cool," he heard when leaving the bathroom, in the argot of the time, an argot with an implausible longevity.

Hmm, yes.... But at first he doesn't respond to the strange summons, it was a little uncanny, he had gone with Rob "out of curiosity," he told himself, indeed told Rob, off-handedly, not yet willing to admit the depth of his own spiritual hunger — though what does that mean, "spiritual hunger?" — his sense that his life is whirring into confusion, both hyperactive and aimless, a phosphorescent compass trapped in a caved-in mine, his involvement in the peace movement has ranged between private enthusiasm and public skepticism, that of a sympathetic if oblique fellow traveler: he reads with approval as much Hegel's aesthetics as Marx's economics, as much Kaufmann as the ephemerides of revolution, Ortega and

Hoffer as the ravings of "Ramparts," enjoys William Buckley's rhetoric far more (a guilty pleasure!) than, say, Jesse Jackson's. He hates what the movement hates, but doesn't yet love what the movement loves. Or claims to: rock, grass, totems of third-world fashion, tie-died tops, jazz slang, anonymous group sex. And he is congenitally incapable of lip service beyond the totems of politeness. But he knows what he hates: the hell of the war, the hypocrisy of the fight against civil rights, the worship of money and power whatever the cost in social chaos and personal despair, the violence, smugness, and mindrot his country celebrates among its pieties. The chronic nightmare of his age he saw not only at home but throughout his era, in Europe and Asia as much as here: war, hatred, fear, death, sex without love, power without responsibility, money without conscience, cruelty and pride, lovelessness a badge of honor, cold the shield of choice, the self the only god. And here was a chance to address the age in the only language it understood: the language of power. Which was?

He will, he decides, find out.

The phone number burns like a bright candle on his desk. It beckons like the siren of the time. It's the historical moment making its gesture. *Make a difference, stand up and be counted,* change *it.* It sits like a spot of sunlight on his desk, waiting for him to wake up. He mentions it to his friend, the priest in anarchist's clothing.

Call him up, he won't call you.

That trap.

Almost a week passes before he takes it and, without thinking of the time (what time is it, then? I can't see daylight, so it must be evening, and it is still spring), dials.

Andrei … No: At first Andrei doesn't remember him, or pretends not to, then, out of the blue, he bawls him out, accuses him. *Are you a narc?* Morgan is startled, offended, but, paralyzed by the good manners his parents nurtured in him instead of religion, keeps listening, insulted, angered, fascinated that someone his own age or only a little older, is treating him like a cop, a principal, a father — it is both humiliating and strangely elating, as though a male peer were finally taking him — no, as though *he* were finally taking himself — with complete seriousness. It was like the insult a sergeant makes a new recruit at boot camp.

Andrei suddenly orders him to meet him at a diner half a mile away.

Who the hell … But "no" is not an option.

This "Andrei" (a real name? a personal brand? a panache?), when they meet, doesn't look him in the eye, nervously balls, thumbs, tears to pieces, one flimsy dispenser napkin after another. You feel intimidated after the phone bawling out, but you notice that it isn't the act of a seasoned tyrant, but an amateur, a beginner. It makes you feel even more timid in his presence. *What am I doing here?*

He sounds you out, getting your "history," weighing you up in those blue, opaque eyes of his; grins, for the first time offering something like an actual smile, however snide, at the story of the train "hijacking," then, still grinning, repeats what he just heard: *You said you were masked.* You reassure him — somewhat mollified, even relaxed after he has listened to you — as though it were both important to be sure about this and, at the same time, a joke — *after all, who could possibly care?* — no one who had been on the train could possibly recognize you now. Andrei's grin holds longer than it should. You suddenly feel a need to prove something to this guy, you don't know what. Mouth and diaphragm tighten.

They leave and walk toward Andrei's car, and the vulpine (suddenly he has become vulpine, yet Morgan doesn't seem to mind — it's *interesting*) the vulpine youth asks him if he wants to take part in an "action" the following month. Then *maybe* …

Action: you are being asked to "act," rather than "behave," which has been the immemorial injunction, lapping you in chains of deeds that had nothing to do with you. "Action equals reaction equals action," you think irrelevantly, Newton's physics still fresh in your mind from high school, out of the mouth of hapless Fuzzy Schwartz. It's salt to the wound of your passiveness, if you but knew. Though you don't like this fellow, this "runner," you'll take this offer to "act," see where it leads.

Without even asking who or what the group is, or what the "action" is going to be, you say, with an eagerness in your voice that surprises you, however nonchalant you try to make it, clipped, sharp, not overly impressed: *Sure. Of course.*

Andrei slips into an old battered Nash. *Don't talk about it. Don't talk over the phone about it. If you need to talk, call to meet somewhere, we'll have coffee, bullshit, then leave, talk in my car.*

Secrecy shall be my shield and charge.

Days, a week, two weeks. No word. He telephones him; no answer. He is ... What is he doing that is typical and urgent? Ah yes, studying for finals when, late one night, you get the call. Now, that sounds tendentious enough. They meet at a park twenty minutes later on the other side of downtown. You don't feel intimidated now; now you feel you might yourself, not long from now, be intimidating to someone else. It is a nice feeling, like being drunk.

Andrei is almost rudely silent. After a time watching headlights pass, and looking (Morgan thinks) ridiculously obvious, they go to the Nash and, as they drive, Andrei explains, in a drone, as if talking to someone else or about something totally irrelevant, how you'll be needed. It's extremely, suspiciously, simple: standing near a certain residential intersection for an hour as though waiting for a bus, walking across one of the streets if you catch any sign of police, a siren in the distance, etc. You'll have to wear a certain piece of clothing, of a certain color. That's it. That's "action." You feel queasy, afraid you're being set up. You ask for details.

Andrei throws you a blank look.

No details. If it goes okay, you'll find out what happened later. The fewer people know what's happening, the safer for everybody. It's happening tomorrow. So are you in? — I have a final tomorrow. — What time? — Eight to ten. — You have time to get there. — Well if I bust ass ... — Then bust ass.

Again the phony dictator-in-training look in Andrei's opaque eyes.

The car pulls up to the broken curb outside the foulness of

Morgan's apartment house, a peace sign posted in a window.

What about after? — Depends.

You hesitate before leaving.

You hardly know me, why are you trusting me with this?

How do you know I am. — And he suddenly grins. — This country is a lie. You said so yourself. It has a lot to hide, and it does it in full view, but its game is that it doesn't. You said that, remember. There are ways to tear it down. Ways to force it to show its real face. And the people once they see it will tear that face to shreds. Tear it down! But to desire the end is to desire the means to the end.

You grin: Good Catholic doctrine!

You do not actually recall saying precisely this, but you are often quoted back to yourself with inconvenient accuracy.

I'm not a Polack for nothing.

You shake hands in the high-five ghetto style, though without the thumb tap-dance clamp at the end, and you're surprised at the warmth of the look passing between you. You suddenly see into Andrei's hooded eyes. This is different from the "Merry Pranksters," with their endless ruminations, childlike openness, washed faces, and silly actions: there is, underneath the soft youthfulness and playacting amateurishness, a hardness here, determined, willful — a little frightening. Exhilarating.

You wonder again if he's queer, and wonder for a moment if you might be yourself. This thought usually terrifies you; now it is just a thought bearly weighted with a feeling.

So you're in.

Morgan doesn't answer this question, inflected now like a statement, almost an order, and the question behind the command is as vulnerable as it is equivocal. He doesn't answer but waves the car down the block.

Then a surge of energy passes unexpectedly through him, rising from his legs to his skull, and in a few minutes, after tossing his jacket on the top of the stoop, he's jogging a mile, feeling his strength coursing like the blood and air through his body, counting his paces to his breaths as the lights stagger and blur around him along the black, nearby river.

When he gets home, still panting, he tries to remember what Andrei claims he said. *I said ... what? I don't remember saying that, but what was it, this country is ... this country ...* and finally drifts asleep, still not remembering.

The columns meet the entablature where the circle meets the rectangle, though in this light it could be a square. A pale yellowness illumines the scene, though not the spaces between the columns.

Did you know that there is only one traffic light in all of mighty Rome?

The "action" goes well: Morgan takes his stand, in the right rags, at the appointed time and place, and the police make no sign. He calls Andrei that evening and Andrei rewards him with a laugh, a quick, dry slightly condescending flip of the trachea, and he realizes he has passed.

The group that Andrei, and now he, is part of is composed of half a dozen radicals who scorn the Frankfurt School of Social Research, in particular Erich Fromm and Herbert Marcuse, Theodor Wiesengrund-Adorno and Max Horkheimer, for the "purer" revolutionary analysis of the early Bolsheviks. Their shelves combine Lenin's writings in the cream-covered, Moscow-printed English paperback translations and Mao's "little red book" with *One Dimensional Man* and *The Sane Society, Soul on Ice* and *Love's Body* — orthodox manuals of revolution and typical "romantic revolutionary" examples of contemporary false consciousness.

They meet regularly in the basement rec room at the downtown home of a young man named Maks, from a wealthy family (his father is vice president–accounts of a locally based chemical company), and discuss Marxist-Leninist theory and practice in light of the "wars of liberation" now being staged globally, with debates on the fine points of Maoist and "Castroist" doctrine and the "contradictions of capitalism"

412

as applicable in Western representative "democracies." Régis Debray is a hotly debated author — *Révolution dans la révolution?* keeps them arguing for weeks. The main division in the group is over whether or not the United States of Amerikkka (the approved spelling) has *already entered*, or is *about to enter*, "an objectively revolutionary *situation*" (meaning revolution is imminent or, with certain dramatic interventions, can be made so) or merely "an objectively revolutionary *phase*" (meaning revolution has become a practical possibility if other conditions are also met) and, if either case is realized, what actions would be appropriate either in response to it or to help bring it about.

Morgan is almost certain that the "clown master of liberal reaction" is not about to launch a revolution, though he plays with the idea on late nights when he hears the sounds of fights in the slum streets or a weaving of sirens approaching from all directions, his heart racing fantasy in anticipation. But he is, as he puts it, "grimly optimistic" that America (he is still too respectful to spell it otherwise in his own mind) is heading toward "fundamental political and social change": civil unrest increases monthly, sometimes weekly, and "revolutionary consciousness" — an assumption that revolution is inevitable, and a collective consensus on the reasons justifying one — seems about to seize the minds of "the young," his contemporaries.

After an hour of debate or planning future "actions," most of which bog down in bickering over tactics and procrastination, the room disappears in a cloud of marijuana smoke.

Yes. I like it, God help me, I liked it then, and even more so now. O tempora, o mores.

Morgan speaks little at these sessions but listens hard, absorbing the poisons around him. The imaginary bomb he has often felt ticking in his pocket seems to have at last acquired a purpose: he imagines suddenly swinging it, toward the monuments of modern civilization that line the streets of the city throwing their vast, lanky shadows over the streets; toward the hard voices of middle-aged men who speak or do not speak on television or in the rooms that let him in grudgingly and with a smirk; toward everything and everyone that has denied him, softly or harshly, subtly or flagrantly, wrongly or, for that matter, rightly, with contempt or without, with the kindest or the meanest of intentions, smiling, sneering, scowling, weeping, angrily, rejecting. And the scattering smoke of the silent explosion fills him with a hard and empty rapture, a dry pride and contempt, a metallic pleasure that shines like glass, brittle thrust of triumph. He can feel his face change, without even looking in the mirror. His favorite word is "rage."

What next? Was it not inevitable? As in "historically inevitable?" Though it's difficult to trace exactly how the group slips from debates and more or less innocuous "actions" to robbery, theft, embezzlement, vandalism, sabotage, arson, and other crimes that would one day be labeled "terrorist" if for no other reason than they were not crimes committed for their own sake or merely money, but attacks carried out in pursuit of a political cause and fueled by a sense of outrage. Maks had a weakness for faux Latin; at the end of every speech he gave (and he gave a lot), he would repeat his favorite line: "Et Amerik-k-ka delenda est," apologies to Cato's ghost which must still haunt these purlieus. And the phrase quivered, in recognition, in Morgan's ear: he was not certain just how far Maks's dream of destruction was meant to reach. How far was "America to be destroyed"? The glitter in his eyes and the flat smile disturbed and thrilled him. He woke in the middle of the night with a nightmare on his tongue. *Maybe all of it.*

The slipping into subterfuge beyond the lèse-majesté of rhetoric happened gradually, with a feeling of the inevitable, without anyone having raised an objection, or if so, one that was easily overturned by the rhetoric and momentum of the hour: Morgan did have a twinge of conscience the first time they planned an actual robbery — he imagined the blank fear in the faces of the victims, people he had never known or met, and only agreed because they were, supposedly, rich and so wouldn't deeply regret the loss of a drawerful of jewels once they got over the sentimental side, if any. It was successful — it was as easy as saying the first lie — no one ever discovered who had done it, even though Maks was a close friend of the family and had dated one of the daughters in high school. Perhaps it settled an old debt. The ease of it, of the only apparently trickier problem of "fencing" the stolen jewelry — which in fact took longer than the period between the first idea and the "action" itself — the successful disbursement of cash (naturally, a good less than predicted but respectable even when split seven ways), and the ease with which the money was spent (and not only on revolutionary "necessities"), made the next "action" that much easier to contemplate. Plan. And execute. And the next. And then the next. Until it became a habit, a way, almost, of life. They had begun to call themselves the "Revenge of Che," or ROC, after their hero, killed and displayed in a tub by soldiers of the latifundistas in the mountains of Bolivia.

It is not enough, said Maks, to lead revolutionary actions against the bourgeoisie. — Maks, a big young man with thick hair sprouting like a burning bush from his scalp, with delicate hands that waved through the air like those of a drunken orchestra conductor, and a smile that always seemed to patronize a face on the other side of his listener's head, waffled the air. — That is not enough: it must also be *seen to be revolutionary!*

Like Caesar's wife!

But only if conditions are objectively ripe for revolution, Andrei points out. — Until then keep actions anonymous.

And let them squirm, added a flame-haired, freckled youngster called Rick the Red who somewhat theatrically hated his father and indulged in rhetoric more fiery than he intended and more revealing than he wished. He barely concealed the pleasure he found in the ringing sounds of his own voice or the wince that his more catastrophic phrases pinched in the face of his listener. — Or, to pick up your point, pre-revolutionary. They can twist the knife into a cry for blood. And that will ignite the streets.

If, said Maks, with finger raised, but only *if* they are clearly identified with the revolutionary struggle. He paused. We need to sign our crimes, gentlemen.

Carve our initials into our next victim. It might be all they need.

Maks grinned drily. Don't spoil a good idea by overdoing it, Ri*shard*.

Morgan listened patiently. He was adept at waiting, listening for the whistle on the hob. His passiveness was his strength, for when he finally did move, the world seemed to shift on its axis. To him, naturally. Only to him. He added a pinch now.

The only good idea is an extreme idea.

The only good idea is a *dead* idea.

He had forgotten the childish need to one-up.

Gentlemen, gentlemen!

There's something to be said for that. As a gauge for action. The extreme idea offers a measure for actions that can never meet it, it sets a limit we can continually strive toward, extending ourselves to touch it without the disappointment of a too-easy success.

So (grand pause for effect), how extreme shall we become.

Even grander pause for impressive closure.

As *extreme as we dare.*

They sit staring at each other complacently through a screen of ganja.

That is another of those words — "extremes" were in the air at the time. Only the *radical* was truly interesting.

So this part begins, seedily enough, of that life you might one day have called your own.

Then there was Sean — or Sohrab! — no, no, let's call him Peter, God-haunted, God-hungry one. Yes. Raving in his purity. Peter, let's say, splits off from the revolutionary cell, the "Pranksters," whatever, unpersuaded, not of the justice but of the ultimacy of their cause. What if they succeed, he thinks, despairing — *so what if they succeed?* It will leave everything *else* exactly where it is, and that, precisely, is the problem: the sun will terrify the sky with equal inescapability. The shabby misery of life will only be palliated, another rag added to the damage. The scar might be pleasingly marked with sequins, sparkles, and foundation. The wound's lips will kiss the air of the same poisoned morning.

He tosses between ultimate goals, like a bean bag. He calls himself "the bean bag," with an only seemingly cheerful contempt. The needles of an unanswerable skepticism never bend or blunt: they make any answer impossible. And yet some answer is required, however provisional, to get him out of bed each day. So he makes one up: today it will be a cheesesteak for dinner at Bailey's, today it will be a chat with Katherine in the legal library, today it will be to pass the anthropology final, today it will be to fill one more day to graduation, when he will finally have to decide what his real life must be about, today it will be to ruin his mind for the orgy of a week's studying, today it will be the distant corridor of a dreamless night's sleep. But at the end of each day, that reason splits open to display a hollow rot, it must be tossed into the garbage with the bad fruit and stinking meat: a new one, fresh and untoothed by the mind's insatiable questioning must be found, invented, or chipped however it can from the brazen air. Until today when all his options have dried up and withered: today when there is no reason, however trite, nerveless, and banal. And these todays accumulate, like dead insects.

One of those todays had exploded in revolution, another had blossomed into religion, and each had towered above him with open and demanding arms, hungry for a new follower, wrathful with regard and offer. Earthly or unearthly absolutes of transcendence, choices for watchfulness and abrupt bending into a destiny, a service beyond the meager mortalities and ineffable fatuities, the deep futility, of the self. Worlds on offer, this one with a web of obedience and power, that other with the unutterable holiness of a sanctified but possibly illusory love: wild happiness and mortal terror, for they demanded more than just a single day's fulfillment. The reward they offered was total: the world, beyond the world; and the demand they made was total: his soul and mind and life. They wanted him. They wanted his choice.

Yet the criticism he could not refrain from applying, like compulsive pincers, to himself he could not refrain from applying to them, the conspirators of his future. And thus the continual tossing between them and the bitter solitude outside. For the demand for totality would not abate nor the heckling in his mind abandon it.

One day ... no, that's too easy. Everything happens one day, and yet, after all, nothing does but only seems to, after monumental and obscure preparations, analyzable by the quantifiers and data analysts, the statisticians and historians. But not by us, who are them: we must suffer in the dignity of ignorance and silence, pixels vanishing from the screen a moment at a time, one day. Hardly a profound thought; it can hardly be called a thought. In the gutters of the mind.

One day, Peter ...

Peter, one day, ...

Decides? But that is precisely what Peter can*not* do! He walks into a huge church, he scarcely knows why, and prostrates himself before the high altar, his mind a wilderness of silence. No: a long, quiet, a single, tone wraps his thoughts in an almost ease of blurry and sweet enchantment, a hand holding him like a baby, for the first time since his childhood, though he does not know this. He is overwhelmed, it frightens him and he gets up and walks quickly outside, into the winter light, sharp with snow and mud. And he walks for miles through the winter streets, holding the memory of that moment in his mind, examining it as the bliss slowly fades and leaves behind a question, pointed directly at him. By the time he gets home he has returned to his desolation and the heckler in his mind is demanding why he is taking himself and his thrilling nervous system, his youthful self-absorption, his famished ego, his delusive wish to have the world focus for an hour on him, so seriously as to believe he had any right to think he had experienced something like "god."

Yet of course ... no, not of course. He keeps his experience to himself, returns to his radical friends scoffing at the belief of the "straights," the "believers," the uneducated churchgoers, the cop-outs and the co-opted, the stooges and propagandists of wealth and power. Occasionally he sneaks into a church and kneels furtively at the altar rail, hoping to repeat his experience. But it does not happen; he kneels staring at the brass railing, and beyond at the dangling end of the altar cloth, feeling nothing, seeing nothing, thinking nothing but how foolish he must seem to someone watching him, someone like himself who scorns the folly of unreason and disdains the weakness that requires faith and spiritual hope because it cannot establish a material one. And he leaves disappointed, vaguely disgusted, and yet puzzled, because his memory of that other time remains so clear: he cannot convince himself it was simply a delusion — its sharpness he can reconstruct, a moment at a time, and its overpowering sweetness. It was more real than himself, though that is not saying much (he ruefully grimaces). It was more than just peace: it was a taste, though only the faintest taste, of a, of an *absolute* fulfillment, of becoming translated into being, of a wholeness he had known in early childhood and had almost forgotten, but that was now made fully conscious, like the sound of a bell humming through his body.

Whenever he passes a church he looks expectantly up at the cross standing at the top of its spire against the sky. As if it might signal him or beckon.

When a child, he had learned to listen, to look; to savor the moment as if each moment held a message for him. This thing could pierce him through at any moment, from any side, in solitary moments especially. But it could also leave him be and abandon him. If he let it. He must open himself, like an eggshell, and keep pressing it open, because it continually froze over again, like the ice over a winter pond. But if he did, it might caress him like a zephyr, a wind witch over the rippling water. And then as he crawled and climbed and thrust his way out of childhood, it disappeared in the tangle of egos and bodies and choices and selves he had to confront and unknot with each day's further press and twist. Even solitude became crowded with the spirit of demand.

And now, years later, it has once again happened, at the foot of that silence within the darkness of an old building, a darkness slanted with winter afternoon light.

He goes to a service, sitting at the back and leafing through a hymnal, nervously looking around him as if afraid to be seen. The sounds and smells nauseate him slightly and yet hold him in a kind of soft clasp that will not let him go: he thinks about leaving, escaping before it is too late (too late for what?), he remembers the attacks on the churches, the siege of the bishops' conventicle, he remembers Jeremiah and the voice of God, but he can't escape, the walls hold him in a sort of thrall of courtesy — wouldn't it seem unforgivably impolite to leave a church service just before it begins? — the trefoils and the clerestory, the transept and the pylons, the austere flaring pillars and the lacy stone roof, the marching figures in the tapestries along the nave aisles, the colored jewels of the glass in the narrow windows staring down through the sun and the soft beds of gemstones on the flinty granite floor, the white altar and the gold cross writhed with the sagging body of the dead god. And all around him sad, sagging faces pinched with pious smiles and strangely terrified looks. What are they afraid of? Of *you?*

He fled. He walked as fast as he could, almost beaking into a run, as far as he could go, walked to the center of town and sat in a snowy park for an hour until he was certain the service was over, then, without thinking why, walked back to the church and walked in, kneeled next to a pew near the front of the empty church still reeking of incense, and started crying.

And a voice spoke within him and a hand rested on his head, and the voice says, *Don't be afraid.* And the hand strokes his head. And he feels arms folding around him and his mind stills to a vacancy of luminous peace as his sobbing slowly quietens.

He gets up and stares stupidly around him, the only other person there, a tired, middle-aged woman mopping the floor at the end of the nave, then he quickly leaves the church and walks home through the winter twilight (how long as he been there? yet the question does not even occur to him), a decision having been made with more calmness than he can remember ever having had.

The next day he advises the university that he is leaving, the following day he applies for catechism classes at a Catholic school in his neighborhood with the ultimate goal, he announces to the principal who peers at him oddly, of joining a monastery of the Benedictines.

Richard had known Peter, did I tell you? How could he not. He had followed his progress, or "regress" as he chose to consider it, with alarm. Richard presents himself as an old-school Voltairean, *écrasez-l'infâme*, Enlightenment rationalist, a neopositivist with no time for the antics of faith, belief-systems, credulity, superstition, mythomania, religiosity, the cult of the irrational, and contempt for reason. His happiest phrase is "Non credo." His strongest condemnation is "dishonest." His constant suspicion is "self-deception," and he is at least sometimes aware of how vulnerable that suspicion makes him! He calls science the only religion that works and, though he knows almost nothing about technology (not even owning a car), calls it the only magic worth practicing. He detests churches — he joined the church attacks for that reason alone (he told himself), playing God was a nice twist to the irony — except occasionally for their architecture, and considers the elimination of religion to be the next goal of "enlightened man." And he uses the word "man" deliberately, being a contented and sarcastic chauvinist (though the term had not yet been invented) who thinks of women as useful but expendable stepping stones in the self-fulfillment of the male.

No, he is not queer, though his sexuality puzzles himself as much as it sometimes does others: it is almost completely depersonalized, based on soft-porn and fantasy females, though he professes to scorn real ones: there is disappointment and frustration sublimated into physical self-sufficiency concealed — or is the more apt word "betrayed"? — in his little pinched sneer.

He despises Marxism and communism for the same reason he despises religion — a "religio laici" he calls it, quite as irrational as the eschatologies of heaven and hell it replaced. *There is no way to change the world*, he insists, *but through the individual*.

Yet he is no Ayn Randian either (brilliant, he thinks, but a moral monster — she has learned all the wrong lessons from Nietzsche), nor is he a capitalist — the cult of the dollar earns a contempt equal to the cult of God.

Knowledge is the ecstasy of our time, he writes in his notebooks (he is fascinated by summing up bits of reality in a phrase, though he is too well-mannered to drop too many in conversation). *To act only in order to know, because to know is the secular form of salvation. And to coin enameled phrases is our proof of grace. Not God but Man, not sainthood but genius.*

And: *Whoever seeks power seeks his own impotence, but whoever seeks out impotence discovers there the only power there is: liberation from the desire for power.*

And: *America worships failure in its unforgiving pursuit of success. It is the empire of the lie, ignorance, slavery, self-deception, and failure — in that order. It is afraid to admit its "dream" is an unrealizable wish-fulfillment fantasy, so it declares victory over and over, until all, citizens, adversaries, masters, slaves, are convinced it must be true. If anybody calls the lie, it declares war on them.*

And: *Self-sufficiency in all things: of the mind, of the heart, of the pocketbook.*

His favorite reading is Nietzsche and Walter Kaufmann: he is dazzled by the will to power, which he understands as ultimately a will to self-conquest and self-command. He plays variations on his favorite thinkers: *It is not how powerful you are that matters — it is how powerful you feel. Politicians seek power out of a sense of weakness: hermits and saints seek to be alone in the wilderness because they are overwhelmed with the strength they have achieved: they mistakenly bow before their god in order to get rid of the power that god has given them. Whereas what they should do* ...

But there Richard stops: he isn't at all sure what they should do, and by extension, what *he* should. Make a fortune, like a philistine? Conquer a country, swollen with self and majesty? The story of Napoleon fascinates him: a completely fulfilled man: his tragic fall *completed* him, made him, curiously, unconquerable: ensured his fascination for as long as there are men to be fascinated. Yet he senses a flaw even in that ultimate destiny. The stories of other magnificently triumphant men whose actions haunted the future also draw him: Leonardo, Michelangelo, Shakespeare, Balzac, Wagner, Beethoven — *heroes of their own lives.* Or those who had died on or near the threshold of their fates, knocking hopelessly to be let in: Keats, Shelley, Baudelaire, Rimbaud. And yet, what triumph has become theirs, had they known or had full faith in *their* stars! It's worth a dozen Roman Empires, a thousand conquests of Gaul — Alexander's conquest of the world, glorious as it was, was worth less than a line of Sappho, like a thread of the genetic code of genius, Richard's substitute for the sacred. But this is the sort of destiny he can only dream of, as he tosses in the middle of the night worrying over his own life and afraid of the future. He can still dream of this dream, his own "wish-fulfillment fantasy," he thinks, mocking himself, and, in a modest way, furiously proud (he knows the paradox of a humble pridefulness, a sincerity that burns with self-respect), serve it. He is obscurely aware he is living in a past that places little if any pressure on the present, but then he holds the present in a healthy contempt — *just look at it!* — and sees the future as little more than a march into darkness. The past was all that counted, in the end, because everything ended up past: the present, that nothing that did not even exist, was no more than a kind of set of teeth that ate the future, a future that was unknown becoming known in the past through the unknowable present, which was past as soon as one thought it; the present was itself, in this sense, no more than the future's past, the future no more than time waiting to become past: only the past, paradoxically enough, was forever. That, anyway, was his idea. And what had happened to his belief in science, technology, enlightenment? What indeed. How explain this strange slip from resonant optimism in the rational and secular to an unfathomable hopelessness in a worship of the past? He could not come up with a resounding phrase to explain that.

And where could he live such a life as he now hopes to live, he asks himself, and is somewhat disillusioned by the answer: right where he is, in the concrete and glass groves, the stone womb, of academe.

Oh no. — He stares above his desk at a ruined patch of wall as it hits him, what he must do next. — *God!* — Then the next moment flips the anomaly of a future that must look like the immediate past into a strange discovery. The walls rising around him protect a garden from the shouts and wailing of the streets. He stares at the patch of wall until the shouts fade into the sound of wind in trees. And in his books he finds a smell almost like flowers.

But it takes some time for the lump in his throat to go.

He turns his back on the fiery sun and signs up for a major in history, with a minor in psychology, an inspiration. Only in that dark, twinned like paired black holes, does he hope to find something like light. And who knows? Maybe he'll get lucky! We leave him in the turmoil of his certainty — not entirely convinced. The nagging thought that he is choosing a shadow for a substance will not respond to his petulant demand to name the substance.

Deep is the moon above the Palatine. It always amazes me to see the moon in the middle of the city streets, when one is unable to see a star.

Well now. Don't suppose all his friends let Richard get away with his retreat into the academy. Let's call him "Paul." Paul has a … No, I prefer "Quinn" — Quinn has a ferocious argument with Richard — one almost as fierce as the one he had with, what did we call him, "Peter." Oh boy, did he! *One of you becomes a priest, the other becomes a professor, and you both become eunuchs!* Quinn knows Morgan too, of course, they move in the same circle, so to speak, and he approves the starkness, resoluteness, and *radicalness* (another favorite word of the time!) of his action, if not entirely his choice (Marxism? Leninism? are you in the right century?) — *if you're going to choose, make it a passionate choice, stop being such a coward, for God's sake it's your life, don't run away from it, you're trying to force entry into the wrong uterus.* And he grins at the tastelessness of the image. But then, Quinn enjoys the rhetorical grimace, the *vomissement* of a phrase.

His studies of French have given him a special fascination for the *poètes maudits* and their heirs: Baudelaire, Verlaine, a bit of Artaud, above all the ruined career of Rimbaud. He burns fanatically in his room, gagging his way through mountains of cigarettes and gallons of coffee while plowing through volumes of poetry that twist his own mind into fleeting moments of a gossamer-fine ecstasy that flees with the turning of a page, the felling of a book back onto the thud of a desk. He hallucinates odes and recreates epics among stars of flesh and cries as he walks long nights down the tree-bound river or through the back alleys of half-lit slums. He pulls his mind into ever keener knots of the impossible and crude, damns his moments in a half-crazy search for psychic intensity, scorns sleep and food. He can taste the sweet frenzy that continually eludes him. And yet it is *there*, as much there as his own body breathing in the dusk beneath the yellowish light. By the window twilight. At the scattering emergence of one more dawn after a night vanquished by the yawning mouth of a word: a book contains only a single word it breathes from beginning to end. And it's the reader's work to *conspire* with it. And thus, in its most concentrated form, thus above all: the poem, the bounding of grace in the word's mystery, captured, recurrent yet vanishing in the moment, sacredly periodic and secularly unique, attuned to the soul attuned to it: a palpable heaven marked in stroke and breath and the inner vibration of the spoken. Yet there was a point stronger even than that, one that the poem points to as a continuous possibility: the strongest point of all, the only true victory: and that is to live it, live the poem continuously, from this point on, to whatever climax to come of ecstasy and extinction. Therefore his unforgiving attacks on his needlessly weakening friends. For they, in their separate ways, are giving in to the world itself, rather than refusing it, defying it in the name of the moment's imanence in transcendence, life itself in its sensation even in thought, the sun's ever-opening rose.

(He would take revenge on her for leaving him by turning her into a *word*.)

As *you* are doing! Richard reproves him sarcastically.

Abashed only for a moment, Quinn replies: Only as I may *aspire* to do — and you've stopped even *trying* to do! You've given up, and that is the only unforgivable sin.

He grins.

Given up *what*, for God's sake? If you could only tell me that. Richard is grinning back at him. This is not the first time they have had this argument.

Living now, rather than putting off to some after life, or dreaming about a lost past, where living sometimes took place!

(Nor will it be the last.)

How do *you* know? You don't know what I *do* let alone what I have "stopped trying to do."

You're transparent. (A smirk followed by a feint ...) But then, maybe not. (... reversing into an undermining triumph). Though you can't *know* that I *don't*. In you I see my own escapes, maybe that's what works me up so much. I want to run away too, and when I see my friends doing it, I can barely hold on, myself.

You sure don't make it clear what it is you're trying to hold on *to*. What's this point of honor you're so crazy about?

If I haven't made *that* clear, it's hopeless.

I guess it is.

The point of honor is the point of the moment's transcendence in living it.

So you're religious too.

It's a religion sine ecclesiam.

Translate your pig latin please!

It's a faith without a religion!

Or god, heaven, priesthood, savior — except you, of course! And only a *hell* ...

... for those who turn their back on the redemption of the moment.

Which is?

Contained in the moment, for its own sake.

What?

And abandons the self to it.

So how am I supposed to live!

You're asking me?

But you're the one with all the answers.

All I have is questions, but the point is to keep the questions in play without allowing easy answers to forestall them. The thing is to insist on what one doesn't know, and hold it to you like the Spartan boy the fox that ate his belly.

Do you have a "sacred text" at least?

Only the one I am trying to create myself.

That's very convenient! Not to say megalomaniac.

Every man his own savior! Every man his own Christ! Every man the son of God who must be crucified before he can be resurrected, *before he can truly live!* There are writers, poets, miscalled "romantics" ...

But not by you!

It suggests people who are running away from reality, but in fact they were the ones *facing* reality, they have seen that truth is passion, an act of confrontation, a choice and a battle, a reveling blindness, an imposing of will, not a detached investigation: the academics who study them (*sorry*, Richard!) can't bear the challenge the *romantic* sticks in their faces, and so they neutralize him by categorizing him, stick a label on him that warns off the poison, cast a pall over him and his like, leave them powerless in libraries, undermine them so nobody will ever take them seriously again. Because if people did, they wouldn't rest until they had *overturned the world* — including the world of the academics, professors and gelders of poets, the hogs of academe who think, in their pompous, cowardly mendacity, their smug, unforgiving mediocrity, because *they* are hogs there are *only* hogs — until they have overturned them, *stuck* them, *grilled* them and *eaten* them, in the name of humanity itself.

Richard slips on his seat, laughing.

What a rallying cry! "Up against the wall muthafucka! And stick the hogs of academe!" — what a bumpersticker that would make.

They giggle at the ridiculousness of being twenty, able to talk nonsense, and laugh at it.

But Richard soon renews the charge: But what … (catching his breath) but what if that is all a body *can* do?

What, besides stick hogs?

What if all you can do is keep alive those ideas that, that, otherwise, would die, what if that's the only life we can offer? Academics are not all sanctimonious, hyper-trained, pompous, fixated clods, though a lot are, you're right — not many would admit it, in fact they'd deny it up and down the faculty conference room till kingdom emeritus come, but the best of them are *priests*. Yes, *priests*, don't sneer, they keep the past *alive* so it can nourish people like you who think the present trumps everything just because you happen to have been born in it.

So we can *feed* on them, no doubt!

And what's wrong with that? Want to starve yourself? Go ahead!

Nothing. Everything. I love to eat corpses.

I *know!* But you're missing the point, they aren't dead, they are texts: embodiments of life that once was lived. And they can offer the future codes, semaphores, emergency messages, plans for action, possible ideals. They reveal actual, *because once lived*, possibilities. And academics, no, *scholars*, keep those possibilities alive. I know all the vileness that academics are capable of, but abuses shouldn't condemn a whole profession.

But the abuses have *become* the profession, open your eyes. Look at what the university is doing to the study of literature — turning it into science, for Christ's sake! Literature can be a *science* about as much as it can be a cuisine, it's no subject for the cortical functions alone, it is a way of life, it addresses emotion, feeling, and will plus thought, the senses *and* imagination *and* intellect in a glorious feast, it cannot be reduced to the categories of analysis, the rigors of logic, the ethos of reason, or the sanctimonious mendacities of politics for that matter! It is not meant to be understood without being felt and acted on, whereas academics stop at "understanding" — and end up by understanding nothing at all: this is why literary academics end up *being unable to write*, they can't even use their own language effectively! Ever think about the bizarreness of this? It's like a physicist who can't perform an experiment, a math prof who can't count, a doctor who only kills his patients! They are unable to use their own language: such a position is a lie told constantly to oneself, and they are excruciatingly aware of it, though it only dawns on many when it's too late and they are committed to the concentration camp of academe — it twists them into caricatures of themselves. Academics despise and seek to kill literature because they realize it cannot be made to fit their rubrics, their analyses, they blame their subject because they can't afford to blame their theories, their theories are what justifies their diplomas, their tenure, their careers, and that's the real problem, they want to supplant their subject with themselves, *they want to own literature and not let anyone else get near it*, and then quietly destroy it in the name of an abstraction. Whereas literature is fundamentally inclusive of all human functions, it appeals to our common and to our exclusive humanity, and the academic is exclusively intellectual, abstract and donnishly murderous, *he seeks to keep out anybody who does not have a credential*, yet literature is sovereign because life is sovereign, literature is a reflection of life itself and not only one aspect of it, neither life nor literature will let itself be destroyed in the name of an idea, however heuristically powerful; rather will it destroy the idea in the name of its own autonomy, its sovereignty, *even if that destruction endangers its own survival*. With guardians like our professors, who needs book burners! They seek to destroy the very culture that made them. They are our very own, our personal *fascisti*.

If I didn't know better I'd call you a budding fascist, myself, of the Lawrence wing! But listen: without academics, inept as they are, literature would die at the hands of venal publishers and the barbarous public: they may demean literature but they also keep it alive, from century to century, millennium to millennium. Who else keeps the classics breathing, ancient and modern, who else keeps poetry being published if not academics! Academics, far from killing literature, are its only salvation in our age of barbarians! Look at what people do with themselves — read Cervantes, Chaucer, Homer, Keats? No! Fill in with the title of the latest best-seller! Is that what you want?

So: better humiliation and survival in a maximum security detention camp guarded by philistines than a quick, proud death in hand-to-hand combat with vandals in a back alley!

At least it keeps it in play, a cultural gene that hasn't been lost, alive if not always kicking, and so it gives some hope. Think of the Irish monasteries in the Dark Ages! They hardly knew what they were copying, and might have been properly horrified if they thought about it: but they kept it alive all just for *you!* And who knows, maybe tomorrow *one* academic will see the light. And he'll be grateful for people like you stinging our consciences and reminding us of our failures!

Quinn laughs dryly.

That will be the day. "Stop me before I murder another poem!" No, you be the academic, and I'll be the poet, and one day we'll meet on the battlefield and trade weapons. And then bombs.

And both of us will perish beneath the bright winter sky.

Boom — we're dead. You have just committed a poem.

Finis. It was a beautiful civilization while it lasted.

They go on, of course. This is the meat and drink of their lives, this debate over the point of their futures, Quinn trying to justify himself, in reams of verse he writes all night long and in fuliginous rants against the very people who keep poetry alive in a thuggish culture; Richard trying in his turn to defend a parasitic profession that sometimes tried to kill the thing it fed on, to "supplant" it, as Quinn said, and in so doing, itself perish in an evil that saw itself as intellectually rigorous, morally superior, and *politically correct*, a phrase that would confuse and mislead many of the well-meaning in years to come. Both, of course, in their impossible, youthful ignorance, a presumptuousness too innocent to resent, "breathtaking" indeed, reflecting the contempt with which their host culture, that disease of the mind and soul of the planet, treated *them*.

Et America delenda est. He was reminded of that, from the old days with *her* and of his flirtations with "the revolution."

And of course, it will be destroyed, eventually, one need only wait: every empire dies by its own hand. Note: the moon is touching the columns of the Temple of Peace. And how long did the Pax Romana last? Just enough to fill a column in the Encyclopedia Britannica.

There was an air of desperation in Quinn's choice of a future, as though he already knew he was choosing a life devoted to frustration, shame, and failure, a long and perilous ascent up an invisible and unrecognized escarpment whose obscure triumph might never be noted by anyone but himself. As he once said to himself, half-mockingly, *Being a poet in America is like choosing to be black, female, and queer.* And yet it seemed to be a choice he was not so much entitled, as ordered by some unknown agency, to take, and persist in, for the rest of his natural life: it was a prison sentence, a marriage. Folly? But how so, when the views across the world the climb laid at his feet would be of an irreducible authority, whatever the final result? Or so he thought at the time.

Is anything worth missing a chance to gaze into the very heart of reality? Abyss though it may be.

For that was the promise, and perhaps the con. As well as a chance to erect a music unheard anywhere else, out of the heart and mind's astonished meeting with that strange, even horrifying, god. What mere worldly success could compare to the splendors of that adventure, tragic as it might turn out?

Pride? Vanity? Ego? Well, naturally!

And yet, to actually believe all that, even as a remote possibility, smacked of willful self-deception. Was this a prospect remotely reasonable, intelligent, wise, merely prudent? And how would you pay the rent, O angel of prosody? *Teaching creative writing?* Oh, fatuousness piled on futility!

What if the entire enterprise failed? and failed ignominiously?

The defeat would be total, the mortification, smirks, condescension, and contempt (if anyone were allowed to *know*) unbearable, the self-contempt even harder to withstand. And yet, having faced this choice, having known the rush of words through your veins like a drug, a drug that sharpened, not dimmed, perception, a drug that made you pay but gave back a hard diamond of light, a machete made of words, to run away from that, having known it, would strip you of the last rag of self-respect: having been offered the vision on the hillside in a bed of fire on the mountain ridge above you, it is contemptible to choose the house in the suburbs, serviced by two cars, in a sheltered cul-de-sac. He had no choice but to take it on and scratch his nails into the rock's inscrutable face. And slowly crawl up into the air.

So what did he do, our unhinged romantic? What choice did he have, after all, with his convictions? He did the obvious thing — he quit school! As simple as amputating your left arm with your right. Folly? But of course! All choosing is folly, as if it made any difference in the end. So take your foolish choice and pay the unforgiving consequences.

He did. He buried himself for six months in a vacancy called freedom, then went to Europe on his last money, and tramped, a young bum, across France and Italy, sleeping in train stations and pension dorms and inventing odes to crumbling or tarted up monuments whose history was vanishing in the attempt to clean them up. He loved it, he loathed it, he was living his romance while not even realizing it: he kept thinking it was coming, in an alms box called the future.

That policeman is looking oddly at us. What does he think we are, a gay pickup? Avanti, carabiniere! Go find a fascist or a whore! Bury your nose in the anal fold of the Roda Brigada! He's dreaming of his pension and spending some time in Milan over the holidays. The past has no hold on him, and even the future is no dream, it is no more than a well-managed pocketbook. If Caesar could see his city now, his ghost caught in this zoo!

Then there was "Gabriel." I've always liked Gabriel, at least the name, and now I have a use for it. Gabriel knew Quinn? How could he not? Indeed, how could all of them not know the others, all of the others, more than he would care to, more almost than he knew himself! Hush! I tread too heavily.

Gabriel visited Quinn just before he left for Europe and the vanishing traces of poetry. There is no *poetry* in America, Quinn told him. *Modern American poetry* is an oxymoron along three axes! — You stand self-condemned, returned the ironic Gabriel. — I'm not American. I had to be born somewhere. — No, you didn't! — If I were to be born at all. — Well, in that case … — And I hereby secede, I renounce my cultural citizenship, I am the Flying Dutchman, I belong to no country, to no shore or land, I belong only out of this world! — Wagner, Baudelaire, you're becoming quite a compendium of quotations, allusions, plagiarisms. — Fuck you. — Oh, I will, I will!

It was an age for such fatuous honesties, the vulgarities of sincerity. I envy them, almost. No, I envy them, period. We know no better, though we pretend to. The future is as dark for us as for them, only they faced that darkness with a sometimes ridiculous courage, whereas we have a more gracefully cynical cowardice: the future will still despise both of us, for our grotesque ignorance of it, and our powerlessness to survive.

Gabriel the ironist took none of the plights of his friends — shall we call them "friends" or "enemies"? — seriously. He had already seen through them, or seemed to, or thought he had, or convinced others that he had. And seen, he thought, to the other side. He was certain he knew — what? All he needed to. The point of the circus, the pinnacle of the moment, which was, quite simply, without cavil or guilty hypocrisy, the immediate and continual gratification of *himself,* in any way he could manage, in any shape it formed. He was a continuous appetite, and he would feed it with whatever wandered by his jaws.

This was not, of course, so much a philosophy as a bent: it

hardly needed formulating, and he was already living it, in a small way, between classes, even during them: the only thing that stopped him was a natural timidity, a shyness before others, though not, luckily, before himself: he was lucid as to what he wanted, which was simple immediate physical gratification, the filling of the void of the moment with the warmth of the flesh, and nothing else would be seriously required but what was needed to defend that gratification from impedence or loss. The impulse was at work in him. And the determination not to be denied, especially after the humiliations he had already been treated to. Was he aware of how deeply the spirit of revenge was working in him, as well as simple appetite? Probably not. And he probably didn't care.

His principal obstacle, of course, was himself: no one else cared enough to stop him! He wasn't a bad looking fellow, his eyes were too small and the little fold over them gave him a funny look, there was something feminine in his visage that sometimes put women off, turned others on, often the wrong others, his face was acne'd from over-active sebaceous glands (and, he suspected, overindulged hand jobs!), and his shyness made him surly at times, his failures made him depressed, but he was bright, once relaxed into trust, and could engage the hour with flights of a mordant and extravagant wit that won him more women than he knew at the time. What was lacking yet was, not the knack, but the conscious decision. And that required a gain as well as a loss: the discovery, beyond the means, of an imperative. Since all youth needs an imperative, no?, particularly when it seeks the naked assertion of self. It wants to tear its hole in the air with a good conscience. And why shouldn't it?

He shook his head at Quinn's peculiar flavor of idealism, his crazy trust in the written word and the redemptions of phrase-making. But his scorn occupied much of his relations with Richard as well, his hiding in the cement skirts of Cacademe, to say nothing of what he opined about Peter's copping out into the church or Morgan's disappearance into revolution. Though he had enjoyed the church attacks, the aborted train-hijacking, the playing at God, the twitting of Jeremiah too, for that matter: he knew all their weaknesses, as they knew all *his*. But they had all missed the point, as far as he could see it, of the absolute nullity of the human race, the vacuousness of history, the emptiness of nature, and the pointlessness of change: the cesspool would simply be mixed into a new pattern of filth and dead bodies. Whenever he asked them, when he had the chance, and he frequently did, why they were bothering, they could never give him a coherent answer: they "babbled o' green fields," asked rhetorical questions he felt under no obligation to answer, condemned him for his shallowness, and then clammed up. No: what they said, when they could find their tongues between their teeth, is that, if he could not see it, they could not show him. And he would laugh mockingly at their condescension. He noticed that none of them claimed anything for their bodies, which for him was the principal fact, sometimes repellent, sometimes consoling, but never deniable to an honest man: masturbation was his steady consolation, even when nothing else was. They spoke of the sacred, of history, of society, of ideas, of the mind, even, a little embarrassedly, of the "soul" (no one was supposed to talk about the soul, even those who believed in God, without fencing it in with quotation marks), and they talked about sex in a way that was both falsely worldly and patronizing, just as they patronized their own bodies: they used them and despised them, you could tell by how they treated them — they weren't convinced they were body through and through, they would have treated their bodies with more respect otherwise, they would have worshipped their own health. But no, not at all, they hated their bodies, secretly or not, insisted they were something other than bodies, were superior to their bodies, they despised their bodies the way masters despise slaves, they *had* them but *were not* them, bodies were women, and women were to be desired and despised, even, *a fortiori*, by women. Whereas Gabriel ...

Well, Gabriel had reached a truce with his body: he would take its humiliations by exacting the price of mastery and pleasure in return. He exercised, jogged, swam several times a week, in an attempt to break his body into something malleable and responsive to his will. He ate sparsely and carefully, smoked rarely but only the most expensive tobacco, experimented with drugs to test himself and pursued only those that cradled him gently back into the "straight" world with a renewed feeling of strength, kept away from the ones that, for all their blissful highs, exacted a price in the morning: the goal was always the same, an access of personal power, the ease of attained domination of the moment. Not of others, however; of *himself.*

It was a kind of detached and calculated narcissism, what he was pursuing — though he may not have used that name for it: "self-fulfillment" was the cliché of the hour that would have served; he himself liked the term "self-realization."

Curiously, you might think he'd have turned into a jock: not at all! Just as he felt no respect for his more idealistic friends, he felt none for either the athletes or, significantly, what one might call the "realists": those going into business or law, in order to establish "careers" in the real world. Them he despised even more than the others: he could see no sense in climbing to the top of a heap of manure, which is what he considered society to be: or, as he put it, manure without the merit of fertilization. If ideas were an exercise in futility, money and power were exercises in mockery: one might be a fool, but the others really had no excuse. Many years later, he saw an ad campaign in the city where he lived, on which large posters decked the sides of buses throughout the city for several months. The posters read, in huge black letters: "$0 - 0 + (0 \times 0) = 0$." He chuckled to himself when he read that sign: it summed up his judgment of human life, formed in a corner of a university campus so many years before.

He had a weakness, of course: for one who worshipped the body, one can hardly imagine what else it might be but the female version, with its hidden promises of physical bliss. Little else about her, not the inflexible mind or the polymorphous heart, the quirky opinions or the brittle personality, the strange character or the stranger soul, not after what he had been through with *her*, but the body, the soul's tomb, had an absolute fascination.

He collected faces in the archive of his mind like a museum

collector: the piquant blond, the searing redhead, the sullen brunette, the flashing jet mane, the haggard sleepless face, the bedroom eyes, the pillow cheeks, the drawn stare, the flustered lady, the forever child, the angry goddess, the closeted witch. He watched their walk, a predator stalking the bush with false insouciance, spuriously blind, a gawky animal immersed in the imaginary terrors of self-consciousness, a broken doll, a queen in exile, needy cat, disdainful dog: he kept tabs on his favorites in school, the slightly masculine one with the sneer atop a stunningly angular body, the serene cold looker with the mouth that said "come" and the eyes that said "die," the perky blond with the baffled smile, the gypsy in her scarf and maxiskirt, the pre-Raphaelite beauty who stopped his heart by walking tranquilly across a lawn, the Botticelli who seemed blind to her own beauty and to pity the entire world. They ignored him, they had richer prey in mind, but he spied on them, their friends and boyfriends, the lesbians, and even the grinds, the fat ones, the ugly ones, the helpless failures with their piles of books and grim smirks. He watched how they handled each other between giggle and sparring matches, he sneaked up to the tables where they held court and eavesdropped on the wars of wit and false cynicism by which they sought to conquer each other and hold high their own radiant torches in the glare of the afternoon. He listened for the slippery sounds of flirtation and promise, the illusory barbs of hope, the small squeak of desire and its answering shiver, the tremble contest between desire and desire, and the faints and sleights of hand, the undertones, the overtones, the false tones, the right tones, the word play and the insults, the smirks and the simpers, the humiliations and the triumphs: he longed to join in the game but his shyness blocked him at every turn.

Shyness! A martyrdom! Imagine being nailed slowly to a wall, or even better being suffocated gradually in a lightless room, and you cannot get out and you cannot scream: that is what it is like for a shy person to go to, say, a party. And to strike up a conversation with a stranger is the equivalent of being impaled on a burning stake: in fact, the latter is preferable, since it still allows for a martyr's dignity, whereas the conversation merely threatens to make you look like an idiot. And that, of course, offers the proper insight: the shy person is monstrously proud, all molten and skinned ego, and the one thing the ego cannot bear is humiliation. It would rather die, or so it thinks, though the actual alternative it sometimes chooses is that it would rather kill.

How the night has deepened here: the moon has moved in a solid arc across the sky, an arc of triumph above the triumphal arch, lighting the ghosts along the Roman avenues. I sometimes tell myself that if I listen closely enough I will hear the murmur of togas and the clatter of sandals, the muttering and laughter of old Romans, the ghosts of a people who spoke perfect Latin daily, and used it to buy lemons and wheat, to bargain over leather and salt, to talk about the weather and make bad political predictions. The empire is dead, long live the empire!

Gabriel might have lived a cruelly vacant life had the loss of the Austrian girl not forced him to revise his understanding, not alone of humanity at large, and of women in particular, but of himself and what he might make of himself as a result of insight and will-power. In fact, that's precisely what he did learn: he must *learn to see* and *learn to act*, and all would be well. Or so he thought! Who says life can't teach us lessons! The problem, of course, is not learning them but applying them. Any monkey can learn. It takes a higher primate to apply. And Satan Ludens to appreciate the results.

He had been shattered by the loss of her. And for months afterwards he wandered through his life like his own ghost, barely responding to the gentlest call or sharpest command. Life slipped from him like slime, like a snake's useless skin, like an amniotic sack, afterbirth bloody and stinking. He loathed what the mirror reported each day: the changeless wall of his rejected face. He loathed, however, more than what he seemed — he loathed what he was. It was precisely that individual he could not escape being that roused his detestation and despair. Suicide was for months an idea never far from his mind; only the thought of how it would hurt his broken, crippled family, kept him from considering it seriously. But the thought of oblivion, of peace, of ending, of destroying his oppressor, *himself*, nagged and goaded like a hope and a promise.

It struck him, or rather he was slowly persuaded of the following thought: he could not change what he *was* but he could change how he acted, how he behaved, what he *did*; he could not change the face but he might be able to change the mask. And who knows? the face might follow, like a dog. He could learn how to dissimulate, like everybody else. He could learn to lie, and become a martyr for honesty. Though this was not clear at the time; hardly so, or he couldn't have gone through with it. Action requires a certain intentional stupidity regarding consequences: if I actually allowed myself to "know" the consequences of speaking these words, and of your hearing them, would I have the gall to pipe up with them? Yes, I'm asking *you!*

Ah well. Silence is not necessarily consent, I know. Even beneath the deepening night of Rome.

But back to Gabriel's *Bildung*. Ever since he hit puberty, he had been watching older males, from a few years older to a generation, out of the corner of his eye, sometimes consciously, often unconsciously imitating their gestures, speech, accents, inflections, phrases, walk, stance, even opinions. He watched movies with this in mind: the unconscious question being, how should I behave? how should I act? what should I become? how should I *be?* And he began to watch with a conscious sense of what he was doing: looking for another self, to be, to become, to hide behind, to hide within, to eradicate the self he had come to detest and wished to overcome, even eliminate. There is no disappointment like disappointed love — especially self-love. Sorry: I am becoming sententious. The imperial air does that to one.

He cobbled together, from rag-tags of watching movies and television political talk shows, visiting music clubs, judging his teachers, a mask for himself that pointed in the extreme opposite of what he had hitherto been: haughty, assertive, mannered, arch, artificial, a little dandying and foppish, in the manner of the time: theatrically male yet with a certain self-regarding female streak that was actually exceedingly male, though this was rarely conceded. There was a new swagger both in his walk and in his accent, a crisp clarity of diction after his old, mushy, shy mumble, a distending of the polysyllabic he learned from watching William Buckley on television, a playing with vowels that fascinated some and irritated many, and a tone that his entire personality began to exude of the artificial, the contrived, fragrant with illusion and self-conscious intention. It was not much different from his memory of being onstage in a high-school theatrical years before: except that he wrote the script, designed the costumes, and directed the blocking as well as starring in the show, and his applause was the weirded-out look in his classmates' gaping eyes. And the occasional collapse into laughter at one of his witticisms, an alarming if gratifying development, because one of the rewards of his personal transformation was the discovery that he could be, actually, on the spur of the moment, almost without thinking about it, funny. No? Yes. Astonishing. If also a heavy responsibility.

Because one does not always plan for the consequences of such unlooked-for success.

They began to fall into his bed. Not literally, but figuratively enough to engage his attention at maximum tension.

Shyness? What shyness? Surely not theirs.

It became a weekend gamble, the weekend gambol, a bargain he made from the back of the week to the following Monday morning, in history. Either way he won, though if he lost, he swore. But surprisingly, he swore less often as time went by. And his shyness became a thing, not so much of the past, as of the parallel life he lived on the other side of the sheet.

He dropped out in his junior year. He had won the only diploma worth pursuing. He got a job as an assistant manager in a downtown hotel that catered to an international clientele. His Austrian girl friend's favorite novel had been the *Confessions of Felix Krull, Confidence Man.* He remembered this as a peculiarly subtle form of revenge. Yes — he began to enjoy the recognition, the salt taste of the vendetta.

Richard was disgusted, Quinn was horrified, and Peter refused to have anything to do with him. Morgan had long vanished into his own world and saw his erstwhile "friends" as more or less useful object lessons, examples, and waste-products, so much grist for the mill of history — I mean, History, for which he needed no Monday morning triumphalism. The only one of the whole odd bunch who almost understood him, and nearly forgave him, in the end, who indeed even kept up with him, out of misgivings, curiosity, a rueful sympathy, and a strange envy, was Alan. ("Alan"? It would make more symbolic sense to call him "Adam." So ...)

Down the Via Sacra you can see the Arch of Septimus Severus — look there, in the shadows — and not far from that, just a little way, see that hulking brick box? The Curia, ugly chamber of the Senate in Mussolini's piously repellent restoration. The Temple of Saturn and the House of the Vestals ignore one another like ancient relatives at a funeral. Scattered, marching, decrepit, down the way remain, for all to gape at and scorn, the Arch of Titus and the Forum of Nerva, the House of Cicero the eloquent vetch, the ravaged Porticus of Gaius and Lucius, the Temple of Divus Antoninus and Diva Faustina, whose memorials one finds everywhere in this eternally decaying city, sacred to the adepts of matrimony and the manes of the family, the despoiled Lacus Curtius and the withered spring of Juturna, and at the dead heart of the ancient city, the scotched and ashen eternal flame of the vanished Temple of Vesta. My favorite member of the Forum's collection of scars on the pavement of the Tiber is the ancient Umbilicus, navel of the Empire. And only after that, the Cloaca Maxima!

Adam the clean, the good, the fair, the honest, the decent, the sane: he retained something of the clear-eyed rationality of childhood, even in the raging psychosis of post-pubescence, the explosion of hormones and the labyrinthine warfare of adolescence. At first it made him seem stunted, emotionally arrested, what was in fact a providential and precocious maturity. He didn't seem to suffer enough, frankly, to his friends, associates, classmates, and they could not forgive him the hiddenness of his wounds. They would make him suffer if no-one else did. But their barbs bounced away, their sarcasms wilted on their lips: his maddening serenity even infected them, if only temporarily. On the other hand, his teachers sighed, for years, with relief — while, paradoxically, holding their breaths. Such miracles do not last, not in this country, not in this age: the fragile victory of reason and sanity must perish in the general madness of the world, the human, the contemporary, America. After all, the fascists, I mean capitalists, won, didn't they.

Adam, however, was unperturbed: he followed the rules of school, the barely contained rituals of his fragile and wounded family, the orders and hierarchies of the middle-class background he had grown comfortable in, the assumptions of college, career, wife, and children, the move up the ladder of a highly successful company, the physical gratifications of a well-cushioned way of life, and the purpose drawn carefully in the wet clay of his future of bringing up his children, in particular his son, as he had been, though with certain additions and subtractions, in order to assure the maintenance of that way of life he so certainly and unquestioningly loved. Yes, loved: he loved his life, the life he had had up to now, despite the many pains it had lately inflicted on him: he wanted to keep it alive. He played with the idea of reincarnation, an idea he had gotten from his step-mother, the woman who brought him up in lieu of the mother who had abandoned both him and his father during his earliest childhood: the idea of reliving the life he had known, in these circumstances, with slight variations, more or less forever: the comfortable home in the country, the one he had lost, become part of the myth of his happiness, his childhood: lushly and elegantly but not extravagantly furnished, the art, the books, the music, the exquisite dinners, the views across fields and woods down a plaiting of valleys and hills toward the aerial dimness of the horizon, the summer house by the seaside beach, the leisurely life between sand and waves, dunes and surf, sunrise and moonrise, the smell of earth in the fall, the briny spice of ocean in the summer, the white cold of the snowed-in winters, the muddy brilliance of the spring, and the warmth of the family when it had been happy, he had retained in the heart of his mind when the family moved to the bitter accommodations in the middle of an ugly and violent city and, later, when the family nearly bled to death after his father left and the carcass stank and rotted in a tiny house in a dark alley under the yellow of sodium street lights. He held that memory of what life had once been for him, for his family indeed, and therefore what it might be again: the family that might have avoided the tragedy and known the happiness it had taken so much for granted, for the length of all its days. And this he held onto, not only as a memory, but as a promise. And the collapsing world around him only determined him even further in the goal, from the past, that he had set himself. And yet, at the time, he hardly knew this himself.

Oh, of course, he was swept up in the tumult of the period: who, of intelligence and sensitivity, to say nothing of someone who had known that thin but deeply cut share of meaningless suffering that he had, could not? He was torn? He was torn. The price of such serenity is clarity of vision: he was less distracted by his own internal warfare and so could not easily dismiss the battleground on which he found himself: the warfare of love seeking love and failing to either find it or make it, or having once found, or worse created it, abandoning, trashing, losing it, like a grotesque heirloom from a long-outdated taste that has overstayed its welcome. And what he saw determined him not so easily to abandon what he saw he could have, as he thought: the delicacy of love behind a hard and almost invisible shield, a narcissus in a bowl of water, sealed behind glass.

But for that he must grow the shield behind which the flower might flourish, without losing the means of attaining and nurturing it. And the search for such means drew him into himself, away from the battlefield on which he staggered slightly, peering at the horizon through the smoke, judging the forms of the wounded as they hobbled into the darkness. He must preserve himself as a farmer preserves his seed, for the next cultivating season, for the coming, for it must come, of spring.

His friends called him Clark Kent, slightly mockingly but with a certain secret envy: things went too easily for him, they thought. He smiled to himself at the charge: who, after all, was "Clark Kent" really? And then, things did not go particularly easily for him: he simply did not readily display the damage or his injuries. He had them, but had also learned that suffering feeds on itself. If given no nourishment, its cries wither into a kind of squeaky moan that can be ignored for hours at a time: it doesn't quite die, but it goes numb. What is left is not exactly joy, of course, and sometimes the numbness longs for the sharp knick that tells it it is alive. But that, he found, is a temptation to the ultimate vice: the vice of self-destructiveness, the unforgivable sin that touches suffering with a delusive but well-nigh irresistible sense of triumph.

As long as he held on to that idea, he was safe. He thought!

The storms of the time rose to meet him, as it rose to meet everyone alive at the time, and especially his peculiarly unprepared generation. Unprepared? What generation is prepared? We survey the monuments to the dashing of that illusion, unless we need visit the Peloponnese: a generation could have hugged the fox to its belly to teach it unrelenting defiance of the invader and still not known how to handle its own dissolution, the relentless fall to an invasion of barbarians from within.

Imagine a nation that grows its own barbarian hordes, a civilization that educates Mongols, that preens and prunes and primes its own Genghis Khan, and then unleashes them upon itself and the world — that was ours, that was their country and time. Who needs Visigoths and Vandals when you have *us?* Adam was horrified at first, then, like the decent fellow he was, backed off and wondered if there were indeed something to justify the onslaught. And of course, there was: there always is — the horrors of systematic injustice, of a hypocrisy that had fueled the country for generations, centuries, a systematic and sanctimonious rapacity that portrayed itself as common sense and that nothing could stop, and a horrific and pointless war that the leaders would neither pursue to a ruthless end nor cut their losses and escape. The young barbarians simply responded, in the naive litany of youth, to the barbarism practiced more genteelly by their elders. They were simply more brutally consistent about it, enslaved to the aesthetic, in love with purity, honest. The mirror deserved its face.

He was pulled, briefly, into the chaos of their righteousness, was even in danger a few times of being pulled under: the boundaries between layers of rebellion and self-destruction weren't as easily recognized as they became later. But some living instinct spared him the ruse of history's fatal tongue, its cunning and vicious pitilessness. He slipped in and out with his detachment secure, he did not go over the edge of a perfervid belief enough to ruin his judgment and torch his homestead, as some were doing. Was this partly due to what he saw happening to his "friends"? Ah! Maybe. The reptile of the time sneaked up and dragged one after another under, for cogent reasons, it seemed to them, and Adam could hardly have gainsaid them either, though the sound of hissing beneath the river waters caused him to pull in his own feet with a snap.

Quinn was gone on a fantasy called "poetry"; Richard was retreating to the death of academe; Gabriel had abandoned himself to the most specious of all possibilities, the body's; Peter had given up the ghost for the sake of the greatest ghost of all; Morgan sought to bring it all down in the name of a future illusion. That their choices might well be right for them was clear to him, he was enough of a reflexive liberal to believe that, but the utter wrongness of them in some abstract as well, to him, personal sense was also glaringly clear, the sheer lack of humanity presupposed by their particular choices, the horrific results that were likely to obtain, and for what, nothing more, really, than a hypothesis: it almost made him give up the moral possibility of choice if actual choices could seem so pointlessly and maddeningly wrong.

But he didn't, because he was convinced of the necessity, the inevitability, at certain times in one's life of making fundamental choices about how to live in future, and these years of his life and the lives of his friends included that responsibility. The choice would be made, consciously or unconsciously. Since he was aware of this, it would have to be a conscious choice of some sort, it was too late for him to "sleepwalk it." If the choice turned out to be wrong, one must stick with it until it led to Elysium or disaster or, more likely, some muddled nondescript fate; or at the very least had been exhaustively explored. Thus, his "friends'" mistakes might lead them to deeper truths than his waffling (which is what he, for a time, accused himself of doing), which might save him a few bruises, but also some ultimate, saving wisdom.

All this mental torture didn't help him decide anything, of course.

Ah. He had his weaknesses. The strongest, in that era, was politics: here was what pulled him up morally, emotionally, and philosophically, with a start, and pointed to both the need for choice and the near impossibility of choosing — the injustices of power and how they needed to be accommodated, fought, used, defied. This had pulled him into the "Pranksters" and their sincere sillinesses. What fascinated him was precisely the struggle between the demand for justice and the drive for power: that they were, in essence, two independent powers, themes, drives, "vectors," with rules of judgment and penalties for defiance, and bore between them an almost intolerable tension, was clear to him, and intrigued him as much as he saw how they might each make him, personally, suffer. They were, essentially, two mutually inapplicable tyrannies that ran the soul and the world, and the trick in society was to balance them and not make a misguided attempt to equate them. Much of the horror of his time, indeed of his century, seemed to him to be an attempt at just such a horrible miracle: the marriage of justice and power. The result was a level of global injustice, played out over the previous century, that the world had never seen, and the future seemed accordingly of a bleakness almost unbearable to contemplate.

What gave him the little historical hope he had was the question itself, and his certainty that justice and power could and must contain one another: the sense of justice, always failed, always awaiting its dispensation on earth, turned against power when it least expected it, just as power turned against the sense of justice when that sense became too trusting. In the patches of silence and darkness between battles, an honorable, if secret, life might be lived. Out of the shadow of society itself, he would create his own. Or so he dreamed.

He dreamed, that is, of building a life out of the shadows of the perpetual war he saw all around him: he would, following the advice he came across in an eleventh-grade French class reading of Voltaire's *Candide*, "cultivate his garden." Not that he had any intention of having a real garden: he had done enough work on the soil in his childhood, he never wanted to look at a lawn, orchard, flowerbed, or vegetable patch again. But the metaphor, as long as it remained a metaphor, appealed to him mightily. He would have a house, on a hill, in the country, with a wife (source unknown; she had an invisible face but a quiet presence off in a corner of his mind, and of the house! — she was wearing an apron and a lock of hair fell across her forehead with a curious combination of the provocative and the domestic) and two or three children (he could only see His Son clearly; he was teaching him something, how to tie a knot, how to read, how to build a model ship, how to walk through the woods and make the most of what he found there). And he would drive to work each morning and come home each evening, and leave the world behind him as the gravel crunched beneath his car. The greatest drama in his life would be the weather. The world would celebrate at his coming, at which he would grin bashfully and, modestly, proudly, demur. In other words, he would recreate, and triumphantly maintain, the family of his that had perished.

It was childish, he knew it was childish, this attempt to recreate his childhood, in which he could be both parent and child, father and son, adult and baby. And he enjoyed the idea immensely, as one does fantasies one knows have no danger of realization, although he was still young enough to feel guilty about wanting it: the unpretending, apolitical middle-class domesticity of it was an offense to the moral insanity of destinies that heralded their public and private subversiveness at full cry, at the time. And then, of course, one has to become an adult before one can abandon adulthood.

Whereas it takes a child to know, and truly love, the world in all its anarchic bounty.

And he was still an adolescent, at home in neither world: he still "believed in reality"!

But at the time, he was still waffling. How is this for a conceit, as my friends the English majors might have put it once in their bad old graduate-student days? To say nothing of their vain-glorious *professori!* Once upon a time …

One day, Adam went to a scruffy student diner where he and his "friends" had hung out in their first years at the university before being drawn and quartered by the horses of destiny. Let's say he had just finished a battery of tests in his junior year, it was spring, and he wanted a smoke and a soda to wring out the tension (not realizing that the combination worsened it) before seeing an Austrian girl he was to have dinner with that evening. As Adam was pulling himself onto a counter stool, he saw someone who looked like Morgan in a booth at the back, mulling over a sandwich and a textbook. They hadn't seen each other in more than a year and this person looked very intense, in strangely nondescript clothes, wire-rimmed spectacles, and a Trotsky goatee distorting his chin in wild, awkward patches. Adam himself hadn't changed his look since high school, except he had let his hair grow down his back, knowing he'd have to cut it after he graduated, and not caring much. He was nearsighted but wore his glasses only when driving.

Morgan.

No hesitation, no hint of embarrassment, just a common, youthful yell of recognition and a brace of open-faced grins bloom as Adam slips in opposite his old friend and they pass a laugh of happiness and callow gestures of surprise.

So! what government building have *you* been blowing up lately?

Another outburst of laughter, this one a little nervous.

Not so fast! — Morgan glitters at the bourgeois-in-training. — They pay our bills still — even if they don't know it. Only bite the hand that feeds you after you've found a *replacement*.

Cynic! Whatever happened to all that *selfless idealism?*

No such thing, it's just good politics. Anyway "idealism" is just one more self-indulgence of uptight middle-class suburbanites like *you*.

Adam's grin freezes slightly.

At least the revolution is getting good role models.

And what are *you* doing?

Getting a wishy-washy liberal arts degree, something to set me up for an entry-level management trainee program in some faceless company.

You mean you're not going for an MBA? *You're* the one we'll be shooting in five years. But the useless degree is Peter's. Yours is downright malignant, like *cancer*.

The two grins brittlely mirror one another across the torn yellow formica. A blade of hostility flashes and disappears across the table.

I feel *so guilty*, what am I to do, but there's no way I'm joining the Che Brigade, sorry! Ever see Peter around? — His eyes unlock from Morgan's, flitter blindly around the dimly empty diner. — He's brave or crazy, headed for a seminary, a monk's hood, or *brain death*, whether he knows it or not.

The religious maniac and the bomb thrower, the terrorist and the saint? I don't think Peter approves of me, for some weird reason, I don't see him going in for liberation theology.

You wouldn't want it any other way.

Hunh!

Approving of you.

He's my conscience, if I ever saw him.

Conscience!

If he ever smiles at me, I'll know I'm *bending* the wrong way.

They are about to crack up over the innuendo when a shadow hoves across them.

So what are you two bums arguing about?

What are *you* doing here? Sit down. We need a chaperone. *You* need a chaperone.

Gabriel, always the dandy, always slightly overdressed, this time with a red bandana around his neck, a moustache bushing his undernostrils, floats ironically at the table end like a spook called up to a seance. A smell of sandalwood wafts from him.

Only for a sec, I've got an appointment.

I'll bet you do, what's her name?

Seriously.

I *am* serious. — Richard! Over here.

What, I thought old home was next week.

Richard, thick-bearded, growsily hirsute, and looking unkemptly professorial already, his arm around a backpack cubed with books, turns stiffly from the counter.

He's trying to convince me to become responsible. Like *he* is, naturally.

How sick. You still balling for dollars?

Loweth bloweth.

Having come closer to gaze at the miracle, Richard looks wonderingly over the faces reflecting his own surprise.

What are you gentlemen doing in the same booth! I thought napalm wouldn't bring you three together.

No, Richard, it's pompous philistines like you who don't talk to anybody. (Morgan.) Sit *down*, man, there's plenty of room, we have no prejudices here, even against cop-outs and uptight middle-class ass-wipes.

Shut your trap or a fly will get in. I'm not copping *out*, I'm copping *in*. (Richard plumps down into a seat.) If I brown the nose on occasion, so do, have, and shall all of us, estimable comrade! (Tu quoque! chimes a voice.) Somebody's got to work the system, to do that, you've got to be inside it, am I correct, *Adam?*

Where's a liberal when you need one?

What? Who? Where? (Gabriel.)

I thought that was the one thing we all agreed to hate. The wimp of the tolerable. (Adam.)

String 'im *ha-agh*, boys. (Morgan.)

Just wait one dad-burn cotton-pickin' *minute*. And if anybody knocks me for that remark, I'll smash them as thin as their politics, we all hate the system as it is, fine, excellent, I just want to work it from inside, corrupt the minds of the young, show them the corruption of the system, make them hate the society they're joining. Who's the real subversive here?

Do I detect a hint of defensiveness?

Co-optation begins when the fifth column starts to eat the enemy's food.

Explain yourself.

If you join the system, you become the system. Don't overestimate your own strength, capitalism is a co-optation machine, look what it's done to the word "revolution"!

Maybe, but Richard doesn't speak for *me*. (Adam.) The system isn't *evil.*

No!?

It's bumbling, well meaning, perverse, *radically stupid*, the way groups of human beings always are. Just look at a demonstration, the brightest people in town march down the middle of a street and turn into a mob of six year olds.

So what's your point?

The country is made up of bright people behaving en masse like idiots. Welcome to society! I can't speak for Richard, but I'm looking for a corner *out* of it.

Avoidance! Like I said, copping out.

But there's no other way! You bastards will blow yourselves away, or at least you'll try to, along with the rest of us.

That is not precisely what I meant. (Richard.) The "system," and I'm not sure I like that word, it suggests things are more coherent than they are, is more than just bumbling, it is, among other things, a collection of powerful people, arrogant, unresponsive, self-perpetuating, and unnecessary, who have deliberately created a mass hysteria of patriotism, self-delusion, and hypocrisy. But there are cracks in the system that'll open if a root takes hold, there's hope if only in the ideals it purports to hold that you can shame it with, and there's always the possibility of future minds to form. I haven't given up entirely on trying to *change* it, like our Adam has. Unless his diet of the fruit of the tree of the knowledge of good and evil has been unexpectedly enlightening? Despair is the cardinal sin, whatever it is you *don't* believe in....

Silence as they grin, glaring at each other, fascinated and repelled by their own contradictions staring them in the eye.

Anyone seen our monk in training? — The reference to cardinal sin had stirred Morgan's memory, even nostalgia. — And what about Quinn?

The saint without portfolio, and six stanzas in search of an author.

Believers!

I believe in something. *You* believe in something. We *all* believe in something. But what something, and at what price? What effect will it have in this, the most real of all possible worlds?

Nothing so inconvenient as a conscience. — Who spoke? One can't always tell when they are all talking at once.

Right! Materialism, historical materialism, dialectical materialism, anal-compulsive materialism, I-want-my-teddy-bear materialism ...

And what *about* Gabriel?

What's your excuse?

I breathe, I eat, I sleep.

Like a well-trained animal, a good middle-class pet.

Sounds like heaven.

Four cokes?

Three cokes. *One* Pepsi.

There's one in every crowd.

"We — are — the world ..."

Hélas!

Quit showing off your French, you sound like Quinn.

Did I hear my name taken in vain?

Speak of the devil!

They go silent and look up at the spook hovering at the table's end.

Pleased to meet you!

A spare face inside a cloud of hair above an anorexically skinny body, with eyes burning with druggy memory, extemporizes a crazy smile above Richard's bearded visage. A magniloquent smirk arching his lips, he leans with arched spine against a nearby chairback.

We're comparing mutual recriminations.

No we're not, we're comparing dicks.

So we're all faggots now. Interesting. I can't say I'm surprised to see Morgan here, but where did you find this *canaille?*

If you don't sit down, I will personally line your ribs with caesuras. (Morgan.)

You might graduate to surrealism yet. — Quinn remains budgeless and arches a little more both back and smirk.

Modernism is dead, long live modernism!

According to whom?

The English Department, which knows everything by claiming everybody else knows nothing.

Ach! The trivia of the bourgeois! This place stinks of ...

God?

Peter?

No. Leon Bloy, actually.

Words, words, words.

Will you sit down, I get a crick in my neck trying to look up at you.

I was on my way.

Oh no you're not! You don't get off the hook that easily! (Richard.)

The hook from which you currently dangle?

Is there any other?

You'll never be so lucky till you've got a poet to mourn you, in the immortal words of the mortal poet, "poets are the unacknowledged legislators of the world," the poet rules man through his imagination: history is the making, the working out, the justification, of metaphors! All men are created equal: a metaphor! SPQR: a metaphor! *Liberté, égalité, fraternité:* a metaphor! From each according to his abilities, to each according to his needs. Our words are our passion, proles, slaves, masters, they give us all life's clues and goals, they build, destroy whole worlds. What's the world but a word, what's the world but the Word with an "l" — as the cockneys call it, with a "hell" — added! The world is a whisper on our lips, no more real, *and no less!*

The booth is divided between glares and giggles. Richard breaks the silence.

I guess we're here to lecture to each other.

The indifferent waitress approaches with her green pad out. She smiles.

Cokes?

And one Pepsi.

Two more cokes.

No, I'll have ginger ale.

Before or after it's been cursed? Oh no! Oh God! Who let the frigging saint in? — Unknown speaker, but he spoke for the table as a whole.

They all look at Peter with a strange, wondering air; short-haired, bright-eyed, clean-faced, strangely clothed in black blazer and plaid shirt, he looks down at them in the clutter of vinyl-covered seating and chairs around the formica table, Quinn still leaning off to the side; with a grin at once beatific and mischievous, as though he had been planning this for ages.

Shit! — Damn! — See, Peter, the effect you have on our vocabularies? — And we had just been discussing the sanctity of language! — Infuckingcredible. — We invent, we are invented, we are inventing. — Truly eerie. — Any *more* coming? — Any more *there?* — Is this ... — A rehearsal for a Rotsy Nazi rally? — Non sequitur! — Non compos! — Non credo! — Nondum!

Peter signs the cross over their heads, still smiling.

Ora pro nobis.

Jesus. — Does this mean I'm a Catholic now? — Or are we entirely lost to God?

Who could lose us but ourselves? (Peter.)

It's a good question, but are we exactly ready for it? (Morgan.)

They're all good questions and we're *never* ready for them. (Richard.)

Being lost is human, it's being found that's beyond *us*. (Adam.)

And what if all the revolutions were over, they had all succeeded, we were free as birds to do as we like, we had good incomes, good work to do, good games to play, with all the physical pleasures we wanted, security, children, love, we were as creative as Leonardo and powerful as Napoleon, our egos were stroked regularly, and we lived on feasts of gratified desire. (And Peter paused.) Wouldn't that awful phrase "so what?" sneak up on us, wouldn't the one thing we are not allowed to conquer because we are created beings, the inevitability of death and the destruction of everything we make, the erasure of everything we do, the deflection of every aim into its opposite, the reversal and defeat of every goal — wouldn't the realization of that spoil every happiness, every satisfaction, hope for the future, pleasure in the present, and make our lives one long nostalgia for what is forever gone in its very passing?

Unspeaking snarling looks greet Peter's sermon, his haunted smiling face, its mischief not gone but transformed into a kind of redemptive malice.

And isn't that what would throw the most successful man in the world into the arms of a god, *any* god, unless, of course, he has succeeded (like so many of us so much of the time) in killing his mind and living the lie he has been telling himself all his life?

You offer us despair, living a lie, or God?

I don't offer anything, I'm just describing what I see.

Morituri te salute, et tu Brute, requiescat in pace! Gabriel intones.

... and fuck your mother. — Who got the last word, hissed with a sincerity, a lack of deflating sarcasm, as plain as it is hostile? But they will, *we* will, never know.

Silence. We stare at each other, frozen for a moment between a laugh yet to sound over an anticipated punchline and a riot about to leave a small neighborhood in ruins. The hair rises on our heads and the air sparkles blindly with uneasy ego and grinning outrage: all six, six faces of the same self as it were, broken in late adolescence, the years straddling high school and college in that epoch of chaos and madness and hope, facing each other with a kind of alarmed contempt and hopeful appeal. The waitress brings the final beverages, we eye her as though she represented some sort of escape, though she does not and is too harried to notice the gridlocked conference of loquacious ephebes and self-important puppies with the striking resemblance. Ignored by the goddess of the place, we giggle nervously as though deciding collectively to ignore what has just happened, and sip through our straws, or chug down quick and hard, and try not to wonder at the splinters suddenly falling all around us through the spring air.

There was another one, of course, who had been there since the beginning, hugging a dark corner modestly as was his wont (yes, he was the sort of person to use the sort of word as "wont" — *quelle surprise!*); he was one so quiet his very name had been forgotten, though he had not forgotten them. He had had the least ambition of them all, the least desire either to imprint his name on the world's accommodating desire or to take what the world had to offer in as copious a measure as he could handle. No, if he had any positive ambition, it was to be left alone by the world (as if that were a realizable goal) and to leave as little mark on the earth he tread as he could (as if that were a realistic hope): to do as little damage as possible and disappear with the stainless purity of his conscience intact. As though one could live in this world without damaging the very air one breathes! (*Can* one? I'm only asking.) He was the most hopeless of the lot; perhaps he knew it, and kept silent and still, in the unlighted corner, and watched them from the side, half envious of their ardent and careless willingness to live and impose their wills on their lives, half pitying them the futility he sensed bound them together, like survivors of a shipwreck chained together by life preservers, and never let his presence be known.

Ah, the night grows deep in this valley of Rome! A cat from nearby, one of Trajan's no doubt, pauses on a slab of shaved column and licks its belly nonchalantly in the eerie public light. The air is still, both moist and dusty as it moves toward the dew of summer morning. The pope has fled to his August villa, and only the tourists are foolish enough to walk the afternoon streets here, before the sigh of the scirocco that deepens even the heat. The traffic died long ago, and it is just ourselves waiting for the Roman ghosts to rise, hopelessly, from the Roman dust. Like ourselves! more modest ghosts in the making.

How do they live? How can they not! They will never meet again — why should they. They talk a little longer, trying awkwardly to ignore the insult spoken at a weak moment, they make poor jokes at each other's expense, half envious of one another, half contemptuous, tightly wrapped in an earnest insincerity, then, perhaps it is Gabriel off to his new girl friend, perhaps Adam to meet the Austrian for dinner, one after another they stand and part, with hardly more than a casual good-bye, as if they will see each other shortly, in class, in the cafeteria, in the library, in the streets, at a party, at graduation, in the restless cities that ingest their lives, at the crossroads of their turning toward, apparently so violently diverse, actually so similar fates; but they do not meet again, not, anyway, in ways they might, had they been "real" to begin with, but in other ways yes, ways they will never recognize, so changed and yet the same they shall become and be, ever become and be, in the fullness of time.

The torrents of history and the currents of their lives send them off to unknown points of heaven, continent, ocean. Morgan moves ahead into the battle against the capitalist empire, for justice, ostensibly if obscurely, for the right of history, an idealist despite himself, or rather despite his theories, a scion of anger and hope: he hopes to sow fire and fury wherever hope hasn't died in the hearts of the ordinary, aims to become, confusedly, an aristocrat of democracy. The slightly ridiculous ROC, small as it is, grows a few more members, then splits into factions: moderate and radical ("more radical than thou") over strategy, the moderates, less optimistic, opting for the infiltration of "sleepers" into corporations, government, as social workers, lawyers, local politicians, aides; the radicals, both more sanguine, not to say sanguinary, about the times and suspicious, with good reason, that infiltrating will eventually co-opt the "sleepers," arguing for the immediate use of violence to promote a right-wing reaction which, according to theory, will provoke open rebellion among the already radicalized, accelerating, with the right direction "from above," into widespread revolt, co-optation of police and military units, the National Guard, and, at the right moment of crystallization, of workers, urban disaffected, youth groups, and police and military cadres, with politically astute leaders and a highly organized militant group timing an accelerating series of raids and takeovers, based, optimistically, on the actions of Lenin, Trotsky, and the Bolsheviks in Petrograd in October 1917, leading to coup d'état and revolution: something similar had almost happened in France. *Wait longer,* they charge, *and the entire country will become co-opted, politically neutered, and shift right. We have to act now while there's still hope — in five years, it'll be gone and we'll have lost a generation.*

Whereas the moderates replied that by using violence too soon, *fellow travelers, fence-sitters will be scared to the right, the progress we've made will be lost: the system will have won not only the tactical but even the psychological advantage on people we need on our side. The only possible action for us is grass-roots work, slow and tedious, but consistently applied, pressure in alliance with liberals and moderates until the limits of working within the system become clear even to them — and only then will militant action bring down a beast everybody will see is not about to let itself be killed behind its own back.*

After days and weeks of anguished thought, Morgan, temperamentally averse to physical violence yet fascinated by it as an idea, sides with the radicals, the dangers of moderation seeming even greater than those of action, the political and social costs of passiveness looming ever larger, the penalty for delay without mercy and without appeal, and parts company, surprisingly, with his mentor, Andrei, who withdraws into a moderation at variance with his earlier rhetoric. They argue the point long into the night, always ending where they started: the argument between a swift, violent intervention, pushing the advantage immediately, with the possibility of igniting revolution or of overwhelming failure, or waiting, growing slower but deeper loyalties, yet possibly missing the chance through too much caution and finding one day that the enemy has grown too powerful to defeat, metastasizing like a cancer.

But you were the one who recruited me for *action*, right? — Morgan, smiling at his friend even as he passionately debates him. — And now you want to pull back?

There's a difference between the occasional job and a campaign, which is what *you* want. We can't do this alone, we don't have the support, don't have the workers behind us, only middle-class students, misfits ...

We'll have *black* workers behind us, and that'll be enough once white workers, hardhats, rednecks see what they've been missing, which is just about everything. Look what's happening in the cities. Blacks are just waiting for some encouragement to tear the country apart. If you listen to almost any black analysis of current conditions, you'll see they know *exactly* what's going on. All it takes is a spark, at the right place and the right time. And the whole thing will blow.

Up in your face and send us back to the thirties! Don't mistake a few riots for a revolution, remember 1848, remember 1905 — they looked great at the time, but all they "empowered" was the police!

And in 1917, Russia was in the middle of a hugely unpopular war, so are we, Russians had already *had* 1905, it gave them an idea of *their* power: the civil rights movement has had the same effect here …

In your dreams!…

And so it went.

The violent faction, renaming itself, cheekily, Left Field, for both its politics and its intended tactics, is led by Rick the Red, Maks leads the moderates, and a struggle begins between the factions almost as much as between the two factions and the "system": after all, they are a better match for each other and can inflict more satisfying harm. It is only years later that Morgan learns that Maks has, all this time, been a double-agent for the FBI.

In the meantime Left Field, left to itself and its dreams of anarchy and glory, begins a campaign of petty robberies and holdups of small banks in cities across the river in New Jersey.

It's peculiarly exhilarating, the rush of panic that follows the hold on yourself and your rifle, a 20-gauge shotgun, at the bank's entrance, the feeling of the black bandana beneath your eyes, the sweaty ski mask tickling your face, the fear that you yourself might be shot at any moment mingling with the knowledge that no one knows who you are but looks at you, at your shoes, from where they're lying on the bank floor, with terror in his eyes, in her face: you feel a tinge of pity muted with contempt for them, even through the scattering of your nerves, they're only trying to get through an ordinary luckless day in a luckless life with its occasional bright moment, this not being one of them, though, who knows, it'll make a thrilling story later on, how the gang charged into the bank yelling at everyone to lie flat and keep their faces down, this is a holdup, like a goddam movie, it'll give them a little halo of romantic excitement in their circle, in their own minds, in a life generally gray, colorless, too cold or too hot or too humid, empty and lonely except when they are hating something in a group, like your own, you think, but you brush away the thought as though it were a gnat trying to get into your head through your eyes, thinking is not encouraged now you have chosen action, doubting, speculation, wondering are luxuries you can hardly afford at the moment, the only thought possible is getting through this without dying or killing anyone, then planning for the next, organizing communications, ordering future priorities, arranging hideouts, travel, codes, masks, propaganda, attacks, escapes. And he pulls the shotgun closer to his chest, hoping, as he sweats, that he won't have to use it. The first action was over in a little more than ten minutes that felt like hours, and they were out, after marking the walls with revolutionary slogans, "All Power to the People!," "US Out of America!," loping heavily down the street with the canvas bag of bills and into the half-busted VW van so fast they didn't catch the sound of the police siren till they gunned the van, driving off with a lurch before settling into an inconspicuous cruising speed as they crouched in the back, tearing off their sweat-soaked masks and bandanas and hiding their weapons under a smelly green tarp. The stash was disappointing, only a few thousand dollars, but Rick grinned in his grim way: *First crawl, then run,* the sweat of excitement and fear evaporating with its peculiar smell in the ratty basement apartment where they regularly met. The bills were unusually crisp, green bills with the gray faces of Washington, Lincoln, Grant looking bemusedly off into the distance.

It was pathetic how little gun practice any of them actually had, of course: most of them (there were only five in the beginning) had never fired a gun; two had owned BB guns as kids. Someone had the idea to practice by going hunting in the countryside in the fall: they wouldn't stand out from the surrounding barrage from hunters in the bloodlust of autumn. But this was a long way off and they needed to get to work soon. They had pulled off three bank robberies without any of them having to pull a trigger in the service of the revolution before they finally packed into a pickup one weekend and headed into farm and woods country northwest of the city.

Harsh, man, said, oh call him "Abbie," their driver, a Russian

Jew in background, intense, bearded, likable, competitive, indeed clearly competing for the role of leader of the group in case Rick ever showed a weak hand. He handled the shotgun gingerly, then suddenly sniffed it. It smells as dangerous as it looks, he smiled. — He handled the gun with some distaste and seemed to want to get rid of it as soon as possible; anyway, as driver, he didn't join the actual attacks: he handed it to Case, an Irish Catholic onetime speed freak who had given up religion for drugs, and drugs for the drug and religion of Maoism, who took the gun, aimed it at a thrush on a branch of a nearby hickory tree, and shot, scattering the bird into a brief cloud of feathers and a blot mangled at the foot of the tree as the branch on which it had perched swished back from the discharge. Case pulled himself up from where he had fallen to the ground, to hawking laughter from his cohorts. After they stopped nearly choking with laughter, they examined the small, half-obliterated bird corpse, tracing the lines of the pellets where they could see them in the leering half-flattened body. Morgan touched it with his boot. He remembered the dying chick in the locker.

It was abruptly sobering, this small, belittling lesson in a weapon's blunt and stupid power — it showed Morgan what manner of thing was the power he held in his hands; it brought him, too, down to earth, before soaring upwards into ever higher dreams of mastery. On the ride back in the pickup, he daydreams about destruction — flipping between the victim's and the aggressor's points of view, the hawk's and the pigeon's, the bomber's and the village's, victim's and victor's, tumbling between horror and pity and guilt and a kind of sober thrill, feelings of complete vulnerability and of absolute power *at war in the same action,* unable to reconcile them, to imagine them *together* — as the slipstream pummels and caresses his hair.

The results of their "actions" are even more effective, according to first predictions, than expected: the reaction by the establishment is swift and hard, however groping, random, vicious, and mindless: various radicals are arrested, interrogated, threatened, released, then one of their own, Dan, a pasty-faced Welshman, is held for three days before being released and returning with stories of being held naked in a cell with the light kept on all the time before being questioned and warned, and the group is now under surveillance: Morgan feels like a hunted fugitive before the revolution has even begun. He moves from home, drops out of school, shares an apartment with a law student who is rarely home. The group organizes several bombings of vacant government buildings and random vandalism of federal buildings. But as a result, the group is forced further underground, breaking up, the others living in slums, hidden behind menial jobs as they are hunted first by police, then the FBI, even as COINTELPRO is beginning to be investigated, the press is unsympathetic, there is no rebellion, no hint anywhere now of the hoped-for "pre-revolutionary stage," they find themselves ridiculed and reviled by the "media," the butts of late night TV show comedians, the targets of fake liberal editorialists, detested by the majority, despised by the intelligentsia, denied by the "responsible left": they are, like many acts of unfettered conscience, at once shaming, for the purity of their motives, and shameful, for their impracticality. You move into the local barrio, the actions wind down, money dries up, the group stops meeting even clandestinely, and you move out of the city, west to a small town in the Alleghenies, working as a night clerk in a motel, getting coded postcards and letters from Rick once a month, then every six months till they finally stop, the last letter telling you about Maks' long stringer work for the FBI, so that was how they found out so soon, hearing from no one else, letting yourself go in a deep depression relieved by after-work drunks in the mean and sarcastic dawns. One or two girls show interest in you, but you don't care: you have too much to tell and too much to hide, anyway their unquestioning patriotism, fed by network television and local radio, leads to political sympathies that are dangerous for you. You never hear from Andrei, Abbie, Case, or the others again. You hover in numb despair between your room and your job. When you see copies of the books that used to raise your hopes as high as your anger, you want to throw them in the trash. When you see the TV report about the first mail bomb blowing off the hands of a university professor, you raise your beer bottle in a wild salute and let out a rebel whoop. Then, with a gag of disgust, you stop: *I have gone out of my mind*, you think. You fall back in your chair and sit, staring at a spot above the television set, trying to remember something. What you see is a crack in a paint blister. But it reminds you, though you don't remember this exactly, of the smeared body of a thrush.

Peter becomes a novice at a Benedictine monastery among the brindled, glacier-scraped, and wind-eroded hills of southern New York. He pulls himself awake for matins, lauds, milks the cows as dawn brushes its face past the barns, walks the genteel monastery in his novice's modest robe, nods to Brother Peter with the stoop and Brother John of the aimless smile, obese Brother Matthew and squinting Brother James, and dreams in his small dark cell, streaked with light in the morning, furred with candle-light in the evening, of the levels of beatitude and the spheres of grace, the seven-storey mountain of joy whose price and staple are guilt and sorrow, the awareness of one's unworthiness before the ground and heart of Awe. He learns to pray for hours between the stables and fields and the tall chapel, between song at the altar foot and the promise of study, of *lectio divina*, in the well-kept library, still and book-smelling and restlessly restful, serene in its demands, and listening in the airy refectory, with its windowless height except for the clerestory shafting the sunlight through the shadowy air, to the melodious voice of Brother Pius as he reads from Erikson or Küng or similar authors to the monks at their repast of garden vegetable and orchard fruit from mug and dish of pewter, as for centuries past, silently bowed over their plates (no talking allowed while eating) before him. He learns to live on the delicate fare of hope — the hope that hope is joy. And that all the world rings round, in its sadness and grief and pain, with love, because of love. The rope around his waist, gathering his robe around him with its knot, holds him like a pair of arms.

He stays there five years, becomes a brother after his time as postulant and novice, the obsequies of avowal, the peculiarities of petition and acceptance, the first evening at the abbot's making his request, the potato-eye-glassed abbot's brief, grave stare and reluctantly friendly, *do you have any idea what you are doing?* standing doubtful in his look, *probably not, father,* should have been the answer rather than the somewhat overzealous and certainly questionably honest, too-sincere gaze of majestic innocence and trembling piety, overmastering his sense of the ridiculous, which he felt his face broadcasting with awful hypocrisy back. Then the supper and the introduction to the novice master, a lean, canny corrupter of men with a bitter underlip and hard, smiling eyes, the weeks learning the details of the abbey's life, the hours and their celebration, the punitive awakening at three in the morning for vigils, to "stand in the presence of angel choirs who they chant" prayers in night wind and the darkness and silence of the countryside deeper even than his young man's dreams in this the first of the hours of the divine office, then two hours of darkness in prayer and holy reading of psalmody and scripture, followed by lauds as the sun glints like metal over the wooded hills, radiating the sky, driving its splendor like a herd of wild horses into the day, the sun celebrated as a herald of the Son, then the homely toiletries before prime, the hasty breakfast, the short prayer before the day's physical work around the cloister and chapter house, cleaning chapels, refectory, the kitchen while avoiding the swinging pots and wayward utensils of the first kitchener, then the cow stables and neighboring dairy with its tubs and tubes and vats of swirling milk and the zinc pitchers dipped into them, then the short prayer and psalm or two and the mutual admonition *age quad agis, do what you are doing,* at terce as the sun swings up the sky, followed by more chores about the farm, maybe cleaning the bathrooms and the cells and the corridors, perhaps a ride to the little grocery store with the verandah down the road for provisions for the main meal of the day, and the ride back passing staring farmers and wives in station wagons or on tractors chuffing and stinking the air around them, then sext at the hour of the noonday devil, and the bell chiming the angelus to all who care to listen, not always many in this Protestant country, and the short, private prayer for peace and steadfastness takes on a certain urgency, for the day is half gone and the sun is marked for falling, and the monks gather for the noonday meal, silently held in the elegant but shadowy hall to the solitary sound of the day's reading by the clear-voiced, calming Brother Pius, then on to the afternoon's work, in the fields perhaps, helping the cowherd with his lowing charges between the rough-hewn fences, or repairing gates, stiles, fences, cleaning and sharpening tools, or working the big vegetable patches, till none's brief prayer and psalm and the return to the cloister and the last dusty hours of the afternoon spent in divine reading or private devotion in cell or chapel till vespers ring and the monks gather to sing the magnificat of the Virgin, then supper in silence, and more reading and prayer followed by compline, the last day's meeting in the gloaming chapel and the singing at the end of the day of Salve Regina, Regina Coeli, Alma Redemptoris Mater, after the abbot, Dom Ambrose with his thick glasses, sprinkles the community with holy water, then on to bed in the small dark cell with its narrow pallet and bed table and cross and bit of straw rug, in the countryside's silence and darkness once again.

And this was only the beginning, three times the Rule of Benedict was read to him over the course of his long novitiate, and the harshness and severity of the monk's way of life, its eye-blearing monotony, its strange mixture of loneliness and lack of privacy, its denial of the autonomy it had been the law of the world outside to train him in and impose on him since he was a child, the inurring of him to obedience, the withdrawal of luxuries he had long taken for granted, the unrelenting pressure, was impressed on him. And the young monk in training was oddly happy to hear this: the last thing he wanted was an easy life, his pride demanded he conquer his pride, to say nothing of need for comfort or ease, at least of the physical kind. Spiritually he was in seventh heaven, no pun intended: *I will never be so happy again*, he often thought. It made him almost dread the future.

His inordinate ambition, never frankly admitted to himself, was to rise to the highest level of sanctity, to attain the most complete holiness he was able not only to reach himself, but to imagine might *be* reached, and to whet his appetite he studied lives of sanctity, from the gospels to the lives of men he thought of as modern-day holy men, such as Thomas Merton or the Berrigan brothers. These last gave him a large bone to chew: their combination of holiness and sense of worldly, above all political, responsibility, excited and disturbed him, at times made him feel guilty and self-doubting: had he, *hadn't* he, entered a monastery not to confront reality and find his place in it, but to run away from it, avoid reality and his responsibility for it, hide from a world grown terrifying to him, uncertain and brutal, thuggish and blank? Wasn't precisely what the Berrigans were doing something he could not do, at least not now and perhaps never? The harshness of the order seemed of little account compared with the drab misery punctuated by violence of the world he had left — and yet *the possibilities for sanctifying his life* (the phrase, and the idea, had filled his mind with a sense of moral direction, imperative, and hope in the months leading to his novitiate) seemed now more remote than ever. He began to flagellate himself — in secret, since it was discouraged by the order.

Once, Brother Ian, a fellow novice who had a neighboring room, broke in in the middle of the night.

Why are you doing this? he asks, looking down on you kneeling naked on your straw mat lashing your back with the rope used to bind the buckram robe.

You look up.

Because I have to.

Brother Ian's eyes glitter strangely at you.

Do you want me to help you, he says softly.

You stare at him, not knowing what he means, and shake your head. Brother Ian, looking a little disappointed, quickly withdraws.

The years passed in silence and singing, darkness and pain, drudgery, monotony, and prayer. He took his first vows, his final vows, his head was ritually shaved one more time, and you lay in the chapel beneath a long embroidered shroud beneath chanting and incense and the words of grief, welcome, and admonition of the final ceremony of all before the entire community, in which you died to the world, and were reborn to your new brothers in Christ. His family came for the ceremony, even his estranged father, a man who despised religion of every kind: he sat away from the other family members, near the back of the chapel, and wore an elegant suit with a brilliant tie, flamboyantly and silently defying the place, its inhabitants, and its meaning, "as if it could *have* one," he said acidly. He left without speaking to his son. His abrasive if well-intentioned stepmother made a brave show but clearly wanted to cry over her "strange boy" who was joining, for good and all, those obscurely horrifying Catholics. His half-brother and half-sister went along for the ride and the reception afterwards; they shrugged and asked if they would ever see him again. Peter turned from them (his new name was Brother Pachomius) with relief and a sigh and joined his new brotherhood in more than mere symbol: he joked with Brother Ian that it felt like getting married "and the in-laws already hate each other!" He watched his father slip out of the chapel with a taste of bitterness that wiped out the peace of the communion wafer and wine.

The years passed. He became ordained and was now called Father, moving about in the black robe of the order, careful always to bathe alone so no one would see the long, crimson welts on his back from his nightly self-punishment. He had once thought his groin would docilely accept his vows once and for all, that all he need do is command it to withdraw its willful and exacting demands and it would curl up in a corner and sleep his life away, not that every night he would waken with his penis stiff and demanding and his hand itching to relieve it, which hand to relieve the scarlet and black hardness in his groin, beat his white back even harder, into bars of black cherry. And when one night Brother Ian came in again, silently this time, and drew your sheets back and slipped into bed beside you and took your penis in hand and gazed softly at you, you wept — *No, no, no, no* — until Brother Ian, alarmed, slipped out again and away: your worst nightmare was being proved true, your haven from the world had become what your own body had long been, a nest of vipers fanging your heart, a blade flaying the skin of your mind.

And the years passed, not only monotonous and unchanging but suspicious as you learned to doubt and then began to learn the extent of the unscrupulousness of your fellow monks — who else was living in sin, who else might grope you, request sexual favors, perhaps try to blackmail you, and the petty thefts, the financial tricks to keep the abbey functioning, the underreporting to Rome of income, the political games between the abbot and his charges, the intrigues between gatherings in the chapel that belied the holiness of the chapel's rituals, the battle with the world and yourself enjoined even more intimately and more humiliatingly here, in this place, where no one had the right to fail, yet failure flourished in secret everywhere you looked if you merely opened your eyes, where you had no distraction from your own continual, defeated struggles yet no certainty they were even witnessed let alone approved, and if witnessed, not mocked; even your confessions seemed pointless and gagged your mouth like charred wood despite the understanding of your confessor (what did he know of what was going on nightly in the cells, in the accounting books, in the backstabbing gossip behind the stables, in the constant backbiting and jockeying for petty advantage even here, such as who stood closest to the chapel entrance during the hours, who avoided toilet duty for a week, who got to ride with whom into town for groceries for feast day shopping, and the revenges exacted in return, the monstrous pettiness of it, a vengeance of mosquitoes locked above a swamp in a perpetual summer?), despite the confessor's questionable sympathy, often doubtful advice, penances ordered and endured: hours of prayer against the sins of the flesh and of the mind, and your nightly purgatory, his knowledge of how these sins and others, more venial yet more gnawing, were practiced within the monastery's walls searing your conscience with a still harsher pain, where could you flee if even this haven was corrupt? You must stay and fight, and you must endure or fail; there was no where else for you to go.

Why have I done this? you sighed in the night. *What am I doing here?*

And the years passed. A sense of futility dogged him, for he felt no progress, only a growing fatigue in the monotonous round whose point, he began to believe, was meant to be, however unsuccessfully, anesthetic, a means of numbing the perpetual wound of living through ritual gesture and exhausting labor, even in this haze of gnats. For a time, he hardened, swallowed the necessary hypocrisy of the order, and moved his way up the short ladder of promotion, in ten years becoming the house's novice master in turn, trying to daunt the few postulants they received from the path they were starting on, with a shudder he watches the young postulants and novices with their soft faces, sometimes alarmingly soft brains, and fearfully hopeful eyes look into his, with a torture of remorse and the terrible knowledge of their future, a future he cannot pretend will be different from the past, for it never is, he now knows, the belief it might being the great illusion of the age and the country they carry with them: the belief that the future will be different from both present and past; cavalierly unknowable and so just the place for a preposterous hope. How can he tell them that they still believe in the future, when it is the eternal — that is to say, when it *is the timeless* — that they should believe in, that he wish he could believe in, that he prays one day to believe in, if only it would allow him its grace.

He sometimes thinks he can no longer bear it and decides to return to "the world," though what would he do there? Nothing there allures him either, he would end up a beggar or a tramp: there was not much demand, he was sure, for a vegetable gardener with a specialty in marathon praying, self-flagellation, and shepherding simple-minded young men into monkhood.

And years pass.

He walks the barren corridors of the monastery, asking himself obsessively over and over until he falters into silence: *Do I do any good? Does anyone care? Is there a God to care? Is there anything there? Do you hear me? Can you hear me?*

And lets himself voice his despair aloud in the night alone, whispering to himself in the dark.

Who would have thought the night would be so long? Who indeed, not you or me! There's no noise of traffic, the mighty empire is dead to the world, the mighty city sleeps. Look, another carabiniere, over there! Nodding where he leans against a wall, like a resentful nightwatchman. Where's a crime when you need one? I have heard no traffic in an hour. Perhaps you are fatigued? I am fatigued, I have lived almost too much in hardly having lived at all. A conundrum? Only one more....

Richard, at first, was almost happy among his books and research papers, classes and seminars, conferences with professors, debates with classmates over cups of bad coffee in the automat, continual rethinking his major and retooling his class schedule: the odor of a university campus filled him with reassurance, its combination of Styrofoam, cut grass, Saran-wrapped sandwiches, and plastic butterfly chairs, its air of student lounges, overpopulated lecture halls, crowded hallways, blasé carefreeness and flushed earnestness, its excessive energy and deficient seriousness, or rather call it an earnestness that confused itself with seriousness, to say nothing of the gullible girls and the overawed freshmen, the easy clamber to status via incomprehensible jargon, stream-of-consciousness monologs, and yearly promotions, an almost shamefully easy superiority even sophomores, especially sophomores, could indulge in. It held him in its clasp like a woman he desired and who desired him but who wanted to play with him a little longer before letting him have her — and he knew precisely (he thought!) what to do about it. He had never been so flattered, continuously, by his surroundings: everything seemed to conspire to welcome, encourage, seduce him. He felt the world holding him up, like a great hand. He was, when he chose, the classroom's dominating student, forever correcting, modifying, expatiating on the contributions of fellow seminar mates, even sometimes, rewarded with a warning glare, at which he twinkled insouciantly, from his teachers; his classmates found him strange and irritating, the girls either dismissed him or set out to seduce him, his professors either loved or loathed him but could do nothing about him either way, he aced his exams and his papers were exasperatingly bright. And he knew they were, and he knew all this, as well as the volatile ambiguity of his status. For his future was being charted with the uncanny infallibility of an institutional mission: it was precisely for his type that the university has been made and molded, *foraminens perpetuus*, student and teacher by the human of the human for the human, in all its grotesque splendor, its gaudy noble and ingenious awfulness, its crass assertiveness, its almost accidental beauty. And this was precisely why he had chosen it for his future, when he thought of it: it fit him like a second skin and it flattered his hopes for himself as well as for the uncanny possibilities of the human "project."

For he was not just a careerist and opportunist, an apple-polisher and grade grind, though some thought that about him: he was *an idealist of the human*, though it was an idealism haunted by a sense of the squandering waste of human life; too aware of the war abroad, the assassinations at home, the bloody-minded defenses of injustice in his own country, the drab misery of the city in which he lived, to rest easily in any optimism about people, whether "the people" or any remarkable elite. *Human beings*, those monkeys of the absolute, troubled and astonished and amazed him: what they, what am I saying, what *we* had done, what we were doing, what we could do, in the mass and in the case of unusually gifted, intelligent, energetic, and lucky, individuals. At one time, our power — *yours* and *his* and *mine* — for good and evil made him look at his own hands in wonder. He had once worshipped genius as a believer might worship a saint; indeed, had felt genius was a form of natural and historical *grace*, an accidental gift that exalted the bearer — that geniuses of the past and present were "secular saints," sanctified by achievement and the awarding of their gifts and given honor in human memory as the highest possible reward, the only kind of "immortality" human beings can hope for. And he retained this faith like an afterimage on the retina, long into his later youth, long after the impression of human degradation and futility had grown like a shadow across the sun. Deny the sun that can't be hidden or the shadow that cannot darken it.

Or the moon, which set long ago. Has the sky grown darker, or are mere *stars* going out? When the eyes that see the sun fail to see anymore any sun, has the sun disappeared along with the vision that saw it? Are we thus the creators and the destroyers of whole worlds?

Richard was aware that this basic faith in the human, "humanism" so-called, went against the current of the time, the mutterings of posthumanism, post-"modernism," and the like, he even *understood* it — he once asked himself, echoing the hectoring Adorno, "How is it possible to be a 'humanist' after the Holocaust?" The age, perhaps more consistent, went in for a methodical destruction of its past heroes, past hopes, values, and ideals, of hope, value, and ideal themselves, like disappointed and rancorous children, and of the past itself, as though the vileness of the present were the fault of the past and not its own: there was no more consistent barbarian than a certain kind of academic intellectual who, sometimes with the best of motives and a cringing conscience, sought to destroy belief in a civilization he had lost faith in before (he hoped, she dreamed) destroying the civilization itself. At first, Richard scorned the trend: the presence of "genius," of "greatness," by which he meant admirable actions, ideals, values, and works of every kind and not just the individuals who concentrated in themselves and historically personified them, could no more be denied than the sun: these goods were, to him, self-evident, and so, at first, the trend troubled him only slightly. He had not, as *we* do, the example of Rome to terrify, and reassure, and terrify him again!

But you did discover that the sun could, in a manner of speaking, be denied, and *was* denied, vigorously, rigorously, repeatedly, angrily, with an envious and nasty pleasure in an obscurely motivated spirit of revenge: we cannot bear to live in the light for long and know moments stretching into years, decades, lifetimes, eras, when only darkness, ugliness, and filth will feed us; you found out well enough that no one's moral, intellectual, even physical, vision can be assumed, even between sunup and sundown, *not even your own*, it warped and crumbled with the passing of an hour, a bad night's sleep, a poorly digested meal, a drink, a drug, a peer's smirk, a woman's refusal; you discovered there was no good that could not prove intolerable, even despicable, to somebody else, even to yourself the next moment; you discovered that no good was or even *could be* beyond doubt or suspicion, distrust, even hatred: every good was provisional and ripened, and rotted, with time. And the undermining of what had once been your essential assurance began, and you were left, a blaze of nerves, in a deliberately cultivated, almost conscientious, state of unease, tension, and intellectual insecurity, riding wolves of anxiety. Though to some it might have looked more like a neurotic parrot, always quick to cover yourself with an arcane quote.

Beware the ideal of honesty, of truthfulness, even more than the ideal of truth. This Richard learned too late, long after the snake had infected him and drove him to the mad dance of his mind over the following years. It was the dance of honesty, like St. Vitus' dance in that it allows no pause for rest, no place to put the sick, tired head, no formulation to rest secure in, together with the compulsion to find an adequate formulation of discoverable truth, dependable value, sovereign and unquestionable good. His mind was on perpetual fire.

There is nothing like the imperative to doubt everything — even the imperative to doubt — to leave one a mental wreck. So it almost happened to him, until he realized one day where he was headed. As usual with him, the realization was the result of an almost whimsical insight, an idea in three almost laughably clear parts that struck him as he was walking home from a delicatessen one curiously warm winter evening: life, he decided, was a matter of setting and meeting limited, clearly perceived goals — simple idea number one. And goals required the making of conscious decisions: deciding on a goal, deciding how to achieve it, and then deciding *to* achieve it, that is to say, acting — simple idea number two. "Deciding a goal," since abstract reason by itself could not give definite answers as to what is desirable, had to be based on feeling, what *felt* most desirable and still seemed possible. To keep a person from crumbling in uncertainty and anxiety at every moment, he should keep to his goal until *feeling* told him the goal was either undesirable or thought told him it was impossible, at which time the entire process had to be repeated.

The point was that he (Richard told himself) must listen to feeling rather than to thought when it was a question, generally life's thorniest, of *purposes*, the one thing that thought alone, *analytical reason*, could not (he believed) decide; and to thought rather than feeling when it was a question of *means* — also tricky, given that once feeling is listened to, it wants everything. That night he ate the best roast beef special on fresh rye he had had in a long time (the beef was just the right pink, the bread still warm, with a luminous crust), and thanked the delicatessen, mentally, for its unexpected generosity.

Simple idea number three (which came to him while sipping his postprandial coffee) was that he should save his doubts for his, and other people's, *theories only*. Leave the doubting once the action begins. Hamlet needs to become Laertes the moment Ophelia dies.

Simple, to some of us obvious, to others helplessly question-begging, most of this, but not to our thinker, who had been trying to live conscientiously according to reason and tying himself in knots as a result!

And Richard sat back, as over a good day's work, thinking he had solved his essential problem: how to make decisions. Hmh!

These ideas did *not* save him, but they did stanch the internal bleeding caused by his anxiety. And he moved ahead, after that attack of common sense, or simple-mindedness, into the arcana, not always given over to *le sens commun*, though very impressed by the French, of his profession, the one that felt right to him as well as possible: surprise, it was the very one he had chosen already, history (to study mankind — or humankind in the rigorous patois of an hour already dead and despised, just as *you* despise *me* — that species he belonged to that he found as fascinating as he did frightening) and psychology (to study himself, frankly, as well as the motivations that made extraordinary personalities stick out from the mass like terrifying signposts aiming the way to grandeur and disaster).

Age quad agis, as the Benedictines put it to Peter.

And so he applied himself to his studies, his classes, his books and journals and research services and library resources, at first fascinating, then intriguing, then merely interesting, then annoying, in the end pointless and nauseating, the warrens of the library, the dust of archives, the lengthy research, the typing of papers, the wrestling matches with footnotes (not always won), the arguments with sources, the suspicion of sources, ultimately the loss of any source that might in any way have been written by someone without an ax to grind, and that meant all sources except birth certificates and death records and lists of exchanges of deeds, and even they were suspect in certain places at certain times, no one could be trusted not to be lying whenever anything was written down, *including when one did it oneself*, which meant that one's own writing would be met with the same suspicion for the written word found everywhere else, thus ruining one's relationship with the reader and ultimately one's own writing, aha that is why academic writing is so awful, he thought, they are all second-guessing their critics, competitors, rivals, *their only readers*, what a hell for both writer and reader, the running of the obstacle race first to the bachelor's, then on to the master's, then — with increasing recalcitrance, less welcoming, a sudden cold from his fellow graduate students, whom he rarely saw anyway and with whom he had none of that sense of comradeship he had had with his undergraduate schoolmates, that sense of being part of a freemasonry, an "us," a warmth of fellowship and shared enemies and shared laughter, but rather the permanent cold of perpetual competition, his professors who addressed him with increasing irony, and his advisors, who seemed ever more challenging and harder to please, a defiance of his courage, a twisting into obscurity, pointless thorns and barbed wire, a testing beyond knowledge or patience but whetting his determination despite them, that surprised him — to the doctorate, the theses increasingly on issues of less and less importance to you, issues forced on you by your advisors since your natural interests were considered irrelevant, worse, outdated, boring, "articulated in a bankrupt discourse," as one of your advisor's colleagues put it, so that, in order to get credit toward your degree, you had to follow a dustier path than you could possibly have imagined, in the hope, in the end, with the doctorate behind you and tenure awarded, in a few years, you would be given your head to pursue, despite the petty fascisms of the profession, the studies for which you had joined the profession in the first place, but the years dragged on and pulled you farther than ever from the goal, the goal behind the goal, *the study of mankind, extraordinary human accomplishment, and the people who had pulled from the dust and ennui of daily life a shining vitality, the shimmering light* that had brought you in the beginning into this cavern of dust and the darkness of texts, back when you had made your choice, according to feeling, until now you had almost forgotten it, five years, ten years, and the dissertation was not even finished, you had acquired the habits of your generation of historians like a disease, you went to, say, Salem, Massachusetts, to study the history of property acquisition in the area at the time of the witch hunts when you wanted to bury yourself in the Vatican library to study the careers of Pius II, Julio Romano and the artists and humanists of Rome, but there was no money for another study of Renaissance popes, and anyway wasn't that better handled by the art history department these days?, their historiography is hopelessly behind the times, and your attempts to apply your psychology degree (acquired on the side) was nixed by your department as irrelevant speculation, "psychohistory" was already passé and there was nothing deader than an old-fashioned trend in a history department.

And he woke up one day, while digging for the hundredth time through some old records about people he had no interest whatsoever in knowing or knowing about, but the study of whom he had been able to get a grant for a year ago for reasons he had long forgotten, a study that would end up in an unreadable and unread book burdening a shelf in a college library and pretending to glorify his curriculum vitae should he seek a new academic position elsewhere, doing the same thing, since he would only be allowed, that is to say *be paid*, to do what he already had a "track record" doing, and he looked up in alarm and disgust at his profession, university, culture, country, era, himself, and asked *What in God's name have I gotten myself into? What am I doing here?*

Making choices that seemed reasonable at the time, even unavoidable, until life made no sense at all.

You could not even expect sympathy: didn't you have what no human being outside the civil service has, permanent security? What you had was an envied combination of physical comfort, professional autonomy, and a sense of self-disgust (so, take the cake at that price?), plus an inability to imagine how else you could make the living you had grown accustomed to, or indeed *live* at all. Easy to mock, as you input one more unreadable page into your desktop computer.

It looked easy to, ah yes, *Gabriel* to live a life of unfettered desire, like a mouth unconnected to a stomach, a sensorium uncaged in a body: all he had to do, he thought, was open out, and the krill of delight would feed themselves to his maw, once he'd learned a few clever tricks. Of course, these tricks were still down the road a bit, just around the bend; patience, attention, and availability were the watchwords. All he had to do meanwhile was attend to the strange, wild light of the here and now of enchantment, and sharpen his appetite for the future. He had chosen, he believed, the easy route; problems, difficulties, troubles, and other obstacles would be mere seductions to triumph.

There was really just one skill to master, and that was the manipulation of other people: make *them want* to do what *you want* them to, the American talent par excellence, though he had not mastered the lesson entirely yet. It wouldn't teach itself, of course, and he had to be in the right place at the right time just to discover what the loss he was incurring was, even that it was a loss at all: there is no more thorough a defeat than the one you learned you've had only long after the battle is over; a maxim that was itself the essence of the lesson. Appetite has its austerities, its northern face, pinnacles and cliff-falls, martyrs, heroes, victories out of space and time, and secret audience of applause. It has its history, rites, tutelage to masters, obscure but unforgiving rules and penalties without appeal. Desire is a kingdom and fulfillment its ruins, or rather desire is a war to increase its kingdom, and fulfillment the insatiable annihilation of its enemies, frustration without end, fulfillment that only increases an ultimately unappeasable desire. But this would be a tiger to ride in future.

He didn't see himself as a predator — far from it; more like a votary of longing, a believer in desire for desire's sake, an almost religious libertine. Longing was almost an act of prayer, desire was worshipful, an opening up of the body as obedient and patient as a soul, an orison of yearning that was as humble, self-abnegating, abject as the obeisance of a believer. In this crooking of the knee to his own desire, the thrill of his body, he found an almost religious ecstasy, an orgy of happiness that, to him, was sacred. What looked to others like all groin looked to him like all heart, and encouraged him in his stubborn attachment. Desire was love and love was the law. His predation was not only not forbidden, it was mandated by life, by Life, itself.

The world is a vacuum of desire, he thought, or felt, or imagined — it funnels itself into itself like a whirlpool, a cyclone. That sound you hear even in the middle of the deepest silence is a soft moan, of desire. What else is the world? Desire awaiting desire, fearing desire, hating desire, denying desire, longing for desire, panting with desire, fulfilling desire, forgetting desire, remembering desire, desiring desire. There is nothing but desire.

So he opined and rationalized making desire, its continual excitation, the search for stimulating and fulfilling it, his primary law, the purpose and fulfillment of each day: a day without movement along the closed arc of desire was a wasted one. You assume I am speaking of sexual desire, naturally, and everyone assumed Gabriel was a male nymph, a satyr, but they were the "shallow" ones; they only half understood his religion, philosophy, theory. For Gabriel, sexual desire was the acme but not the entirety of desire: the body and mind were a musical instrument on which desire and fulfillment played the role of dissonant chord and cadence. Every human act and reflex could be translated into this language, the continual use of which led to continual happiness, in swells and waves, currents and tides, a constant flow and flux of ever-varied pleasures and fulfillments of the self, incarnate psyche in carnate body, in time itself; indeed, it was happiness's long-sought secret. These pleasures included each and all of the senses and the mind itself: indeed, many would think Gabriel an intellectual, given his pleasure in literature, philosophy, history, music, theater, art, not knowing that his interest lay in the pleasure alone afforded by these things, and only insofar as they afforded pleasure; once they bored him, he dropped them till the well of desire once again moaned with the wind hurtling above it. Others would think him a slacker and loafer, not knowing the feats of thought and spirit he was performing in the strange concentrated raving of his mind. Others thought he cared about was power, ignorant of his cynicism regarding that futile quantity: he realized there was no "power," but only the sensation of it. Others thought him a lover, others even thought him, of all things, a money grubber; all wrong, even those who thought he was just a garden-variety egomaniac. He sacrificed himself daily on the altar of desire and had so little sense of himself in the flaring of his senses and fire of his mind that he often teetered on ruin and loss, in danger of being found broken and mutilated at the bottom of a cliff of flesh. He hardly felt himself as existing at all except in the sweet torture of a barely fulfilled desire, a hope just out of reach, a happiness that blinded and frustrated him. The acme of desire was the frustration of desire, just as the greatest happiness was the hope for happiness.

No: he discovered, almost too late, that there was a greater happiness yet — *the memory of lost happiness*. Yes, that strange and excruciating and soul-expanding ecstasy, even as it, even *because* it, tore the little hard ego of the self into a thousand pain-wracked fragments. This was so violent a joy that at first you didn't, couldn't, recognize it for what it was: one of life's most magnanimous gifts. You had known it most conspicuously when you "lost" the country for the city — lost it for a time to all but memory, a muddy, cold, wet paradise of forest, field, hill, insect-infested, messy, dead-littered green, lush in summer, gray stark in winter, ice-covered and snowbound and rain-streaked, smothering with wet heat in July, budded with tight blossoms, drunken with spring smells, treacherous with charm, small wild flowers in shadows, plaintive hoot of the whippoorwill and bloodcurdling owl shriek, the reports of distant shotguns in the autumn, the hanging wing of cirrus suspended above the winter landscape, there where you had been happiest, traded for the stinking squalor and grinding, unceasing snarl, cold stare and contemptuous smirk, casual pitilessness and background hysteria, the proud, unyielding ugliness of a world made by man to live in, his mirror of ego and faeces: your tangled misanthropy began at that hour when you saw the sky hanging helplessly above the city's filth and knew the wild ache and weeping joy of the memory of happiness. And you would lie, half flung across your bed, abandoned to anger and nostalgia.

Hope! *you* say. How can one lose hope at so tender an age! But there is no despair deeper than that of a child locked in a city he hates in a home he can't escape and a time that allows no knowledge of his future beyond the knowledge that all he has is fantasies. And he despises them almost as much his situation, his era, and himself.

The very greatest happiness of all he learned, years later, and not just temporal years, was actually something quite different from the memory of it, though it relied on such memories: the greatest possible happiness was exactly equal to the greatest possible suffering, and that was losing the hope for happiness before fulfillment ever came. In that case, the hope, the illusion, of happiness remained intact and secure against the future: the fulfillment of hope, as he discovered from more than one experience, leads to one thing — disillusionment; only unfulfilled hope protects the idea of happiness from being destroyed by its *realization*, that is to say by *reality*. But this happiness was, in itself, close to unendurable, it burned the self in a hot white light, drove you to incoherence, the impulse to escape at all costs, finally to a craving for nothingness and death because it made life itself seem a mean-spirited and humiliating charade, a cruel exercise in fantasy and disappointment, a huge waste of energy, hope, effort, love and hate and time. And he collapsed in his room, shaking and weeping in a corner, and remained for weeks hidden from family and friends.

What pulled you back was the same old song that played in the same old groove: desire sang, and you heard desire, and hope returned, and a certain stubborn self-respect, great good ego, that found suicide even more mortifying than being snookered by life's scam — an admission of defeat — ego raised its head and glared back at "life," its clown face smeared with sweat, sperm, dung, tears, blood.

And so Gabriel lived, trying to outdo "life" in machination and conquest, manipulation and adroitness, lunge to the jugular and sneak attack over the harbor hills. Pleasure, even the lightest, was the sure sign of being on top, and he pursued it like a daily grail. Most days ended in victory, however discreet, and he slept in the arms of his angels.

Yet woke one day in time to come, after years of constantly irritating, mocking, playing, humoring, denying, trying to outwit, attacking, sublimating, and fulfilling the sharp little nerve of desire, to something he had not entirely calculated because he could not precisely foresee it.

You were living in London at the time, working for an American company as an account executive during the day, going to clubs at night: you had four girl friends you rotated regularly, sometimes in sequence, sometimes together, mixed parties being part of the pleasure, and they gave you the same generosity, so there were no hard feelings as long as no one brought the issue up, and no one did. You saw them when you saw them, and when you didn't, well, everyone was free to love whom they wanted. You were doing cocaine at the time, your acid days were behind you, and marijuana had never given you the buzz it seemed to "gift" everyone else. You also liked alcohol, the range of English gins delighted you, the fortified wines of Jerez, brandies from France, vodkas from Finland and Russia when you were less patient for a rush, but especially a well-aged single-malt scotch, aged 20 years in oak, Glenmorangie, Macallan, Laphroaig. You drank bottled water during the day to whet your appetite for the night's florid intoxications.

You had money to spare and traveled many weekends, to Italy, Paris, Scotland, Prague, sometimes further to the Balearics, Marrakesh, the Greek islands, Istanbul. The only thing missing was anything to regret: wasn't it Jane Austen who said that something had to go a little wrong to make a pleasure perfect? Though you, Gabriel, would have rejected any reference to that clear-eyed mocker with contempt purse-lipped with unease. Life was proceeding with a majestic and smiling smoothness, you lived in perpetual transition between pleasures fulfilled and pleasures planned, with only the occasional bite, or rather *gumming*, of boredom, your office job providing just the right balance of tedium and security to serve as a frame to the little dramas of your Real Life, as you called it. You had before you as many pleasures as you could absorb, and many you couldn't, from the most refined to the most vulgar, sublime and delicate, profound and exquisite music, art, literature, drama, dance, film, thought, the most daunting and noblest of mankind's aspirations paraded before you in dark or glory, or you could escape to the most vicious and crudest dens of debasement, disgust, and revolt against man, God, and love whether inside or outside the bounds of the law, whenever you had the craving. You were free to do whatever, *be* whoever you dared, as you chose for that hour in that place, in a radiance withed with a wilderness of narcissus, lilac, lavender, or a stench layering your mouth with selectively chosen garbage.

He was standing in his bathroom one mild London Sunday afternoon, shaving, when he saw it just behind him, hovering above his shoulder like a moth caught awake in the daylight. He stopped and stared, razor in one hand, his cheek half shaved in an arced rectangle, like a clear-cut hillside seen from a distant plane. It was a face, a familiar one, collapsing in on itself, sucked in in sink holes beneath the skin, a hairnet of wrinkles covering the surface in little squares of thick dirty yellow, the eyes popping out in lozenges of dull blue rimmed with deep pink whites. The teeth appeared like a row of fangs and the whole shrunk to a filthy skull hanging by a fistful of dry white hair. Then it was gone.

He stared at the space where he had seen it. I've been taking too many drugs, he thought. Then he looked at himself.

A hollow, ashen pit faced him with a gray cool face: a pallor that had long begun covering the landscape met his eyes, eye to eye, just as the city with its throngs, the vintage on his table and meat to his lips, the bodies of girls, the bed beneath his back. He saw, in a moment, his body corrode, the edges crack and line fractures appear in the joints, it groaned and creaked like an old car. Calm fell over the clamoring of nerve end and hormone, the dragons that snorted in fire through his sleep, his harem of ghost lovers, desire's phantoms.

He had, before now, discovered behind the false bottom of fulfillment the false bottom of indifference, found himself unable to desire a way out of apathy that was not itself apathy. Ataraxia — detachment and indifference, a peace without feeling or thought — a word he found in the Stoics, described not so much a state to be cultivated as a description of the room that enclosed him, now and forever. Even his destruction in old age and death meant nothing to him. He stared at it with detached fascination. He sat in the middle of emptiness, an empty quantity in an empty room, surrounded by an empty landscape across which towered the ruins of a city burned and bombed out by the life in which he had made his home. There was no wind. There was no sound except for a thin, high whine against his ear.

Who would have thought one could see stars from the middle of all-conquering Rome? What greater proof of the vanity of human pride, ego's flaunting vacuousness! Yet what are those lights glinting like broken glass in a mouth of velvet if not stars cutting through the smog, unless the airport is lining up a continent of airliners before letting them land on its weed-cracked airstrips. Don't put it past the Romans! They'll do anything when there's a strike on.

I ask you: how is a poet to live in America? He becomes an advertising copywriter! Quinn realized this, rejected it, returned to it, reviled it, reviewed it, reminded himself of it, remanded it to the metaphysical attic of rejected careers, and remembered it in the solitary years to come. The teacher course he abandoned, thinking nothing worse than curling into the womb of the university, melting his bones to the pig iron of Cacademe: he had seen that active among the resident fungi of the campus where he schooled: the lost lyricist gently beating his butterfly wings in the poisoned grove, the hopeless token poet, the bundle of nerves quivering in a formica seminar room. The poet was the natural enemy of all Quinn surveyed, the savage prose of American life, the layered prison term of laddered career success, the labor camps in the suburbs, the tinkly bells of good behavior, productivity, and promotion, the trading in of the absolute for a low mortgage rate, a regularly renewed car, discreetly extended vacations, a growing retirement account, and breeding of the next generation of helots. Freedom! That was America's promise. He should have rejoiced, shouldn't he, the ungrateful brat. He should have kowtowed to the gods of the balance sheet and the investment portfolio and sung his songs in his morning walks to work, like Stevens, or on weekends, like Eliot, he should have been mature, realistic, responsible, and resigned. The hole of being needs daily filling, and a petulant adolescent demand fills neither holes nor pockets.

But that was precisely what stuck in his throat, made his gorge rise in disgust, contempt, revolt. No compromise was possible. The name of the enemy was reality.

Self-absorbed adolescent idiot! He will deserve everything he gets.

I accept nothing, he whispered angrily to the empty room he inhabited with the phantoms of his poetry disappearing even as he wrote them, like disappearing ink written on air. *The only truth, only good, only beauty, the only* reality is *the* dream, he wrote and immediately forgot. And yet tried to live as though it were the only truth he knew.

Live the dream! What a lark, what a nightmare. This was not something the Romans can be guilty of ever having tried, hm? Not those level-headed, power-conscious, lusty materialists with their heads of marble and souls of iron. Until they fell, that is, to the savagery of an even starker power than they dared cultivate, and then decided, in a senile act of revenge against a reality that no longer had any use for them, to invent — the Church? But that's Gibbon, or something like him. No: level heads do not always prevail nor do the unforgiving facts obliterate the beckoning of the dream. Especially when that dream denies everything *else*. The candlesnuffer descends on the single candle flame burning in the large dark room. It shall not be true! Snuff! And lo, it was not. And only what you dream in the dark shall be true, *at* the moment you dream it.

And it was so. In that dark you would have believed anything.

Wonderful, what words can do.

Seem to do.

Pretend to do.

Promise.

Every promise, or no promise, is a lie, properly considered, of course — or rather a mortgage on the future, as long as expressed with sufficient vagueness, a salutary ambiguity.

Quinn dove into the ocean of language like a swimmer who had never heard of drowning. He had the gift of verbal intoxication: dangerous as any drug, treacherous as any vice, delusive as any deity. Yet at the center of that drunkenness, keen as any dream he might believe higher than any reality, was a whirling silence bent beneath an intolerable weight, a lintel of air, cloud, and hammer, a hammerhead bearing down on an anvil of mercury: there was nothing for him to grasp but a sensation of perpetual drowning. And he grasped at ropes of words to save him: as though the cries of the drowning were themselves the sheets they clung to. Every day required a new redemption, a new construct of meaning and hope, of possibility into a crystal of flashing reality, a new dream blanking the relentlessness of the sunlight, out of the splintering of the night's demolitions, the nightmare of unyielding yesterday, ruthless today, blank tomorrow. The push and pull of the tidal winds inside him were irresistible, and came to seem commendable, badges of reward for his survival in the weltering of his ever-collapsing sense of self, world, being. He was a kind of fist clutching at air and drawing himself up into a maelstrom that at the same time sucked him down.

His faith, for he had a faith, could be summed up as follows: books, writings, art, music, film, dance, theater, etc. — in fact anything produced under the control of an exploratory imagination, intellectual inquiry, and aesthetic judgment — did not just *express* but *constituted* the basis of our distinctively human reality: a spiritual, in the sense of *immaterial*, reality based on, yet separate from, our bodily one, and often in conflict with it. And in that "spiritual" reality — one that would eventually be called "virtual," however real as the other — which is above all a sphere of purpose and meaning, human beings were most at home.

The *natural world* Quinn understood as his and humanity's ultimate source, his parent in a more real sense than his actual ones, it was what *had caused* him, as it had caused them and their parents' parents, down the slippery evolutionary tree, past the messy clustering of quarks and quanta, back to the Big Bang and, who knows, beyond, producing all his, and their, earthly, organic, somatic, mammalian, synaptic, semiotic, peculiarly human quiddity. And he saw nature as a direct reflection of the divine, that center from which all creation emanated: order, matter, energy, laws of physics, life, consciousness, from the dead stars to his own living flesh, from the laws of nature to his own mental world. And the divine was mirrored more indirectly through artistic and cultural undertakings, symbolic systems, though it also appeared, though with less immediate clarity, through every human undertaking and every human act, insofar as every human action was *symbolic*.

Quinn understood artistic and cultural works, those concentrated symbol systems, as, by the same token, the richest and most complete forms of communication between human beings aside from sexual love. Love was the fullest and richest indeed, but also the most unstable, least dependable, most prone to being a delusive opportunity for communication rather than its most perfect embodiment; one that, by holding on its razor's edge the physical and spiritual ideals, often ended by cutting them both apart.

The social world, in which mortal humans met each other and their risible fates, was — with its constraints and its play of power relations between elements, ourselves that is, which are ultimately, laughably weak, helpless before nature's docile but unconquerable force, however our technologies temporarily fool us — the social world is a constant source of danger to the individual human being's making contact, and maintaining it, with nature, the divine, other people, himself and his destiny, and therefore with a sense of meaning and purpose, for a similar, glaring reason: the human being is fundamentally flawed, shattered, in constant battle with himself, timeless spirit at war with fatal body, blind body at war with unyielding spirit, and this unabating battle at the center of the human being and clearly expressed in every human creation, *including the most spiritual,* is reflected in society at large and its institutions, which, through the difficulty human beings have in accepting graciously their personal unimportance and transience in the world — *their annihilation except in contributions to meanings that transcend them* — place themselves in continual opposition to nature, the divine, each other, and themselves, in a futile but ever-renewed attempt, successful enough to fool them into more inane hopes, to control nature and *conquer* death, that is to say, *conquer time and the continual change time at once creates and measures*; and that, unfortunately, is the equal of saying: *conquer existence itself.*

The only way of doing which is to destroy it.

In our futile attempts to carry out this hopeless project (Quin thought), human society acts out, in generation after generation, a ritual of self-destruction that claims most of its members with grandiose delusions based on an unrealistic hope for ultimate freedom and power, even immortality: the madness of such institutional religions as Christianity and Islam, or of political and social ideologies from Fascism, to Communism, to free-market libertarianism, are obvious examples (he believed). Some escape the collective mania, though at a price of rejection and distrust, and they, oddly enough, sometimes achieve, relatively, what their societies seek absolutely and fail at each time: they outlive their time, leave behind works, mementos, actions, marks on time, society, and history, memories that fascinate the humanity that follows them, firing those of the future with a longing for their own dreams of happiness and a hope for some lasting truth, even if it is only the apodictic sneer that there is no truth and no salvation.

And for yet brighter delusions of immortality!

When you're evolving a broad and, you think, original, if over-general, philosophy of life, and at the same time holding on to existence by the thread of a syllable, anything else might seem comparatively trivial. And so it seemed to you. Pay the rent? Eat regularly? Sleep? *What?* Survival itself seemed frivolous, if not contemptible, if not damning or at best beneath regard, a process that required daily humiliation, the relentless insulting of your pride. Well, yes. And the sooner, the better, *you*, my listener, will say, no doubt! Out of cloud cuckooland, into the streets! Best thing that could happen to him. It'll test his philosophy, too: if it survives *that* abrupt descent, it might survive the termites of the critics — though, to be honest, nobody survives them.

Of course, the one thing that almost saved him, after all, was his other motto, besides not accepting reality, a mark of mulishness if nothing else: "I will not be beaten."

Well, he was. But the story is too depressing to tell: the slow, relentless demands of appetite, the seductions of comfort, the threats of cold and dark and hunger, the need for money, however little, the mortifications required to achieve that little, and the long petty grind that wore him down, yes, not in two years, or in five years, or in ten, but eventually, especially when he learned just how ambitious he was, how desirous of recognition, respect, even fame, of success, and the absolute contempt with which his fledgling attempts to express himself were greeted, unless he played the game, a game he despised and despised himself for playing, and even then the success was hardly worth the effort, and still he was despised, cordially, as he learned that it was not only himself but what he believed in that had no place in the society and so-called culture of his time, it was despised because it was reject-ed, like a foreign body by antitoxins and leukocytes, white corpuscles defending the body politic from ideas that might poison it, demoralize the helots, depress the markets, if they got out: useless ideas, unmar-ketable ideas, impractical and untimely. And yet they were also ideas that the "loyal opposition" rejected, for the opposition was even more lockstep in its thinking than the ones in power: they feared nothing so much in their ranks than freedom of thought, because that would eat away at their own greatest fear, the fear that they were wrong. And the weak need at least one thing to believe in: that their ideas are the right ones. The powerful don't care: the only ideas they need are the ones that keep them where they are. The rest are for parlor games.

So Quinn was doubly outcast: he couldn't even get along with his fellow poets, whom he deemed for the most part what they were: incompetent slanderers of literature, smug, presumptuous, untalented know-nothings that he realized he was, himself, in constant danger of becoming.

Yes, he was insufferable. It was when he was finally offered a com-fortable, well-paying job working in a publishing house in his early 40s, gotten through no fault of his own but almost by accident, you don't spend twenty-plus years writing away without learning a little about things like spelling and grammar — it was then that, in this pleas-ant job, with these pleasant people, publishing pleasant, insignificant books (specializing in horticulture and gardening needs, cookery and house decor, and the pretty fripperies of suburban lifestyles), and mov-ing into a nice co-op in New York, that it hit him with terrible force: he had been holding out against a delusion, but it was his own, not the world's: he had been, all this time, less warrior for truth and beauty, for literature and art, for the spiritual in human life, than a pretentious (a word constantly being hurled against him and which he constantly rejected with a snarl — and yet, it summed him up, he thought with a kind of self-disgust: pretentious!) and sanctimonious prig. He was going gray and the prospect of old age frightened him: and his "ideas," so long his staple and faith, his staff and rod, his own small certainty, crumbled beneath the onslaught of a suddenly sweet and easy life. His curious feeling of blank, blind-sided, botherless, carnal contentment made him, well, queasy. Women? He had had women, though he'd always thought he despised them, especially after the dogmas of feminism became mandatory social tender: actually he desired and feared then, fearing above all that they would either abandon him, as his mother had done, or turn into a version of his stepmother and, protesting her love for him, work at every point against him and everything he cared about. But suddenly, the neurotic tug of war between attributive delusions abandoned him, the fatigue of the struggle no longer warranted the strife: he wanted one of his own, as he might want a pet, to add to his comforts, to soften the graying of the air to say nothing of his temples and the straining of his joints, the little, accumulating betrayals of his body. In brief, he got one: a secretary who believed in him more than he did, more even than he *had*. He treated her with great politeness and a distant, absent-minded affection. Even married, she never quite knew where she stood with him.

One day not long after his marriage he put his writings into storage: whenever he felt tempted to *write* something, he left his apartment in a rush and stalked down to the Hudson, pacing up and down the riverside and glaring across at New Jersey, until the mood passed and he had stamped it into the cement. He saved the lines that would not go away for e-mails to the advertising department.

The mood would not stay stamped, of course, the muse is a witch and harridan not so easily abandoned, she came back, under other aegises and other guises, and he would fantasize in the night of what he had lost and what gained, opening his arms to dreams.

I accept reality, I've been beaten, he repeated to himself like a mantra while staring into his chosen lightlessness, in an obscure hope that capitulation might redeem him and chanting the phrase until it dissolved into meaninglessness, working a new enchantment, and resign him, at last, to the real.

Working in publishing does wonders for writers: it kills your belief in the written word while turning you into a fanatic for linguistic form, you become disgusted with language and its endless futilities, you fall out of love with your muse, though it be the muse that has fallen out of love with you: but you recognize this too late, try to pull your old MSS out of the back closet in hopes of picking up inspiration from where you dropped it like a thread in the past, but the papers have been eaten to dust by mites and you are left with dreams you can no longer remember.

Is there any more deluded mind than that of the reformed, the recovered, delusionary? He who is convinced he finally knows what it's all about, has put aside childish things and fully accepted reality! Which is the greatest delusion of all, am I right? No? Not even that? Oh no, you mean I too am a victim!

There has not been a sound for hours. Even Rome knows sleep, unlike the temporary mania of New York. You must be tired, your eyes are heavy, your patience is kind, admirable, you let me run on all night. You wonder where the story is leading, or you have given up and wait patiently for the end. But the story has no ending and the drone of my voice is no more than silence made visible to the mind. Maybe I am a figment of your imagination? Have you thought of that, with a spasm of contempt and disgust? Among these spirits of ruined columns, cracked in serried lines along monumental stones, memorials to human vainglory and pride and the ruthlessness of time and the power of air and rain and grass against hides of marble and fists of lime, you could hardly have expected something more original: your own double come to pillage and burn your city of dream until the end of the long-coming night. You can almost hear the sizzle of carbonate in the dew of morning, one more molecular layer of dissolution, a skin of decay on rejected bone. Slippery and treacherous as, well, as life itself, since, like stoned teenagers, we have reached the hour of pseudo-profundities and eloquent ridiculousness — the hour of the gaze in the watery mirror, there to spume and splinter and smear.

Was he indeed the wisest of them all, or only the most to be pitied? Adam, the modest, even humble, insofar as Americans are allowed the privilege if they expect to get a salary, unless we are referring to its false equivalent, which is a different matter altogether. And he expected to make at least a salary, though he was not hugely concerned how, at least not too dishonorably, he thought at first, just enough to pay for the mortgage on the house he would require for his wife, his children, and himself, probably in the suburbs or as far in the country as he could manage the commute, he was sick of living in the city, though he did not examine his dislike very closely since it might have destroyed the moderately liberal gentility he ascribed to himself and always supported in political discussions among his friends; not wanting to explore his instinctive dislike of poverty, Hispanics, blacks, and other "others," calling it to himself when he had no other choice, a hatred of exploitation what was actually a distrust of the exploited. He did not after all think he was, and did not want to be, a hypocrite, even though hypocrisy is the compliment that vice, etc. If he was at all cynical, it was still the mild, passive variety of cynicism, the defensive cynicism of the young who still believe in the moral standing of their ideals and are still impatient with the moral implications of pragmatism, the adult philosophia perennis par excellence, to mix languages reprehensibly, alas, but we live in a mongrel age, the dark age of the cur.

After the last meeting with his friends, Adam went off to have dinner with the Austrian girl, that girl who has haunted my mind all my life. It was unsuccessful, as it turned out: she went home to her lonely bed and he to his. But it wasn't in the end a total loss, as these things normally are, except for the residual lesson left like a tack in a shoe: through the Austrian girl, he had met an American girl, a school friend of hers, and it was not long before they in turn started to date, as a result of his turning to her for advice and of her giving it to him, warmly. All being fair, etc. And so it was.

They were both in similar situations, being essentially good-natured and decent, vaguely idealistic, young persons (they had met at the "Pranksters," had both left at the same time, together — they had had their youthful fling with political idealism, it was nice to feel noble for a semester or two, and wasn't it cool to be paid for it into the bargain, but it wasn't really going anywhere, really, was it?), not entirely clear about their own motives perhaps, more than a little baffled by their times, to say nothing of their own reactions to them, troubled by the domestic and international crises though not to the point of destroying their own lives (the hard little nub of self-preservation had not shattered for them as it had for many others in their generation, see our previous examples); practical issues, after all, had to be considered, and that meant, first of all, finishing college with a useful degree, perhaps pursuing some graduate studies, and preparing for careers. Yes, two careers, since both of them felt they should both earn incomes, though naturally Adam's would take precedence (they lived in the yet early dawn of Friedan feminism), regarding where they lived, for example, since his earning power would be so much greater (practicality trumping purity, naturally). "Carol," let's call her, didn't seem to mind this, at first anyway: it was practical, it was sensible, and she felt she could work around it. So she went for a liberal arts degree, and she advised Adam (he needed the advice, even more than he realized) to take a business degree in preparation for a masters in business administration in future. At first he balked: not *business!* Not yet! Not *now!* But Carol was insistent: it was never too soon to start: "We aren't in high school anymore, we have to think about the future." And that was something Adam rarely actually thought about, preferring, far, to dream. Still, though recognizing her superior wisdom in this, he agreed to it only partially: he would major in political science, one of his fascinations,

and minor in economics, with a few courses in accounting: if he
did well in both general subjects, he argued that he would be able
wriggle an acceptance to a business school, or even law school (Carol
approved enthusiastically when she heard this) in future. Thus they
were both happy, with each other and, above all, with themselves.

It hardly occurred to them to be surprised that they both, in
that era to end all eras, had such old-fashioned aims: a family with
two, maybe three, children ("a child needs at least one sibling"), a
house in or near the suburbs, two cars, a flower and vegetable garden,
a summer house at the shore (or in the mountains — their one point
of serious contention), a steady rise in income, a secure retirement on
fully owned property. As little to do with the neighbors as possible
but "close" (which meant distant) ties to "outside" family members.
Horror of horrors! they were in the wrong decade. But did they care?
Why should they, as long as they could pull it off.

Adam was doubled; Adam was halved. But we are getting ahead
of ourselves.

The awful thing is that it worked — that is, as well as it did
— and it had no right to work at all. The world had changed, the
country had changed, they had changed, but it seemed to make no
difference. They would follow an old pattern, Adam would follow
an old pattern, immersed in this soft warm world of women and
children whose sole currency was the yes of us, in which his only
contact with his peers would be in the chilly and sardonic air of
"work" whose only mercy was numbers. The line fracture was already
forming down the middle of his spine; his skull was already broken
into several fragments, his skeleton rode a maze of splintering. It
looked appalling already, but he did not let himself think that for
more than the passing nightmare: at least he would be spared the
hurricane of screaming ice that the world beyond the nest he was
building had become, and, maybe, he would shatter cushioned. He
could visit the wilderness outside, even regularly, should he need to,
to breathe. He began to understand why married men craved war.

And he wasn't even married yet!

But that was the plan between the wife and the man, and we know what plans turn to, at least for mice and plowmen. Within a few months, it began to unravel, for Carol, intrigued by Friedan's poking at the mystical powerlessness of the feminine but by turns disgusted and fascinated by "women's lib," as it was quaintly called, one day shed her bra after a spirited colloquy in class over Lessing's *Golden Notebook* and announced to Adam out of the blue that other well-meant cossettings and corsettings by marketplace and social code were really cages meant to keep her strapped to inferiority, though one she had never hitherto suspected. The practical bossess became, within months (she was a quick study), a screaming rebel, the level-headed suburbanite a militant shrew: she insisted, and indeed showed with much physical responsiveness, that she "loved" her Adam as much as ever but she also demanded "equality" and stared down every impolitic act of politesse as though it were an act of subterfuge, a subtle undermining of her autonomy. Adam was baffled and didn't know what she was talking about. He tried to read Friedan and Millett, and even the gargantuan theses of de Beauvoir, like a conscientious moderate liberal (which he professed to despise) and dropped them as if scalded by an acid bath. At first writhing in a kind of historical guilt, much like what he had onetime felt for underprivileged non-European groups, he soon began to believe that in this case, he was in danger of becoming his own most vicious enemy: what happiness he might hope for in the one life he knew was being attacked (he felt, he thought, he was convinced, his nerves thrilling to the free-floating paranoia of the times), even his hope for happiness, and he was being painted as a historical villain, an unconscious lackey of a grand historical conspiracy of one half of humanity against the other half, his every impulse under inquisitorial scrutiny by his own peers, most of whom (he suspected) were as blind as, when not blinder than, he. Fine, he thought, let them gape their fill from the suddenly vacated orbits in their heads. He would fight back and beat them in the common darkness, and if the fight required injustice, so be it. Justice be damned if it required his sacrifice.

9

Hero of self-fulfillment or unscrupulous wimp? You decide!

Carol would have to go: though a lover, she was neither a friend nor the helpmate he would need in the war for simple happiness, which is what he now understood life to be: she was at best his loving enemy. It was an extremely painful loss, like many supposedly required ones: the sex had been glorious, the talk a continually renewed drama of debate over truth, politics, revolution, morality, coercion, the conflict between private and public good, when morality had a right to destroy and a duty to kill; the emotions ran from simmer to boil to spikes of hot lead shot into brief paradises of thorns and roses. When he left her she raged at him for an hour then collapsed in tears, and he was certain, briefly, that he had made a mistake. Then she pulled herself up and walked calmly out of his apartment, never acknowledging his existence again, even when he tried to be friendly, almost hoping to win her back, much later: she looked through him as though staring at the shadow of his head against the wall behind him. Two months later he learned she had joined a lesbian collective on campus. He walked around for many months like an amputee carrying his dead limb under his arm: he hadn't realized how much the break would damage himself before, finally (the young suffer only till they heal, and that is almost mockingly swift), beginning to look for what he thought he, in fact, needed: an ally, as in a war, against the *barbarians of the good*, as he called them. And he began shedding his liberal scales with frightening speed, as though scraping off not only a mistaken ideology and erring belief, but a suspected guilt toward himself as much as toward one who loved him.

The parade of lectures, seminars, visits to the homes of professors, lunches, debates, swatting over sleepless weekends, examinations, office visits with his favorite teachers, meetings with grad students, research sessions over long evenings, readings and reports, arguments and laughter swept him through the worst of his trauma by giving him little time to wallow in it: the problem was the women, all the best of whom — the smartest, the prettiest, the sexiest, the most talented, daring, demanding of themselves and life — were hypnotized by feminism and the outrageous promises of revolutionary change, the grand vision of a paradise of power and plenty on earth that horrified Adam as the hallucination of a certain Apocalypse destroying, from the little gnawing of its relentless critiques to the Armageddon of its highest desires, the little happiness and good that the limp and crippled earth allows and human nature can tolerate, like a generation of Eves in love with their helpless autonomy as they reached for the apples just beyond their reach in the tree of the knowledge of good and evil: they were not about to latch themselves to a Candide of the modest and reasonable, the limited hope and moderate range, a historical simpleton who did not respect the wave of the future or the mandate of the moment and not only thought but stated viva voce that any man who called himself a feminist was either an idiot or a hypocrite.

The corybantes ran shouting with laughter through the melee of cowed and awestruck junior males of the campus or to the patronizing amusement of the calculating alpha males who strutted at the head of classrooms and stalked superciliously through the halls, their weapons of grade and charm, reproof and promise, flunking and flattery held in light yet empowered and empowering grip at the back of their middle-aged spines. It was often precisely these males the most militant of the feminist horde were sucked to, like filings to a bar magnet, pummeling them with propaganda in a show of bravado that made them giddy with a feeling of false domination, falling to the basilisk's gaze with all the more effrontery for their certainty, confused with that of their allure, of their righteousness. And Adam watched, amazed and appalled, confused himself at times, even at times pulled into the whirlpool of resentments and righteousness, both the sophistical moralisms and the hard, sharp bone of compelling and respectable cause, however thwarted from unarguable "articulation" by the pious angers that suppressed it, even though that cause itself, however just, was not only not his cause but would require his abeyance, if not defeat, for a fruition that was not and could never be his: he could hardly justify his own suppression in the here and now because of some half-imagined, half-imaginary suppression against others by some of his own accidental type in the debatable contingencies and enormous vagueness of the arguable past, *history*, with all its glaring uncertainties. How could he do that just because some group was claiming it had a right to — even when, *especially* when, that group was essential to his own fulfillment as a human being, as — horribile dictu — a man. He felt sorry for them, in his calmer moments, but he was not about to commit suicide, either quickly or slowly.

He graduated cum laude and marched off to business school, almost on automatic, and there he found … well: would he even have discovered her there had it not been for the feminists encouraging the plunge? He never asked himself that, of course: he had left introspective questioning behind when he graduated from the university — from now on, all questioning was to be aimed outward, with the goal of mastering the Thing outside. And, of course, being a business major, she never let on: feminism was left wing, and that was communist, and that was the enemy of everything the business school stood for and believed in, so, no: she would never, ever call herself a feminist, but she would learn and know how, and never fear, to take control, of her own, for her own, ever again, notwithstanding.

Adam fell for her without quite knowing what had happened: she pulled him into her life as easily as laundry into a basket — and he struggled about as fiercely, rumpled as he was and in need of laundering and an iron. He asserted his masculine rights feebly enough when faced with a woman who never denied them, merely negated them with a smile and a compass made of a domestic rose and a magnetic star: she bravely sailed him toward his own ease, letting him seem to wear the bell of the leader to his own satisfaction and falling into his plans as easily as if they had never been her own. Barbara ironed him without starch, but iron he surprised himself by becoming: he steered his degree through a shoals of competition with an alacrity that almost alarmed him. Her hair was blond as gold.

"Barbara" — well, after all, Yvette and Ivy are much too obvious — married him before the ink on the degree was dry — *her* degree, that is. It was at that point that Adam realized he was no longer living essentially one life with outliers: he was divided in half like a knived peach and was from now on only half his own. He told himself he liked it, and that, like any merger, it would thrive on synergy. And indeed he could only live the life he wanted, with all the accoutrements of a Candide of Outer Suburbia, by taking the compromise: after all, hadn't he always professed to despise the "autonomists," whether feminist or otherwise? Wasn't he more of a communitarian type anyway — he even liked the provocative connotations of the term, with its echo of "communist." Nice kick for an MBA already getting offers from two multinationals! Of course, when Barbara got an executive account job in Atlanta, he had to give those up, but heck, the luck that showered on one showered on both, that was marriage after all: they packed and gallivanted south without apparent demurrer on his part, he was all sweet encouragement, and worked as a Kelly Girl (how he laughed for six months at that designation!) while Barbara found her feet in a glass office 35 stories in the air. At the end of the seventh month he was offered a permanent position as a secretary — well, why not, at least it gave him a leg up, a foot in, a toe well cooled in the water. His ego stood at attention behind his grin at Barbara at breakfast, as she smiled happily telling him about her more obnoxious clients; Adam could only think of his pleasant, condescending boss, and the mild terror of the thought that he was being ghettoized in assistant administration at the tender age of 25. His Masters was aging already: would he be taken seriously among the cohorts of recent grads now that he had instantly taken one of the grooming positions first offered. And promotion? There were no promotions for secretaries, even of the male persuasion, though there might be an occasional raise. He began feeling what he knew was an almost childishly impatient resentment, but then he could not see where this was headed except into a deadly inescapable corner. He was not even the gardener of his own garden; he was more like a chipmunk.

The employment market was in one of its stagnant periods so there were no job offers and having a job of any kind was considered a sanctification of one's efforts sufficient to require hymns of gratitude and hosannas of praise to the god of the market, the one god not only worshipped but actually followed, by the least pious as by the most. Adam vegetated at his post and Barbara throve at hers. They bought a house, on her salary, and moved in, decorating it also on her salary and therefore with her taste: Adam's heart sank in despair. His job was not his own and his home was not his own. Maybe he would have his own children.

"And throw my career into a cocked hat? No way," was Barbara's succinct response. Then she saw his face collapse, and smiled, bending to him on the sofa. "Well, not just yet. Give me a few years, sweetie."

A few?

"Well. No more than five. I promise."

Five years came and five years went. Barbara was offered an irresistible post in another company, in Chicago, so up they pulled what shallow roots they had laid and replanted them in Oak Park, from which they both commuted to inside the Loop, she to her senior executive in marketing position, he to his senior clerical post at an insurance firm near the Art Institute. He would visit the galleries during lunch with other office peons and stare plaintively at the swaths of painted cloth depicting apples and oranges on serene stretches of linen, suspicious Flemings staring at their depicters and incurious audiences, cuts and slashes of paint and brush, pencil and knife, knots of black against anarchies of color, spots of serenity amidst blasts of hopelessness, and wonder how utterly idiotic his own life seemed, despite his having gotten so much of what he had thought would make him happy.

But I was wrong! he thought, staring at a statue in a corner, beaming through its radiant dust beyond him. — But what would work, then — what would make me *happy*?

Barbara was as good as her word, though you thought otherwise, didn't you! Yes, her company was progressive, they actually had a fairly generous leave policy for pregnant women and she was encouraged to take it, especially by the men in her department. "Go on, we'll be here for you. Don't hesitate. This is what the policy is for." On almost the exact day five years after her promise, she turned to Adam, who was gamely trying to hide his sense of being crushed by hopelessness amidst plenty, and, grinning at him with that girlish, unsuspectingly but overwhelmingly sexy look that had won him immediately almost ten years before, she said, or almost said, being struck with a sudden and untypical wave of shyness that left her tingling: "Shall …?"

He stared at her sweetly uncharacteristic blush.

Shall *who what?*, he whispered and grinned back. Then he realized what she was really saying, and felt his old hopes flood back, saw the young man (because the first one would be a boy, *natürlich*) standing in front of him taking instruction and laughing wildly at his jokes, and then dipped trustingly into his beloved (because she was beloved, even though he sometimes hated her) wife's arms.

They began as they often began their lovemaking. Adam would commit the hoary palindrome and Barbara lie with a pretty rhyme.

Madam, I'm Adam.

"I believe I'm Eve."

Eight months, three weeks, five days and thirteen hours later a girl spanked up out of Barbara's open and exhausted thighs and Adam gazed in impotent dismay at the miracle of birth, at once flooded with pride, giddy with wonder, and cut off with a detachment as severe as the scalpel cutting the umbilicus that connected, for the last time, the nameless one from his vanishing spouse. He held her only much later (when they had finally found a name for her, Judith, which Barbara insisted must never be corrupted into "Judy"), with dazzled glee, weighing her in his arms with insistently anxious premonitions: the future had suddenly received a face, and its helplessness raised an alarm that from then on would not cease ringing.

It had effects on him he would never have predicted: at first, it made him feel Responsible, and made him insist on that responsibility in the face of doctor, friend, counselor, relative, even Barbara, such that it surprised him. Empowering? He had mocked the term, but now he felt what it meant: not only stronger almost physically, surely psychically, but authorized to use that new-found strength, he felt both braver and more "validated," like having a signed driver's license. Barbara wasn't sure she liked this new side in him: it meant he was taking over, and "taking over" had always been Barbara's job, especially with the sanctions of the mothers of the Revolution. At first she didn't take it too seriously, assuming it was a passing attack of maleness that would be stifled with a few well-aimed pussy whips when she got her strength back. But she had not calculated on how exhausting Judith would be, nor for how long, especially when, with only a mere two months of leave, she had to report back to her job. At which she found a small but well-placed knife stuck in the back of her chair, right between the shoulder blades, with the bad news hanging from it, like a ransom note: she had been reassigned to a dead-end department and a remote corridor, a small account list, and half a secretary; she was no longer automatically cc'd important internal documents, was regularly forgotten to be invited to important meetings, etc. She complained, was told she needed more time for her child, would not have to put in the excessive hours and travel that otherwise would have been expected, and eventually have caused "conflict" and therefore "problems" for "everyone"; it was a move in "everyone's best interest" and of course her "options" would change as her "circumstances improved" (she glared at the verb; as if having a child was assumed to be a kind of breakdown, an existential regression). She added it up: it meant at least two years out of the (lowercase) loop. She smiled acidly, recognized the wisdom of it, resented the intrusion into her own decisions, suspected the culprits but could not flush them out. Her male colleagues were exacting their revenge; and she began a counterstrategy that involved, somewhat unfairly, undercutting Adam in his new potency. She was beginning to feel the trap tightening around her: nature, her home, her work were acting in concert to bring her into the fold; the edge of her anger, never far from the surface, began to slice the air around her in random sweeps.

Adam was only aware at the second degree, as it were, of the state of his wife's mind and the steadily increasing painfulness of her position: for the first time in his marriage he actually felt in control and was even, almost, though professionally balked, happy, at first, at least at home, until Barbara began to take her revenge on the only person she was able to. And the serene and unsuspecting weapon was Judith, giggling and crying by turns up into the vacant, babbling enormities, the sun and moon, of her parents' faces.

The devolution of married life into its cold and isolated constituents is not a pretty thing to witness, especially when it takes time, and in this case it took an excruciatingly long one. A failing marriage is a peculiarly vicious form of hell in which the victims and their demons are the same and, so, the avenues of escape almost impossible to trace let alone use. Especially where there once was something like love, a love that each party hopes desperately even at the times of greatest despair to get back because, superstitiously but not incorrectly, they doubt if they will ever, no, are certain that they will never find again that love, a love that, once flourishing, made life, as only love can, worth, well, living. And they are right, of course, despite the ever-renewed possibility of new love, since every love, the one we know, is unique and dies with itself, and possibility is only that, as maddeningly real as it is so often misleading. How wise I am becoming, and how lucky you are to imbibe it.

No, I don't have the heart to detail it. Take it as read, the ten years and more of deepening misery at the heart of Adam's dream of happiness. They compounded their errors by having more children and having Barbara leave her job for what turned out to be a permanent sabbatical rather than rage every day over her humiliation; Adam's prospects suddenly improved, for mysterious reasons, partly no doubt due to his growing self-respect, but Barbara did everything she could to undercut him, she could not bear to watch him wax in strength and serenity with every passing day as she felt herself grow weaker. Eventually the three children — a girl and two boys — became her weapons of choice; a bad move, since the children already leaned heavily toward their father; something that actually compounded Adam's problems, as the growing financial burden of the family was no longer so easily met by an income that had been gradually halved. Adam's appearance of satisfaction, relative success, and gratification of his distant dream was deceptive: he was sinking into a kind of strenuous hopelessness. He could not relax for a moment, the clamor of the office, with its barely suppressed panics, arrogance, wild-eyed infatuation with computers, e-mail, the Internet, its luxuries of euphoria and despair, its promotion of the *false promise as a way of life*, played leapfrog with the clamor of home, the raucous good cheer, crying bouts, neediness, and donnybrooks of the children inching their way through the jungle of childhood, and the bitter good will of his wife clawing at him between the darknesses of bedroom and dream. There was no exit from such a life until at least the kids were out of the house — and the prospect of almost twenty years of this felt like a prison term in a forced labor camp. Yet it was also one that the prisoner was not even willing to admit to himself, and so add the clamor of unmet energies, the lies he had to tell himself to keep himself together, to the external clamors of the world he had, he could quite believe, made himself, from the cautious and modest prospective fantasies he had woven for himself in the early light of his sophomore spring.

No, it could not last. Though the sudden collapse came as a surprise only to those involved, not those who had been watching. Shortly after Adam was reorganized out of a job, he also realized what he had not yet let himself think: he had built himself a prison of dreams, duties, debts, and duplicity, and he could lock himself in it permanently or seek a way out. And being aware of the choice as well as the condition bloomed into the beginning of the end. He took it out at first on his boys, being a helpless pawn of his flirtatious daughter, who was using him in her war with, just as he was using her in his war against, her mother and his wife — poor Barbara. His boys' weakness and their helpless desire to win him at any cost made them ready victims and easy marks for his frustration; they also haunted him with himself, being little mirrors of his own most detested attitudes, gestures, poses, and pretensions. He beat them with less compunction as they aged toward teenhood.

Then he began The Affair — we knew this was coming. Of course, she was everything Barbara could never possibly have been: a dancer and a poet, bisexual, theatrical, intense, politically alert, conversationally provocative, in long skirts and wild hair, with a crazed look in her eyes and the attractive powers of a vampire, a temp worker in his office who promised him exactly nothing beyond a way out, though he fooled himself into thinking she offered him a way back to that sophomore spring when he made such a foolish, bourgeois mistake as to place all his hopes for happiness in — a hope for happiness.

He left Barbara, Judith, Henry, and David for Skyler and woke up one day with neither Skyler nor Barbara, Judith, Henry, and David, in a cheap room in downtown Chicago, still unemployed, feeling free and overwhelmingly alone, staring at a ceiling that refused to give him an answer. The bad taste in his mouth went as far back in his throat as his tongue could reach, and gagged him. The sun shone and he was where he had started, only older. What had he learned?

What else is there? Ah, you're not letting me off the hook — there's still the silent one who watched off to the side at the student diner, the one noticed by no one but us. What happened to him? Yes, what did happen to him? He had no name, he was not even recognized by his "buddies," his "friends," his coevals at the tables of choice and the future: he mutely stared and listened, watching, waiting for the crass moment of lucidity after all the brave hopes came crashing down, to count up the fragments and the cost, the rewards and the ruins, the leftovers and the bill. He waits still, as the game is not over yet and the first disillusionment is by no means the last, each choice has ramifications that never cease, that blossom into the future along myriad paths of vectoring choices that themselves bouquet toward infinity. He waits, watching us play out our hand, listing points lost and won, for amusement's sake, even as the scorecard burns. And it makes a pretty fire, don't you think, curling into yellow umbels and blackened petals on the table?… Are you there still? Are you still listening?

Yes, it has been a long night, which you have shortened for me by your kindness, your patience, in listening to an old man ramble about his, well, shall we say, his "lost opportunities." And in the long night I have grown old indeed. The sky closes above the ruins of the capital. And, by Jupiter, where is the sun, has it gone for good? Where is the light of even false dawn, so gentle in its easy deception? Not there? Nothing but gray, black night? No, not to worry — it will come again. If only in the mind, it will brighten the eastern hollow of an opaque sky, soar up from the sleek horizon like a god in his chariot, his horses blazing, as if two thousand years had never been, as if they had never cancelled his glory and his power, his majesty and his beauty forever — and it will blind the waiting city, it will dazzle the white bones of its ruins with the morning. Yes. It will come. It must come.

Kiss me.

10

No.

... where ... what ... who ... now ...

No. Not here. Not now. Who did this. How did it.

... voice ... from how ... long ... now here? no ... dream ... dream on ...

They told me you were bad but not how bad can you hear me?

... who knows ... is it you it can't be ... can't be you ...

Scavenger of happiness.

I came as soon as I heard I wasn't far. Nod your head if you can hear me. If you can hear me. Or move your eyes. No?

... world spins when I nod splinters if I open ... my eyes ... whirls ... like then ... how long ...

No?

... no ...

Oh stubborn. My poor. Arrogant and blind then how humble now. How sad you seem! How could you expect anyone to listen to you then but now ...

A ghost ...

... a ghost sent to punish me again? ... you can't be here too good to be true too awful ... if a little late ... yes? ...

You must think I'm a ghost if you can hear me at all. Hear me at all. Come back from the dead to punish you. You can't hear me. You can't hear me or see me you couldn't then. And you can't now. Can't now. But can I see you?

The taste of your name ...

... hand on my brow ... your fingers ... cool ... dry ... no ring though ... the softness behind the hardness behind the softness inside softness.... that light southern drawl under the hard leather sheen a little unsteady now ... but that! ... tenderness trembling in the angry eyes ... and that! ... tenderness of a wound ... now my cheek ... Venus fading in the ... horizon headlights moving down a far hillside ... now my chin ... distant shipwreck ... raging in the west ... now ... touch my lips ... please ... please ...

Are you comfortable at least? What a question to ask are they taking care of you? Do you have what you need? It seems so hopeless talking to you! It's like talking to God.

Murmured God not knowing what she said ...

... you were always bringing him up ... the shoe now on the

other foot ... the trap the pain will go as deep ... promise! ... oh my love ... if it is you ...

I didn't expect to find you so changed. Balding and white and shrunken with tubes coming out of you all over. I hardly recognized you I didn't recognize you. You were such a pretty man once. With your wicked politeness and comfortable smile. It fooled all the girls! Especially this one. Such a smart man a beautiful man a nice man a good man. And it was all true.

... if only I could see you you you if only I could ... open these dead ... eyes ... measure the distance ... between us ... again ...

... in a language he had not mastered.

I couldn't believe my luck. The life you'd led was enough to fill six!

... seven ...

You were far too good for me. And you knew it but you were too good ever to admit it. Even to yourself. That is what I meant when I said you didn't when you asked how you deserved me. It was a grim joke I hoped you would never understand. My. Poor one.

... murmured you not knowing what she said.

... as I did then for years measuring the distance never reaching the end ... such waste of years hoping you would come back ... remember Italy? ...

... murmured you ...

I couldn't measure my luck. I thought I would lose you. I knew I would lose you. So like a fool like an idiot I threw you away.

… murmured you …

… we were happy in Rome weren't we? for a time … the swinging bells in the church nearby … calling us to mass … in that city … built over millennia pockets of light where the past spied on the present between the averted faces … of the blessed …

Why did you let me?

… don't say don't say you were never happy with me … too bitter to say you were never happy with me … the only time I was ever happy … as a man! … as a man …

… murmured …

Though I never did know you. Not really. I never understood you I can tell you now I couldn't then I was too proud to admit it. Though it wasn't my fault alone. You so liked being misunderstood it gave you prestige in your own mind I guess the man of mystery nobody could figure out. You might suffer for it but how much sharper you must be than everybody else. A strange game for a middle-aged man to be playing. It was very adolescent of you but then we were both locked in adolescence weren't we. In love with not growing up with failure as a way of life.

… twist the blade in the old wound isn't it late to play the old … so what if you are right if you are wrong … I can only give you the silent treatment now anyway! …

You always did like to give the silent treatment that was your favorite weapon. Now we're both stuck with it. Withdraw into angry silence. Or just into silence. And let them go crazy trying to guess. It's the most effective one of all.

… you used it against me for decades … I raged pleaded begged damn my pride … did everything did nothing waited hoped fool! … for an enraged door slammed in my face … over and over … until even I … saw the light rather saw the night impenetrable black … and slunk off to lick my broken heart scalded ego … the only woman I had ever loved with all my heart mind soul body … if I have no soul I yet loved her with all my soul she created the soul with which I loved her … if you are her … if … bless damn you …

Like a pillar of darkness …

It was one of the first things I noticed about you after your charm. Yes you were very even dangerously charming but you knew it you practiced it a compulsive flirt. No what I noticed was how much you withheld. Usually people leak something about themselves when you sit with them first for two hours but you said almost nothing. Responded and asked questions and made little comments and smiled. Such a warm smile you had! A little shy with penetrating eyes and very direct. But you said nothing whatever about yourself. Even a direct question got a one-syllable answer. Or a shrug with a little grunt. It was charming. But it said nothing it did make me wonder. If that was your plan.

… my plan did I have a plan … how long ago yet I can see you yes in the café with that mutual friend … accomplice … madman with the grin and bellowing voice cantankerous brilliant ego-famished … you sat next to him … spare elegant woman with engaging grin … charming yourself! … with similar ends in view! … ballerina … at one time … writer of poetry who didn't discuss it … wore a long full peasant dress tight bodice large glasses made you look like a sexy librarian … broad pale hat made you seem from an era just outside memory … haunting the collective dream … I felt at ease with you … I was enchanted … you reminded me … of who …

No I misunderstood you even then. Your quietness should have warned me. Still waters run deep? And not cold? Or shark-filled? Or treacherous with rip tides? Or otherwise betraying?

... I told you once I didn't lie outright silence my way of lying ... stupid candor ... that was our love game truth or dare I was holding my breath ... when faced with your love of music dance books ideas philosophical ... pugilistics moral passion political mudslinging the debates we had over the lunch table ... food flying as we made one crazy irrelevant point after ... your uncertainty about yourself the meaning of your life the meaning of any life but you were determined to find out ... the scattering of your purposes your confusion strange insistent ... hope ... your hatred of cynicism devotion to truth and beauty or only honesty and desire ... your almost cruel sincerity a virtue ... you scorned ... ruins of your family love-hate for your father abandonment by your mother dying as abandonment ... your wild hope for love search for ecstatic vanishing ... fear of madness death ... I found a mirror in you no another self pure injured soul my other half hungry for some stable ... something like ... like being ... my self in you I found in one insistently other ... my own fears and loves hopes despairs echoing back to me in the music of your ... of your voice ... we were so honest it destroyed us ... remember? are you listening ... you remind me of ... of ...

... a pillar of darkness in the wilderness.

... it was as though you didn't know how to give. I never saw anyone reach out so little as you. You sat there and smiled stood there and smiled lay there and smiled nothing could penetrate that maddeningly calm look. It was a sham but it was a good sham. A gracious sham. Consoling like a pillow I could talk to all night.

... yes ... no ... not then later maybe you're misremembering the beginning ... you liked it at first you called me dangerous because of it ... and you knew I would like being called that ...

So I called you that called you dangerous on the walk back. Remember? All men like to hear that. You pleased me even then. Especially then. I could project on you. As you could on me.

... right we were a mutual projection society! ... laugh damn you it's a joke ...

Silence.

I don't know why I'm talking to you like this. You probably can't hear me. It's like talking to myself. Or my therapist. Long gone!

... how I wish I could see you again ... or maybe not you must ... have changed like me ... I want to remember you as you were ... a little worn in your tired angry beauty graceful gestures bending from your ... military carriage ... high cheek bones serene forehead piercing depthless hazel eyes ... froth of chestnut hair ... incised brows superb nose with its little bump ... like the bending of a bow ... delicate features painful furious look in your eyes ... maddening vulnerable desirable thrilling ... my personal poison ...

Or like beating off! This mechanical thingy even looks like a vibrator. I guess you don't get good sex in here.

... what is that ... I heard about it once ... oh yes that is something we once did together ... we invented it ... a long time ago ... it belonged to us ... alone ...

We certainly didn't.

... don't ...

If you remember. Though God how you tried. I guess you know you never made me come. You have guessed that I hope. You weren't that much of a dork not to have guessed that! Didn't it occur to you that might be a problem?

... don't ...

You thought I had? Have you ever seen a woman come? I mean outside the Internet.

... please ...

I'm sorry but I had to say it. I wanted to love you. But I had to get something back.

... any more exquisite torture than sexual humiliation ... or more pointless ... I have become something ... I can't go back to being nothing and building everything again from ... even if it becomes the same city to destroy in the same catastrophe all over again ... thrown from a shell into a jail ... with a single flip of a key ... that is what it does to you ... sticks your nose in your own face ...

And you gave so little. A little in bed a little over the table a little face to face. Too little.

... maybe ... and then you gave nothing ... a generous trade ... I was waiting ... for you to speak to me ... now you speak when I can't answer ... the perfect woman for me! you never let me in you dragged me into shape-shifting caves echoing with anguished cries ... that made me love you deeper and harder it damaged me ... with pity ... you gave too much I was overwhelmed drunk on your gift ... too much it became nothing at all ... I was lost in you ... I thought you had guessed that ...

We knew nothing really of each other that's what's strange. Do men and women ever know anything of each other really? Is it even possible for them to know each other to know each other's hearts? Are we condemned to be strangers to each other forever? Even when we love each other especially when we love. Is this raw longing nagging torture we put ourselves through to communicate clearly with each other a hopeless act of stupidity? Get over it admit it can't be done and accept being locked and damned in your ignorance like an adult? Are we all in comas to each other! Do you know? It would be better to know the worst and give it up. Better to drown in our invisibility to each other than screaming like maniacs for a relief that's never to come.

... maybe not ... I sometimes thought so ... kept hoping it wasn't so ... that with one more try ... you were the saddest person I have ever known I wanted to ... reach you ... discovered when we became lovers ... remember we were friends for years lunch coffee friends though you let me know more might be possible just enough to give the air a little ... thrill ... you ... made me smile dream for the first time in years ... about the future ... who had always been afraid of the future spent my time dreaming about the little past I had ... victim of nostalgia at the tender age ... of thirteen ... now I was fifty and dreaming of the years to come ... happily! ... my folly ... I should have stuck to what I did best ... regretting the past ... now I am all past ... hearing you makes me want to dream of the future again ... one that might have been ...

I've never been proposed to in a bathtub before. That was interesting I wasn't quite expecting it. You looked so sweet with your hair plastered flat on your head and a drop of water hanging from the tip of your nose. Like you had the sniffles.

... lying curled in each other's arms in the cooling dirty bathwater I should have suspected an omen ... you with your alarmed crazy eyes your bony pale body shifting in the deceptive water ... but you don't remember you were first months before you asked me to marry you ... almost as romantically we were lying in your bed after making love what a sappy word for it ... screwing fucking having sex all wrong too vulgar clinical sappy oblique ... nothing comes close to its strange terrifying beauty ... common as grass yet intolerably unique ... the body's sublime ... its contemptuous power ... and when you asked me I lay there at peace beside you I went dead silent amazed I had never been asked never thought about marriage seriously before not once ... I didn't yet know how much I loved you ... your no stabbed me with the first thrust ... that after a dozen lost battles in bewitchment and disbelief destroyed my ... trust in you ... finally ... even though you withdrew it at once ... leaving behind a false hope like a smear of soap ... on a wet floor ...

I don't remember how I reacted. I was very tempted. But I was also frightened. Your intensity when you did speak made me uneasy you weren't loose about anything. There was a purity about you. You were God-ridden but the dailiness of being around you hung like a raptor in a desert sky. It could plunge at any moment. You reminded me of my father.

... I hated your father almost as much as ... even as your love for him consumed ... a love requited in a way calculated to destroy you a love that missed the point a love all I ... I never wanted to meet him I don't know what I would have done ... though I had only your word ... believed you crazily then as I believe you crazily now ... in the collapsing honesty you collect each day ... like sand ... fathers why so hateful ... my own ... abandoning ... even when they try to love bruise and welt with their ... scorn ... leave starvation for a love maybe it's true no man can ... no matter what we feel how we give ... always tainted we hate procreation so much ... mirror of ourselves ... unanswerable shaming taunt ... my father the reflection of my face in his eyes as he saw what I saw in him ... the weight of a paralyzing light ...

I wasn't sure I could take that. For long for very long. You were sailing at levels too high for me if I fell I'd break. I felt broken I'd been so broken everyone I had ever loved had betrayed me left me violated me died. Abandoned me. So I had to act like a cunning animal to survive. Furtive as a night creature. A raccoon scavenging trash cans in the dark. I know it seems unforgivably selfish. But I couldn't trust anybody. No one. Even you. I couldn't trust anyone who claimed they loved me. Especially them. Can anyone understand that. Can you understand that.

... I don't know not now not then ... at the heart of you I heard a young child perpetually weeping ... I couldn't reach her ... especially when she withdrew behind that face of rage you wore a flimsy primitive mask meant to terrify the enemy ... and then there was no reaching you at all ...

How can I expect you to understand what I barely can myself? I remember telling you stories about myself. I was such a slut! All those lovers you looked so alarmed. But you had so few anybody else looked like a slut to you. You were the straightest person I've ever been with I didn't think they made them anymore it was part of your attraction at first then a challenge then a bit of a burden then exasperating your constant look of shock. You needed so many lessons. And you were so reluctant. Where had you been in the 70s. Holed up in a library I guess. And when I told you about my girl friends I couldn't tell whether it turned you on or appalled you. Or both or neither or just stumped and dumbfounded you. You had never been with a bisexual before now how strange is that. At first I thought you had never heard of such a thing.

... part of my hatred of life contempt fear ... all life seemed to require of me was my dignity and pride I wasn't willing to give them up for an occasional roll in the hay is that quaint enough for you most women I couldn't stand anyway they were in it for the babies they claimed they didn't want nature trumped their intentions and they ... hated it ... and men's sexual fever was a fantasy when real nature's way of getting back at our so-called autonomy that joke ... the women I knew I could barely tolerate until I met you ... feminism made the best of them sanctimonious bitches the rest were idiots or Christians ... all of them incapable of giving me what I needed ... I thought ... and what was that ... now here's selfishness for you the fulfillment and realization of my self the working out of my possibilities within the limitations time and space and nature afforded me ... I thought! ... I could provide my own sex thank you very much ... I thought! ... fantasy was better than reality on almost every front anyway the definition of reality was *what disappointed* ... women no exception ... until you ... opened me like a tin can and spilled me out into the light and I saw dazzling in the brutal lashing sun all the wonders I had missed in my solitary quest for self-sufficiency ... my hatred of love ... oh I was not reluctant I just needed a more patient tutor ... you wanted too much from me too soon ... you wanted me to make you happy and all you did was send me into ecstasy you were the only reality I knew as wonderful as a dream maybe you were a dream ... I was insufferable but so is any man worth his salt between the ages of eighteen and twenty-six ... thirty-seven ... eighty-four! ...

... we couldn't go on that way. Going to Italy was a fine idea being in Italy was wonderful we could forget everything in the wonder of the villa cathedral palazzo museum caffè trattoria gondola mistral tramontana scirocco of the moment but we couldn't stay there forever though for weeks we pretended to and home waited for us at the far end of the landing platform like a blocked cave. It was only a matter of time. But why am I defending myself to you? Why have I come maybe I should go ...

... don't go ... you don't know and maybe don't care how happy it makes me to hear your voice ... again ... thought I would never hear it ... again ... your music surround me ... my torturer enchantress ...

I wanted to see you. I wanted to explain why I left you. I felt I owed you that I thought you wanted to know. If you can hear me. If I can hear myself. I wanted to see you again. Can you believe that. I wanted to see you before now even then I did for a long time. But I couldn't. I couldn't bear seeing that look on your face. That look you once gave. I was startled to see it on a middle-aged man. The look of a beaten frightened child begging and defenseless. It was unbearable.

... never wanted you to leave at last I understood what love meant yes the overcoming of no wait the suspension of self the self no longer so terribly important the reward a kind of strenuous joy what sex could be not just a pleasant physical spasm followed by a short relief from tension but binding to another human being someone ... who made my life a feast treasure a palace a garden and gave it a meaning that no longer had to justify itself moment by moment but was clear even to me the meaning of life is love I saw it I held it in my hands for the first time ... the only time ... and knew if you left I would never have it again ... that was something I thought I couldn't bear ... and didn't want to bear even if I could ... didn't want to survive as I had before locked inside myself ... after such a loss it was like being spat out into the desert after having a taste of paradise better never to have known it than be given a handful of water a large cold mug of beer and then returned to die slowly of thirst ... but my incorrigible will to survive thought otherwise and kept me alive even as I died again and again in the years to come ... years to come ... intolerable years ... I managed to tolerate ... knew all that would happen I couldn't face the idea that is why my face crumbled into childhood ... my hopeless attempt to keep you ...

That look in your face almost held me. It almost made me pity you so deeply I couldn't leave you. But I had to leave you to survive. Me. I must not give in to my pity for you. You were holding me like a claw and dragging me down. You needed someone so desperately. So did I. And so I left you and didn't speak to you again slamming the phone down and the door in your face whenever I knew it was you on the other side to make it absolutely clear to you I did not and would not and could not love you as you wanted me to. No matter how you loved me. A silence I have held until now like my breath. When I can hardly be said to be speaking to you.

… it was me who turned blue don't forget … am I still? … God knows what color I am now … pink and white like undercooked pork probably … stewing in the silence never broken between us for decades on your side now on mine …

And now you aren't speaking either. You're abandoning me. As I always knew you would. God knows you have cause. I was a sick crazy bitch.

… how right you are I just happened to love you … wanted to share your air on occasion would have been content to have coffee with you once a year sit across from you listen to you rave and watch you shimmer … if you had let me … I would have looked forward to it like Christmas … living with you was like living in a carton of crushed eggs … with shells made of glass …

A sick crazy bitch with revenge in her eyes. The vampire ballerina! Dancing with the shadow of herself.

… maddeningly lovely dancing shade …

You were crazy to love me. Love is stupid and crazy and a punishment there is no greater crime than loving someone who doesn't love.

… can't love …

What is love do you know? Can you tell me? Open your eyes so I can look inside.

… who are you are you who I think you are? … is anyone was anyone how many women did I love after all … not many … are you one or all or none of them … you keep changing your voice changes … in my mind … no you can be only one I thought the one I did love the only one I did love of all the ones I thought I did … there was still only one … of them all … the one you remind me of …

If I look inside your eyes I'm afraid I'll see our child. That is why I could never see you again. Because that child was my last chance. Can you understand this? A year later two years later it would be too dangerous. Deformities Down's syndrome stillbirth they increase with age after a certain point. That I was well beyond. Part of the curse of womanhood the narrow gate for childbearing. Or blessing in disguise who knows. Deep disguise.

… your child my child … myself … my only willing chance at being a father … your last safe chance at being a mother … I had never wanted a child in this world not the burden of it blame for creating another sufferer mouth to feed on the mobbed earth member of a criminal species … until I met you and crazy hope … returned … last night in Rome … last time we made love … in that pension near the Termini … with the shutters open we didn't care if everybody saw us we impaled our bodies shamelessly under the moon … bitten like a crust of bread in that hot August night as we sweated into each other … smell of your skin … twisted sweetness of your mouth planes of your face dancing with pleasure … softness of your body in my hands … cushioned softness of your breasts brown smoothness of your nipples sweetness of your navel long plain of your belly with its little mole elegance of your calves your handsome … austere feet nobility of your knees smoothness of the inside of your thighs … thatch of reddish hair around your pubis mount of Venus salty taste of your clitoris moist gentleness of your vagina … I never made love to a woman again after that night … I thought I had forgotten … you said then that you knew … immediately … as we lay sighing and sweaty against each … feeling the night wind come in cooling us off drying our sweat it was the first time I had actually liked the smell of sex usually it repelled … watching the moon disappear behind the top of the window frame … I froze of course said nothing I couldn't face it … like so much else … after we returned home something happened … you began to turn your back to me … like the closing of a vault … relentless slow … at first I barely saw it … a few weeks later you started getting sick …

I got so sick it terrified me I had to go home. You were no help to me you hid from it you hid from me. I went home and hid in my old room and cried for two days. My sister took care of me. I couldn't face anyone. Least of all you. If you had called I would never have come back. I lost the child I never told you how. I told you I was going to keep it. I killed it. And then I couldn't bear being anywhere near you. I never told you I was sorry. I was sorry. I am sorry. Can you hear me.

… you didn't kill it it died you didn't kill it … it died … you didn't kill it … don't blame … for the next week I cried … for the death of my … our … child I wanted … and would have fought anyone to keep alive … except you … because it was your child as well … your selfishness in this as in all things was beyond my understanding as though the child was entirely yours you had planned this pregnancy I found out later from your friends you wanted a child so you used me to get one then acted as though I had nothing to do with it it was despicable of you … I didn't care I loved you so you could do whatever you pleased as long as I was allowed to be there … but you went dead on me for a month after you got back … and then one day piled your belongings in a car and vanished no forwarding address no number nothing you were gone without a good bye and when after months … I finally tracked you down even your friends left me ignorant and crazy with grief bafflement … it hit me leaving me a plain of wreckage in flames … everyone I had loved and wanted to love me left me my father that girl so many years ago my mother not that not now now you you refused to speak to me beyond a strangled cry of anger and a shout through a closed door the insult of a phone …

No what drove you insane and terrified me was when I told you I was certain. We had been back from Italy a month inured to our routines again I had to tell you what only now I knew.

… but I was forgetting it's beyond me to remember I can't bear to look at …

You had just got back from a day flying with a friend you were exhilarated and stumbling over your words describing the excitement of piloting the plane the views of country and town and city and you had said there was someone else beside you the whole flight through and you looked at me with a horrible trust. And I had to tell you then there was no more waiting possible.

… how could you have done that did you have no heart at all … nothing where you might keep such a thing as a heart … did all you have was principles? honesty! … what is the point of honesty … without love …

I told you. That I was going to have a child.

… you told me oh you told me all right … you sent me into the heaven whose floor I had just scratched with the wings of the plane … vaulted I soared! … couldn't you see it in my eyes … I was drunk almost whooped with joy immediately started planning what next …

I couldn't bear to see you so happy. With so little cause. Because it was based on a misunderstanding. You thought I loved you.

… so you told me … like an earthquake … palace of joy I had built in a few moments weeks months … fell … you made me the happiest man I had ever been … immediately a ruin …

You whirled up and stood there like I had just struck you with a hammer. Then you staggered out of the room into the kitchen. When I tried to go to you you growled like an animal and slammed the door in my face. I heard you leave a few minutes later it was the middle of the night you didn't even have on your shoes I didn't hear you come back for hours.

... walked the mile down to the beach up and down shouting at the waves then walked an hour to a bench outside a restaurant and sat staring into space till four in the morning ... with a blank mind ... then went back ... didn't notice my lack of shoes till I got inside the front ... door you had locked yourself in the bedroom ... I fell asleep on the couch at dawn ...

From then on I was afraid of you.

... from then on there was silence between us ... we spoke only when we had to ... the rest followed ...

Long silence.

I sometimes wonder what would have happened if we had been luckier. You didn't hear me out. I said I was not in love with you but sometimes I was because that was true and it was important to be absolutely true at that time and I did. I did love. In my way. But you could only hear the first. And you drove me away. Your weakness was what I couldn't bear.

... if we had been luckier ... what a thought ... I wouldn't have been I you wouldn't have been you ... and yet we would have to have been to fall in love for the short time we did ... because we were in love ... for a time ... you cannot say we weren't don't say we weren't ...

... *Because I did love you. In a sense. Once. I was in love. Once. Well I thought I was and isn't that enough. I thought you were strong enough to take me on. And I needed someone strong enough for that. I was amazed by you by your kindness and patience with me your willingness to be with me after so many had run away I couldn't believe how lucky I was finally you had come after all these years of waiting.*

... couldn't believe how lucky I was after all these years of waiting ...

If only. If only other things had worked. That we were better in bed together. Though that wasn't the main thing. Our awful living arrangements!

... the sublet from hell those roommates we never failed to ... we were too old for that but it was all we could ... those debts ...

Our lack of privacy everything we did or said was heard or we thought it was. It was like living onstage and having to hobnob with the audience at all the intermissions. Every look carried a snide comment on the performance it was awful.

... so imagine we had a decent place to our ... unseen by anyone ... but us we aren't on parade ... can relax as we had in the beginning ... when we were ... oh that we could have stayed friends ... that had given me hope ...

The first rule would have been: have your own place. Maybe if we had done that and visited as in the beginning and not broken our own rule not to live together for at least a year. We broke our very first rule!

... or that! ...

We meet regularly have real dates have sex maybe you would even learn gradually to satisfy me you had it in you you were certainly enthusiastic enough. And I thought I loved you then and I knew you loved me. And I knew that was rare for you your own awkwardness proved it. In my world you would be practically considered a virgin! You could be so sweet when not threatened.

... was hungry enough ... we live apart well all right ... but meet often ... I'm habit's slave I have a spot for hot meals I go back ... we make love ... regularly I improve ... you said I was good at foreplay and afterwards gentling you back ... we always landed well ... in bed even if you didn't quite touch paradise ... you yourself said coming wasn't ... everything ...

We become domestic. We have our routines. We have our rules. We make our little plans and have our little disagreements have our little fights that always end up in bed. We laugh a lot. I sometimes cry you look sad and concerned and let me have my way then we argue and you triumph over me and I settle down. You know how to manage me you handle it well I learn how to manage you I handle it well. Very well! After a year we find an apartment together and since we have practically been living together for six months already either in your place or mine the transition is almost perfect.

... almost ... except our tastes in music ... or the timing ... you insist on playing light classical at all hours Bach at his least learned to Schubert ... I like silence or Stravinsky ... with heavy metal for bedtime Mendelssohn is not my idea of a film score to orgasm ...

Another year passes. And another. Soon five years have passed and we get along like a house on fire. We burn. We have made the little adjustments we trust each other implicitly we have learned to hold our truths till they must be spoken and when they must tell them as softly as possible.

... we have learned love needs more as well as less as well as other than ... honesty ...

Leaving tough love for self-love. Maybe. And then the miraculous happens. We get married.

Silence.

We get married. Your first my third but what of that it just took you a while to find me. And me a little longer to find you. We ... merge.

... we marry no we do not merge we reinforce what each is ... we are not the same do not want to be the same ... honor are happy in each other's no ... because of each other's ... difference ... our walls fascinate us because we would not exist for each other without them ...

We merge into the whole I have always sought to be. I am happy. Sometimes I make you miserable but that is part of being happy but never for very long. I reward you. We have wild sex and we have it everywhere. We are in love and there is no end to it.

... there's an end to it but it's gentle ... there are no children we waited too long but we have each other that is enough ... we think ... we are both aging and the illusions of youth are making way for the illusions of age ... the myth of the plateau of disappointment and reconciliation with life's limitations ... myth of the fulfillment of our early years' strivings as if that might ... content us ... part myth part truth ... reality ... but we ignore reality ... our dream is so intense ...

We waited too long to have children and I am sorry I missed my chance. It is the one other thing I have wanted out of life and I shiver whenever I see. A couple with children. Especially young children. I can't endure seeing babies. You wonder why I shiver so you think I can't stand them. What I can't stand is the fact they aren't mine.

... we get older ... the passion leaks away as it must but we had begun as friends light trusting laughing lucid frank and after everything else is gone that remains ... if things had gone a little better if luck had bent just an inch on our side ...

We age well together. I calm down. I calm down as if I could ever calm down! But age brings fatigue it is simply too tiring to be crazy all the time. We take vacations to the Canadian Rockies to Baja to New York. We go to concerts of classical music and jazz and popular stalwarts who age as gracefully as we like to think we do. We visit fashionable resorts we are not rich but we have two middle-class incomes and only ourselves to spend them on so we live well on organic gourmet cuisine mid-priced wines on sale at specialty food stores mix-and-match handy-me-down furnishings for the living room and modern modular for kitchen bathroom and bed. We have a state of the art entertainment center with a large flat-panel TV a wall-panel sound system and Wi-Fi for our laptops. We both drive the new VW bug mine pale yellow yours steel gray. We are the kind of couple it is fashionable to despise but we don't care anyway we are getting too old to be envied. Our friends like us and we like each other and we like our lives and we are content. We have two cats and one dog. We live in a gentrifying neighborhood of a major west coast city. It would be almost ungrateful not to be content. Looking at us from outside people might think our lives are empty. Morally. Spiritually. Our lives are not empty.

… our lives are not empty … our lives are so full we can barely keep up with them … we vote Democrat or Green depending on … whether or not the Republican running has any chance of winning … like all good Democrats we both register as independents and condemn the Democratic candidates before voting for them with a disgusted sigh … retire early when parents on both sides die leaving more inheritance money than we had counted on … we travel admire the ruins of old civilizations … consider retiring to a cheaper country where our income will stretch further especially when Social Security kicks in … Greece? Portugal? Mexico? Poland? excuse me! …

You are the first to retire then five years later I do. Having gotten used to having you as a house husband cleaning house and cooking all our meals. What luxury! We are in good health and nothing can stop us. We buy a house outright and move to horse country. I buy a horse finally after all those years wanting to and at the hale age of 66 start riding it at its stable three miles from our backyard.

... scaring me to death in the process what is the woman doing now dressage and leaping fences with her hair gone white ... so that is the source of most of our fights I was wondering ... how to spend our meagre retirement income and our remaining time on the daedal earth ... we bicker we get along ... sometimes time hangs heavy ... we both drink more than is good for us though we both quit smoking long ago in our fifties must have been ... not long after our second visit to Italy ... though we avoided Rome ... we loved Venice ...

Age creeps up on us. The old phrase sums it up. Sleep begins to disappear or no it starts taking over gone from the night it appears throughout the day. I catch you afternoons on the sofa with your mouth open snoring like an old tiger. If an old tiger snores! The cataracts come the cataracts are operated on the cataracts go. The arthritis scare. The diabetes scare. The heart attack that was only extreme indigestion. The cancer scare. Plural scares. The increasing feelings of frailty of the vulnerable walls of our home being gnawed at by some hidden enemy. Ourselves!

... ourselves ... was it by anyone else then ... all this time ... our enemies our selves ... though that seems far too broad after all ... did we make ourselves? ... hardly ... I wasn't there at my own creation ... I will not be there at my destruction ... was I there in between? ...

Then one day I come home from the stable where I was visiting the horse I no longer ride and find you lying half on the floor your mouth open but no snores come out there is a foam of saliva around your mouth and you are gagging

gagging for breath you call the ambulance they're almost too late my heart had stopped but they pound on it for long minutes I can feel them … at the back of my frozen mind pounding away and I seize up and gag up a clot of phlegm it tastes like blood

pull you onto the gurney after they get you to breathe again haul you all officious alarm competence kindness to me their irony the scorn hiding the fear the living feel for the dying squatting in the corners of their eyes into the ambulance they let me get in beside you hold your hand in mine only now do I realize how much I love you I had always thought it was you who loved me and I fondly let you but I can't bear the thought you are dying

I can hear the ambulance screaming down the afternoon streets … we were lucky to have bought a house so near the county hospital our calculations were right I feel you take my hand then I'm suddenly hauled off with a bounce and a groan … into a white-lit building with a smell too clean an undertone of some nameless chemical suddenly plugged full of needles and tubes and masked with a rubbery plastic glove and air is pumped into me … I am suddenly fully awake but strange can't move I can't speak

they keep me outside the ICU for hours that feel like days before they finally let me in to see you and there you are lying motionless wordless stuck with tubes and wires with a beeping machine at your side and I don't know if you can hear me and I don't know what to say I can't even get near enough to hold you and I want to hold you I want to hold you in my arms

and I want you to hold me in your arms how I have longed for that to feel you at my side beside me again before me in my arms again you in mine again I in yours again as once so long ago remember standing in the night street for hours or was it days … cradling each other kissing fondling holding hugging gentling reassuring each other making each other sigh and laugh … when later all we did was make each other cry … or fear … or hate … crazy as we were … my only possible love … cradles the dead one like a child folds around it its arms taking it in … tenderly … flowers falling to his hand … he dreams … until he disappeared … some day some hour … the hunger of being in pursuit … the eyes turning to him as he sleeps … winter twilight … deepening weft of light and dirt … fabric carpet spell … the tingle of a cobweb against my cheek as I walk between two apple trees … whistle of wind through an old bone the vivifying odor of decay … death it said a justice not a punishment I missed the point if I … the dogwood blossoming in the picture window the lights in the house across the night field. Convinced he had been made to be happy a difficult prejudice to shake. Home. Drafts of letters never sent. A lance across a windowsill. At the time. What was to come something unknown that defined him. Me. You. You turned your heel in the doorway. And found yourself spinning. For years. A flare of darkness woven with flashing. Disdainful minx in the sand cards spread on the table acrobats of sticks and platters surfers in the tunnels of waves the girl on the beach with the ocelot. Yes. Without grief or guilt though obscurely frightened. How happy we would be how happy. There was nowhere that was not here. That darkness nameless with radiance her undeniable pain. That he gazed at paralyzed with pity and longing. With only human love. She danced and whispered in his mind's theater its separate tiers hidden balconies generous stage. Deflections of stillness and domination. Suns. A smear of light and twilight across what may have been a life. What a theater it is what I said and embarrassed and happy she said our life. Oh yes that yes our life I said should we be grateful she said or ashamed.

I don't know when it began but soon there was no turning back. Turn to her embrace her take the beloved face between your hands and kiss. Take the fiery iron in your hands it will scorch the skin from your hands like paper but it will also illumine. The night that lies behind her eyes. But you must act says the voice. Or burn in unforgivingness. It was now clear. Nothing appeared as grand as what had never been but might be. Are you listening or have you too fallen asleep.

There was amazement in the day. Anything could happen anything did happen. Her body shifted with the tides died in the arms of the moon then in those same arms was reborn her body was her lover was her tyrant her betrayer the fault line passed through her she was the problem no one could solve.

Birdsong emptiness.

She does not love you he said to the morning and grew calm. Not joy not despair anything but joy and despair.

The unmerited punishment of love. Savage and unforgiving. What then was. What I was. What I lived. If I lived. If he lived. Pursuing what. What he would never have. Because pursued unpossessed. System hangup and the boot. Crash. Virus or worm feeding from the frail node. Rotting the network its lush and fragile web of electronic liana rancid with chemical wash and stink of rubber and ozone. Crushed silica hammered silly in a rush to savage the one connection left. To one's own lost point. Going forward the flesh may no longer need fear. Soul be lost or mind crack for downloadable entelechies might then be available. The immaterial self will be all the rage cloning become primitive. A perfect spiritual existence at last made possible by a perfectly realized technology. God the machine. Woven from our own hands. Music holy and eros. Almost triumphant at last. And this sticky mess of dying will be the lot of our unhappy ancestors they knew no better. Pixels flash with memories. Virtual reality at last what we have always suspected i.e. reality *tout court tout prêt tout près* to pray to to prey on.

All was in suspense it had been thrilling at first and for long after not knowing or caring to know not seeing ahead more than the next curve in the road. It was a dream you wanted to wake and were not allowed to. Only further on and in. Under. Till you drown. Retreat the ignominious word. A phase transition out of being. Byss fitted to abyss like a sleeve. A hole waiting impatiently for the shovel that built it yes built. The big rip slicing through everything like a many-bladed knife a Swiss knife of the primordial jamming to the heart of a smoke-ring of strings. Darkness of energy and mass invading then sucking

down the dream of light luminous dust on being's hide. You don't even
know where you are let alone what or who or. How. Or. Why. Groping
at our hands like the Carmel monk in his stinking cell (Viola fecit) in
a windy room slashing a slideshow of whipping mountains. Thinking
you are in universal space locked in a dust closet called time. In bars of
light. Wrong even this guess you will never know how far wrong only
that wrong you are.

Shovelling down for more seed.

Collapsing around him every conceivable reflection each assertion
decaying in the gross undergrowth of language its irresistible history.
Fading from a fairy spark the flashing crystal tossed on the dung
heap. Another year another theory. Gone. Another man another
woman. Gone. A twist of the kaleidoscope brings a new but is it new
pattern of randomness and mirrors.

I was a small winner as is without much ado I managed to
leave nothing alive behind no ungrateful fool to blame me for its
generation in this. Casino cathouse above the shambles. Is the silence
mine now only mine. I hear nothing. He hears nothing. You. Hear
nothing. Far away or in imagination or in memory or in dream. All
dream now. Nothing but. A sound of hammering. No. A homeless
man yelling in the night. No. A sound of weeping. Why. Do not
weep for. The fishermen and the sea and the baited hook and the.
Caught fish. Yes. Held up for the camera still flailing as though.
Escape were a possibility. The long climb out of the valley of nettles
and ice streams toward the. Village on the summer. Hill. You make
your way as though it were desire's maze. Into a map a circuit board
of currents carefully engineered to offer you. A way out or at least the
thought of. At least the thought.

Gesture of powerless wings. Murmurs god not knowing what.
Murmurs all not knowing. Murmurs you.

Oppositorum. Scintilla. Caligine. Fascinans.

Disk of flaming radiance.

The lamb against the white wall of the alcove. The surprise of it
the wonder of a prayer. But by that time love will be unendurable.

They will be showered with blessings they will receive with clenched hands the gifts. Between starlight and the seapaths of the moon.

A blade sweeps the strings of a harp. Distant bark. Ice cross of the moon blanching the winter fields of what will once again be your home. Compline. Vespers. None. Sext. Terce. Lauds. Vigils. Money power sex love truth goodness beauty. Folded clothes locked in a winter closet. Ocean. They never forgive the mirror its serenity. Their lives are pratfalls of faith.

Precession of paradoxes.

Idealist of the human.

Terrorist of love.

For thou art. Glory.

Thin high whine against my ear.

Corruptor of men.

I accept nothing.

The smell of drying oils.

Windmills.

Evensong.

The theory of chaos that after all is not a theory of chaos.

She turns from him appalled no one like you should have desire she says. His heart commits suicide several times. To erase the memory of love with great slowness.

Daydreams spinning into sunlight.

A language he has never mastered.

You will move from temple to temple seeking a god adequate to your worship the source of a deepening sadness the thought you will never be adequate to your love.

You will almost be ashamed of your happiness.

The heavy snows the first promise of spring. And they will become at last kind to themselves.

Assault of laughter.

The nave turns round itself in the choir. It is strenuous and there is no standard of success. Delayed resolution of the chord. As long as possible.

Come to the end point of land in the sound there is nowhere to turn but back. And in that moment she disappears.

Is it love. At last. At long last. It may even be love.

Facies zone. The rangers stand watch in the tower of spiders. Before the conquest. Teneo te terra. Divina. Nothing more a threat than the moment of incarnation.

Legerdemain of power hostile examination of language.

They lift like the ash of a burning moth.

Outgrown toys from a table.

Skein of clues and forgotten lines attack of stage fright in a hermit's den.

You will play with the ambiguity of morning. If you can.

Before coldly turning back toward safety.

Birth of innocence.

Snow the frame for our wonder.

God is in the wind no sooner doubt that than doubt your doubt of it. Our lives are unfolding symbols lined with promise and warning vast green and enormous blue.

Into the trash of a life.

This is the story he had to tell. The last definition of. The freedom of.

Text for midrash.

Is there motion toward is there possibility you don't know when you set out you simply go. Who it is that rests now in the recollection of the maple tree. Depending on the whim of the time. At the time. Or all time. If any or if so.

Thralled parataxis metaphor.

Wilting tea rose in a bud vase.

Two worlds locked in each other's arms.

A spider suspended in a bathroom doorway.

The taste of her name in your mouth.

Twenty years will pass before you wake. In the barranca. Inhabited by only the shy natives of the past.

Residue of night birds.

The sea's children heard almost laughing.

Vast twilight.

No island there.

Cries of crazies in the alley will revert to witticisms in the café.

The main events will be scanted the relief will be of trivia against a background of confusion. They will seek in vain for a persuasive justification. In the memoirs of the assistant nothing will be revealed.

They will dream of each other for years.

They will stalk each other like prey.

Jerusalem cross targets. Yes. Towers.

Far far away far flung.

Their feet in the water their eyes in the clouds their mind in the city their heart in the forest.

The kaleidoscope twists between thumb and forefinger. Chaos in a mirror. Become.

Exterior. Day. Sun.

If they listen they will be able to make out what they are shouting on the beach.

The little girl drops her fork. To the restaurant floor. The peacock shrieks beneath the willow.

Green blur of roadside whipping past.

Plunges into the forest darts of sunlight on flashes of meadow shafts of brightness ornateness of leaves netting of branches dropped wildflowers weave of birdsong.

Hand riding the slipstream. Yes!

Hand riding the slipstream.

Velocity.

Acceleration....

Crack of a gunshot.

And they will race each other to the bottom

heart's stone   head eaten   salt heart   smell of panic   could he not love   crowded with joy   shrunk to naked   cloud chamber   so they can   some day some hour   tragic of happy   empire of holy   be made floating hovering   shied glanced acknowledged caressed   whole again   in embryo   moving toward birth   weakie thrashing in the bucket the pole left   in its sand socket   fisherman gone buckets thrashing   with the catch   thunder shore   crying gulls   flatworm cut in two   resurrected twice   remember that   that heaven   live over each instant of life from birth to dying   over again   and over again   forever   that hell   the pilot at the ferry landing   collecting his bribes   the village at the bottom of the road   where the rooster could no longer be heard   sharpness of the bell   wore his hopes like a life jacket   brief eulogy   deny the words   before they are spoken barren plains   attack into sleep   crows   cell   caused   velocity freeway   saccade   flickering   Tantalus   echoes   gridlock   Petra   the solitary one closes his book   whoever is waiting   the result never in doubt   MacGuffin ahead   cast party in the Balkans   velocipede overturned in the driveway   parry riposte   life death   and you never

knew what hit you   so hold on   let go   hold on   that you have
been given many of   gifts   the air harried with humiliations   no
hosannas   whitecaps   taste of seawater   flash of water skis an arm
waving   exhilarating scent of compost   keys clattering to the floor
turnoff to Lock among the ghost towns   encrypted in panels of
sand   crumbling as he reads them   the boy not seen that day   bone
shell cage jail   wings   let it pull you through as you approach   the
threshold you grow immense and slow   never to be seen   to attain it
the screen goes blank with beauty it was   so great a joy   he vanished
the solitary one moves across the bottom of the aquarium   collecting
trace bubbles rising from the oxygenator   a glint of bluefish through
the tidewater   the air rising from two open hands   surprised the
egg of the lark   the sky opening like a long-clenched fist   light from
every compass point   dazzling   where the solitary one sat long ago
in a back corner against the rotting   joists   staring into the shadows
of the rafters   the smell of rot piercing   piercing sweet   smelling of
the earth his mother   whom he has never known

◐

A plain of rubble stretches on each side to a near horizon long street
blocks of wreckage the remains of walls in dust and gray in fractals
like pressed clouds abandoned quarries a revenge of mountain
against the geometries of order lumps of concrete wrenched from
streets away into opaque patterns twisted iron frames groping
like fingers windows lined with glass an occasional single window
untouched by the devastation shining in the map of a wall door
frames opening high in the air stoops leading up to sudden pits
of cellar girders exposed through the skin of walls like bones of
dead animals through rotting hide. A black end to a tortuous
career. Condemned to docility a passive agate a corrupt amethyst.
Shattered glass sparkling in the gutter mortar and brick strewn
tangles of splintered wood slabs of drywall ripped in sheets the
metal webbing revealed like the layer of glands beneath the skin wet
vulnerable soft. Skeins of wire lying loose and tangled like a dead
woman's hair. The torn trunks of a tree its roots clotted with mud
dug up in the pass of an explosion's shock. The sign of a drugstore
prostrate near a fire hydrant a hillock of decaying fruit outside the
remains of a grocery a shattered beauty parlor the charred remains
of a firehouse. Further stress proves the intangible strategy was at
fault. On the wall of a building across from him stuck like toys with
glue high in the air a bathroom sink and medicine chest and pipes
a pattern in the wall showing where a bathtub once stood and next

to the sink apparently untouched the toilet like a serene attendant ignorant of the death of its employer. Torn wall paper. These leaves. Graphic illustrations presented for uncertain reasons. Not that they mean more than we willingly begin by humoring. Patterns of room and stairs drafted in detail against the still-standing walls so that with little effort he can imagine not only the vanished interiors but also something of the lives that went on within them. A city stripped to its bones by catastrophe. No to its nakedness so long hidden from the eyes of the wondering. The shell of a church stands at an intersection of destroyed streets. A silence of quartz. Office towers in the distance shaved of their windows and standing black and shining beneath the sun. The scene of the disaster is like an enormous arena spreading out from him in all directions with him at the center the focus of a vanished populace of eyes. He picks his way carefully ahead impressed by the uncanny beauty of this ruined city terrible beauty the words of the poet revolve in his mind a smashed car partly bars his way he steps on the gnarled bumper where it meets a tilting dumpster and balances himself along it to the other side what he sees is a gutted kitchen a refrigerator with its door blown off a mangled stove cabinets irrupting in splinters and a cascade of china and glass piled on the torn remnants of the linoleum the dull warped blade of a cleaver sticking from a broken platter. Above him he hears a fluttering and snapping and he looks up to see a miraculously unbroken facade and a long yellowed curtain blowing from a window. And it hits him was it war or storm or earthquake that struck and pulled the city down was it a wrathful god or merely some lonely misery suffering in a corner that could no longer bear it and reached out and pushed with all its strength until the world collapsed over it in ruin. The execution rose. A pattern of cedar leaves shadows on a summer porch the pistils of the moon flower a preamble of a kind. An unpaid debt of stones. A storm in prospect snow forbidding evergreen. He had saved it from the likelihood of disappearing he opens his eyes and collects what he sees like so many fragments for future restitution or as the elements for the construction of a new order. Never having said never again he thinks. Always. Though nothing has yet come of it despite the strange return. Drop it in. A broken pattern takes an unusual revenge. If he plays the game. Yet happily. Then moves ahead. Dim soft sounds of shouting and laughter. The trash burning in the tower of stones. Yellow rocks. Smear your tongue with the ash. The spy in his kingdom the king in his ruins. The child in its grave. The dead in its cradle. Was. Alas. So happy. Tag. A sudden expansion sucks him out flings him outward beyond him far flung so that he is no longer what he was or is or could be. Ever. As before. Never. Always. Again. Now.

Your turn.

for Z.

Christopher Bernard spent his formative years in Pennsylvania, New Jersey, and Mexico. He has published poetry as well as fiction, essays, and criticism in literary magazines and periodicals across the United States and in the United Kingdom. A founding editor of the literary and arts magazine *Caveat Lector*, he is also a playwright, with works produced and radio broadcast in the San Francisco Bay Area. He lives in San Francisco.